The Book Club Hotel

SARAH MORGAN

CANARY STREET PRESS

**CANARY
STREET
PRESS™**

Recycling programs
for this product may
not exist in your area.

ISBN-13: 978-1-335-00512-0

The Book Club Hotel

Copyright © 2023 by Sarah Morgan

Canary Street Press
22 Adelaide St. West, 41st Floor
Toronto, Ontario M5H 4E3, Canada
CanaryStPress.com

Printed in U.S.A.

Praise for the novels of Sarah Morgan

"Morgan's latest Christmas tale will delight readers and give them the perfect excuse to snuggle up for a few hours with a cup of hot cocoa."
—*Booklist* on *The Christmas Escape*

"A journey of love and festive cheer."
—*Woman's World* on *The Christmas Escape*

"The ultimate road-trippin' beach read and just what we all need after the long lockdown."
—*Booklist*, starred review, on *The Summer Seekers*

"Warm, funny and often insightful, *The Summer Seekers* is a satisfying dose of escapism with plenty of heart."
—*Shelf Awareness*

"Morgan expertly avoids cliché and easy fixes, resulting in a deeply believable portrait of a family relearning how to love each other. Readers will be delighted."
—*Publishers Weekly*, starred review, on *One More for Christmas*

"Morgan's gently humorous aesthetic will leave readers feeling optimistic and satisfied."
—*Publishers Weekly* on *A Wedding in December*

"Packed full of love, loss, heartbreak, and hope, this may just be Morgan's best book yet."
—*Booklist* on *One Summer in Paris*

"The perfect gift for readers who relish heartwarming tales of sisters and love."
—*Booklist* on *The Christmas Sisters*

"Her lovingly created characters come to life, the (dialogue) rings true, and readers will fly through the pages and then wish for more."
—*Library Journal*, starred review, on *How to Keep a Secret*

To Margaret and Alan, for being wonderful friends.

ONE

Hattie

"Maple Sugar Inn, how may I help you?" Hattie answered the phone with a smile on her face because she'd discovered that it was impossible to sound defeated, moody or close to tears when you were smiling, and currently she was all those things.

"I've been planning a trip to Vermont in winter for years and then I spotted pictures of your inn on social media," a woman gushed, "and it looks so cozy and welcoming. The type of place you can't help but relax."

It's an illusion, Hattie thought. There was no relaxation to be had here; not for her, at any rate. Her head throbbed and her eyes pricked following another night without sleep. The head housekeeper was threatening to walk out and the executive chef had been late two nights running and she was worried tonight might be the third, which would be a disaster because they were fully booked. Chef Tucker had earned their restaurant that coveted star, and his confit of duck had been known to induce moans of ecstasy from diners, but there were days when Hattie would have traded that star for a chef with a more even temperament. His temper was so hot she sometimes wondered why he bothered switching on the grill. He could have yelled at the duck and it would have been thoroughly singed in the flames of his anger. He was being disrespectful and taking advantage of her. Hattie knew that, and she also knew she should probably fire him but Brent had chosen him, and firing him would have severed another thread from the past. Also, conflict drained her energy and right now she didn't have enough of that to go around. It was simpler to placate him.

"I'm glad you're impressed," she said to the woman on the phone. "Can I make a reservation for you?"

"I hope so, but I'm very particular about the room. Can I tell you what I need?"

"Of course." Bracing herself for a long and unachievable wish list, Hattie resisted the temptation to smack her forehead onto the desk. Instead, she reached for a pad of paper and pen that was always handy. "Go ahead."

How bad could it be? A woman the week before had wanted to know if she could bring her pet rat with her on vacation— answer: no!—and a man the week before that had demanded that she turn down the sound of the river that ran outside his bedroom window because it was keeping him awake.

She went above and beyond in her attempts to satisfy the whims of guests but there were limits.

"I'd like the room to have a mountain view," the woman said. "And a real fire would be a nice extra."

"All our rooms have real fires," Hattie said, "and the rooms at the back have wonderful views of the mountains. The ones at the front face the river."

She relaxed slightly. So far, so straightforward.

"Mountains for me. Also, I'm particular about bedding. After all, we spend a third of our lives asleep so it's important, don't you agree?"

Hattie felt a twinge of envy. She definitely didn't spend a third of her life asleep. With having a young child, owning an inn and grieving the loss of her husband, she barely slept at all. She dreamed of sleep but sadly, usually when she was awake.

"Bedding is important." She said what was expected of her, which was what she'd been doing since the police had knocked on her door two years earlier to tell her that her beloved Brent had been killed instantly in a freak accident. A brick had fallen from a building as he'd been walking past on his way to the bank and struck him on the head.

It was mortifying to remember that her initial reaction had been to laugh—she'd been convinced it was a joke, because normal people didn't get killed by random bricks falling from buildings, did they?—but then she'd realized they weren't laughing and it probably wasn't because they didn't have a sense of humor.

She'd asked them if they were *sure* he was dead, and then had to apologize for questioning them because of course they were sure. How often did the police follow *we're sorry to have to tell you…* with *oops, we made a mistake?*

After they'd repeated the bad news, she'd thanked them politely. Then she'd made them a cup of tea because she was a) half British and b) very much in shock.

When they'd drunk their tea and eaten two of her homemade cinnamon cookies, she'd shown them out as if they were treasured guests who had honored her with their presence, and not people who had just shattered her world in one short conversation.

She'd stared at the closed door for a full five minutes after they'd left while she'd tried to process it. In a matter of minutes her life had utterly changed, the future she'd planned with Brent stolen, her hopes crushed.

Even though two years had passed, there were still days when it felt unreal. Days when she still expected Brent to walk through the door with that bouncing stride of his, full of excitement because he'd had one of his brilliant ideas that he couldn't wait to share with her.

I think we should get married…
I think we should start a family…
I think we should buy that historic inn we saw on our trip to Vermont…

They'd met in England during their final year of college and from the first moment she'd been swept away on the tide of Brent's enthusiasm. After graduating, they'd both taken jobs in London but then two things had happened. Brent's grandmother had died, leaving him a generous sum of money, and they'd taken a trip to Vermont. They'd fallen in love with the place, and now here she was, a widow at the age of twenty-eight, raising their five-year-old child and managing the historic inn. Alone. Since she'd lost Brent she'd tried to keep everything going the way he'd wanted it, but that wasn't proving easy. She worried that she wasn't able to do this on her own. She worried that she was going to lose the inn. Most of all she worried that she wasn't going to be enough for their daughter. Now Brent was gone she had to be two people—how could she be two people when most days she didn't even feel whole?

She realized that while she'd been indulging in a moment of maudlin self-pity, the woman on the phone was still talking. "I'm sorry, could you say that again?"

"I'd like the bedsheets to be linen because I do struggle with overheating."

"We have linen bedding, so that won't be a problem."

"And pink."

"Excuse me?"

"I'd like the linen to be pink. I find I sleep better. White is too glaring and drab colors depress me."

Pink.

"I'll make a note." She grabbed a notepad and scribbled *Help* followed by four exclamation marks. She might have written something ruder, but her daughter was a remarkably good reader and was given to demonstrating that skill wherever and whenever she could, so Hattie had learned to be mindful of what she wrote and left lying around. "Did you have a particular date in mind?"

"Christmas. It's the best time, isn't it?"

Not for me, Hattie thought, as she checked the room occupancy. The first Christmas after Brent had died had been hideous, and last year hadn't been much better. She'd wanted to burrow under the covers until it was all over, but instead, she'd been expected to inject festive joy into other people's lives. And now it was the end of November again and Christmas was just weeks away.

Still, providing she didn't lose any more staff, she'd no doubt find a way to muddle through. She'd survived it twice, and she'd survive it a third time.

"You're in luck. We do still have a few rooms available, including one double facing the mountains. Would you like me to reserve that for you?"

"Is it a corner room? I do like more than one window."

"It's not a corner room, and there is only one window in this particular room, but it has wonderful views and a covered balcony."

"There's no way of getting a second window?"

"Sadly not." What was she supposed to do? Knock a hole through the wall? "But I can send you a video of the room before you make your choice if that would help."

By the time she'd taken the woman's email address, put a hold on the room for twenty-four hours and answered the rest of her questions, half an hour had passed.

When the woman finally ended the call, Hattie sighed. Christmas promised to be a nightmare. She made a note under the reservation. *Pink sheets. Linen.*

How would Brent handle it? It was a question she asked herself a million times a day and she allowed herself to glance at one of the two photographs she kept on the desk. This one was of Brent swinging their daughter high in the air. Both were laughing. Sometimes, she'd discovered, remembering the best of times sustained you through the worst.

She was about to search the internet for pink linen sheets when someone cleared their throat in an exaggerated fashion.

She looked up to find Stephanie, the head housekeeper, glowering at her.

Stephanie had been another of Brent's appointments. Almost all the staff had been Brent's choice. Before Brent had recruited her, Stephanie had been head housekeeper at a renowned hotel in Boston. *Her credentials are impeccable*, he'd said after he'd interviewed Stephanie, *and she's ferociously organized and capable.*

Hattie had agreed with the *ferocious* part. She'd pointed out that Stephanie's manner had bordered on rude and that she might be difficult to manage, but Brent had dismissed her concerns and assured her that he'd be handling the staff so it wouldn't be her problem. Except that now she was handling it, and it was her problem. Everything was her problem.

"Do you have a sore throat, Stephanie?" She knew she shouldn't have said it, but she was ground down by the woman's relentlessly negative attitude. Dealing with her was energy sapping. Stephanie had respected Brent—there had been moments when Hattie had wondered whether she'd been feeling something more than respect—and responded to his unbridled enthusiasm for everything, but clearly found Hattie's more gentle nature nothing but an irritation.

"I have bigger problems than a sore throat. That stupid girl somehow gathered up a red item with the bed linen when she was dealing with the River Room."

Hattie pretended to be clueless. "I'm not sure who you mean."

"Chloe." Stephanie's mouth was a tight line. "She's a disaster. I have lost count of the number of times I have warned her to shake out the linen to make sure guests haven't left anything in the bed. I warned you not to hire her and I have no idea why you did. And now this has happened."

Hattie had hired Chloe because she was friendly and enthusiastic, which she believed to be important qualities. An establishment like the Maple Sugar Inn survived on its reputation, and that was only as strong as its staff. Chloe made people feel nurtured and important. Stephanie was more like a Doberman guarding a compound.

"Chloe is warm and helpful and the guests love her. I'm sure she won't do it again."

"Brent would never have hired her."

Hattie felt as if she'd been kicked in the stomach. "Brent isn't here."

Stephanie had the grace to flush. "I do realize the last few years have been hard for you, Harriet, and you're not a natural manager, but you have to be firm with staff. You're the innkeeper. You're the one in charge now. Your problem is that you're too nice. A good manager should be able to fire someone."

Hattie had no intention of firing Chloe. She was one of the few members of staff who didn't bring tension into the room with her.

"This is her first job," Hattie said. "She's learning. Mistakes happen."

"This is supposed to be a quality establishment. Quality establishments don't tolerate mistakes."

The whole venture was a mistake, Hattie thought wearily. *What were you thinking, Brent?* "I'll talk to her. Where is she?"

"In the laundry room, crying. I just hope she's not blowing her nose in the sheets."

Maybe they could cry together, Hattie thought as she made her way through the welcoming reception area and past the open door of the library. She gave the well-stocked bookshelves a longing look, wishing she had time to snuggle down in an armchair in front of the flickering log fire and escape for a while. The library was her favorite room and nothing pleased her more than seeing someone curled up on one of the sofas with a book.

Occasionally, she envied her guests, who were pampered and cared for, their every need anticipated, their every wish granted. Her guests did seem happy and most of them booked again, so maybe she wasn't doing such a bad job as an innkeeper even if she was a terrible people manager. Was she a terrible people manager? Or was it just that she wasn't good at managing terrible people?

She headed downstairs and found Chloe exactly where Stephanie had said—in the laundry room.

Her eyes were red and she scrubbed her face with her hand when she saw Hattie.

"I'm sorry," Chloe muttered. "She told me I had to change the bed in four minutes, so I was going for speed. I messed up, I know I did, but Mrs. Bowman frowns so much that she makes me nervous and flustered and then I make mistakes."

Hattie wondered if she should confess that Stephanie Bowman had the same effect on her.

"Don't worry about it." She patted the girl on the shoulder. "Everything is fine."

"No, it isn't. The bedding is ruined." Chloe's face was scarlet. "It's supposed to be snow-white, and now it's pink. And not pale pink, but *pink*. I'm going to try washing it again, but I think the color is stuck fast. It will have to be thrown away."

"It really doesn't—" Hattie let her hand drop. "Wait a moment. Did you say *pink*?"

"Yes. It was a hat. I think it was part of Mr. Graham's Santa suit. He hired it, and it obviously wasn't colorfast." She frowned. "And it's weird, because I could have sworn I'd packed the whole suit away for them, including the hat. I was very careful, but somehow the hat was mixed up with the laundry so I guess not."

Hattie blinked. "Santa suit?"

"Mr. and Mrs. Graham from Ohio. They spent two nights in the Cider Suite. He told me that Mrs. Graham's fantasy was to spend a night with Santa, so he hired a suit to surprise her."

"It's November."

"I don't think he cared about that. He also bought a festive-themed sex toy, but I didn't ask for details. I thought it might ruin Christmas for me."

"Indeed." Hattie was so fascinated she momentarily forgot how tired she was. "How do you know all this?"

"People talk to me," Chloe said, "which can sometimes be a little alarming, to be honest, but it does lead to interesting revelations."

"And pink sheets." Hattie grabbed a box of tissues from the shelf in the laundry room and handed her one. "Stop crying, Chloe. You might just have done me a favor."

Chloe took the tissue and blew her nose. "I have?"

"Yes. There are guests who would apparently love to sleep in pink sheets. They're soothing, didn't you know?"

"No—" The girl looked dazed. "I didn't know."

"Well, now you do. Put the pink sheets to one side. Do not throw them away." Hattie hurried back to the reception desk, where Stephanie was tapping her foot.

Hattie took a deep breath and smiled, hoping to reduce the tension and soften her mood. "All sorted."

Stephanie paused the foot tapping but didn't look remotely softened. "You fired her?"

"No, I didn't fire her. It was a mistake." Or was it something else entirely? Something Chloe had said niggled in the back of her brain. "Odd, really, because she seemed convinced that she'd packed the red hat away with the rest of the Santa suit Mr. Graham brought with him. She couldn't figure out how it got mixed up with the rest of the laundry."

Stephanie's expression didn't flicker. "Probably because she's careless. You're far too lenient. Brent would have fired her."

There was no way Brent would have fired Chloe, but he would have found a way to manage Stephanie.

She had a feeling that Stephanie wanted her to fail.

"We're a team," Hattie said, "and our job is to support one another." Fortunately for her, Gwen and Ellen Bishop, two sisters in their eighties who had been regular guests since the inn had opened, chose that moment to wander into reception. Hattie had never been so relieved to see anyone. "Excuse me, Stephanie. I need to attend to our guests."

She hurried across to the Bishop sisters and greeted them as if they were a lifeboat in stormy seas. "How was your breakfast?"

"Delicious as usual." Gwen beamed. "The maple syrup is the best we've tasted anywhere. Everything here is just perfect as it always is, and it's all down to you, dearest Hattie."

If only everyone were so good-natured and easily pleased.

"We'll give you a bottle to take home, Miss Bishop. I'll arrange it right now."

"I've told you so many times to call me Gwen, honey." Gwen patted Hattie's arm gently. "You're looking tired. You're not sleeping?"

"I'm fine," Hattie lied and Gwen gave her a compassionate look.

"Keep going," the older woman said softly. "One day at a time, one step at a time. That's what I used to tell myself when I lost my Bill."

"I used to tell you that, too," Ellen said and Gwen nodded.

"You did tell me that. Daily. I wanted to tip my breakfast on your head."

"It's what sisters are for."

Hattie felt a pang of envy. It would have been nice to have a sister, but her mother had died a week after Hattie was born, and her dad had never married again. She and her father had been close and she still felt the loss, never more so than when Brent had been killed. *I need you, Dad.*

She especially missed him at Christmas. Her dad had always made Christmas special.

"The problem," Gwen said, "is that people are sympathetic at the beginning, and then they think it's time for you to move on. They don't realize that grief never leaves you."

Hattie nodded. Usually, she saved her tears for when she was alone in the shower or walking the dog, but Gwen's kindness had loosened the bonds of her restraint and for a moment she was afraid she might howl on the spot. Emotion gathered in her throat and bumped against her self-control.

"That's true. I still miss my dad," she confessed, "and he died seven years ago."

Gwen reached out and squeezed her arm. "The people we love never leave us, not really."

People said that, but it wasn't true, was it? Brent had definitely left her. And he'd left her with a ton of problems to handle.

"The weather is looking good for our trip home." Ellen briskly changed the subject. "But before we leave, we have a little something for that treasure of yours."

"Delphine," her sister said as if Hattie had numerous *treasures* to choose from.

"We'd love to say goodbye to her."

She pulled herself together.

"She's reading a book in my office, with Rufus. I'll find her." Rufus, their four-year-old Labrador, had been one of Brent's better ideas. As well as proving himself to be a dedicated and reliable babysitter, he was also a source of unconditional love and affection. Hattie had shed so many tears into his sleek golden coat over the past two years that he barely ever needed a bath.

"Delphi?" Hattie popped her head round the office door and saw her daughter lying on her stomach, carefully turning the pages of her book while Rufus lay next to her protectively. He lifted his head, ever watchful, and thumped his tail on the floor. Delphi looked up, too.

Her face brightened. "Did you know that a T. rex had sixty teeth?"

"I did not know that. You are always teaching me something."

"Did dinosaurs go to the dentist?"

"No, they didn't go to the dentist." She had no idea where Delphi got her obsession with dinosaurs but it made for non-stop entertainment.

Hattie's heart suddenly felt full. The child was her whole world.

She was lucky and she needed to remember that.

It seemed like only yesterday she'd discovered she was pregnant. Her daughter was growing up so quickly it was scary. "You can tell me more about the dinosaurs later, but right now the Miss Bishops would like to say goodbye to you."

"They're leaving? No! I don't want them to go." Delphi scrambled to her feet, her skirt sticking to her tights. "I hate it when people leave."

Hattie felt her chest ache. "Me, too. But they'll be back in a month. They're coming for Christmas, remember?" Providing life didn't have a nasty shock in store for them, like a brick falling from a building onto their heads just as they were walking past.

She had to stop thinking like that.

She was turning into a catastrophist, and she didn't want her daughter going through life afraid of everything, anticipating disaster at every turn.

Delphi sprinted out of the office and hugged the Miss Bishops tightly.

"Don't go. I want you to stay forever."

"Things move on, honey. That's life." Gwen stroked Delphi's hair gently, and Ellen's eyes grew misty.

"Dear child. We'll be back soon and in the meantime, we have something for you. A gift."

The sisters took turns to hug Delphi and then gave her a prettily wrapped package.

"A gift?" Delphi's eyes widened and she took the package carefully. "But it's not Christmas yet."

"This isn't a Christmas gift," Ellen said. "In fact, it's hardly a gift at all. It's a book, and my sister and I think of a book as a necessity rather than a luxury."

"What's a necess-ary?" Delphi stumbled over the word.

"A necessity is something you need," Gwen said, "like food or water."

"Sometimes Rufus thinks books are food." Delphi fiddled with the ribbon. "Can I open it?" She looked at her mother for permission and Hattie smiled.

"How very kind. Yes, you can. And what do you say to the Miss Bishops?"

"Thank you." Delphi tugged at the ribbon and tore the paper. "Thank you, thank you."

"I know you love books, dear," Gwen said and Ellen nodded. "Books can take you to a different world."

A different world would be nice, Hattie thought. She'd like to be in a world that still had Brent in it, and also her dad. And with luck, her alternate world wouldn't include Stephanie or Chef Tucker or anyone who used shouting as their primary form of communication.

She helped the Bishop sisters with their luggage and when she returned to reception the phone was ringing again.

She was about to reach for it when Stephanie stepped in front of her.

"This issue is not resolved. Either Chloe goes, or I go."

Hattie resisted the temptation to say *Go! Right now.* She couldn't afford to lose anyone, and besides, firing Stephanie would make her feel disloyal to Brent. She was trying to hold together what he'd started, not let it unravel.

The phone was still ringing, and her insides tightened with stress. If she moved to answer it, Stephanie would think she wasn't taking her seriously.

"I hope you know how much I value you, Stephanie." Her palms itched to pick up the phone. "You're an important part of the Maple Sugar Inn family." She shuddered. The thought of Stephanie as *family* was a step too far.

"Then something needs to change or I'm going to have a meltdown." With that warning, Stephanie stalked away and Hattie stared after her.

I'm going to have a meltdown, too.

She turned to answer the phone but Delphi reached it first.

"Maple Sugar Inn, Delphine Maisy Coleman speaking," she spoke carefully, enunciating every word. "How may I help you?"

She glanced guiltily at her mother. She knew she wasn't supposed to answer the phone but that didn't stop her doing it.

"Mrs. Peterson!" A smile spread across her face. "I've got books! New books."

Hattie listened as Delphi told their neighbor about her latest gift, stumbling over the words in her excitement.

"Mommy can't talk now because she's having a meltdown."

Hattie winced. Had she actually said those words aloud? She needed to be more careful, particularly in front of Delphi, who was like a sponge, soaking up everything around her. Everything she overheard was stored away and then repeated at the worst possible moment.

She held out her hand for the phone and Delphi handed it over, slid off the chair and headed back to the office, where Rufus was waiting patiently, his head on his paws.

"Hello, Lynda. How are you?"

"I'm fine, honey, but how are you? We haven't seen you for a while. Delphi said you were having a meltdown."

"She misheard. It's a new dessert we're trying in the restaurant," Hattie improvised wildly. "It's a chocolate pudding filled with melted chocolate. We're calling it a meltdown."

"Sounds delicious. I can't wait to try it. I know I say this all the time, but Delphi is a delight. You're a wonderful mother, Hattie, and you're coping so well. Brent would be proud."

Would he?

Was she coping? She was surviving, but was that the same thing?

She knew she was lucky to have neighbors like the Petersons. They owned the farm adjacent to the inn and supplied produce to the kitchens, and also the Christmas trees that Hattie used to decorate for the holidays. What had started as a business relationship had turned into a deep friendship.

Lynda had once mentioned how much she would have loved

to have a daughter, and Hattie had been tempted to reply, *Adopt me, I'm available.*

"Hattie?" Lynda's voice was gentle. "Are you doing okay, honey?"

"Yes. Absolutely. Brilliant."

"Because if you need help, you know we're here. Noah can be over there in a flash if there's something that needs fixing."

Noah.

She grew tense and her heart pumped a little harder. "He doesn't need to come over. Everything is good."

Noah was the Petersons' son, and he worked the farm with his father.

He'd been a good friend to Hattie, until a few weeks earlier when she'd ruined everything. It had been the night of the Halloween party that the Petersons held every year on their farm for the local community. The children dressed up, there were ghost hunts and spooky experiences, and plenty of sugar-loaded treats.

And there was Noah.

She closed her eyes. She'd promised herself she wasn't going to think about it again. It was just a kiss; that was all. She'd been having a *really* bad day, feeling lost and lonely and a little afraid of the future and he'd been there, broad shouldered and solid, kind and, yes—she was going to admit it—sexy. She was a widow—she hated that word so much—and Noah was single, so there really wasn't an issue except that now she felt embarrassed, and horribly awkward and not at all sure what she'd say when she saw him again.

Worst of all she felt guilty. She'd loved Brent. She still loved Brent. She'd always love Brent. But she'd kissed Noah, and that single, earth-shattering, mind-blowing kiss had been the best thing that had happened to her in the past two years, and also the most confusing.

"Don't send Noah. Nothing needs fixing, Lynda." Except her. She definitely needed fixing. Why had she kissed Noah? She could blame the dark or being spooked by the ghost noises the kids made in the forest, or the glass of "witches' brew" that had turned out to be a great deal more potent than she'd imagined and guaranteed to knock the most hardened witch right off her broomstick. But mostly she blamed herself. "Are you calling for a reason?"

"Yes. Noah wanted to know if you've decided on your Christmas tree order for this year. He'll want to reserve the best for you."

The fact that he hadn't called himself told her he regretted their encounter as much as she did.

"I need to have a think, Lynda, but I'll email Noah soon."

"Email?" Lynda sounded mildly bemused. "You could just tell him in person, honey."

She could, but that would mean actually looking him in the eye and she wasn't ready for that. She was pretty sure he wasn't, either. She knew little about his relationship history. He'd lived in Boston after he graduated and had worked for a digital marketing company. Seeing how comfortable he was working outdoors, she struggled to imagine him in a glass-fronted office staring at a screen, but apparently that was what he'd done until his father had crashed one of the tractors and narrowly escaped with his life. Noah had returned home and he'd worked the farm with his parents ever since, spending any free time he had converting one of the barns into a home for himself.

"He's busy, and I'm busy and I could call obviously, but email might be easier." Also less awkward for both of them.

Lynda paused. "Whatever is best for you, of course. When you decide, just let us know. And you and Delphi should come up here that first weekend in December like you did last year. We'll be doing sled rides and snowshoeing. The two of you could help me make some of the wreaths and garlands and then you can head out into the forest with Noah and pick a special tree for your own living room. I'd love to see you, and it would be fun for Delphi. Remember when she used to call Noah 'the Christmas tree man'?"

"I do. She still thinks of him that way." Maybe she could somehow arrange for Delphi and Noah to choose a tree together and she could help Lynda in the kitchen.

"The Maple Sugar Inn is always a picture at Christmas. I know it's a busy time, so you're to promise me you'll reach out if you need anything."

"I will." Hattie was touched by Lynda's kindness. "Thank you."

"It has been tough for you, I know. Life has pulled the rug out from under your feet, that's for sure, but there's some comfort in knowing that you're living your dream."

No, Hattie thought, she wasn't living her dream. She was living Brent's dream, and it wasn't the same thing. But she couldn't possibly tell anyone that. This place had meant everything to Brent, and all of their savings had gone into making it what it was today. In the beginning she'd had a few ideas of her own, but Brent hadn't thought they would work so they'd followed his plan. She was the caretaker of *his* dreams and the pressure was crushing.

What if she messed it all up? She loved the guests and enjoyed making their stay special but managing the staff was killing her.

Perhaps that was why she'd kissed Noah. For a brief time she'd wanted to throw off the weight of life and feel young, and light and lost in the moment instead of weighed down by responsibility and anxiety for the future.

She was twenty-eight, and most of the time she felt a hundred.

Having assured Lynda again that she absolutely did not need help, she ended the call and felt Delphi's arms wrap around her legs.

"Mommy, are you sad?"

Hattie pulled herself together. "I'm not sad. This isn't my sad face. It's my thoughtful face."

"Are you thinking about Christmas? I think about Christmas a lot."

"Yes, I was absolutely thinking about Christmas." Not Noah, or the seductive pressure of his mouth, or that fleeting moment when she'd felt that maybe, just maybe, life might be good again one day if she could just hold on. "Can't wait."

"Can we get a tree tomorrow?" Delphi gazed up at her hopefully and she stroked her daughter's hair, feeling those soft curls tickle her palm.

"Not yet, honey. We have to wait until the first week of December, otherwise the tree will be—" She paused. *Dead* wasn't her favorite word right now "—tired. It will be tired by the time Christmas Day comes."

And the tree wasn't the only one who would be tired.

As the Bishop sisters would say—that's life.

She needed a miracle, but those were thin on the ground so she was willing to settle for a chef who didn't have anger-management issues, a housekeeper who didn't have a permanent sense-of-humor failure, and friendly guests.

TWO

Erica

Was she really going to do this? It broke all her rules. It was everything she avoided.

Maybe turning forty had blown something in her brain.

Erica lay on her stomach on the bed, feeling as if she was about to step over a cliff edge. Her laptop screen displayed an image of a picture book–perfect inn, surrounded by snow and bathed in a holiday glow. Lights shone from the windows. It was described by reviewers as *magical* and *romantic*. Erica didn't believe in magic, and she wasn't romantic. She stared at it and felt her heart start to pound. Doubts burrowed into her brain and nudged at her resolve. Once she did it, that was it. There was no changing her mind. No rowing back on the decision.

Muttering under her breath, she stood up and paced to the window of her hotel room. Beyond the windows the city was alive with activity. People walked quickly, heads down, wrapped up against the bitter cold. In the square below people seemed to be setting up some sort of market.

She leaned her head against the glass.

What was wrong with her? She was a decisive person, and

she'd made this decision the same way she made all her decisions, by considering pros and cons. There was no logical reason to feel stressed. And yet, here she was, stressed.

On impulse, she reached for her phone.

If she was doing this, then she needed her friends there.

Feeling shaky and a little unsteady, she tried Claudia first but it went straight to voice mail, which worried her a little. Claudia's ten-year relationship had imploded six months earlier and she'd been having a difficult time. Erica called her frequently to check on her, and usually she picked up right away.

But not today.

She tried calling again, and this time considered leaving a message, but decided against it. What would she say? *Hey, it's Erica and I need you to stop me doing something I'm going to regret.* Claudia had enough problems of her own.

She called Anna instead.

Her friend answered almost immediately.

"Erica! I didn't expect to hear from you today. I thought you were traveling." There was a clatter in the background. "How does it feel to be forty? Is it any different? I'm not sure whether I should be dreading the day or not. Will I need a therapist? I can't wait to get together so I can celebrate with you."

Erica waited until her friend paused to take a breath. "Forty feels no different from thirty-nine." That wasn't quite true, but she didn't intend to dwell on it. "Thanks for your birthday message. Your singing is still awful, by the way. Took me right back to college and having to use earphones whenever you took a shower."

"Pete would sympathize with you, but I *love* singing so I'm not going to stop for anyone. So what's wrong? Tell me."

"Why would anything be wrong?"

"Because you don't normally call me at breakfast time," Anna said. "You're usually in a meeting."

"I'm in Berlin. It's lunchtime."

"Berlin? I'm envious. Are you visiting the Christmas markets?"

Erica glanced back toward the window, wondering if that was what was happening in the square below. "Of course I'm not visiting the Christmas markets. This is me you're talking to. I'm working. There's a conference. Also, it's November."

"Christmas markets are often open in November. You could sneak out, surely."

How could two people who were so different be such good friends?

"I could sneak out, but why would I?"

"To enjoy yourself? To get in the Christmas mood? Any of those things ringing bells? No, I guess not. Never mind. Claudia and I have long since given up trying to fill you with festive joy. So if you're not calling to make me jealous with talk of gingerbread and handmade crafts, why are you calling?"

"I'm calling because I've found the perfect place." She sat back down on the bed and stared at her laptop screen. It wasn't a lie. It *was* the perfect place.

"Perfect place for what?" Anna's voice was suddenly muffled. "Hold on—"

Erica winced as a loud crash came down her headphones. "What's that noise? Do you have intruders in the house?"

"Do my kids count as intruders?" Anna sounded distracted, as if Erica's call was just one of ten things she was doing simultaneously. "If so, then yes—wait a second, Erica, you've called at crazy hour."

Was there a moment in Anna's household that wasn't crazy hour? It seemed to Erica that whenever she called, her friend was neck-deep in something. Supporting with homework, supervising music practice, washing sports kits, cooking dinners, making packed lunches. Her friend was basically a one-woman room service.

She heard laughter down the phone and then Anna's voice, slightly distant.

That's brilliant. So funny, Meg. I love it. But just because you're a talented artist doesn't mean you're allowed to leave your bowl on top

of the dishwasher! I know your father does it. That doesn't mean you
have permission to do it. Now go—I'm catching up with Erica.

Conversations with Anna were always the same—noisy and
disjointed, punctuated by a background of family activity and
interruptions. Part of her found it frustrating—how did Anna
stand it?—but another part of her was grateful for moments
like this because they made her feel better about her life decisions. Not that she often questioned herself, but occasionally
she did. To be in Anna's house was to be engulfed by warmth,
wrapped and supported by those closely intertwined threads
of family love. It made Erica feel unsettled. It made her question decisions she didn't want to question. It made her wonder
if she'd made all the wrong choices.

But she knew she hadn't. Everyone thought that having a
family was the best thing. But was it, really? Would she want
what Anna had?

No, she would not. Yes, there were occasions when she envied her friend her warm, stable family and at other times—and
this was one of them—she was grateful for her independent,
uninterrupted single life where her only real responsibility was
to herself.

She felt a pleasurable rush of anticipation as she contemplated
the afternoon and evening ahead. After this call she'd do the
work she needed to do, then she'd be heading to the hotel spa
for an indulgent massage before dining alone at the table with
the best view in the restaurant.

She didn't have to cook her own meal—someone would do
it for her. She didn't have to launder clothes—the hotel would
do that, and return them perfectly pressed. She didn't have to
worry about loading the dishwasher. And as for being alone—
well, alone didn't worry her. She'd been alone for most of her
life. She knew that some people pitied her, and their sympathy made her smile because they had no idea just how good
alone could feel.

In her case it was a choice, not a curse. Right now, listening to her friend trying to extract herself from domestic demands, it felt like the best possible choice.

In her life she was her number-one priority and for that she had no intention of apologizing.

"Are you still there?" Anna was breathless. "Sorry about that."

"Bad time?" She said it lightly. "Shall I call back?"

"No! It's been ages since we talked. I really want to catch up. But Meg just drew this brilliant cartoon—I'll send it to you. Oh, wait a minute—*Meg, don't forget your art project!*"

Erica sighed. She probably had time to check over her presentation while she waited. Or maybe even write a novel. And why was Anna reminding Meg not to forget her art project?

She knew nothing about raising children, but she did know that encouraging dependence helped no one. Her mother had never reminded her about anything. If Erica forgot something then she was expected to take the consequences, and if those consequences were harsh then it would serve as a reminder not to forget next time.

Erica's father had walked out on them when she was born, apparently after seeing Erica for the first time—she tried not to take it personally. He'd left Erica's mother with heartache, a baby, and a bundle of stress and anxiety. Although she had no memory of him, Erica had, over the years, witnessed the impact of his behavior. She'd watched her mother struggle, and understood and admired her determination to never again rely on anyone.

She also understood that her mother's experience had impacted the way she'd raised Erica. She'd insisted that Erica do everything herself, from homework to tying her shoelaces. If she fell over, then she had to figure out a way to get up again. Her mother refused to pick her up. If she failed an exam, then her mother told her to work harder. If Erica had a problem, then it was up to her to find a solution. Her mother never solved anything for her.

And it seemed like a good upbringing to Erica. After all, she'd turned out just fine, hadn't she? Thanks to a powerful work ethic, she was financially independent. She didn't have to clear up after anyone, or share the controls of her wickedly indulgent media system. There were no fights about laundry or homework. No putting herself last as women with children so often did. She didn't expect anyone to do anything for her. And she didn't need a man to make her life complete. She'd seen her mother work herself to the point of burnout to compensate for her father's deficiencies. She'd played the role of both parents, thus proving to Erica that men were like candy. Fine as an occasional treat, but not necessary for survival.

Thinking how right her life was made her wonder why she was about to do something that felt so wrong.

"Anna?"

"I'm still here! Don't hang up." Anna's voice was barely audible above the sound of running water and multiple conversations. "*Do not feed that to the dog or our next trip will be to the vet!* Wait a moment. I'm going to lock myself in Pete's study."

Erica reflected on the fact that the only way her friend could have an uninterrupted conversation was to lock herself in her husband's home office.

Anna was nothing like Erica's mother. Anna was one of those mothers you read about in books. If her kids fell over, not only did she help them up, but she also gave them hugs, kind words and cookies. If they needed help, she offered it willingly. She considered it her job to cushion her family. Erica had no doubt that Anna would fling herself in front of a car if it meant saving one of her children. It was all very nurturing and safe, but it was a world far from Erica's experience.

"Where's Pete?"

"Not in his study, fortunately. He's back in the office three days a week. I miss not having him around, to be honest." The clattering and banging faded and then a door slammed and Anna sighed. "Peace. Finally. I don't suppose you want to swap lives?"

Erica tried not to shudder.

"We both know you love your life. So…what's going on with you?"

"Wow, where to start?" Anna sounded breathless. "It's been busy here. Pete got a promotion, so that's good but he's working longer hours. Meg won an art prize and—get this—she's started knitting. She says it relaxes her. Expect a new sweater for Christmas. I've already told her that I'll tolerate reindeer, but I'm not wearing a giant grinning Santa. Daniel is doing fine, although he's been a bit quiet lately. I'm sure something is going on but so far I haven't been able to persuade him to talk about it. If something is wrong with Meg she just lets it all out, but boys are different. I really encourage him to express his feelings—I don't want him to be one of those men who just won't talk—" Anna rambled on for another five minutes and eventually, Erica interrupted.

"What about *you*? What's happening in your life?"

"I've just been telling you about my life."

"No. So far, I've heard about the kids and Pete. Nothing about you."

"This is my life. The kids and Pete. And the house, of course. And the dog. Don't forget the dog. I know, I know, you think I'm boring, but honestly I love it."

They both laughed and Erica wondered whether if she'd met a man like Pete on her first day in college, her life might have turned out differently. "You're not boring. And you two are ridiculously cute together, even after all these years."

Anna herself wasn't boring, but Erica had to admit that sometimes her life seemed boring. She tried to imagine a day without international travel, the buzz of work, the high she got from securing a deal or being called in to handle a crisis situation when everyone else was floundering.

"Well, thank you, but that's enough about me—I want to hear about you. I want to know more about your birthday. And what are you doing in Berlin?"

"I'm speaking at a conference on crisis management this afternoon." Erica glanced at the stack of papers on the table by the window.

Anna gave a moan of envy. "I shouldn't have asked. You're no doubt staying in a five-star hotel with room service and an incredible spa."

Erica thought about the massage awaiting her. "The spa is good."

"Tell me all about it, but start with your birthday. Please tell me you spent it with a gorgeous man."

Erica smiled. "I spent the evening with Jack."

"Sexy Jack the lawyer?" Anna gasped and then laughed. "Tell me! And do not leave out a single detail."

"Nothing to tell. Jack and I often hook up if we both happen to be in town and have an event to attend. You know that. It's not serious, and it's how we both like it."

"Erica, you're forty. Hooking up is for twenty-somethings. And you've been sleeping together for at least two years. It's time sexy Jack started leaving a toothbrush at your place."

It was such a typically Anna response that Erica rolled her eyes. "I'm not sure who would be more horrified by that idea, him or me. And could you stop calling him sexy Jack?"

"Why? I've seen his photo. Claudia and I looked him up. He could defend me in court any day. So you're saying he didn't stay the night?"

"He stayed until about three in the morning and then took a cab home." She didn't confess that he'd suggested staying and that she'd almost agreed. Force of habit and relentless discipline had stopped her, but the impulse had shaken her.

Turning forty had definitely affected her brain. She and Jack had an understanding, and staying overnight and enjoying leisurely breakfasts was an intimacy neither of them wanted. They'd met when she'd needed legal advice for one of her clients, and had enjoyed each other's company sufficiently that they'd started seeing each other casually. A dinner here. An event there. There was no routine to it and no assumptions of commitment.

"You should invite him to stay. Go away for a weekend or something."

"Anna, stop."

"What? I like Jack. Jack is perfect for you."

"You've never met Jack."

"I feel as if I have. And I love the fact that the two of you have a relationship."

"We don't have a relationship. We're both too busy to nurture a relationship with anyone, which is why if he needs a plus-one for a work event, he calls me. If there's a play I want to see and I feel like company, I call him. He has a quick brain so occasionally I'll talk through a work issue with him. That's it."

"You've missed out the sex part."

"Yes, we have sex. Great sex. Happy?"

"Very. And so are you, by the sounds of it." Anna still had the same filthy giggle she'd had when she was eighteen, and Erica couldn't help smiling. Deep down Anna was the same person she'd always been. Maybe they all were. Age didn't change that.

"Calm down. Jack and I are strictly casual."

"Don't. You're breaking my heart. You're forty, Erica."

"Could you stop slipping that into every sentence?"

"Sorry, it's just that I want a happy ending for you."

"This is my happy ending. This is how I want my life to look."

Anna sighed. "How long are you in Berlin?"

"Two nights." Erica glanced at her laptop and felt a twinge of guilt. She probably ought to be working. On the other hand, she could give her presentation in her sleep. She'd built up a good team and started to delegate more, giving herself the opportunity to pick and choose how she spent her time.

"I could give a talk on crisis management," Anna said. "My life is one big crisis, although never of the exciting sort. Yesterday the freezer broke, and the day before that the car died.

Anyway, you don't want to hear about that. You said you'd found the perfect place. For what?"

Erica kept her voice casual. "For our book club meetup in December."

"Oh." Anna's tone changed.

"What? We talked about this. We reserved the date."

"Provisionally. But that was back in the summer because Claudia was a mess so we couldn't make our usual week. No one mentioned it again so I thought we'd all agreed it wouldn't work."

"Why wouldn't it work? The basic ingredients are all the same. We are the Hotel Book Club. This is the point where I remind you that I wanted to call it the Luxury Hotel Book Club just so that there could be no confusion about where I wanted to be staying, but the point is all we need is a hotel, a book and the three of us. That's it."

"It's not the book club that's the problem. It's the time of year. It feels weird going away so close to Christmas. Christmas is family time. Buying the tree, wrapping the presents, decorating the house. We have a routine. Traditions. Sorry, I know you don't do any of that. Am I being tactless?"

"Why would that be tactless? You know I'm not sentimental about the holidays."

"I know, but that date you picked is when we head to the forest to choose our tree. We've done it every year since the kids were born. It's their favorite tradition. I'd hate to disappoint them."

Erica tried to relate and failed. For her, Christmas was just another day of the week. Growing up, her mother had encouraged her to fly the nest and live her own life as soon as possible. Never once had she suggested they choose a Christmas tree together.

"You just had Thanksgiving together."

"Christmas is different."

"Get your tree at the beginning of December. That way you'll be able to enjoy treading on fallen needles for longer.

Your kids can't be your life, Anna. That puts pressure on them, and on you. And they're adults now."

"Ha! You wouldn't always know that," Anna said. "Do you have any idea how complicated a teenager can be?"

No, of course she didn't know. She'd never been in a position where she'd contemplated having children, and she had no regrets about that. Her career was exciting and constantly stimulating. Would she have been prepared to sacrifice that to stay at home and argue about loading a dishwasher and feeding the dog? No way.

"We're talking about one week, Anna, that's all. You'll be back before Christmas, so you'll have plenty of time to deck the halls or whatever it is you do. Friend time and family time. Best of both worlds."

"I need to think about it," Anna said. "It's my favorite time of year and I really want to feel Christmassy. No offense, but Christmas stuff makes you shudder."

"I promise not to shudder." Erica didn't have much clue what *feeling Christmassy* involved, but she was willing to do some research and provide whatever was needed to keep her friend happy. Surely you could book these things as *extras* in a hotel? "And if you want *Christmassy*, then you're going to love the place I've found. It's idyllic. Quaint." Her heart beat a little faster. "Even Santa would drool over it."

"I don't believe you. You choose sophisticated boutique hotels that make me want to redecorate my home. You don't do quaint."

"This time I have, but fortunately I've done it without sacrificing luxury. It's the perfect compromise for everyone."

"Mmm." Anna clearly needed convincing. "What about the book? Have we decided what we're reading? These days I fall asleep standing up so reading takes me a while. Did you talk to Claudia about doing book club in December?"

"I tried. She's not picking up. I'll call her later. She sounded really down when I spoke to her a few days ago so I want to check on her. After everything that has happened this year, a week away somewhere might be just what she needs."

"You're right. It's time to help her get back on her feet," Anna said. "But much as I love Claudia I do *not* want to plow my way through another biography of a chef or a politician as our book choice."

Trying to find a book that appealed to all of them was always a challenge. Anna loved romantic fiction, Erica enjoyed thrillers and true crime, while Claudia preferred nonfiction.

"I was going to suggest the new Catherine Swift. It's called *Her Last Lover.*"

"What?" Anna choked with laughter. "I'm officially worried. First, you tell me you've found somewhere Christmassy to stay, and now you're reading romance? Is this what hitting forty has done to you?"

"This isn't a romance."

"She's a romance novelist. I've read every single book she has written, most of them more than once. And you said the book is called *Her Last Lover.* That's romantic. The last man she ever loves."

"It's not romantic. He's her last lover because she kills him."

"Oh!" Anna's shock reverberated down the phone. "Are you sure you have the right author? Catherine Swift?"

"I think she's writing this one under L.C. Swift or something. But the book is a thriller. The reviews are excellent and the movie is already in production."

"I didn't know she'd switched genres," Anna said. "You've just broken my heart. Her last book was brilliant. Made me cry. That *ending.* Is this one scary? You know I don't do scary."

"I haven't read it yet, but I promise we can keep the lights on if you're scared. I've ordered you both a copy. Arriving tomorrow."

"Does it have blood on the cover? I hate books that have blood on the cover."

"No blood. Just a wedding ring and a very sharp-looking

knife." She could almost feel Anna's shudder. "I'll cover it in snowflake paper if that helps. Aren't you a little intrigued as it's Catherine Swift and she is your favorite author?"

"I don't know. But I'm a little relieved you haven't had a personality transplant overnight. I was starting to worry. Now, tell me more about this place you've found for us to stay."

Erica felt something uncurl inside her. "I've sent you a link. Check your email."

There was a pause and a sound of keys being tapped. "Okay, now I'm sure you've had a bang on the head," Anna said. "This is—wow. It looks like something from a fairy tale."

Fairy tales often had grim endings, Erica thought, and felt another stab of doubt.

"You approve?"

"Yes, although—" there was another pause "—this really doesn't seem like you."

"What do you mean?"

"You're a city person," Anna said. "This place will be all about snowshoeing and cozy nights in front of the fire with hot cocoa. I'm the one who loves fresh air and walks in the country. You're all about bright lights, cocktails and designer shopping."

"That's true, but I do that all the time. This is an escape."

Escape? Who was she kidding?

"But you don't usually want to escape. Nothing frustrates you more than being in the middle of nowhere. Remember that summer we booked that hotel in the Catskills? You left a day early."

She'd forgotten how well Anna knew her.

"There was a crisis."

"Mmm. I seem to recall that the crisis was that the phone signal was unreliable, which is why we've done city breaks ever since. This place you've found looks amazing, but it's not you. What's going on?"

For a moment she considered telling her friend the truth. All of it, including the real reason she'd chosen this place. But if she told the truth, Anna would ask her lots of probing questions that Erica wasn't ready to answer.

She wanted to tread cautiously. Anna would dive right in like an out-of-control puppy, creating havoc, and Erica would risk losing control of what happened next. She didn't want to lose control. Whatever happened, or didn't happen, she wanted it to be her decision.

"Nothing is *going on*. I knew the only way to tempt you from your nest at Christmas was to produce the perfect Christmas getaway complete with all the festive trimmings. Instead of the No-Phone-Signal Hotel Book Club, it's the Christmassy Hotel Book Club. Do you want to come or not?"

"We've known each other for twenty years, Erica. I know when you're keeping secrets."

"Twenty years? There you go again, reminding me of my age. Pretty soon we're going to be the Retirement Hotel Book Club." Her phone beeped with another call and she checked the screen.

Jack.

Her heart jumped. That, she had *not* expected. Why was he calling her? He knew she was traveling this week.

She had a brief flashback to the night of her birthday, the long, leisurely dinner in a restaurant with jaw-dropping views over Manhattan. The food had been memorable, the wine delicious, but best of all was the company. Jack had made her laugh, and he'd made her feel fabulous. As if being forty was the beginning of a whole new exciting stage of her life. After dinner they'd gone back to her apartment...

She frowned, remembering. The sex had been different. Slower, more intense, more—intimate?

She stared at her phone. If Jack needed her company at an event he would have mentioned it when they were together. Or maybe it was something that had just come up, in which case he could leave a message.

She let the call go to voice mail and turned her attention

back to Anna, who was still questioning Erica's choice. "How did you even find this inn?"

She could imagine her friend's reaction if she told the truth. *A private investigator.*

"I was reading a feature on cozy winter stays." And now she was beginning to wish she hadn't suggested it. She could have gone on her own for a weekend to find the answers to the questions that were buzzing in her brain. She didn't have to involve her friends. "I can find somewhere else if you prefer."

"Don't you dare! This place looks perfect," Anna said. "Special. And we both know Claudia will approve because it has an award-winning restaurant and that's the only bit that matters to her."

"Right."

Deep down had she been hoping her friend would express a preference for somewhere in the city? Or decide that she didn't want to do this at all? That she would somehow stop Erica making what could turn out to be a huge mistake?

But far from talking her out of it, Anna seemed won over by the place.

"They have three rooms vacant. I just checked. Would they reserve them for a short time while I talk to the family? I want to see if they're okay with it and I don't want to lose those rooms in the meantime."

Erica tried to imagine having to get three people's permission before doing anything. Total nightmare. Apparently, hitting forty hadn't changed her that much.

"I can call, but it's only a couple of weeks away so no guarantee they will hold the rooms."

"Your powers of persuasion are legendary. Twenty-four hours," Anna said. "That's all I need. And anyway, we can't confirm until you've spoken to Claudia."

"Fine, I'll call them."

She felt like Pandora, about to open the box.

If they lost the rooms, then that would be it. Decision made.

But if the rooms were available then this was actually going to happen, and in a few weeks she'd be checking in to the Maple Sugar Inn.

Which might turn out to be the worst idea of her life.

THREE

Claudia

Thousands of miles away in California, Claudia drove her fists into a punching bag.

Her thoughts worked in rhythm with her punches.

I—hate—you—John.

She pivoted and punched again.

I—hate—myself—for—trusting—you.

"Relax your shoulders." Michelle, her trainer, was frowning. "Watch your form."

Claudia stopped punching. Her hair was sticking to her forehead and her neck, and her heart was hammering against her rib cage.

"Drink," Michelle advised. "And take a breather."

Claudia tugged off her gloves, reached into her bag for her water and saw that she had two missed calls on her phone.

Erica.

She drank deeply and then dropped the bottle back in her bag. What would she have done without Erica the past couple of months? Most people knew Erica as a successful business-woman with a reputation for plain speaking and ruthless focus. They didn't know Erica the friend. They didn't see her kindness and her loyalty. She checked on Claudia all the time. The weekend John had packed his things and moved out, leaving her in a state of shock, Erica had canceled her appointments and flown to California to be with Claudia. Claudia was a mess, but Erica had insisted on staying with her. In a crisis, there was no one better than Erica. She'd forced Claudia to take a shower and get dressed, she'd made her soup—a loving gesture, which Claudia had returned by eating the soup and managing to keep it down—Erica was a terrible cook. She'd helped box up the rest of John's things and then she'd had them shipped to him to ensure he had no reason to come back. Claudia still remembered her words—*you shouldn't let rats into your apartment; it's bad for your health.* She'd had the locks changed, just to be sure. Most importantly, she'd turned off her phone and listened to Claudia. She'd listened for hours while Claudia had sobbed and ranted and tried to figure out how a relationship that had lasted ten years could suddenly end without warning. She hadn't glanced at the time, or told Claudia to pull herself together, or seemed impatient to be somewhere else; she was just *there.*

And even when Erica had flown home and back to her busy schedule, she'd stayed in touch. *If you need me, call, and if it's urgent tell my assistant and he'll get me out of whichever meeting I'm in.*

Claudia hadn't had to call Erica's assistant—she could just imagine the embarrassment associated with that—but in her worst moments she'd been comforted by the knowledge that Erica was there if she needed her. Knowing that had been enough. Anna was there for her, too, but Anna had her family to care for and Claudia didn't want to bother her. Erica had no actual blood relatives. Her friends were her family.

And on the whole, Claudia had been doing okay, until last week when she'd lost her job. Which just went to prove that whenever you thought life couldn't get worse, it got worse.

Merry Christmas, Claudia.

Michelle raised an eyebrow. "Do you want to talk about it, or do you want to work out?"

"I want to work out." She pulled the gloves back on. "Particularly as I won't be able to afford you after this session. Punching is the best therapy."

Michelle gave her a sympathetic look. "You're my favorite client. I'll give you a reduced rate."

"No, you won't. You have a business to run."

"We could call it my Christmas gift to you."

Claudia managed a smile. "We won't be calling it anything because I won't let you give yourself away for free."

What did she want for Christmas?

She wanted life to stop throwing bricks at her. She wanted to wake up in the morning and be excited about the day ahead. Was that too much to ask?

Losing her job had been a horrible end to a horrible year. A year of rejection. A year of losing what was familiar to her. A year of people telling her she wasn't good enough.

And she knew that it happened to millions every day. Relationships ended. People lost their jobs, particularly right now when so many businesses were struggling with the rising cost of living and closing their doors, but that didn't make her feel better.

People told her she'd bounce back, and perhaps in her twenties she might have done that—would she? She wasn't sure—but she was only a few months away from her fortieth birthday and she felt more broken than bouncy.

Forty.

At forty you were supposed to be settled. You were supposed to have life all figured out. Erica had a great career. Anna had the perfect family. They'd each made their choices and had done well.

What did she have? Nothing. She had nothing at all to show for the past twenty years apart from excellent knife skills and an almost permanent headache from working in a full-service, high-volume restaurant. Oh, and she had short hair because John had told her once that he much preferred women with short hair. She'd had long hair at the time.

After thanking Michelle for the final time, she picked up her bag and headed to the shower room, her mood low. Yet another ending. Another change that wasn't her choice.

Enough! She had to pull herself together. It wasn't even as if she'd loved her job that much. The executive chef had been a bully. Most of the time you could have cut through the tension with a very sharp knife. All the kitchen staff had been paralyzed with terror half the time, and Claudia had been no exception. If filleting the boss hadn't been a crime, she would definitely have considered it as an option. She'd stood her ground, but that didn't mean it wasn't unpleasant. But although in no way was it her dream job, it would have been nice to leave on her own terms. It had been a year of endings, all of them forced on her.

The changing room was empty and she stripped off, showered and pulled on clean clothes. Then she pushed her way through the revolving doors of the gym and into the Californian sunshine.

The day stretched ahead of her, barren and unstructured.

She resisted the urge to call Erica back and off-load on her. She'd done more than enough of that. It was time to fix herself. But how?

The lack of routine was unsettling. Usually, she was far too busy to think about her life, but now she had all the time in the world and she was thinking far too much.

Over the past few days she'd thought herself to the point of exhaustion.

She didn't know what she wanted or where she was going in life, and shouldn't she know that by now?

She used to love everything about cooking. The excitement of working with the best ingredients, the creative buzz that came from preparing something delicious. Cooking relaxed her. The sizzle of garlic in hot oil, the scent of fresh herbs, the sense of satisfaction that came from hearing a diner say that the meal she'd prepared was the best thing they'd ever eaten.

But working in a stressful kitchen had killed her love of cooking, and that felt like a loss every bit as big and shocking as the ending of her relationship. Cooking was everything to her, or it had been. But now she no longer felt even a flicker of excitement when she contemplated experimenting with ingredients and flavors. She couldn't be bothered to make anything more complicated than scrambled eggs and toast. She felt numb and tired.

So now what?

She walked the five blocks to the small apartment she'd rented with John and tried not to snarl as she opened the door.

They'd chosen the place together and being here made her think of him, even though she didn't want to think of him.

Simmering with emotion that ranged from anger to misery, she made herself strong coffee and switched on her laptop.

Mug in hand, she started to search for jobs. Maybe she didn't love cooking right now, but she needed to pay the bills and this was the only thing she was qualified to do.

A leading hotel was advertising for a sous-chef so she clicked on the link and checked what qualifications they were looking for.

Two-plus years in a five-star property.

So far so good.

You're passionate about food.

She used to be passionate. Did that count?

You're flexible, able to work weekends, nights, holidays and early mornings, and you're able to energize the team.

No way.

Claudia flipped her laptop shut.

The thought of throwing herself into another busy, impersonal, stressful kitchen exhausted her. There was no way she'd be able to energize a team. She couldn't even energize herself.

And she just didn't want to work those stupid, inhuman hours anymore.

She had to build herself a new life, and how was she going to do that if she was working all the time? When was she supposed to have a social life?

She'd left everything behind to follow John to California two years earlier when he'd had a big promotion, and since the day he'd walked out on the life they'd built together, she'd been horribly lonely. She didn't know anyone here, and she hadn't had time to meet anyone. Her life had revolved around work and him.

If she was living on the east coast, it would be different. It would be easier to see her friends. She missed her friends. When she'd lived in Boston she would occasionally meet up with Erica if she was in town for business, or visit Anna for a weekend. Here in LA she'd been too busy working to make new friends.

But now she was no longer working.

She reached for her phone and hesitated. She needed to call Erica back. She needed to tell her that as well as losing John, she'd lost her job, but she couldn't bring herself to make the call. Erica had done so much already. She didn't need to hear more of Claudia's woes.

She sat slumped in her chair. She hated herself for it, but she was envious of Erica. She'd made such a success of her life. So had Anna.

Claudia had failed at the two most important things—her relationship and her job. Her entire life was like a disaster movie, with no happy ending in sight.

She checked her emails and found one from Erica. The subject line said *Christmas Book Club*.

She'd forgotten they'd talked about holding their book club meeting at Christmas, which said a lot about her state of mind given that she was the reason they'd had to cancel their usual summer gathering.

She clicked on the link Erica had sent, expecting it to lead her to the website of a fancy hotel in Manhattan that Claudia wouldn't be able to afford, but instead of an exclusive hotel, she was looking at a cozy inn in Vermont that looked chocolate-box perfect. Snow clung to the pitched roof and the surrounding forest. Lanterns glowed on either side of the front door.

She felt a pang.

When had she last seen snow? When she'd first moved to

California she'd loved the sunshine, but lately she'd started to miss the stunning fall colors and the crisp winters she'd enjoyed as a child growing up in New Hampshire.

She scrolled down and read the text.

Nestled in a picturesque corner of Vermont, surrounded by rugged mountains and meandering rivers, stands the historic Maple Sugar Inn. Originally an eighteenth-century lodging house, it was rescued from its dilapidated state by Hattie and Brent Coleman who lovingly converted it into a boutique hotel. Sadly, Brent died suddenly a year after the inn opened to the public, and it was left to Hattie to continue the work alone.

"Oh. That's horrible." Claudia stopped reading for a moment, thinking about Hattie Coleman. Someone else whom life had tried to flatten. Living her dream with the love of her life and then—wham. All over.

According to the article Hattie had moved from London with Brent, who was American, with the purpose of settling in Vermont and living their dream. As someone who had moved across the country to be with a man, Claudia sympathized with how Hattie must be feeling right now. Was she missing home? Wishing she'd never moved? Had she bought a plane ticket back to England?

She felt a stab of sympathy and enlarged the photo of Hattie and her husband, Brent. They were smiling. They looked so happy. And they had a child, a toddler with curls and a big smile. Now fatherless. Why did life have to be so utterly cruel?

Her throat felt full and she closed the photo and went back to the website.

"It has been a labor of love," Hattie told us as she served us a perfect apple and parsnip soup topped with a swirl of cream and toasted parsnip crisps. With log fires, four-poster beds and spectacular views, it is considered the place for a romantic winter getaway away from it all.

Salivating at the thought of toasted parsnip crisps—she might have added a few shavings of aged parmesan—Claudia frowned. Romantic? Away from it all? The place did not sound like somewhere Erica would choose.

She picked up her phone, but instead of calling Erica she called Anna.

"It's me. I've had a strange email from Erica. Is she okay? I'm worried she has had a bang on the head."

"I said the same the moment she mentioned Catherine Swift."

"Is that her book choice? I hadn't read that far in the email. I was talking about the Maple Sugar Inn."

"Oh, that. Cute name, don't you think?"

Claudia could hear clattering sounds in the background. She could imagine Anna busy in the warm fug of her spacious kitchen. Cooking for her family.

She felt a stab of envy. It was sad that being a professional chef had sucked all the joy out of cooking. "Since when did Erica like cute things?"

"I said the same thing."

Claudia stood up and poured herself another coffee. "And?"

"And nothing. She said she thought the place looked great. But there was something not quite right about the whole conversation. Do you think there's something going on that she's not sharing?"

"I don't know." Claudia sat down at the table and thought back to all the time they'd spent together lately. She felt a flash of guilt and then shame. Had she even asked about Erica's life? "Do you think something is going on?"

"I'm not sure, but this seems unlike her. But whatever her reasons, it does look like a gorgeous place. If we do it, Erica could pick you up from the airport and the two of you could spend the night here. Pete and the kids would love to see you. Then we can all drive together the following morning."

"If? Are you saying you might not be able to come?"

"I need to talk to the family. They might not want me to go. Christmas is family time for us."

Of course it was. Christmas at Anna's was like something out of a movie. A perfectly choreographed festive celebration. Her life was a cheery candy cane, whereas Claudia's resembled gray melting snow.

She felt a thud of misery. Last Christmas she and John had decorated their apartment together. They'd stuffed stockings with gifts and watched old movies. She'd served a mouthwatering roast partridge with a sauce made from fresh blackberries.

This Christmas would be just her, alone in the apartment they used to share.

She tried to focus on her friend. "What does Pete think?"

"I'm going to talk to the whole family tonight. If they're really disappointed, then I might need to rethink. I don't want to ruin Christmas for them. How about you? If it happens, would you come?"

Claudia added up the numbers in her head. A room in the Maple Sugar Inn in December wouldn't be cheap, and then there was the flight. It would eat up the last of her savings.

Still, it did look magical. And after the rotten few months she'd had, she deserved to treat herself.

The idea of a week with her friends was too tempting to turn down.

She'd have plenty of time to worry about money when she was back.

And maybe being away from the apartment would clear her head and help her make decisions about what to do next.

"I'm in if you are. But I'm not reading Catherine Swift. I hate romance at the best of times, and this isn't the best of times."

"It's not a romance. Erica says it's a thriller. She has sent us both a copy, which should be arriving tomorrow. It's called *Her Last Lover.*"

Claudia typed the author name into her search engine. "Here we are. Yes, her latest book is a thriller." She scanned the details. "Ooh, he's her last lover because she kills him. I could get on board with that. It's about a woman getting revenge on a man."

"Sounds totally awful," Anna said. "I might have to bring Jane Austen as an antidote."

"I think it sounds good. I can think of a few men I'd like to kill, starting with John."

"Has he been in touch?" Anna's voice was gentle.

"No, but given that I told him six months ago never to get in touch again maybe that's not surprising. And I don't regret that. I don't want to hear from him. How do people stay friends with their exes? I don't get it. Thanks for sending that gorgeous makeup by the way. It cheered me up."

"You're welcome. How have you been?"

"Mixed." She and Anna were always honest with each other. "At first, I was sad, as you know. Now I'm mostly angry. I prefer angry. I get things done when I'm angry. I'm angry with him for cheating, and not having the guts to tell me things didn't feel right to him. It's disrespectful and cowardly. I'm angry with myself for believing that what we had would last. I'm angry that I didn't notice something was wrong. I wish I'd been better prepared."

"Can you ever prepare for something like that?"

"I don't know. But he forced change on me, and I would have preferred it to be my choice. For a start I would have been more careful with money. Do you know how much more expensive life is when there is just one of you?" She took a deep breath. There was no reason not to tell Anna the truth. "I lost my job. They were losing customers. They had to cut costs. I'm a cost."

"Oh, Claudia, I'm sorry to hear that. Does Erica know?"

"No, not yet. She's done nothing but listen to my woes lately so I thought she deserved a break."

"She won't agree with you, but you can talk to me anytime.

You know that. Do you need money?" Anna didn't hesitate. "Pete and I can lend you money."

Claudia felt her throat thicken. Friends were everything, she decided. "I'm fine at the moment, but I appreciate the offer. My biggest problem is that I feel like a failure." It was hard to admit it. "You and Erica have made such a success of your lives, and what have I ever achieved? Sorry, ignore me. I'm horrible at the moment."

"No, you're hurt and worried and coping with a lot." Anna's kindness was a balm. "I understand that Erica's career success can be intimidating, particularly if you're feeling a bit low and uncertain about your own life, but I don't know why you think I'm a success. What have I ever achieved?"

She couldn't believe Anna was asking her that. "Er—a wonderful marriage and two well-adjusted children." She hadn't even managed to succeed at the marriage part. Claudia felt pressure in her chest. She'd thought she and John would be together forever, and she was still coming to terms with a future that looked very different from the one she'd planned. "I'll tell Erica about the job at some point of course, but I don't want her to have to prop me up again. I need to fix this myself. And don't feel you have to say anything wise. All I need is to hear you agree my life sucks and it's okay to feel miserable."

"Your life sucks," Anna said, "and it's okay to feel miserable."

"Thanks." Claudia sniffed and smiled at the same time. "I can always rely on you to say the right things. You're a good friend. Please come to our Christmas book club, Anna. You're comforting and relaxing to be around. Also, I miss you, even though you have the perfect life and sometimes I want to hate you."

"My life is not perfect. Stop thinking everyone else's lives are perfect."

"Stop trying to make me feel better. Your life is perfect, and I'm pleased for you. Talk to Pete and the kids and let us know."

FOUR

Anna

"Dinner is ready!" Anna shouted from the kitchen as she re-moved a tray of garlic bread from the oven. No matter how busy everyone was, she made sure the whole family sat down to dinner together as often as possible. It was a time to connect. A time when, for a short time, they were all in the same place. And the place where they all came together was the kitchen.

It was her favorite room in the house. She loved the hand-made wooden cabinets and large floor-to-ceiling doors that opened onto the garden and the fields beyond. She loved the way the room gave her light in the summer and warmth in the winter, as if it knew exactly what she needed at all times. Most of all, she loved the large table that she and Pete had placed right by the doors so that they could always see the garden. The table was made of reclaimed wood and she appreciated every notch and mark. The table had nurtured them through all the different stages of family life. It had witnessed those heady days when Anna and Pete had been a young couple—sex on the table, then parents of twin babies—mashed food smeared on the table, parents of toddlers—streaks of crayon on the table, parents of teenagers—moods around the table—and now when they were a family of four, two adults and two almost-adults, it witnessed spirited conversation.

Beyond the window it was dark and wintry and a few flakes of snow drifted down from heavy skies. Anna had switched on all the lights and the honey-gold glow made the room feel welcoming. She always felt grateful for her home and family but tonight, after her conversation with Claudia, she felt it more acutely than usual. Poor Claudia. Her life had been upended and right now nothing was certain for her, whereas Anna's life had a predictability that she found deeply comforting.

Claudia had said that her life was perfect and although Anna hadn't wanted to rub it in by agreeing, particularly when Claudia was low and vulnerable, her friend was right. Her life was pretty perfect. It wouldn't suit everyone of course, but it was perfect for *her* and since she was the one living it, she was more than satisfied.

She glanced at the table, checking everything. All that was missing was her family.

As always Daniel was first to arrive, mostly because he was always hungry. Her husband, Pete, next, because he enjoyed this time of day as much as she did, and Meg last because no matter the time of day, she was almost always talking to one of her friends on the phone and virtually had to be dragged away from the call.

Anna felt a glow of contentment as her twins, *her babies*, sat down at the table.

The scent of garlic and herbs filled the air and she served pasta into the hand-painted bowls they'd bought on a family trip to Italy.

They all settled into their usual seats, Meg facing the garden, Daniel facing Meg, Anna and Pete sitting opposite each other at either end. Anna had given Daniel an extra-large portion of pasta in the hope that he wouldn't need to raid the fridge later.

"Can you believe it's almost December? They're forecasting snow this week."

Her remark earned no response.

Meg was checking her social media under the table even though phones were banned at family mealtimes. Daniel was humming a tune to himself and picking up the rhythm by tapping his fork on the edge of his bowl.

It was obvious that he couldn't wait to get back to his room, where he spent most of his time composing music for his "band." Even as a baby, music had soothed him and now it was his passion. Anna had listened to Mozart when she was pregnant, so she felt at least partly responsible for his musical talents. He wanted to be a songwriter, as well as a performer, and she had to squash the urge to nudge him hard toward a more secure career. Perhaps if she'd spent her time watching medical dramas on the TV when she was pregnant, he might have chosen to be a doctor.

"Maybe you can write me a Christmas song." Although no doubt the idea of writing a song for his mother would be as embarrassing as her hugging him goodbye when she dropped him at school.

He didn't respond, and she realized that he was wearing the tiny wireless earphones they'd given him for his birthday and he couldn't hear her.

"Daniel!"

He jumped and looked up. "What?" Looking guilty, he pulled out his earphones. "Sorry. I'm rehearsing with Ted and Alex later, so I wanted to get this right. We're playing at the school concert on Thursday."

"I know." It never ceased to amaze her that the tiny babies she and Pete had brought home from the hospital had turned into fully functioning human beings. She wasn't quite ready to think of them as adults. Adults picked their laundry up off the floor and generally left the bed before midday. "I have tickets. I'm looking forward to it."

Daniel looked panicked. "You're coming?"

"Of course. So is Dad. We're your parents. We always come to your concerts, plays, ball games—whatever." That was her role, wasn't it? To be there on the sidelines cheering her children on. Her parents had done that and she'd done her best to reproduce that same happy family atmosphere. When she'd had her own children she'd imported some of her favorite traditions into her new family.

"I know, and I appreciate it, but—" Daniel's smile was a little panicked. "It's great. No worries."

What was she missing? She'd learned that with teenagers what they didn't say was often as important as what they did say.

"I thought we could all go out for pizza afterward."

If there was one thing guaranteed to make her son's face brighten it was mention of pizza, but not today, apparently.

"Speak the truth, brother." Meg slid her phone away, sensing conflict the way a shark sensed a drop of blood in the water.

"Shut up." Two livid streaks of color appeared on Daniel's cheeks as he glared at his twin sister.

"Daniel the spaniel."

"Don't call me that!"

"Why not? That's what you are. You wag your tail and please people, just like Lola does. If you don't speak up, people are going to walk right over you."

Lola, their eight-year-old springer spaniel, heard her name and shot round the table to Meg, hopeful of attention.

Meg stroked her soft ears. "He should tell Mom the truth, shouldn't he?" she crooned. "He has a girl, but don't worry—he's still going to love you."

The red bloom had spread across Daniel's face. "Sometimes I hate you."

Anna sighed. On reflection, maybe her life wasn't totally perfect. Sibling spats were normal, she knew that, but that didn't mean they didn't sometimes drain her.

As a parent you were required to be everything from a cab driver to a negotiator.

"Daniel doesn't have to tell me anything he doesn't want to." She intervened gently, trying to remain neutral. "It's important to respect people's privacy, Meg."

Meg's eyes narrowed. "I'm speaking up for the greater good. Daniel would rather you weren't there, but he doesn't want to hurt your feelings. If you're trying to impress someone, you don't want your parents in the front row. Just saying."

Sometimes Anna wished her smart, spiky daughter would stop *just saying*. But she also wondered what was going on with Daniel, who, unlike his sister, had never given her a moment's trouble. She worried far more about him than Meg, who was a born survivor. Whoever this girl was, Anna hoped she was kind.

She paused for a moment, searching for the right thing to say. "We'd like to be there to support you, but of course if you'd rather we weren't there then that's fine."

Relief spread across Daniel's face. "Really? You wouldn't mind, Mom?"

Anna felt a jolt of shock. That wasn't the response she'd expected. "Of course I wouldn't mind," she lied. The frequency with which she found herself lying to her own children in the name of good parenting had come as a shock to her. "We love hearing you play, but if you'd rather we weren't there then we totally understand." Another lie. She didn't understand at all. "There will be plenty of other opportunities."

But would there? The twins would be off to college the following year. Flying the nest.

It was something she tried not to think about. "I hope it goes well for you, honey." She hoped that the girl he was trying to impress wasn't about to break his heart.

When you had a child, everyone warned you about the lack of sleep and physical tiredness that came with parenting. No one talked about the emotional exhaustion. It had been a shock to her to discover that whatever her children felt, she felt. That their pain was her pain. Their struggles, her struggles. That long after you'd stopped being woken for night feeds, you'd be woken by anxiety for their future. Unlike Meg, who had been buffeted by the storms of complicated female friendship, Daniel had kept the same small loyal group of friends since preschool and up until recently he'd been too focused on music to think about girls, but that appeared to be changing.

Pete leaned forward to grab the salt. "Your mother and I will go out for dinner," he said. "Date night. It will make a nice change. You can tell us about it after. Call if you need a ride home."

Daniel shot him a grateful smile; Meg went back to her phone. Anna felt as if something important was slipping away.

She didn't want to go out for dinner. She didn't want date night. She wanted to go and listen to Daniel perform in the concert.

Wasn't Pete at all bothered? Probably not. He didn't seem to feel the passage of time the way she did, and maybe that was because his life wasn't about to change as dramatically as hers. Their family and their children were her whole world, whereas they were one part of his world. He still commuted into his office in Manhattan three days a week, and on the other two days he worked from home, closeted away in his office.

She poked at the food on her plate.

She was being ridiculous, she knew that. At some point her children were going to leave home. That was the way of things. She'd always known the day would come, but it had been a distant worry. Now that day was fast approaching. She almost wished she hadn't had twins. If there had been a gap between her children at least then she could have let go of them one at a time and gradually eased herself into a child-free life, instead of losing both at the same time.

She was dreading the moment she dropped them at college, no matter where that turned out to be. She'd promised herself that she wasn't going to cry, but it was going to be hard. And harder still would be arriving home after.

The house was going to feel empty. Her life would feel empty. She was going to miss them so much. The chat, the chaos, even the bickering.

Suddenly, she envied Erica, who wasn't facing major change. Yes, she'd turned forty but her life would be the same. She would still be doing the same job. Enjoying the same glamorous, exciting lifestyle. Anna's was going to change dramatically, and she had no choice about that.

She loved her life. She wanted to freeze time. She wanted to hold on to life the way it was now.

Claudia was right. She had the perfect life. What Claudia probably didn't appreciate was that Anna was about to lose it.

Panic engulfed her.

"Mom?" Daniel sounded worried and more than a little guilty. "Are you okay?"

No, she wasn't okay, but the first rule of motherhood was to be calm and steady and always look in control. She produced her brightest smile. "I'm fine. Just planning where Dad and I can go to dinner. It will be a treat." She had to stop thinking and worrying about the day when they would leave home, or she'd ruin the remaining days they had at home. She didn't want to make that classic mistake of ruining today because she was worrying about tomorrow. She needed to make the most of the time she had left before they left home.

Erica would tell her to focus on the positives. The fact that her children would be going off to college as independent adults meant that she'd done a good job. She should be patting herself on the back for getting this far.

Her relationship with her children was inevitably going to change as they grew. She'd read a parenting book recently, about how to be a good parent to teenagers. Apparently, her job was to give them what they needed, not what she needed. And right now it seemed Daniel needed her not to go to the concert.

It didn't matter if it felt as if someone had stabbed her in the chest; she had to accept it.

She sat up a little straighter.

Maybe she couldn't go to the concert, but there were other things they could enjoy as a family and this was the right time of year for it.

"So who is excited about Christmas? I know we normally go to the forest to get our tree second weekend of December, but how would you feel about doing it sooner than that?" She ignored Pete's look of surprise. "Does ten o'clock Saturday work for you? I can bake our favorite cinnamon cookies to eat while we're decorating the tree. We could play games. I'll make a special family dinner in the evening. It will be fun."

Meg smothered a yawn. "I'm at a sleepover with Dana on Friday. It's her birthday. I did tell you."

"I know. Pizza and a movie. I have it on the calendar." The photo calendar had been her Christmas gift to herself the year before. Each month was heralded by another family photo from her archives. Meg, aged ten, playing on her sled in the snow. Daniel with his guitar. A family holiday at the beach where they'd all squeezed into the shot and smiled for the camera. Treasured memories layered one upon another, like bricks in a house. That was how a family was built, wasn't it? "But you'll be back Saturday morning so I could make a stack of pancakes for breakfast and then we could go and choose the tree. We always do the tree together. It's a family tradition."

"Dana's mom is taking us ice-skating on Saturday morning." Meg saw her mother's expression and sighed. "I guess I could miss it."

"I have band practice at school in the morning," Daniel said. "But we could do a different weekend."

"No, we couldn't. I have something on every weekend until Christmas," Meg said. "My life is madness."

Every weekend?

Anna felt a pressure in her chest. "Even our usual weekend?"

"Yes. And I did tell you." Meg was defensive, a sure sign that she'd forgotten to mention it. "It's Maya's party on that Friday and I can't not go because I've already said yes to Dana's party so I have to say yes to Maya, too. I can't appear to have favorites."

Had her teenage friendships been as complicated as her daughter's?

"But when were you thinking we'd get the tree?"

Meg squirmed. "I was thinking that maybe you and Dad could get the tree this year. I mean it's not as if the *choosing* part is that big a deal. It's having the tree that matters."

Not that big a deal?

Remembering how Meg used to make a chart to count down the days until they bought the tree, Anna felt inexplicably like crying. The child's excitement had been infectious. *When are we going to the forest? Can we go right now?* She'd been telling herself that there was plenty of time before they left home, but there wasn't, was there? The conversation tonight had made her feel as if they were already halfway through the door.

She wished it were possible to grip tightly to time to stop it disappearing.

Were the lovely family Christmases she cherished so much now a thing of the past? Was that part of their lives gone forever?

"You don't want to choose the tree?"

"I mean, obviously I'd love to if life wasn't so busy," Meg said in a bright voice. "But let's be honest. You usually decide anyway. Dad says *too tall, get a smaller one*, and you say *no, I want a big one*. If Daniel and I pick one it's always lopsided, or not bushy enough—you know what you want and you get it. Same outcome, every year. Cut out the middleman, I say. We don't need to be part of it."

But wasn't that the whole point? Being part of it? Arguing over the tree was part of tradition, but it seemed she was the only one who saw it that way.

She imagined picking up the tree herself when she went to the farmers' market. No input from anyone else. No smiles and anticipation because the whole thing, from the scent of pine to the prick of the needles, was about creating a festive atmosphere. Just another item on her shopping list. Carrots, potatoes, bag of apples—tree. Nothing special about it.

"It's something we've always done together. I don't want you to miss out."

"Don't worry about that." Meg waved a hand. "We'll love whatever you get."

Anna searched for a flicker of regret in her daughter's face and failed to find even a glimmer.

It seemed Anna was holding on to something that everyone else had already let go.

And right then and there she made the decision she'd been struggling to make.

"Right. Dad and I will buy the tree. We'll need to do it this weekend because I'm going away in the middle of December, with Claudia and Erica." Even saying it felt wrong and she waited, half hoping for appalled looks and a chorus of *What? Don't go, Mom!*

That was the week they did all their Christmas shopping, wrapped gifts, decorated the house.

No one said anything, so she tried again. "I'll be away for the whole week. The full seven days. But don't panic."

No one appeared to be panicking although Pete sent her a quizzical look. Although she'd mentioned rearranging the book club when her usual summer trip with her friends had been canceled back in the summer, he'd obviously forgotten that Christmas had been mentioned as a possible date. Or maybe he hadn't thought she'd actually choose to go away at Christmas.

The kids didn't react at all, and for a wild moment she wondered what would happen if she didn't come back for Christmas. If she didn't arrange all the food, and string lights and winter wreaths and garlands around the house, and help everyone hang stockings above the fireplace for Santa. Would they even

bother doing it themselves, or would they just treat it like another day of the week?

She gritted her teeth. "Are you hearing me? I'm going to be
away for a week."

Meg helped herself to garlic bread. "Sounds great, Mom. I
think it's great that people of your age still have friends."

People of her age?

"Friendship isn't just for the young, Meg." If anything, you
needed your friends more as the years passed; at least she did.

"I know. That's what I tell Dana and Maya. Don't sweat the
small things because we're in this for the long haul and we're
still going to support each other when we have wrinkles and no
teeth. Although I don't intend to ever have wrinkles, which is
why I asked Santa for high-factor sunscreen. Have fun, Mom.
And say hi to Erica. Lucky you spending a week with her. She
is *so* cool."

Erica was cool, it seemed, whereas Anna was boring old
Mom whose mere presence at a school concert was an embarrassment.

Hurt gnawed behind her ribs.

"What has Erica done to earn the title of *cool*?"

Meg shrugged. "She's the boss, isn't she? I mean, she flies all
over the world first class, and people pay her a fortune to give
them advice on stuff. She stands up and gives presentations to
thousands of people. That talk she did has had like sixty million views on YouTube. She has focused her life on her career
and doesn't ever apologize for it."

Anna considered Erica's lifestyle to be bordering on the unhealthy but maybe that was because she knew much more about
Erica than her children did.

She knew that one of the reasons Erica had focused on
her career was because her mother, disillusioned and struggling after Erica's father had vanished from the scene when she
was born, had drummed into her that she should never, ever
rely on anyone except herself for anything. She knew that al-

though Erica would never admit it, her childhood had left her so focused—she wouldn't use the phrase *screwed up* exactly, or maybe she would—on the importance of independence that she wasn't capable of sustaining a romantic relationship. Erica never leaned on anyone, or relied on anyone, although she was more than generous with her own time. When one of her friends was in trouble, she was there to provide whatever support they needed.

Anna glanced at Pete and felt a rush of love. If she stumbled, she trusted him to catch her and she knew he felt the same way about her. She didn't ever doubt that he'd be there for her. Some people might have thought she was naive, but she knew she wasn't. She trusted him completely.

She'd felt this way right from the day she'd met him. She'd been working in the college library and seen a gorgeous man with ridiculously long eyelashes so absorbed in a book that he hadn't noticed the girls hovering close, sending him longing glances. She'd just finished the same book, so she'd handed him the next in the series and he'd invited her back to his room to share a bottle of wine and discuss it.

Twenty-two years and two kids later, they were still drinking wine together, laughing and talking about books. Right through college they'd been "Anna and Pete," and they were still Anna and Pete.

Erica, who had flitted from partner to partner even at college, had never understood how the two of them could be so content, but Anna thought that was probably because Erica had never been willing to fully trust someone. She'd never had a truly intimate relationship.

Erica had never put herself in a position where a man could walk out and ruin her life, the way her father had.

Anna thought about it sometimes. She thought about Erica's father and wondered what sort of man would walk away from his wife and newborn baby. She tried to imagine Pete doing the same, but it was impossible to imagine it because Pete would no more walk away from his children than he would walk away from Anna.

Over the years she'd entertained hopes that Erica would meet someone and fall in love—Claudia blamed Anna's addiction to romances—but it had never happened. And now Erica was forty.

Forty.

They'd been close friends for more than two decades, since they'd shared a room in college.

Anna thought about her earlier phone call with Claudia. After they'd finished speaking, she'd taken another look at the Maple Sugar Inn and couldn't see a single reason why Erica would be choosing it. She had a sneaking suspicion that Claudia was right. Something was wrong with Erica, but she knew from experience that Erica would tell them when she was ready and not before.

Meg finished her pasta and put her fork down. "Also Erica has great clothes and is always in great shape. You would never know she was forty. She doesn't look that old."

Pete winced. "Oh, the cruelty of youth. Forty isn't old. Forty is the new twenty."

Meg stared at him as if he needed humoring. "Er—okay, Dad. If you say so."

I'm the same age as Erica, Anna thought. Would people guess she was almost forty? Yes, probably. She wasn't thin, and she didn't stride around exuding confidence the way Erica did. She was suddenly aware of the fact that her jeans were biting into her tummy. Maybe the kids leaving home would be the nudge she needed to take better care of herself. Get fit.

"Erica stays in hotels a lot, so she always uses the gym and the pool." She ignored the little voice in her head that reminded her that exercise was a choice, that you didn't need a five-star hotel or a gym membership to stay in shape. Claudia was proof of that. She ran most mornings, and worked out several times a week. There was no doubt that of the three of them, Anna was the sloth.

"Exactly," Meg said. "Erica puts herself first and doesn't apologize for it. That feature about her last week—what was the headline?" Meg tapped her finger on the table and then smiled. "'What Glass Ceiling?' That's it. About how she'd let nothing get in the way of her ambition. I showed everyone at school. I said *That's my godmother* and they were all like, *Whoa, you're kidding.* And then the teacher asked if I could invite her in to talk to the school. I said I would, but she'd probably be in Tokyo, or London or somewhere glamorous. She's an incredible role model for women."

Anna put her fork down.

She'd spent the past eighteen years trying to be the best mother possible, and now she was discovering that if she'd gone back to work and focused on climbing the career ladder, she might have earned more respect.

And if she'd done that, she'd have something in the future that wasn't about to change.

"I used to work in the same company as Erica. In fact, I was promoted before she was." The moment the words left her mouth she felt embarrassed. What was she doing? Trying to prove that she was worthy of the *cool* title, too? Was she really that insecure about herself and her place in the world? Since when was your worth measured in terms of job title and salary?

"You were promoted before she was?" Daniel's eyes widened, as if he couldn't even picture his mother occupying the same space as Erica. "Why did you give up?"

"You know why." Meg rolled her eyes at her brother. "She had us."

Daniel looked troubled. "But you could have carried on working."

It intrigued her how simple the world seemed to her children. They saw everything in black-and-white, no shades of gray. Maybe that was one of the advantages of hitting forty. You saw things in a more nuanced way.

"I could have carried on working." She smiled. "But I enjoyed being a mother. Our family has always been my priority, and I have no regrets about that." No regrets, but lately she'd wondered how her life might look if she'd made different decisions. "You'll be making these decisions yourself one day."

"I'm not sure I'm going to have children with the state the planet is in," Meg said. "Your generation has broken it. Thanks a lot, Mom."

Anna blinked. Now she was being held personally responsible for global warming.

"Anyway, you can still go back to work. It's not too late. As Dad says, forty isn't *that* ancient." Meg helped herself to another piece of garlic bread. "Priya's mom has just gone back to work in a doctor's office."

Anna tried to imagine herself working in a doctor's office.

That wouldn't happen. She'd been out of the workforce for too long. She had no skills. She'd have to retrain and she wouldn't even know what to retrain as. She couldn't think of anything she wanted to do. Her life stretched ahead, empty and without purpose. She imagined herself walking from room to room, tidying things that were already tidy.

She'd always known this moment would come, so why wasn't she better prepared?

After the kids had cleared the table and helped load the dishwasher—she might be a stay-at-home mother, but she wasn't a walkover—she glanced at Pete.

"It seems you and I are getting the tree by ourselves on Saturday."

"Mmm. I can pick one up on my way home from work on Friday if you like. I pass a store that sells them."

His answer unlocked the misery she'd kept inside. "Sure. Why not just add it to our weekly shopping? Maybe we should buy one already decorated so we don't have to bother with that part, either." She saw him raise his eyebrows and sighed. "Sorry. Ignore me."

"I was trying to be helpful," he said mildly, "but clearly it wasn't a good suggestion. What's wrong? What am I missing?"

"Evidently nothing!" She felt frustrated that he didn't understand without her needing to explain. "Am I the only person in this family who appreciates tradition? Don't you care at all that the kids don't want us at their concert, and that they don't want to join us to get the Christmas tree? A Christmas tree isn't a chore. It isn't something to be ticked off the to-do list like laundry."

He paused. "Anna—"

"Don't *Anna* me."

He rubbed his fingers across the bridge of his nose, the way he always did when he was trying to figure out exactly what to say. "It's not that they don't want to come with us to get a tree. It's that they had other plans. We could do it at a different time."

"They didn't appear to care much. And did you notice that they didn't seem at all bothered that I'm going away? But that's not the point. The point is that the tree has always been everyone's priority. As soon as we hit November, they'd be begging us to get the tree, remember? They wouldn't have missed the trip for anything."

"I remember. I remember the year we caved in and got it at the end of November." He smiled and she smiled, too, because it was a happy memory.

"It had lost most of its needles by Christmas Eve."

Pete nodded. "You can't expect them to want to do the same things they did as kids. And look at it this way—it's great that they have friends they want to hang out with."

"I know, but this is Christmas. At Christmas plenty of families have traditions that they repeat year after year. That's why they're called traditions. I don't see why that has to change. Doesn't it make you at all sad to think we're not going to do it?"

"I haven't really thought about it. But you obviously have."

He was sympathetic. "I know how much you've always loved Christmas. I tell you what. Why don't we go and get that tree together and then we'll go out to lunch at that new place in town? We can make a day of it. Make it special. It will be an Anna and Pete day."

She felt a rush of nostalgia.

After the twins were born, they'd occasionally taken up the offer of babysitting from Pete's mother and enjoyed what they'd both affectionately called "Anna and Pete days." Time when they could be together and focus on themselves, and not the twins. Those days had been precious. They'd gone to the movies in the afternoon and crunched their way through a bucket of popcorn. They'd checked in to a hotel and had sex. Once, they'd checked in to a hotel and simply slept. But most of the time they'd talked and focused on each other.

It seemed like a long time ago.

"It's not the same. It's just me, isn't it? I'm the only one who cares. It wouldn't bother you if we picked up a Christmas tree from the side of the road. You're doing it to humor me."

"I like having a Christmas tree. It's not important to me how we get that tree, but it's important to you. And if it's important to you then it's important to me." His tone was steady as he watched her. "But this isn't really about the tree, is it?"

Her throat thickened. He knew her so well.

"It's about everything changing. About them leaving home. I've dreaded this moment for so long, but I've always managed to bury it and tell myself it isn't happening yet. But tonight I realized it's already happening." She felt emotion build. "Maybe the kids haven't actually left, but in some ways it feels as if they have."

"They're growing up. Taking their own journeys."

"I know. But we've always been on the journey with them until now, and letting them go feels—" She swallowed. "It feels hard. It isn't such a big deal for you, I know. You go to work in the morning and you're busy, and I bet you don't really think

about us. You have something else to focus on, but the kids—
our family—that's my whole life."

"I know. You've created a wonderful home, and it's mostly
thanks to you that we have two happy and well-adjusted kids
who are confident enough to get out there and live life the
way they want to live it. Our role now is to support them as
they do it."

"I want to keep them close."

"I know. But maybe this is the time for you to make some
changes, too. It could be exciting. A fresh start."

It didn't feel exciting to Anna. It felt close to scary.

"I don't want a fresh start. And even if I did, what would I
do? I'm not qualified to do anything, not like cool Erica who
can charge a gazillion dollars just for giving her opinion on
something." She felt a flash of insecurity. "When we worked
for the same company I had a great career ahead of me." And
she still remembered the buzz that came from that.

"Until I made you pregnant." Pete's voice was soft and she
flushed, feeling guilty.

"You didn't exactly do it on your own. We were both there."
A little too hasty, a little too lost in the moment. A little too
young and impulsive to think about sensible, adult things like
birth control.

"Do you regret it?"

"Regret having the children?" She was astounded that he
would even ask. "They're the best thing that ever happened to
me. You know that."

"I do know that. But maybe if we'd had them later, you
would have been more established in your career—if you'd kept
working, even part-time, maybe it would have been easier to
go back."

"I didn't want to work part-time. I wanted to be with the
twins." She knew some women went back to work because
they couldn't afford to stay home, and she knew some women
worked because they preferred it that way. But she'd chosen to

stay home because it had been what she'd wanted. Her choice.
In her mind she'd sacrificed nothing by being at home, and
gained everything.

She didn't find childcare boring or tedious; she found it fas-
cinating. Meg's first steps, the day Daniel managed to read a
page of a book—those were all moments she knew she'd treasure forever. And she knew that she was lucky that she'd had
that option. Pete had helped it happen, and she didn't underes-
timate the impact on him. Yes, there were times when "going
to work" had seemed like the easy option compared to sleepless nights with twin babies, but Pete carried the weight of the
family finances by himself and that was a big deal. Five years
into their marriage he'd lost his job and she'd seen the strain on
his features as he'd worked into the night, every night, searching for something new.

"Come here—" Pete reached out his hand to her and she
went willingly, settling on his lap as she had as a teenager.

"I'm heavy." Remembering Meg's comment about Erica, she
tried to stand up but he tugged her back down again.

"You're not heavy." He locked his arms around her. "I know
you don't regret having the kids. They're pretty perfect kids,
not that I'd tell them that of course, and why wouldn't they
be with my DNA—ouch!" He winced as she dug her elbow
into his ribs.

"They've inherited all your bad traits."

"I don't have any bad traits." He pulled her closer. "What
can I do to make this easier?"

"I don't know." She paused, wondering how to explain.
"Remember when you lost your job? For a while you felt as
if you no longer had purpose, that you no longer knew what
your role was. That's how I feel. The children don't need me
the way they used to, so I'm basically losing my job."

He stroked her hair away from her face, his fingers gentle.
"You're not losing your job, Anna. They're always going to
need you."

"But in a different way. This job—being a mother—has filled my life and now it's ending and I don't know how to handle it. It's all I know. This is what I do. This is what I'm good at. This is what I love. And pretty soon I won't be needed anymore. And what then? When you lost your job you applied for a new one because you had skills. Unless someone wants me to raise their kids, my skills are no use to anyone."

"That's not true." He locked his arms around her. "They're not the only thing in your life, Anna. You have other good things."

He was reminding her that they had a lovely home, and friends and good family. She was hugely grateful for all of that, but it didn't change the feeling of loss. "The kids are the most important thing."

There was a pause, and then he let her go and nudged her to stand up. "Right. Well, I suppose you can either see this as the end of something, or you can see it as a beginning."

She picked up her wineglass from the table. "That sounds like one of those really annoying things they post on social media. Time to stop talking, Pete."

"I'm trying to help." He stood up and headed to the coffee machine while she stared after him in frustration.

"Unless you can rewind time, there's not much you can do to fix this." She'd never understood how he could drink coffee this late in the evening and not be awake for half the night.

He pressed a button and made himself a strong espresso. "So what are you saying? You want to have another baby?"

Anna choked and put her glass down. "Did you seriously just say that?"

"Yes. Why so shocked? You love babies, and you're telling me kids are the only important thing in your life. So I'm taking that to mean we should probably have another child." He sipped his coffee, watching her from across the kitchen.

The conversation felt jarring. And she hadn't said the kids were the *only* important thing in her life—had she said that? No, surely not. Did fathers feel the same way about their children as mothers? Was the bond somehow different? It was something she and her friends had discussed in their last book club meeting in a response to the book they'd been reading, although as neither Claudia nor Erica had children, it had been a short discussion. And given that Erica's father had stuck around for all of eight minutes after she was born, her opinion had been heavily biased.

"Another baby? Pete, that's ridiculous." She finished her wine.

"Why is it ridiculous?"

"We always agreed two was a good number, and it just happened that we had two at the same time."

"So? We're allowed to change our minds if that's what you want."

It hadn't even occurred to her. She tried to imagine being pregnant again. Having another baby. The sleepless nights. The chaos. *The fun and the love.* "I'm going to be forty in a few months. And so are you."

"Plenty of people have babies when they're forty. And what we lack in youth, we make up for in experience. We were young when we had the twins. We've learned a lot." He shrugged. "Who knows? We might make half-decent parents next time around. We can consider the twins our practice run."

She knew she was supposed to laugh, but she couldn't find laughter anywhere inside her.

Even if it was possible, would she want that? "The kids would freak out. It would be evidence that we still have sex."

He gave a faint smile. "It will be good for their education."

She could imagine Meg. *Ugh, Mom, no way! Do not pick me up from school for the next nine months.*

"It's not just the kids. I can't keep having babies to solve the problem. There will always be a 'last baby.'"

"I know, but by then you'll be too old to care." Pete drank the espresso and then put the cup down carefully. "Do you want to know what I think?"

"I'm not sure. Do I? Your last suggestion bordered on wild." Feeling shaken and unsettled, she walked across the kitchen and topped up Lola's water bowl. She had a feeling Pete didn't really understand, and perhaps wasn't trying hard to understand, and that made her feel lonely. A ripple of panic spread through her. She *never* felt lonely in her marriage. When had Pete not understood? They talked about everything.

"I think we should get the tree together this weekend," he said, "and then you should go away with your friends and enjoy yourself. You always love your week together. You come back buzzing. You really missed it this summer."

"I know, but summer is different."

"It doesn't have to be. What's cozier than curling up in a snowy inn talking about books?"

"Do you mind me going?"

"Mind? Of course not. You're lucky, Anna. Books have been your hobby forever, and your book club has been a big thing for you since college. Go and have fun. Drink hot chocolate. Argue about plots and characters and inexplicable decisions. Forget about the kids. Christmas will still be here when you're back. It's not going anywhere."

He was right, of course. Books were her hobby. Reading kept her going. Some people exercised, and Anna did try to exercise when she could summon the motivation, and some people meditated, but all Anna had to do to relax was pick up a book and she was immediately transported to another world. And it would be fun to spend time with her friends. Also, she was worried about Claudia and wanted to give her some support.

With that thought uppermost in her mind, she picked up the phone to Erica before she could change her mind.

Her friend answered immediately.

"I'm coming," Anna said. "Book it now."

"Did the kids try and stop you?"

She felt a pang. "They didn't try and stop me."

"Good. You deserve some time to yourself, Anna. Pack your

winter clothing and your snowshoes. You're going to have the time of your life and I promise I'm going to give you more Christmas atmosphere than you can handle."

"That isn't possible. I can handle a lot. You've reserved the rooms?"

"Not yet. I've been swamped with work. Why do companies cut corners and never think about the consequences? Anyway, now you've confirmed I'm going to call them first thing tomorrow because you know how fussy I am about details. Claudia emailed me to say she's in, so I'm booking three rooms at the Maple Sugar Inn. Hot chocolate. Cookies. It will be like those late nights back in college when we all curled up and tasted whatever Claudia had baked. Did you read the stuff I sent through about the place?"

"Yes. It looks idyllic." Anna wondered what it would be like to wake up every day to that view. She felt a flash of envy. "And although it's horrible that she lost her husband, at least Hattie Coleman is able to carry on their dream. I'm sure that brings her comfort."

FIVE

Hattie

"The pillow is too hard. I don't like a hard pillow." The woman glared at Hattie. "I haven't slept a wink."

"I'm sorry to hear that, Mrs. Green." Her apology was genuine, as was her feeling of sympathy. If anyone understood the impact of lack of sleep it was her, but right now even if she slept on a fluffy cloud she doubted she'd be able to switch her brain off. "I'll ask the housekeeping staff to give you fresh pillows."

"Don't give me the ones I had on the first night. They were too soft."

Too hard, too soft—it was like trying to please Goldilocks, Hattie thought. Still, trying to make sure the guests had a perfect stay was the part of the job she enjoyed. She wanted to give them a moment they'd remember forever, because those moments were important. Happy moments sustained you when life was hard.

"I'm going to ask Chloe to bring you a selection so you can choose," she said. "It's important to us that you're comfortable. We'll make it a priority to sort it out, I promise. In the meantime, if you head into the dining room I'll make sure the staff gives you your favorite table overlooking the river and the mountains. We have eggs Benedict on the menu. Chef's specialty. I recommend it."

The phone rang and Hattie waited for Mrs. Green to head into the dining room for breakfast before she answered it.

"Maple Sugar Inn, how may I help you?"

"I'd like to book three rooms for the middle of December. My friends and I meet every year in a different hotel for our book club so three rooms close together would be appreciated if that's possible." The woman's voice was crisp and professional and Hattie felt a stab of envy. What wouldn't she give to be spending a week with friends, talking about books? Before she'd met Brent she'd worked briefly in a bookshop. She loved reading, but these days the only books she read were children's books with Delphi. So far this week she'd read about dinosaurs, sharks and a walrus who hated his tusks.

She was too busy to read any of the novels waiting on her nightstand, and then there was her concentration, which, since Brent had died, had been shot to pieces.

She checked her computer screen. "You're in luck. We have three rooms left for those dates so I can reserve those for you now. My name is Hattie, by the way. I should have said that right away." There was no response and Hattie frowned. "Hello? Are you still there?"

The woman cleared her throat. "Yes."

"Oh, good. I thought for a moment that I'd managed to cut you off."

"You're Hattie."

"That's right." There was something strange about this conversation. "And I have three rooms, if you'd like them."

There was a pause. "What's your cancellation policy?"

Hattie was confused. The woman hadn't even booked yet, and she was thinking of canceling? "We always try to find you an alternative date. If we can rebook the rooms then we just charge a small admin fee." It was all on the website. Was this conversation weird or was she tired? "Would you like to go ahead?"

There was another long pause. "Yes. Let's do it."

Hattie blocked the dates in her system. Maybe the woman was stressed about Christmas. The season did strange things to people. "A book club, you say? In that case, you'll need somewhere to sit and chat. Your rooms are lovely, but the seating area is a little tight for three. Would you like me to reserve the library for you and your friends? It's the perfect place."

"You have a library?"

"Yes. It's small, but it has comfortable sofas, a log fire, and its very comfortable. I'm a book lover myself, and my late husband turned one of our rooms into a library so that I had somewhere to store all my books." And in the beginning she'd had big plans for that room. *Let's host book club weekends,* she'd said to Brent. *Like a spa mini break, only with books.* She'd imagined small groups of women—because book clubs so often seemed to be women—descending on them from around the country, ready to be nurtured by bed, breakfast and books. She'd thought it was a brilliant plan, but Brent hadn't been enthusiastic. He hadn't thought it was a commercially strong idea. And maybe he was right. What did she know? Just because it had seemed like a dream vacation for her, didn't mean anyone else would see it that way. "Most guests prefer to be in one of our two living rooms or outdoors enjoying winter activities, so it would be no problem to reserve that room for you if you let me know which evenings. You can talk to your friends and let me know when you check in."

"Thank you—Hattie."

There was definitely something odd about this conversation.

"You're welcome." Hattie took the details. Erica Chapman, Anna Walker and Claudia Price.

So now they were going to be full for the whole of December. Which was good, providing none of her staff left. If any of the staff left, she'd be in big trouble.

As she ended the call she heard Delphi's infectious giggle coming from the office and the sound of a deep male voice.

Noah Peterson. Here. In person. There was no more avoiding him.

Her stomach lurched.

She'd known this moment would come of course, but she hadn't been prepared for it to be today. She was pleased now that she'd washed her hair. Not that it mattered how she looked, but still—it was easier to handle awkward situations if you were looking your best.

And this was most definitely going to be an awkward situation.

She would have welcomed a large glass of that witches' brew that she'd downed on Halloween to get her through the next few minutes.

She took a quick glance around the empty reception area of the inn and ducked into the back room.

She'd pretend nothing had happened, and hopefully he would do the same.

Noah was crouched down next to her daughter and both of them were peering into a basket. Rufus padded across to investigate but Delphi pushed him away gently.

"Sit, Rufus. You'll scare her." She reached into the basket. "Will it bite?"

"It won't bite."

For a moment Hattie just watched the two of them, man and child, heads close together, dark and light. She felt a pang because Brent had been a great dad but Delphi would never remember that. She'd never remember the first time he'd pulled her on a sled, or the first snowman they'd built together. She'd never experience that special close relationship Hattie had enjoyed with her own father. Hattie was careful to talk about Brent all the time and she displayed photographs everywhere, but it wasn't the same. Sometimes she thought about all the missed moments, all the fun they would never have and all the memories they would never make, but it broke her heart so she tried to discipline herself not to do it. What was the point? She had to stay in the present. She had to live her life forward. That was the example her father had set for her, and the example she wanted to set for her daughter. Stand up. Keep walking. Deal with what was, not with what might have been.

She needed to get on with things, including difficult things. And talking of difficult things...

"Hi, Noah." She made her best effort to sound casual. "I didn't know you were here."

"I dropped off the fruit and veg to the kitchen." He rose to his feet. Wearing jeans and a thick rib sweater, he radiated healthy outdoor vitality. "You were busy with guests. In fact, you've been very busy lately. My mother keeps complaining that she never sees you." His easy smile flustered her. That smile of his had been her downfall. Did he know she'd been avoiding him? Yes, probably, but he'd been avoiding her, too.

Still, he was here now, which presumably was his way of signaling that they should both develop a convenient bout of amnesia and move on.

"I see Delphi has been taking care of you. What's in the basket?"

"Panther had kittens," Delphi said, her head almost wedged in the basket. "This one is going to Mrs. Michaels in the bookstore. She looks like Panther, except for the smudge on her ear. Noah has more kittens at home. Can we have one?"

She so badly wanted to say yes. The intense desire to do anything and everything she could to make her child happy and compensate for the lack of a father was a difficult thing to manage. But manage it, she would. She was barely coping with the inn, a dog and a child, and they were heading into her busiest time of year. She knew better than to add more responsibility or chaos. She could make an excuse, or she could tell the truth. She preferred her daughter to always hear the truth.

"We can't have a kitten, honey."

Delphi wrinkled her nose. "Why not? I *really* want one."

"I know, but sometimes in life there are things we want that we just can't have. And I know it seems hard." Hattie thought about all the things she really wanted. "But right now we have a lot to deal with. An animal is a big responsibility. They don't just need love and attention. They take time and care."

"But we already care for Rufus."

"Exactly. We care for Rufus. And I think you're grown up enough to take more responsibility for him. Maybe this is a good time to talk about that."

Delphi sat up straighter. "I could feed him. And clean his bowl."

"You'd do that? Because that would be a big help."

Rufus thumped his tail and Delphi looked up at Noah. Her hair framed her face in a tangle of pale gold and her eyes were solemn.

"We can't have a kitten right now because I'm too busy to care for it."

Hattie felt an almost overwhelming rush of love for her daughter.

Noah nodded, equally solemn. "That's very responsible of you. You can visit them at the farm and help Panther look after them any time you like."

Hattie appreciated the gesture. "That's a kind offer."

"Can I come today?" Delphi was savvy enough to know that adults didn't always follow through on their promises and Noah smiled.

"If it's okay with your mother, then it's fine with me. And while you're visiting, you can choose your Christmas trees. That way you get first choice."

"Today?" Delphi almost burst with excitement. "Can we cut one down?"

"We won't cut them today. I'll do that just before we bring them over to you. That way the trees will stay fresh."

Delphi gazed at her mother. "Can we go? Please?"

If she said no to this, too, then she'd ruin her daughter's day, and her daughter didn't deserve to have her day ruined just because her mother had been feeling lonely and sexually frustrated and had exorcised those feelings on Noah.

Noah was watching her, his face inscrutable.

"It's up to you," he said steadily. "If you'd rather not, that's fine."

Was he saying he'd rather she didn't come? Or did he genuinely not care either way? Did he think about those wild, mindless moments in the barn or had he tried to forget it? Maybe, for him, that kiss had been the most terrifying thing about Halloween.

She bit back a hysterical laugh. Maybe that was why he hadn't come around for a while. She'd scared him. She'd been so damn desperate, she'd scared a man.

On the other hand, Noah had never struck her as a man who was easily scared.

It was impossible to decode his true thoughts from his body language.

But whatever he was thinking, she needed to reassure him that nothing had changed. He was her neighbor and, before that wild moment of madness, a good friend. She didn't want to lose that.

After Brent's accident she'd been grateful for Noah's constant and steady presence. He'd visited frequently, reminding her that she wasn't alone, that she had friends and neighbors who cared and were looking out for her. Long after other people had given up asking her how she was, he'd still paid attention. Often he brought gifts from his mother's kitchen.

She made too much casserole, so maybe you'd help us out and eat it. My mother has tried this new pie recipe, and she'd love your opinion.

She'd started to look forward to his visits. Unlike others, he didn't tiptoe around her. He seemed to understand that she might laugh one minute and sob the next.

Since Halloween she'd missed seeing him. Was that wrong?

She had no idea what was right or wrong. Life had upended the natural order of things, and she felt as if she no longer knew the rules, or even if there *were* rules. She didn't care what other people thought; that wasn't her problem. Her problem was that she didn't even know what she thought.

But at least spending time with him would be a way of reassuring him she didn't intend to grab him at every possible moment, and that he didn't need to be nervous. Also, an afternoon on the farm would make her daughter ecstatically happy, and if there was ever an opportunity to make her daughter ecstatically happy, then she was going to take it.

"That would be great. Thank you. I did mean to email you about trees, but it's been busy. We've had a lot going on."

His gaze held hers. "I understand."

If that was true, it was really embarrassing.

She was annoyed to find her cheeks turning pink. "We'll come after lunch. I'll ask Chloe to cover reception and she can call me if there are any problems."

"My mother is hoping you'll join us for dinner. She hasn't seen you since Halloween."

Halloween. That one word was all it took for the memories to come pouring back.

She remembered the sharp bite of the cold air, the darkness of the barn, the shadows cloaking the intimacy of the moment. They'd been talking about Christmas trees, or maybe it was the pumpkin harvest, she couldn't even remember, but she remembered the moment she'd dug her fingers into the front of his shirt and tugged him toward her. She'd tugged him so hard he'd had to put out a hand to steady both of them, and for a single breathless moment she'd thought *what am I doing?* and then she'd kissed him. In fact, she hadn't as much kissed him as consumed him. She'd been ravenous, burning up in the heat of the moment. It embarrassed her to remember it, although to be fair, he'd been right there with her, his mouth urgent against hers, his hands holding her hard against him as they'd pressed closer. The whole thing was a dizzying blur of erotic pleasure and guilt. Guilt because she wasn't sure she was ready emotionally to kiss another man; pleasure because—well, that part was obvious. Noah Peterson clearly had skills she'd known nothing about until that moment.

But now she knew.

Her gaze slid cautiously to his and for a moment they looked at each other, connected by the memory of that stolen intimacy.

This was the moment to say something funny and dismissive that would signal to him that everything was fine and that he didn't need to worry about being alone with her on a dark night.

But her mind blanked.

Noah looked at her for a moment longer and then shifted his attention to Delphi. "Can you watch the kitten for me, honey? Your mother and I need to have a talk about a few things."

Hattie felt a flash of horror. He wanted to talk about it? That was the last thing *she* wanted.

Keeping a protective hand on the basket, Delphi looked up at him. "I know. Christmas trees. You have to talk about Christmas trees. Because you're the Christmas tree man."

"That's right." The smile crinkled his eyes and tilted the corners of his mouth. "I'm the Christmas tree man." Giving the child's shoulder a quick squeeze, he walked toward Hattie.

She stared at him stupidly. "You want to talk about Christmas trees?"

"Your order. It would be helpful to know what you need before you come over this afternoon."

"Oh." She forced herself to relax. "Yes. I scribbled it down somewhere. It's on my desk." She grabbed her notebook, ripped out the relevant page and thrust it toward him. "Here—"

"Thanks." He glanced at it and tucked it into his pocket.

"It's mostly the same as last year, except that this year I'd like to put a tree in the library."

"Sounds good. Size?"

Size? *Over six foot*, she thought, because she'd had to lift herself onto her toes to kiss him.

She was so flustered by the direction of her own thoughts that her brain had stopped working. "I don't know."

"Show me the space and I'll find something suitable." He walked through the door toward the reception area and Hattie checked Delphi.

"Don't move. You're in charge. You're basically running the whole show."

"I won't move." Delphi crossed her legs and sat firm, taking her new responsibilities seriously.

She followed Noah through to reception. For once everything was quiet, so she crossed the hallway to the room that she and Brent had turned into a library. "That child is five going on twenty-five. I swear I'm going to wake up one morning and discover she's already off to college."

"She's growing up fast."

"She is. A little too fast. I can't keep up." Thank goodness for Delphi, who was always a safe topic of conversation.

Hattie pushed open the door and instantly felt some of the stress leave her. Books did that to her, and this room was full of books. The shelves were walnut and reached up to the ceiling. A fire flickered in the hearth. Two deep, comfortable sofas faced each other across a low table, which was stacked with more books. What wouldn't she give to curl up on one of those sofas and read for the rest of the day?

"I love this room." Noah reached up and pulled a book from the shelf. His sweater emphasized the width of his shoulders, and a flash of sensation rippled down her spine and settled somewhere deep inside her.

"Me, too." It was a struggle to sound normal and she wasn't sure she managed it.

"I currently have eight books on my nightstand, and with the amount of work on the farm I'm not likely to cut that down to seven anytime soon. Not that I don't love reading, but since

Dad hurt his shoulder there's not much time to do anything except work and sleep. I'm guessing you know how that feels." He put the book back and turned. "So we should probably do this so that you can get back to Delphi and the inn."

Her mouth was dry. "Do this?"

"We should talk about this. Figure out what it is you want."

If she knew that, she wouldn't be in this quandary. She knew she had to move on one day, whatever that was supposed to mean, but how would she know when that day came?

"We don't need to talk about it."

There was a flicker of surprise in his eyes followed by understanding. "The tree," he said slowly. "We should figure out what you want this tree to look like."

The tree. Of course he was talking about the tree.

And now she wanted to die.

Tactfully ignoring her embarrassment, he pulled his phone out of his pocket and took a couple of photos. "You'll probably want to put the tree by the window, so that it doesn't dry out by the fire." He glanced from floor to ceiling and then made a few notes on his phone. "You don't want it to dominate, and you don't want it too wide. Do you have any preferences? Any thoughts?"

She had no thoughts, only feelings. All of them confusing.

"Nothing. But I want it to smell like a Christmas tree."

His gaze lingered on her face for a moment. "Right." He dragged his gaze away. "In that case, I suggest we go with the balsam fir. Good needle retention, rich color, great shape. And firs tend to last longer than spruces."

"Great."

This wasn't awkward, it was excruciating. They were both dancing around what had happened, pretending it wasn't there. Which made it seem bigger.

Maybe she should say something. On the other hand, why draw attention to something he was obviously trying hard to ignore? If he'd wanted to mention it, he'd had plenty of opportunity. "We'd better let you go. I know how busy you are. It's Christmas tree season!"

Noah slipped his phone back into his pocket. "You look tired." His tone was blunt but caring. "Have you been working too hard?"

"Probably. This place is pretty demanding and stressful." She was trying so hard to keep everything the way Brent had wanted but the pressure was keeping her awake at night. She was constantly asking herself what Brent would have done, but seeing as they'd often felt differently on things to do with running the inn, that wasn't an easy question to answer.

He nodded. "How are the staff?"

"As of this morning they were all still here, so I'm grateful for that given that I'm so bad at managing them."

His brows pulled together in a frown. "You're not bad at managing them, Hattie."

"Yes, I am." She thought about Stephanie and then she thought about Chef Tucker. "Brent appointed most of them and he chose them carefully. He was great at the people stuff. He knew when to be firm, and when to encourage. But I'm not Brent. I'm not very…confrontational. Pathetic, I know."

"It's not pathetic. People have different management styles, and good managers have different styles for different people. I'm sure you're an extremely effective manager." Noah paused. "Maybe it's time to stop trying to do things the way Brent would have done them, and do things the way you want to do them. This is your business, Hattie."

It wasn't her business though, was it? She still thought of it as their business; it was just that Brent was no longer around to share in it. She was caretaking his dreams.

For a brief moment she was tempted to tell Noah how she felt, but she couldn't push the words past the barrier she'd built inside her. It would have felt disloyal to Brent, particularly given her confused relationship with Noah.

"I'll be fine."

He hesitated. "I know you're trying to keep things the way they were, but you have to find a way that works for you. You have to make a life that works for you."

Was he talking about the inn or something more personal?

And was she constantly going to look for alternate meanings in everything he said?

However much she tried to pretend differently, the kiss had changed everything. She was thinking things she shouldn't be thinking. And wanting things she shouldn't be wanting. And if she really thought they could move on as if nothing had happened, then she was kidding herself.

There were some things you couldn't forget and some things that couldn't be undone.

"I'm happy keeping things the way they are. Brent had great ideas." Her words shattered the almost painful intimacy.

"Right. Of course." He straightened his shoulders and gave a brief smile. "Apologies if I overstepped."

She had to stop herself reaching out and assuring him that he hadn't overstepped. That she was the one who was confused. But that would just muddle the situation even more.

She wished she could rewind the clock to the time when being with him hadn't felt awkward. But that would have meant undoing the kiss, and she wasn't sure she wanted to deprive herself of that one memorable moment even if it had left her unsettled.

"We should probably check on Delphi," she said. "As much as I believe in her good intentions, I don't entirely trust her not to stuff Rufus with candy."

"We'll see you later, then. Message me when you're on your way over and I'll meet you at the farmhouse. Dress warmly, both of you. It's cold out there."

"We'll do that." And this time, she promised herself, there would be no intimate moments in the barn, no long, lingering eye-meets, no heart-stopping kisses. Just an afternoon of Christmas trees and her daughter.

No problem.

SIX

Erica

The drive from New York to Anna's house in Connecticut took a little under two hours thanks to heavy traffic, construction and an unexpected flurry of snow.

"You have no idea how much I've been looking forward to this." Claudia unwrapped her scarf from her neck and folded it in her lap. "The Maple Sugar Inn looks charming. How did you find it?"

Erica wished she'd thought up a better answer to that question.

"Random searching on the internet." There had been nothing random about it, but this wasn't the time to share that. Maybe this evening over a glass of wine when the three of them were together, she'd open up. She imagined herself saying casually, *by the way, there is something I need to tell you…*

"I keep looking at the photos on the website," Claudia said, "and the menus are inspiring. It will be bliss to eat food I haven't had to cook. I can't wait to be there, curled up in front of that log fire. Given how hard you work, I bet you're feeling the same way."

Erica kept her eyes on the road and her hands on the wheel.

She wasn't feeling the same way. She was feeling a little sick and wishing she'd never booked the Maple Sugar Inn. She could have chosen a nice boutique hotel in Boston and carried on living the life she'd designed for herself, instead of looking for answers to questions she might have been better off not asking.

"Erica? Are you okay? Did you hear anything I just said?"

"All of it. And I'm fine." The lie came easily. "Just tired, that's all."

"Not surprising. Have you even spent a night in your own bed this year? Whenever we talk you're always in a hotel somewhere. It sounds glamorous, but I guess it's a little lonely, too, isn't it?"

"I don't find it lonely." There was something about the blankness of a hotel room that soothed her. She kept her surroundings the way she kept the rest of her life—free of clutter. And yes, a therapist would probably tell her that she had some attachment issues, but if that was true then she was fine with that. She owned nothing that she couldn't happily part with and that, she believed, was a recipe for a happy life.

Claudia seemed to disagree. "With the hours you've been putting in I bet you need a vacation. You need to relax."

"Mmm." She really did need a vacation, but she knew she wasn't going to find the next week relaxing. She was unnerved by what lay ahead. She liked her life, so why was she doing something that could potentially shake it up?

"I'm relieved to be away from the apartment. Everything about it reminds me of John and that's not good. Look at the snow." Claudia gazed at the snowflakes that drifted in front of them, swirling and dancing around the cars. "It's as if the weather is welcoming us on our winter break."

Erica smiled. "I think that's to do with a low-pressure system rather than some cosmic intervention designed to enhance your Christmas experience."

"I don't know about that. I do know it means you'll be building a snowman with me."

"I've never built a snowman and I'm not confident I have the skills. Ask Anna. I'm sure she builds the best snowmen on the east coast."

"What?" Claudia sat up straighter. "You're kidding."

"I'm not kidding. It's the sort of thing Anna would be great at."

"I meant you have to be kidding that you've never built a snowman."

"What possible reason would I have to build a snowman?"

"Er—for fun? Didn't you ever build a snowman when you were a child?"

"No." When she thought of her childhood Christmases she didn't think of fun; she thought of struggle. Her mother's mood had always dipped badly at Christmas. She'd checked the mail regularly and when nothing arrived she'd seemed to lose some of her fighting spirit. *I don't care about me,* she would mutter as she'd hugged Erica close, *but I care about you. You deserve to have a father who is there for you.* Erica had never met her father and knew nothing about him other than the fact that he'd left immediately after she was born. She certainly didn't miss him, and she didn't really understand why her mother was so upset. Weren't they fine, just the two of them?

Her mother had often worked at Christmas. At first, Erica had assumed that was because she was paid extra for working the holidays and they'd needed the money, but later, as she'd grown older and started to understand the nuances of life, she'd wondered if it was because her mother had chosen to keep herself busy. She'd treated the holidays like a survival exercise—*it's just one day, Erica, just one day*—and Erica had grown up knowing that Christmas wasn't candy canes and twinkling lights but something to be endured with gritted teeth and determination. On those days when her mother was working, their elderly neighbor had watched Erica. Her mother would collect her at the end of the day, and they'd curl up together and read books they'd chosen from the library. They'd avoided books show-ing families gathered around a Christmas tree—*it's a fantasy*—and instead selected stories about dragons and unicorns where the heroine defeated evil. In the stories her mother chose, the heroine always rescued herself.

"I volunteer to give you snowman-building lessons." Clau-dia was oblivious to Erica's thoughts. "I can't wait. I miss snow. I miss the seasons. Do you know how exciting it is to be able to wear a scarf?"

Erica was grateful for the change of subject. "You love Cali-fornian sunshine."

"I know. But I miss kicking my way through leaves in fall and snuggling in winter. I miss warming my hands on mugs of steaming hot soup. And talking of soup, I'm starving," Claudia said. "I hope Anna has cooked dinner."

Erica slowed down as the car in front of her came to a stand-still. "When has Anna ever not cooked dinner?"

"Nothing in life is certain. You think you understand some-one and then *wham*, they surprise you. And not in a good way."

Erica thought about her mother. *Your father wasn't the man I thought he was.*

Something shifted inside her. She had a head full of questions but right now the priority was Claudia, who had weathered a difficult year. "Anna is not going to surprise us, and she will not order takeout. I can safely say that Anna cooking dinner is one of life's few certainties."

But it was clear that her friend was feeling raw and vulner-able, and Erica ached for her.

This, she thought, was what happened when you let yourself depend on someone. She was grateful to her mother for teach-ing her to rely only on herself.

Should she ask about John? No. If John had called, Claudia would have told them.

She chose a safer topic.

"How's the job going? Entertain me with your funny kitchen stories."

"Ah, the job." Claudia stared straight ahead. "I don't have a job. I've been laid off. I don't suppose that counts as a funny kitchen story."

"What?" Erica glanced at her, shocked. "When did this happen? Why didn't you tell me?"

"Because you've done enough for me already. You didn't need to hear more of my moaning." Claudia slumped in her seat and fiddled with the edge of her scarf.

"Claudia, you're my best friend." Erica wished they weren't in the car. It was hard to give her friend her full attention when negotiating heavy traffic and falling snow. "There is no such thing as *enough*. You should have called me."

"I'm in denial. I've been hoping to wake up one morning and discover it's all a bad dream. So far that hasn't happened. I feel as if my self-esteem has been run over by a truck."

"What does it have to do with self-esteem? Being laid off isn't personal."

"Maybe, but when it's you it *feels* personal."

Erica tried hard to put herself in Claudia's shoes. "I can see that. Right now you're angry. Upset. A bit wounded. But it's important not to waste energy on emotion. Think of it as a problem to be solved. The best thing is to come up with a plan." And plans were her forte. Even in traffic and snow, this was something practical she could do. "We can discuss your goals and what you want for the future."

"I don't know what I want."

"We can start by looking at your skills."

"What skills?"

Erica was determined not to let Claudia wallow. "This is not the time to undervalue yourself. I've tasted your food. You're an exceptionally talented chef."

"That must be why they told me they no longer needed my services."

This, Erica thought savagely, was why she'd set up her company—so that she was in control of her own future. Also because she wasn't interested in playing office politics. She just wanted to get the job done, and done well. On her terms. "Where have you sent your résumé so far?"

"Nowhere. I haven't put in any applications."

"Because this just happened yesterday?"

Claudia hesitated. "Three weeks ago."

"Three—" Erica breathed. "So why haven't you made any applications?"

"Because I don't know if I want to work in kitchens anymore. I'm almost forty."

"What's your age got to do with anything?"

"Turning forty feels significant. So does losing my job. I feel as if it's a sign."

"A sign?"

"A sign that maybe I'm not meant to be a chef." Claudia turned to look at her. "Does that make any sense at all?"

"None." Erica didn't believe in signs. She didn't believe in fate. She believed in deciding what you wanted and going for it, but she had enough experience with people to know she had to handle this in a way that worked for Claudia. "If you don't want to be a chef, then what do you want to do?"

"I don't know."

Erica thought about the times she'd watched Claudia preparing food. It was like watching an artist at work.

"But you love food. You always have."

"Yes, but I don't love working in kitchens. I love cooking, but I hate kitchens. And sadly, if I want to get paid, the two come together."

"You're feeling this way because you had no control over what happened." Erica came to a standstill in a line of traffic. "Have you thought of owning your own restaurant? Being the boss?"

Claudia leaned her head back against the seat and laughed. "I love you, do you know that?"

Erica stiffened. "Did you have a drink on the plane?"

"No, I did not have a drink on the plane."

"Are you sure? Normally, you only tell me you love me after your third glass."

"That's because I know you're uncomfortable with outward displays of affection, but today I'm appreciating what I have. My friends. You and Anna. The world is a scary place, and you make it seem a little less scary. You're always so positive and brave, and right now I'm not either of those things." There was a telltale wobble in Claudia's voice and Erica felt like a fraud.

She wasn't brave. Far from it. She had a nasty habit of avoiding anything difficult and of making sure she didn't put herself in situations that threatened her carefully controlled life and sense of independence. She'd discovered that about herself only recently, when she'd struggled with the idea of taking this trip. But here she was, doing it. So maybe she was braver than she'd thought.

She focused on her friend. "I mean it, Claudia. You could set up on your own. I've tasted your cooking. I'd invest in you. I'd help you."

"Even if I could somehow pull together the funds, which I couldn't, I'm not sure I want to spend the rest of my life cooking. I don't know what I want to do."

"Then it's a good thing we're having this week away." The traffic was moving again and Erica took the turn toward Anna's house. "Operation New Future."

"Honestly? I'd rather talk about books and forget my problems."

Keeping her eyes on the road, Erica reached across and squeezed Claudia's leg. "It's going to be okay, I promise. This is a rough patch, but you're going to come through it. And talking of books, did you read it?"

"Twice." Claudia reached into her bag and pulled out the

book. "I loved it, particularly the way she made his death look like an accident. Brilliant. I had some issues with the choices she made in the middle of the story, but overall I thought it was great. I'm looking forward to chatting about it. Has Anna read it?"

"I don't know. She was grumbling about it being a crime novel, but was also intrigued that it was by Catherine Swift." She glanced at the copy Claudia was holding. "Looks as if you dropped that in the bath or something. What happened to it?"

"I dropped it in the bath. Bath and a book is the closest I get to a hot date these days."

The traffic was moving again and soon they were entering Anna's neighborhood, driving along a wide, tree-lined road. All the houses were decorated for Christmas, their windows offering the curious a peep at sparkling Christmas trees and hearths draped in greenery.

Claudia snuggled deeper into her seat. "It's magical. Reminds me of my childhood when Dad would string lights all around the house." She gave a long sigh and finally smiled. "Okay, now I'm starting to feel Christmassy. Are you?"

Erica was pleased that Claudia seemed happier. She wanted her to stay that way. But the words *magical* and *Christmassy* simply wouldn't leave her mouth no matter how much she tried.

"It's great." It was the best she could do, and fortunately, it seemed to be enough for Claudia.

"This place is so Anna, isn't it? She lives in paradise."

"I can see the appeal, although personally I prefer Manhattan." Erica swung onto Anna's drive and pulled up outside the house. "This place is great for a visit but it would drive me crazy to have to get in the car every time I want to go somewhere. I want to be able to walk, and leap on the subway when necessary."

"She can walk to the village from here, and the waterfront."

"But can she get to Saks and Bloomingdale's? The Met? Carnegie Hall?"

Claudia grinned. "You have different priorities. Anna wants good schools and green space."

"I know." Erica killed the engine and sat for a moment, pondering the lifestyle twinkling in front of her.

Anna lived in a newly built stone-and-clapboard colonial-style home, surrounded by an acre of gardens bordered by trees. Lights glowed in all the windows and it wasn't hard to see why Claudia had described it as paradise.

"It's not the building, is it?" Claudia was staring at the festive wreath decorating the front door. "It's Anna. Everything about her shrieks comfort. She could move into a barn and still make it cozy. Remember what she did to our room in college?"

"I'm not likely to forget." Their room had been a barren, soulless space until Anna had taken over and transformed it. She'd added books, a stylish rug and pretty blankets. There was always a jar stuffed with fresh flowers on the windowsill. "It took me half an hour to remove the throw cushions from my bed before I could sleep."

But she'd found it oddly comforting. Her childhood home had been functional, but could never be described as *cozy*. Her mother had focused on the practical and on making sure Erica was fed and watered. Cushions were considered a pointless luxury. The point, Anna would have said, was that they were a luxury.

As they were sitting there the door opened and Anna appeared on the doorstep with Lola, the family dog, at her ankles. Her dark hair was scooped up in a messy bun and she was wearing a short dress and knee-length boots.

"She looks great," Claudia muttered. "Like an advert for wholesome foods, fresh air and exercise. It makes me want to move to Connecticut and get a spaniel. You?"

"Not if you paid me." Erica opened the door and hauled their luggage out while Anna sprinted down the steps and hugged Claudia.

"I can't believe you're here! It's been six months." Anna spun her around, warmth exuding from her like a log fire in winter. "We are never leaving it so long again."

"Feels like less because you haven't changed. You never change." Claudia was hugging her back, the two of them locked together.

"I'm older. I have four more gray hairs than I did yesterday. I'm wondering if I should tug them out." Anna turned her attention to Erica. "How was the drive?"

"Fine. Oh—" She felt Anna's arms come around her and was engulfed in the warmth of the hug. She hesitated for a moment and then hugged her friend back, breathing in the subtle floral scent that was so very Anna. She smelled like a summer garden, and for a moment Erica was comforted. Whatever happened in the next few days, it would be good to have her friends there. "I'm starving. What have you cooked us?"

"Claudia's favorite. A lamb tagine with apricots and spices from a recipe book Pete bought me last year. It's delicious. Perfect for this cold weather. And I've made a wickedly indulgent chocolate cake for dessert." Anna was generous with her hospitality, never happy unless she had someone to pamper and spoil. "Come on in. Pete isn't back from the office yet, which means we have time to catch up over a glass of wine."

They followed her into the house and Erica was stopped in her tracks by the large Christmas tree in the entryway. When it came to Christmas, Anna never did anything by halves.

"That's bigger than usual. No chance Santa misses your house."

"That's the plan. Pete and I chose the tree on our own this year, and he was indulging me so there was no fighting me over the size."

Erica tilted her head back. "How did you get the star onto the top?"

"It involved Pete, a stepladder and a lot of bad language. Why don't you take your bags up and meet me in the kitchen? Claudia, you're in the guest room. Erica, you're in Meg's room."

Erica frowned. "And how does Meg feel about that?"

"She has tidied her room for you, which is the closest thing to a Christmas miracle we've had around here for a long time, so I think it's safe to assume that she's excited to have her impressive godmother in the space she normally occupies. Apparently, you're a role model."

Claudia gave a snort. "Role model for what?"

"I love you both, too." Ignoring them, Erica sailed up the stairs to Meg's bedroom. She paused in the doorway, remembering when Anna had been pregnant and she'd helped them paint the room a sunny yellow with clouds on the ceiling.

We want you to be godmother, Anna had said, *then we'll be family, connected forever.*

Erica had refused at first, daunted by the task and not at all confident of her ability to fulfill the role required of her, but Anna had refused to back down.

All you have to do is be there for her.

All? To Anna, whose family had never let her down, or walked out on her, it had seemed straightforward. Erica wasn't Anna. She was convinced this would be the end of a beautiful friendship. She wasn't good with babies. She wasn't interested in babies, and she wasn't sure she could convincingly pretend otherwise. She was going to fail at the task.

And then the twins were born and she'd fallen in love. No one had been more surprised than she was. She still remembered the first time she'd held Meg, hours old with a scrunched-up face and a fuzz of dark hair on her head. The baby wasn't even beautiful—not that she ever would have voiced that thought out loud—but that hadn't stopped Erica from falling hard. She'd fallen in love in a way she never had before. It was a hold-nothing-back type of love. A *prepared to throw yourself in front of a bus to save her* type of love.

"Erica!" A squeal came from behind her and Meg hurtled toward her and threw her arms around her.

Erica managed to stop herself from being knocked flat.

Something unraveled inside her. "Hello, have we met? I was looking for Meg, but she's half as tall as you."

Meg pulled away and grinned. "Kids grow, Erica, providing they're fed. I tidied my room for you."

"So I hear. It doesn't seem fair that you have to give up your room. I'm comfortable on the sofa."

"You can't sleep on the sofa. You're used to five-star hotels. And you haven't seen my room since Dad decorated it last." Meg pushed open the door of her bedroom and turned to assess Erica's reaction. "What do you think?"

Erica paused in the doorway. After the yellow bedroom with the clouds, Pete and Anna had turned Meg's room into a fairy grotto, complete with pink walls and a canopy bed. Now it was a haven of teenage sophistication. The walls were covered in vintage movie posters; in one corner was a faux fur beanbag perfect for snuggling, and her bed was stacked with cushions and warm throws.

It was no wonder teenagers struggled to get up in the morning, Erica thought. If she was cocooned in this bed, she wouldn't want to get up, either.

Did Meg know how lucky she was, having Anna and Pete as parents?

"It's a great room." On a stand in the corner was an old-fashioned turntable and next to it a stack of records. "That's cool."

"It's my record collection. I've been building it up for a year." Meg followed her gaze. "It's more fun than having everything on your phone."

"It really is." Erica picked up the sketch on Meg's desk. "Did you do this?"

"Yes, but I was just messing around." She was dismissive, her face scarlet.

Erica knew insecurity when she saw it. "It's incredible. You have real talent."

"You think so? Thanks. I've been building up my portfolio.

I love art and graphic design. I think I might want to work in advertising or maybe publicity. Look." Meg grabbed a remote control from her bed and pressed a button, and lights twinkled around her ceiling. "They look great when I'm making content for social media."

Erica felt old.

Claudia appeared in the doorway with Daniel and after more hugs and greetings, they headed downstairs to the kitchen.

Anna was in her element, chopping, frying, plucking fresh herbs from the pots on the kitchen counter. Christmas jazz played quietly in the background, and four long-stemmed glasses gleamed in the center of the large table.

"Erica, grab the champagne from the fridge." Anna slid the casserole back into the oven. "Pete just called to say he's on his way, which gives us a good hour to say all the things we don't want him to hear."

"Since when have you kept secrets from Pete?" Erica opened Anna's fridge and stared in astonishment at the array of foods. "How do you find anything in here?"

"What sort of a question is that? It's a fridge."

"My fridge looks nothing like this."

"That's because you never cook for yourself." Anna nudged her to one side and grabbed a bottle of champagne from behind a stack of fresh vegetables. "I was saving this for Christmas, but having you here is better than Christmas. Sit down. I've got this."

"You're too used to room service," Claudia said to Erica. "That's your problem."

"Why is that a problem? There's nothing wrong with room service." Erica took the champagne from Anna and popped the cork. "The sound of celebration."

Anna produced a plate of freshly made canapés. "I'm always nervous to feed you." She offered the plate to Claudia, who scanned the food and chose something.

"I don't know why. You're an excellent cook. And anyway,

there is nothing a chef loves more than someone else putting food in front of them." She bit into the canapé and closed her eyes. "Delicious."

Anna looked relieved. "You think so? Thanks. It's a new recipe. If you were staying for two nights I'd make my cheese soufflé for you tomorrow."

"You mastered it?"

"Yes, thanks to the tips you gave me."

Erica took a sip of champagne. It slipped down, ice-cold and delicious. She felt herself relax as the conversation flowed around her and the warmth of Anna's kitchen seeped into her bones.

The dog padded across, sat down on her feet and looked at her with adoring eyes.

"Don't be fooled. She just wants what you're eating. Push her away," Anna said, but Erica bent to stroke Lola's soft ears.

"I always wanted a dog when I was little."

"We know. We know you, remember?" Anna picked up her glass. "We also know you won't ever get a dog because you don't want the responsibility."

And they were right, of course. She never would get a dog. And they did know her. All those tiny details embedded themselves and became part of the fabric of friendship. It was like having the key to a secret door that no one else had. She spent so much of her life with the door to her real self firmly closed, that it jolted her to be with her friends. With them, the door was open. They saw right in.

She smoothed Lola's silky fur. "You're right. I won't ever get a dog. It would be irresponsible. I'm never home."

"If you had a dog, you might feel like spending more time at home."

"A dog is a big step," Claudia said. "She should start with a houseplant. Maybe an artificial one."

"A houseplant doesn't love you unconditionally."

"But nor does it cause you any trouble."

Erica decided it was time to shift the subject of conversation. "I don't want a dog and I don't want a houseplant, artificial or otherwise. I'm happy with my life, thank you." Although if that was true, why was she about to follow a course of action that would shake it all up?

"Lucky you." Claudia finished her champagne. "My life is a disaster. Maybe I should adopt eight dogs."

Erica wrenched her mind away from her own problems. After all, anything happening to her was her own choice whereas Claudia had lost her relationship and her job. She couldn't fix the relationship part, because she had no expertise in that direction, but she could help with the job.

"When we're away we're going to sit down and come up with some ideas about what you can do next."

"Isn't it obvious?" Anna topped up Claudia's glass. "She needs to find a job in a kitchen that excites her."

"Hello. I'm sitting right here. You don't have to talk about me as if I'm not in the room." Claudia lifted her hand to stop Anna pouring. "And I hate kitchens. I hate kitchen politics. I've given up cooking. I was explaining to Erica in the car—I just don't enjoy it anymore. We need to think of something else, although what, I have no idea. I'm too old to retrain."

Erica caught Anna's eye and gave a quick shake of her head. She knew that the time to talk about it wasn't when Claudia was tired.

"She's twenty-six, did I tell you that?" Claudia reached for her glass. "The girl John is now with. Twenty-six. Fourteen years younger than me. No wrinkles, no gray hairs. Abs as flat and hard as oak flooring. She's nearer to twenty than forty."

"But she's not always going to be twenty-six," Anna said, "whereas you will always be amazing. You're smart and kind and special and if John doesn't appreciate your qualities, then you're better off without him."

Erica raised her glass. "I agree. Also, I bet she can't cook the way you do."

"Judging by how slim she is, I don't think she eats at all."

Anna frowned. "You've met her?"

"Not exactly. She's a TV presenter. Annoyingly perky and her career is on the rise whereas everything about me is sliding, from my career to my boobs. I'm like a soufflé that someone took out of the oven an hour ago."

"Please don't tell me you've been watching her on TV."

Claudia hesitated. "Occasionally. When I feel like torturing myself."

"You have to stop that," Erica said. "It's not healthy."

"I know. Chocolate isn't healthy, either, but somehow it makes me feel better about life. I don't have your self-discipline. Do you know what I really envy? Confidence. I wouldn't have the confidence to take my clothes off in front of a twenty-six-year-old, but it didn't bother John at all. Why is it that men become more attractive as they age and women become invisible?"

"It's one of the many injustices of the universe," Anna said but Erica shook her head.

"Don't let yourself be invisible. I would have no problem taking my clothes off in front of a twenty-six-year-old if I found him attractive."

"That's because you never eat chocolate and look about a decade younger than you really are," Claudia said gloomily. "I envy you being married to Pete, Anna. He's such a great guy. Also, you're guaranteed to have great sex whenever you want it for the rest of your life. I will probably never have sex again."

"That's ridiculous," Anna said and Erica nodded agreement.

"That is ridiculous. I can have sex whenever I want it. Being forty doesn't change that."

"Yes, because you just call sexy Jack," Claudia said. "I don't have a Pete in my life, and I don't have a Jack, sexy or otherwise."

Erica raised her eyebrows. "Jack and I are strictly casual."

"Of course you are." Claudia exchanged glances with Anna, and Erica sighed and put her glass down.

"Why the look?"

"No reason. And anyway, I don't want casual sex. I want relationship sex. The sort of sex where you fall asleep together afterward and wake up still together. The sort of sex where you feel close to someone and know you're going to be seeing them again."

Erica was still thinking about that look. They obviously thought that her relationship with Jack wasn't casual, but that was absurd. She and Jack went weeks without seeing each other.

She was about to point that out when she heard the sound of the front door opening.

Lola barked and went racing out of the kitchen, and a moment later returned with Pete.

"This is good. Our kitchen is full of our favorite people." He greeted them warmly, quietly commiserated with Claudia for her recent woes, and then tugged Anna against him and kissed her on the mouth.

They'd been together for twenty-two years, Erica thought as her gaze slid away, and he still kissed Anna as if he couldn't help himself; as if seeing Anna was the best part of his day.

She imagined the two of them ten years in the future, then twenty and thirty. They'd grow old together, bound by love and the life they'd shared.

"Could you two have a fight or something?" Claudia took a mouthful of wine. "All this marital harmony is a little nauseating for those of us less fortunate."

Anna pulled away, her cheeks pink. "Good thing you didn't arrive five minutes ago," she said as she brushed flakes of snow from Pete's shoulders. "We were talking about sex."

"Damn the traffic." Smiling, Pete helped himself to the last of the champagne. "Sex is one of my favorite topics."

It was unfortunate that Meg chose that moment to come into

the room. "Ugh, Dad, that's gross. Please. You are too old to think about sex. It's disgusting."

Pete grabbed Anna and kissed her on the neck. "I love you. Have I told you that lately? I love you."

"I need to leave home right now. I can't wait until next year. This is cruelty to teenagers." Meg backed away and sent Erica a pleading look. "How do you stand it? Message me when they've stopped." She fled from the room and Pete grinned and let Anna go.

"Works every time."

Anna was laughing, too, and she gave him a little push. "You have to stop winding her up, Pete."

"If ever I want some private time with Anna, all I have to do is kiss her." Pete shrugged off his coat and slung it over the back of the nearest chair. "The kids leave the room so fast. It's my best and only parenting tip."

"They'll be off to college next year," Anna said, "and we're going to have nothing but private time."

"That will be romantic." Claudia slumped in her chair, not even bothering to hide her envy. "You must be looking forward to it. Nonstop date nights."

Erica saw Pete glance briefly at Anna, who was suddenly busy laying the table.

What did that look mean?

When Anna had first introduced them, Pete had been a shy, gangly teenager with untidy hair and a passion for science fiction, computer games and crossword puzzles. But there had been a kindness and warmth to him, and also a sense of humor. He and Anna were always laughing about something.

He'd grown into a quietly confident man, who was a good listener and a rock for his family. He was also, Erica mused, very attractive. Gangly had given way to tall and broad shouldered. The crinkles at the corners of his very blue eyes were testament to the fact that his sense of humor had remained intact.

She knew it for a fact, because whenever she was staying here she often heard Pete and Anna laughing about something. She felt a twinge of envy and the feeling irritated her. She wasn't used to feeling envious. She didn't *like* feeling envious. She was forty years old and happy with her life choices. Wasn't she?

SEVEN

Hattie

"You're fully booked from now until January?" Lynda put a mug of tea in front of Hattie. "That's quite an achievement. Also, a lot of pressure on you."

They were sitting in the Petersons' cozy farmhouse kitchen and thanks to a generous helping of Lynda's apple and ginger cake and the warmth from the range cooker, Hattie was finding it harder and harder to stay awake. Her head felt fuzzy and her limbs were leaden. She could barely string a sentence together. Still, it was good to be with Lynda, who always made her feel as if she was doing a great job and not just hanging on by a thread.

"I don't know about an achievement. It's a relief, that's for sure." She suppressed a yawn and tried not to slur her words. "Providing we don't have staff issues, the inn should be fine for a few months."

"I'm sure the inn will be fine. It's you I'm worried about."

"Me?" Hattie took a sip of tea to wake herself up. She was reaching the point where she was going to have to slap her own face or go and stand naked in the freezing air. "Why are you worried about me?"

"Because you're twenty-eight years old and you're working yourself to the bone," Lynda said. "You're about to fall asleep in my kitchen."

"Your kitchen is comfortable. Also, I didn't have a good night. Delphi's had this cough and then last night she had a bad dream, so I caved in and let her sleep in my bed." Was that an awful thing to do? When she was pregnant she'd read every parenting book she could lay her hands on, but after Delphi was born there had been no time. Now she was making it up as she went along. "She wriggles and sleeps across the bed. Every time I fell asleep last night she rolled over and woke me up. Also, she kept stretching out her arms like a starfish and smacking me in the face."

"Believe it or not I remember those days well."

"Really?" As hard as she tried, she couldn't imagine Noah in any form other than a disturbingly attractive adult male.

"On second thought, forget the tea." Lynda gently removed the mug from her fingers and gestured to the sofa in the corner of the room. "Close your eyes for five minutes."

"Oh, I couldn't. It wouldn't feel right." But that didn't mean she wasn't tempted. She'd reached the point where she would have killed for just one hour of undisturbed rest.

"I think you'll find it will feel just fine." Lynda urged her gently out of the chair and toward the sofa.

"I should probably be getting back. I still have to decorate the library. It's the last room I need to do. I should have done it before now, but things got away from me. I have a group of friends checking in—they're a book club—" her head swam a little "—which made me think maybe we should make that a regular thing locally. Your book club meets in people's houses on a Wednesday, isn't that right? You could use our library. Sorry, how did I get onto your book club? What was I saying?" She stopped, her mind suddenly blank.

"You were telling me you need to decorate the library for guests checking in, and I'm telling you that you'll do a better job if you're not falling asleep on your feet." Lynda plumped a couple of cushions on the sofa. "When I was a young mother the hardest thing was accepting help, but things were better when I did. Put your head down just for five minutes, honey."

Hattie felt a rush of love and gratitude. It had been so long since anyone had fussed over her, and she enjoyed the novelty of being the cared for and not the carer. Sometimes doing everything on your own was hard. It meant you were constantly on alert, never completely able to allow your mind to shut down.

And there was no doubt it would be a treat to just close her eyes for five minutes. But still she couldn't quite forget her responsibilities. "Delphi—"

"I can watch Delphi. I'm just pottering around here cooking and the child is happy enough over there, so snatch a few minutes while you can. I wouldn't be surprised if she falls asleep, too, right where she is."

Hattie glanced at her daughter.

Delphi was sitting cross-legged on a large cushion, two of Panther's kittens in her lap and her favorite soft toy dinosaur on the floor next to her. She looked completely content and Hattie knew that any suggestion that perhaps they should be going home would be met with protest.

Beyond the windows snow fell, blurring the outline of the mountains behind.

Would it hurt anyone if she just closed her eyes for a moment?

"She's fine." Lynda reached for the throw draped over the back of the sofa. "It's been a while since I've looked after a five-year-old, but I'm sure I still have what it takes. It will be good practice for when I'm a grandmother."

"You're going to be a grandmother?"

"One day, hopefully. Now lie down and rest."

Did Noah know he was supposed to be producing a grandchild?

She was too tired to unravel the meaning from the words and somehow Hattie found herself sliding off her shoes and curling up on the sofa. Her head sank into the pile of soft cushions and she was instantly asleep. She didn't even feel Lynda tuck the soft throw around her.

She woke to the sound of voices and lay there, disoriented. Still half asleep, her brain kept trying to drift off again.

"Between running the inn and being a mother—and excelling at both—there is nothing left for herself. The girl is exhausted and that's not good for anyone. Something needs to be done."

"She's not a girl." This voice was deeper. Rougher. Noah. "She's a woman."

"I'm glad you've noticed. I was starting to wonder if you had eyes in your head."

"Don't meddle, Lynda." Roy this time. "Leave it alone. It's not your business."

"I'm making it my business." Lynda managed to raise her voice without actually raising her voice. "She's as good as family and Lord knows she needs people who are as good as family because she doesn't have any actual family. But she has us. And don't tell me to leave it alone, Roy Peterson, because I will not leave it alone."

"Maybe she won't appreciate your interference."

"Or maybe she'd be grateful for it. Just because someone doesn't ask for help doesn't mean they don't want it or need it. Particularly women. Women are so used to coping that sometimes they don't even realize there's another way. We're going to show her there's another way. Good. So that's agreed. You'll take her out, Noah. Thursday works for me."

"Excuse me?"

"I'll have to babysit, obviously. Thursday is a good night for me. Tuesday is my choir practice and Wednesday is book club. The weekends are Hattie's busiest time at the inn, so I'm thinking Thursday is the night that works for all of us."

"Anything else?" Noah's tone was somewhere between aghast and amused. "Would you like to pick a restaurant? Give me a script?"

"You can choose the restaurant, as long as it's somewhere fancy. No burger joints, and nowhere too noisy. You need to be able to hear yourselves talk. Take her somewhere she needs to dress up a little and eat food she doesn't cook for herself or the child. And as for a script, I'm sure you can formulate a sentence if you put your mind to it, but if you need some hints then I'd suggest you give her an evening where for once she isn't an innkeeper or a mother."

Lynda was trying to fix her up with Noah.

This was mortifying.

Hattie was fully awake now, but she kept her eyes tightly closed because this was not the time for them to know she'd overheard the conversation. Behind her closed lids she burned with embarrassment.

If she'd felt awkward around Noah before, it was going to be so much worse now. Particularly as he wasn't exactly jumping at his mother's suggestion.

"Mom—"

"Don't *mom* me in that tone."

"I'm a grown man." His tone was surprisingly patient in the circumstances. "I don't need my mother to organize a date. I can organize my own social life, thank you."

"Well, forgive me for not knowing that. I can only go on the evidence before me, which is that you're slower moving than your father."

"I moved at the exact pace that was right for me," Roy protested, and Noah reached across the table and helped himself to a slice of cake.

"And I'm doing the same."

"When you decided to move back here, we were delighted of course. But I don't like to see you sacrificing your own social life for this place. And I'm your mother. It's not a crime to want to see you happy."

"I'm happy." There was a pause. "Has it occurred to you that she might not want to spend an evening with me?"

"You're a grown man, as you keep pointing out, so I'm sure you're big enough to handle rejection if rejection is coming your way."

Now would be a good time to wake up, Hattie thought, before the conversation got worse.

Fortunately for her, Delphi stirred at that moment and Lynda immediately stopped the conversation.

"The little one is awake. Who knew Panther would make such a good cushion? There, honey, come to Lynda and have a big old hug. How do you feel about chocolate milkshake?"

Hattie opened her eyes in time to see Delphi wrap her arms around Lynda's neck and rest her head on her shoulder as she was carried to the kitchen table.

"Noah, you hold her for a moment while I make the milkshake. I need two hands for the task." She handed Delphi over and Noah took her, settling her on his arm.

Delphi thrust her soft toy dinosaur at him.

"He's called Huge."

"Good name."

"He's a diplodocus. He has a very long neck. See?"

Noah gave Huge his undivided attention. "I do see."

"I sleep with him."

"That must be comforting. He doesn't wake you up?"

Hattie, who had woken to find Huge wedged under her back on more than one occasion, thought she should probably be the one to be answering that question.

And talking of waking up, she decided it was time to officially declare herself awake.

She sat up, dizzy from having slept so heavily. "I passed out. I'm sorry."

"Don't be sorry." Lynda wiped her hands on her apron. "You obviously needed the sleep."

"It's all the Christmas tree decorating." Hattie slid her feet back into her boots. She wasn't going to look at Noah. She didn't dare. "And talking of Christmas trees, Delphi and I really should be going. The tree in the library isn't going to decorate itself."

"All the more reason to have something to eat first. It will give you both energy." Lynda placed a milkshake and a cookie on the table. "We're just having a snack. I made one for you, too."

Lynda had made her a milkshake?

"My dad used to make the best milkshakes." Sometimes memories stung and sometimes they soothed. This one soothed. "Takes me right back to childhood. He was heavy-handed with the chocolate."

"Sounds as if your dad had some serious parenting skills."

"He was the best." Hattie sat down and watched as Noah settled Delphi in the chair next to her. Delphi drank her milkshake, holding the glass carefully with both hands. When she put the glass down she had a ring of chocolate around her mouth and a big smile on her face.

"Oh, look at the little one, covered in chocolate." Lynda fussed over Delphi, who sat on the chair with her legs swinging. "Now then, Hattie, I was thinking that on Thursday I could come over to you and babysit. It will give me an excuse to sit quietly with a book for a while and it will give you a chance to get out and have some time to yourself. You've been working yourself hard. You need a break."

Hattie froze on her chair. She hadn't expected Lynda to be so direct. "I don't really—"

"Noah is going to buy you dinner. He has been working hard, too, and I'm worried about him. You'd be doing me a favor."

Noah frowned. "There's no—"

"You don't have to thank me. You spend all the hours taking care of the farm for us and you deserve a night out. You young things should go and enjoy yourselves. Roy and I will cope just fine, won't we, Roy?"

Roy looked like a man who knew when he was trapped. "I'm sure I can struggle on if I put my mind to it."

Hattie cleared her throat. "I'm fine, really. I don't need a night off."

Lynda gave her shoulder a squeeze. "When did you last dress up and go out?"

"Well, I—"

"Exactly, you can't remember. You're young, Hattie. You should be getting out there and having some adult time. Don't you agree, Roy?"

Roy studied the cookie in his hand. "I think Hattie should probably have a say in it? Maybe she doesn't want to go to dinner."

"Well, of course she does. The girl has to eat, doesn't she? And she doesn't want to eat alone. So that's sorted." Lynda cleared up the glasses and loaded them into the dishwasher. "It's bitterly cold out there and snowing again so you're not walking home. Noah will give you a ride."

Hattie glanced out the window and saw that it was indeed snowing. Big, fat flakes were swirling past the window and she hadn't even noticed. She'd end up carrying Delphi, which was fine for short distances, but after a while it made her arms and her back ache. Also, she didn't want to make Delphi's cough worse.

Noah scooped up his keys and this time didn't argue with his mother. "Good plan. Let's get you both safely home."

Hattie thanked Roy, gave Lynda a hug, and then dressed a wriggling Delphi in her coat, hat and scarf.

The moment they opened the door to the kitchen the cold air slammed into them.

Noah turned up the collar of his coat and turned to check

on her but Hattie had survived enough New England winters to know how to dress for the occasion.

They stomped through the fresh snow to his car. The cold air bit through her clothing, making her long to return to the warm kitchen.

"You don't need to do this. Delphi and I could perfectly well walk. We didn't need rescuing."

He opened the car door for her. "Maybe you didn't need rescuing, but I did. If we'd stayed in that kitchen much longer my mother would have mapped out the rest of my life and not just the next week." He lifted Delphi into the back and fastened her seat belt carefully. "You comfortable, honey?"

Delphi nodded and Noah winked at her and then waited for Hattie to get in the car before settling himself in the driver's seat.

Here in the confines of the car she was even more aware of the size and power of him. She told herself that it was his kindness to her child that was making her feel this intense and almost painful longing.

She wondered if he was annoyed at the prospect of driving her home. "Your parents are so kind."

"They love you. Think of you as a daughter."

"So what does that make you—my brother?" She saw his smile flash.

"Definitely not that. And you wouldn't want me as a brother. I'm annoying. Only child, so terrible at sharing. If there's one piece of shortbread left on the plate, then that's going to be mine. You wouldn't get special treatment. I'd run right over you."

She didn't believe it for a moment. She already knew how generous he was. She'd seen evidence of it repeatedly.

"I'm an only child." And she'd often wished she'd had someone to share the ups and downs of life with.

"There you go. Can you imagine the scene in the kitchen? Both of us fighting over that single piece of shortbread? It could get vicious." He started the engine and headed down the track toward the road. "So, about dinner. What time shall I pick you up on Thursday?"

She glanced at him. "You're not seriously going to take me to dinner?"

"If you know my mother as well as I think you know my mother, then you'll also know that it's going to be easier to go to dinner than to argue about it."

Her heart kicked up its pace. "Do you always do everything your mother tells you?"

"Hardly ever," he said. "Just the things that seem like they might be a good idea. You have been working too hard. So have I. We both need to eat."

"I don't know." She pretended to think. "Are you going to fight me for my dinner?"

"That depends."

"On?"

"On whether you order something that looks better than what's on my plate. If I prefer yours, I might fight you. Does seven twenty-five work for you?"

"Seven twenty-five? That's very specific."

"My mother suggested seven-thirty. It doesn't pay to have everything go her way."

It would have been easy to say yes. She wanted to say yes very badly. Being with him made her feel lighter, even though the load of her life was just the same.

She tried to think through the implications. *Consequences*, she thought. *Everything had consequences.*

"I'm not sure it's a good idea."

"Let's find out, shall we? It's just dinner, Hattie." He pulled up outside the inn and turned to look at her. "Dinner, that's all. If you hate my table manners and decide you never want to eat with me again, I won't bear a grudge." He was smiling and so was she.

"How can you be sure? You might decide to punish me by giving me the smallest, weediest Christmas trees from now on."

"I only grow magnificent specimens."

"You might give me one with a sloping trunk so that all my decorations slide off."

He considered. "That's possible, but you'll have to take your chances. You seem like a risk taker to me."

They both knew she was anything but a risk taker, but the conversation had made her realize how much she wanted to spend an evening with him, just the two of them.

He was making it all sound simple and she was ready to go along with that, even though she knew it wasn't simple at all. But then life rarely was simple, was it? It was full of good decisions and bad decisions, of twists and turns, ups and downs, moments of intense wrenching pain and, occasionally, moments of heightened joy and pleasure.

And when those good moments came, you had to grab them.

"All right," she said. "Thursday. Seven twenty-five."

And she had to hope this turned out to be a good decision.

EIGHT

Claudia

"You could retrain as a teacher," Anna said. "I've always thought that would be a rewarding career."

"I don't want to retrain as a teacher." Claudia was in the back of the car, staring out the window as they left Anna's house and neighborhood behind. She was trying not to remember the look Anna and Pete had shared as they'd kissed each other goodbye. "And anyway, I'm too old to rethink my whole life and start again."

Or maybe she wasn't ready for a rethink. She was still adjusting to the fact that she didn't want to cook. There had never been a time in her life when she hadn't wanted to cook. It was like losing a part of herself. Remembering how food used to excite her, she felt bereft.

"You're never too old to rethink your life." Erica was driving, but that didn't stop her joining in the conversation. "And don't give me drama while I'm driving."

Anna glanced at her. "Are you okay? You seem a little tense this morning. Didn't you sleep?"

"I slept well, thank you."

"Was it the work call you took at breakfast? You usually have a no-work-calls rule when we're away."

"This was an exception, but no, that's not the reason. And I'm not tense, I'm focused."

Claudia shifted to try to get comfortable, but it was impossible. It felt as if they were back in college. The only difference was that they were in Erica's sleek sports car and not Anna's ancient Ford Mustang, donated by her parents and maintained by Pete.

Still, Claudia was crammed in the back as always with her legs pushed up to her chin, or so it felt.

Next to her was the luggage that hadn't fit into the trunk, and a stack of gifts. Anna's were hand wrapped, neatly tied with string and decorated with greenery from her garden. Erica's were store wrapped in shiny expensive paper folded with geometric perfection and secured with elaborate bows. Looking at the expensive wrapping on Erica's gifts, Claudia worried that she hadn't spent enough. She dismissed the thought. Their friendship had never been about money, and it never would be. She'd made her gifts and that, she told herself, made them priceless.

She restacked the gifts to give herself more room. "I have a question. Given that you're not financially challenged, Erica, why didn't you buy a bigger car?"

"I don't need a bigger car."

Claudia tried to find a position that wasn't going to cut off the blood supply to her lower limbs. "Trust me. From where I'm sitting, you need a bigger car."

"Why? Usually it's just me, and occasionally one other." Erica flashed a wicked smile at the mirror and Claudia laughed.

It was good to be back with her friends. Just being with them made her feel better. They made her feel more confident. Happier. Lighter.

But it was also true that she felt a little envious of them. How could she not? There was Erica in her beautiful clothes, so confident and sure of herself and so obviously happy with her life. She was financially secure and was doing what she loved.

And then there was Anna. Anna, with her shiny dark hair and her kindness. She wore her life like a favorite dress that fit perfectly and made her feel good. And why wouldn't she? She had everything she'd always wanted. Pete, the twins and a beautiful home. Anna's home was like another member of their family, sheltering them and holding all their memories. It represented security, both literally and figuratively. A place where they could all gather.

Claudia was genuinely happy for her friends, but that didn't stop her from wishing she was as settled in her life as they were. A year ago she'd been settled. She'd had no inkling that everything she'd built was going to fall apart.

She'd been with John for ten years, and yet when he'd walked out and moved in with someone else, she hadn't seen it coming. How was it possible to be with a person that long and not see that coming? What was wrong with her? It was something she thought about constantly. It nagged at her in the middle of the night when she should have been sleeping.

She'd lost everything and was basically starting again at the age of forty.

Her friends were exchanging banter in the front of the car and Claudia listened, soothed by the familiar teasing.

Not everything had changed. Whatever she might have lost, she still had her friends. They were the glue that held her life together. The cushion that softened the blows.

She gazed out the window, pondering her options. "If you've spent your whole adult life training to be something, is it a waste to throw that away?"

Erica glanced in the mirror. "I assume we're talking specifically about you, not generally?"

"Yes. I spent so many years training to be a chef. It feels wrong to walk away from that."

Erica shrugged. "It depends why you're walking away. If

you're doing it because you're upset that you were laid off then yes, it's a waste. You'd be punishing yourself for no reason. But if this really is about cooking and not about your last job, of course you should walk away. Life is too short to slog at something you're not enjoying."

"Even if I've done it for most of my life?"

"Of course. You don't keep doing something if you're hating it. And whoever said you have to do the same thing forever? People retrain all the time."

She made it sound so simple, but Claudia knew it wasn't simple.

"Do you ever wonder if you made all the wrong choices? I've been wondering that a lot lately."

Anna was silent.

It was Erica who answered. "Never," she said. "And we are not doing this. We are not spending the four-hour drive looking back on our lives and deciding we made all the wrong decisions. What is the point? This is a vacation. The whole point of a vacation is to leave your troubles behind."

Maybe that depended on the size of your troubles, Claudia thought. It was hard to leave hers behind because she needed to make some decisions, and she needed to make them quickly. If she was going to give up being a chef, then she needed to find something else to do.

Anna turned to look at Erica. "Are you *sure* you're okay?"

"I'm totally fine."

Anna studied her. "And there really is nothing you'd change if you could have your time again?"

"Apart from maybe persuading you both to hold our book club in the Caribbean? No. Nothing." Erica gripped the wheel. "If we must have this conversation about regrets, then let's postpone it until we're ninety. Right now we have everything to play for. If there is something you want, then go for it."

Claudia had no idea what she wanted. She wished her thinking were as clear as Erica's.

Anna didn't seem inclined to drop the subject. "You wouldn't change a single thing?"

"No." Erica sounded exasperated. "I don't think like that. I don't ask myself those questions. It's not helpful. So what if you decide you made the wrong call about something five years ago? Nothing you can do about it now. Learn from it and move on."

"I ask myself those questions all the time." Claudia relaxed against the seat, lulled by the movement of the car and the changing scenery beyond the window. "Mostly at three in the morning when I'm lying awake staring at my ceiling."

"That's your problem right there." Erica turned off the main highway and they took a road that led through a forested area. The road stretched ahead of them, clear of traffic. "Everyone knows you never pay attention to thoughts that arrive in your brain at three in the morning. They are intruders to be shut out. You don't listen to them."

"What if those intruders have loud voices?"

"Life always seems at its worst at three in the morning," Anna said. "It happens to me, too. I think I keep so busy the rest of the time, it's only in the middle of the night that I have time to think about something other than the next thing on my to-do list." She glanced at Erica. "You don't find your mind wandering if you're awake at three in the morning?"

"There's only ever one reason I'm awake in the night," Erica said, and Anna rolled her eyes.

"And just like that we're back to sexy Jack."

"Could we stop calling him sexy Jack?"

"I don't think so." Anna stretched out her legs. "Remember all those nights in college where we used to lie awake talking about what we were going to do with our lives?"

"We were idealistic," Claudia said. "We didn't have a clue."

"We were ambitious and bold," Erica said. "And if you can't be ambitious and bold when you're twenty, when can you be?"

"I think what none of us realized," Anna said slowly, "is

that you can plan all you like, but sometimes life just happens. It's unpredictable."

Erica turned her head and flashed her a half smile. "You mean like you and Pete forgetting to use a condom? That was entirely predictable."

Claudia laughed and Anna smiled, too.

It was no secret that her pregnancy had been a happy accident.

"I don't know why you'd worry at three in the morning," Claudia said to Anna. "Your life is perfect. Your marriage is perfect."

Anna was silent for a moment. "No one's life is perfect."

Claudia felt a flicker of alarm. If there was something wrong with Anna's perfect life then that was her faith in the world and humankind destroyed forever. Was something wrong between Anna and Pete? No. It couldn't be anything to do with Pete. He and Anna had a rock-solid relationship. Acknowledging that made her realize she hadn't totally lost her faith in humanity. John had cheated, but she wasn't taking that to mean that good relationships didn't exist. She did not believe that.

For the first time since John had moved out and she'd lost her job, she felt something that might have been hope.

It was like discovering a bleeding wound was superficial and would heal in time.

Watching Pete and Anna the night before had made her think harder about her relationship with John. When had John last looked at her the way Pete looked at Anna? And had she really felt about John the way Anna felt about Pete? Her friends had been together almost twice as long as she'd been with John and yet they were still so obviously in love. How did you tell the difference between love and comfortable habit?

She pushed the question aside, finding it too uncomfortable to dwell on but it stayed there, hovering in the periphery of her thoughts. Everyone's relationship was different, of course, and everyone wanted something different.

She relaxed back in her seat, feeling a little more optimistic.

Resolving to try to nurture that positive feeling, she focused on Anna.

"What do you worry about at three in the morning?"

"Everything," Anna said. "All the things I said that I wish I hadn't said. All the things I have to do. All the things that could go wrong. All the things that are changing that are outside my control. And don't tell me to make a list of my worries before I go to sleep because I've tried that and it doesn't work."

Erica glanced at her. "Why worry about all the things that could go wrong? Why not wait for them to *actually* go wrong, and then worry?"

"I never said my worries were logical."

"What does Pete do when you're lying awake worrying?"

"Usually, he's asleep, but occasionally if I'm really anxious I wake him."

"And he doesn't kill you for that?" Erica shook her head. "That man is a saint."

Claudia realized that Anna still hadn't answered the question. "What's changing that is outside your control?" Anna's life seemed so steady and predictable to her. It was one of the things she envied most.

"My family." Anna was silent for a moment. "Over the years I've had the occasional moment of panic when I've thought about the day when the twins leave home, but I always pushed it aside because it was something in the future, but the other night I realized that the future has arrived. Next year they'll be leaving, and I'm dreading it." There was a quiver in her voice and Erica frowned.

"You're worried about how they'll cope without you?"

"No." Anna swallowed. "I'm worried about how I'll cope without them."

"But the alternative would be to have them living with you forever. You wouldn't want that, surely?"

"I wouldn't." Anna paused. "Or maybe I would."

Erica waited for a break in the traffic and made a right turn.

"You're making no sense. Your job as a parent is to raise your child to be a competent human being capable of independence."

"I know. And I've done that. But that doesn't mean I'm going to open champagne and congratulate myself on a job well-done when they leave. I'm going to miss them horribly. I almost wish Meg and I fought more. It might make it easier to let her go. Maybe I'd be counting down the days until she left. And of course I haven't told them I feel this way. Whenever they talk about college and leaving I'm encouraging and enthusiastic—which is exhausting, by the way—but the truth is I love being a mother. It's what I've always wanted, and now it's ending and I'm—" her voice suddenly thickened "—well, I'm heartbroken."

There was silence in the car.

Erica glanced in the mirror and caught Claudia's eye.

Claudia knew that was her cue to say something. "Empty-nest syndrome. Isn't that what it's called?"

Anna cleared her throat. "Probably, but in the end it doesn't matter what it's called. It only matters how it feels, and it feels awful. And it hasn't even happened yet! If I can feel this bad anticipating it, how much worse am I going to feel actually doing it? And as well as missing them emotionally, I feel as if I'm about to lose my job. The only job I've ever loved." She sent Claudia an apologetic look. "I'm sorry. That was beyond tactless in the circumstances."

"No, it wasn't. I never loved my job." Claudia felt bad that she hadn't given more thought to how Anna might be feeling now that the twins were about to leave home. "Does Pete know you feel this way?"

"Yes, but it's different for him. His life isn't going to change as much because he spends so much time working. He'll miss them, I'm sure, but it won't be as hard for him."

Of course Pete knew. If she had a problem, Anna would have talked to Pete about it. They talked about everything.

John had rarely talked about his problems or feelings. If he'd had a bad day at work his solution was to go for a long run alone, or pour himself a drink. On the few occasions she'd tried to talk about work stress, his response had been *you'll figure it out.*

And that was true. She hadn't ever expected him to solve her problems, but there had been many occasions when she would have appreciated a hug or a few warm words like the ones Pete gave Anna whenever she was stressed.

Claudia felt envious of her friend's relationship. Did she realize how lucky she was? How rare it was to have a relationship where your partner was caring and supportive? "Knowing Pete, I'm sure he had an opinion. What does he think you should do?"

Anna picked at the corner of her nail. "Don't even ask."

"And now, obviously, we have to ask and you have to answer." Erica leaned on her horn as another driver overtook them and almost clipped her car. "Tell us what Pete said."

Anna rested her hand back in her lap. "He asked if I wanted another baby."

"You're joking. That is so caveman of him."

"I think it's caring," Claudia said. "He knows how much Anna loves being a mother. He knows *her.* It's actually very romantic." She felt another twinge of envy.

Erica shuddered. "You have a strange definition of romance. *Here, have another baby. Let me chain you to the nursery for another few years.*"

"You know Pete isn't like that," Anna said. "It's my choice."

"Right." Erica gripped the wheel. "So are you going to do that?"

"Have another baby? No, of course not." Anna stared ahead. "At least, I don't think so."

"You don't *think* so? Anna, you're almost forty!"

"Thanks for the reminder. Women do still have babies at forty, you know. But that isn't the point. The point is that no matter how many children you have, there is always a last child. So I suppose deep down I know this is something I have to face eventually. And only I can do it. If I decide to have another baby then it has to be for the right reasons. And now let's talk about something else."

"In a minute." Erica slowed as the traffic came to a standstill. "Surely the kids leaving has some benefits. For a start you and Pete will be able to have sex all over the house. Imagine the freedom."

"I think that will just remind me how empty the house is."

She wasn't the only one whose life had changed, Claudia thought.

"It feels strange, handling a big change at forty. This should be a time for building on everything that has gone before."

"Yes." Anna turned in her seat to look at her. "And I don't feel I have the confidence to do anything different. But there are so many examples of people who do."

Erica tapped her fingers on the wheel, impatient for the traffic to move. "What are you saying? That the decisions you make when you're young dictate the rest of your life? That's ridiculous. Not to mention restrictive. Some people change a lot between twenty and forty. Look at Jack. He didn't train as a lawyer until he was thirty."

Claudia was intrigued, and not only because it was unlike Erica to mention Jack except in relation to sex. "Really? I didn't know that. What did he do before?"

Erica stared at the road ahead. "Medicine."

"You're kidding. He was a doctor? And he gave it up?"

"Yes and yes. It wasn't for him. He could have carried on and made it his life, but instead he admitted he'd made a mistake and started again."

"That's a very brave thing to do," Anna said.

"It is. But the point I'm making is that it's never too late to do something different."

"I like that." Anna sat back in her seat. "I also like the fact that you and Jack do occasionally talk."

"I never said we didn't talk."

"But you didn't reveal that you've been sharing innermost secrets."

Erica made an impatient sound. "Maybe you should be a romance novelist. There's a gap in the market since Catherine Swift turned to crime."

"You're changing the subject," Anna said. "I think there is far more to your relationship with Jack than you're sharing."

Noticing Erica's shoulders tense, Claudia decided it was time to change the subject. "Any chance of stopping soon? I've lost the feeling in my legs."

"Do you want to swap?" Anna was instantly generous. "I can sit in the back for a while."

"That makes no sense," Erica said. "You have longer legs than Claudia."

"I used to have longer legs," Claudia muttered, "but I've evolved over time to be able to squish into your vehicle. Darwinism or something. Survival of the shortest."

They stopped for lunch at a little roadside diner with a revolving Christmas tree and copious twinkling lights.

"Don't judge," Erica said. "The reviews say the food is excellent."

Trying not to wince at the tinny Christmas music playing in the background and the staff wearing reindeer antlers, Claudia ordered a simple grilled cheese sandwich.

Her low expectations were blown away at the first bite. She closed her eyes as she chewed. "Simple, but delicious. Local aged cheddar and heirloom tomatoes. When you have ingredients as good as this you don't need to invent fancy dishes. Add a little mustard and a splash of bourbon and you elevate the flavor to something spectacular." She heard muffled laughter and opened her eyes to see her friends grinning at her across the table. "What?"

Anna looked at Erica, who shrugged.

"If she can't see it herself, then who are we to point it out?"

Claudia put her fork down. "Just because I can still appreciate good quality ingredients doesn't mean I want to be a chef."

"Of course it doesn't. Could you pass the salt please, Anna?"

"With pleasure, Erica." Anna passed the salt and Claudia sighed.

"You two are—"

"We're what?" Erica emptied an unhealthy quantity of salt onto her already salted fries. "We're good friends? I'd have to agree with that. How did you get so lucky?"

Claudia gave up. "I was going to say *annoying.*" She took another bite of her sandwich. "This is so good. I feel better than I have in months."

Erica looked smug. "It's our scintillating company."

"Maybe, or maybe it's being back on the east coast. Maybe I should move to Vermont. It would be perfect."

Erica shuddered. "Not for me."

Claudia asked the question that had been hovering in her brain. "If it's not for you, why did you choose Vermont for our vacation?"

Erica carefully extracted the lettuce from her burger. "I chose it because it's perfect for what we need for our week away. Cozy inn with snuggling potential, great food and a much praised wine cellar. And because I knew you two would love it, and I try and be a good friend."

She's not telling the truth, Claudia thought, but she knew from long experience that if Erica had something on her mind it always took her a while to tell them about it.

Anna was typing a message on her phone.

"Are you messaging Pete?" Claudia reached across to grab her phone but Anna held it out of reach. "It's not even three hours since you saw him. Stop."

"I forgot to remind him about Meg's doctor appointment on Monday." Anna pressed Send on the message and dropped her phone back on the table. "It's so good being with you guys. This week is going to be great. We're going to sleep, relax, build a snowman, and in the evenings we can settle down and sort out all our problems, like we used to do when we were twenty."

Erica emptied some of her fries onto Claudia's plate. "I don't have problems."

Anna beamed. "Good, then you'll have more time to focus on ours." She took a bite out of her burger and Claudia studied her for a moment.

"How is your hair always so shiny and healthy-looking?"

"It's because I live a sin-free life, full of fruit and vegetables and wholesome thoughts."

Erica shuddered. "I'd rather have dull hair."

"I'm just kidding." Anna reached for a napkin. "It's a fancy hair pack. I treated myself."

"You did something for yourself? I'm impressed."

"I often do things for myself." Anna glanced between them. "What? Why are you looking at each other like that?"

"Because you never do things for yourself."

"I think *never* is a bit strong. It's true that there are some occasions when I don't make my needs a priority but I'm working on that. The hair pack was my first attempt. And given that you like my hair, I'd say it is working." She smiled. "I love our book club week. Has anyone actually read the book?"

"Of course." Erica pushed her plate away, her food half-eaten. "That's the whole point of our book club."

Anna put her burger down. "Since when have we only talked about books? The whole point of book club is that it gives us a chance to talk about life. And isn't that why we read anyway? To learn about someone else's life?" Anna's phone lit up and Claudia grabbed it and read the message on the screen.

"He remembered about Meg's appointment. Oh, and he loves you. That's good to know, because we were all starting to doubt it. Can I reply?"

"No." Anna retrieved her phone and Erica reached for her purse.

"If you two have finished playing phone games, we should

get going. Heavy snow is forecast and my car doesn't love snow. I don't love snow, either. Remind me again why we're not in the Caribbean?"

"I adore snow," said Anna. "Especially when there is no pressure to be anywhere. There's nothing better than curling up by the fire and watching snow fall."

Erica finished her water. "I can think of plenty of things that are better."

"I love snow. I've missed snow." Claudia dug in her purse for money but Erica waved her away.

"Forget it. This one is on me."

Claudia felt her face burn with embarrassment. "I can't—"

"Yes, you can. I'm not giving you a choice. Remember that time you spent the day in my apartment preparing a meal for my date in the evening? I still owe you for that."

"Your date was scared away by your cooking abilities, so does it even count?"

"It counts. You saved me from a dating mistake." Erica extracted her card. "He was intimidated by a woman who ran her own business, enjoyed sex and could also cook. He said to me, *Honey, is there anything you're bad at?*"

Anna laughed and exchanged glances with Claudia. "And you said, *Yes, honey, I'm bad at relationships*," Claudia finished the sentence, "and then you kicked him out the door."

Erica shrugged. "What could I do? Apparently, I shriveled his ego."

"As long as that is all you shriveled."

"Anna! I'd forgotten how shocking you are when we peel you away from Pete." Claudia wriggled out of the booth and they walked back to the car as Erica paid. "Does she seem more tense than usual to you?"

"Erica?" Anna snuggled deeper inside her coat as the wind licked across the parking lot and a few flakes of snow swirled around them. "Yes. But it's probably a work thing. She works too hard. It always takes her a while to unwind. She needs a vacation."

Claudia didn't think that was it, but since she didn't have evidence to support her theory she simply smiled. "I'm sure you're right."

Anna opened the car door. "Do you want to sit in the front for a while?"

"No, you go in the front. I wouldn't know what to do with my legs if I had more room. Also, I know you get carsick."

They drove north, and Claudia gazed out the window, enjoying snow-dusted forests and quaint New England villages full of old-fashioned holiday charm that seemed almost too pretty to be real. Stores and homes were festooned with lights and greenery, and for a brief moment she was transported back to childhood, and the magic and wonder of it. She drifted, remembering, and was brought back to the present by Erica's voice.

"This is it. We're here. Next turning on the right if the directions are correct."

Claudia shook off her sleepiness and leaned forward to get a better look.

A fresh layer of snow covered the streets and people hurried along wrapped in thick coats and scarves, the bulging bags they were carrying suggesting a flurry of last-minute shopping.

The trees that bordered the street glowed with thousands of tiny lights, creating a festive walkway.

"Slow down." Claudia gripped the back of Erica's seat. "They have a bookstore!"

"Great. I can finish my Christmas shopping." Anna turned her head to look as Erica drove past it. "It's called The Read-a-While Bookstore. It's cute. I love the window display. And they have sofas. Shall we stop and visit?"

"Yes!" Claudia felt a sudden urge to go inside. Bookstores always reminded her of her mother, and right now she could do with that warming and reassuring connection. "It would be the perfect start to the vacation."

"Not now." Erica didn't slow down. "We need to do this."

"Do what?" Claudia exchanged a mystified glance with Anna. Erica made it sound like a visit to the dentist.

"We need to check in."

Claudia glanced at her phone. They weren't late. Why the hurry?

But there was no diverting Erica.

She turned off Main Street leaving the bookstore behind them, drove a little way out of town, over a covered bridge spanning a river in full flow, and there, nestled among fir trees and instantly recognizable from the photos, was the Maple Sugar Inn.

Claudia instantly forgot about the bookstore.

The inn stood two and a half stories high, its covered porch and balconies strung with lights and festive greenery. Snow clung to the pitched roof and frosted the windows. The front door was framed by two tall Christmas trees studded with tiny lights. The whole place sparkled with old-fashioned holiday charm.

Erica pulled up and switched off the engine and they all sat in silence for a minute.

"Well," Anna said, her eyes fixed on the inn.

"Yes." Claudia's eyes were fixed on the same place. Warmth spread through her. She'd never seen anywhere so magical. It was like stepping into a Christmas card. "I guess the website and the photos didn't lie."

"It's everything Christmas in Vermont should be." Anna actually sounded choked as she put her hand on Erica's arm. "This is going to be wonderful. Thank you for choosing somewhere so special. I'm excited."

Erica said nothing.

Her hands were clenched on the wheel. Her lips were slightly parted, as if she was trying to remember how to breathe.

Either she was totally overwhelmed by the same Christmassy feeling that had engulfed everyone else—and being Erica that was unlikely—or something else was going on. And if the whiteness of her knuckles was anything to go by, it wasn't good.

Claudia reached forward and touched her shoulder. "Are you okay, Erica? Is it not what you expected?"

Erica didn't answer.

"Erica?" And now her mind was working, sifting through the options. To the best of her knowledge, Erica had never been to Vermont before. She'd definitely never stayed in the Maple Sugar Inn. Had she worked with them in a professional capacity? No, that seemed unlikely.

She looked at Anna, who caught her eye and gave a tiny shrug.

"I don't think we're supposed to park here," she said. "We should probably drive around to the parking lot at the back. That's what the instructions said."

Mention of the parking lot seemed to rouse Erica. "Yes. Right. Parking lot." She cleared her throat. "Good plan. So everyone is happy with it, yes?"

"Yes, of course. How couldn't we be? But are you—"

"I'm looking forward to seeing our rooms and talking about books." Erica checked her mirrors and headed to the parking lot. The road had been cleared but snow lay banked at the sides.

They pulled into an empty space. In the space opposite them a man was unloading logs from the back of a truck marked with a logo.

Claudia squinted. "*Peterson's Christmas Trees.* Mmm. I'd buy a Christmas tree from him any day."

"I'm guessing he's around thirty." Anna picked up her bag and got ready to pull on her coat. "Isn't that a little young for you?"

"Not according to Erica. And he's older than John's current girlfriend."

Claudia didn't want to think about that, so she allowed herself a moment to sit back and simply admire. Distraction could be a good thing.

The man wore a heavy-duty jacket and a pair of work boots that had seen plenty of action. His hair was dark and edging toward his collar, his expression serious and approaching stern. As he steadied the logs he noticed them and gave a quick smile by way of greeting that transformed stern to sexy.

Claudia smiled back. "Now *that's* a man who probably carries a wrench in his back pocket at all times, and knows how to change a tire."

Anna laughed and Erica sighed, apparently roused from whatever dark mood had been gripping her.

"Please. I know how to change a tire. Anytime you want me to change your tire, let me know. I'll happily change your tire."

Anna looked at her. "You do know it's not about the tire?"

"Yes, I know it's not about the tire," Erica said. "I'm just saying I don't need some man to change my tire."

"Even if he's cute?"

"Especially if he's cute. I don't want him getting a false impression of me and thinking I'm helpless."

"It's not about being helpless," Claudia said. "It's about someone doing something for you because they want to. I miss that. I miss having someone who knows all the little things about me. I miss those thoughtful gestures. In the early days John used to bring me a cup of coffee in the morning before he left for work, particularly on the days when I'd worked late at the restaurant. And it was always cold by the time I woke up, but I drank it anyway because it made me feel close to him. Does that sound weird?"

"Cold coffee? Not weird. Disgusting." Erica caught Anna's eye and cleared her throat. "Maybe it's an acquired taste."

Claudia didn't expect her to understand. Erica valued her independence above everything else, and she hated someone doing something for her that she could do herself. It was as if she believed that any selfless gesture on someone else's part would require a show of weakness on hers.

"I liked being a person who someone wanted to do things for. Now if I want tea, I make it myself."

"If I want tea, I call room service," Erica said and lifted a hand to stop Anna's gentle admonishment. "Yes, I know, I'm a heartless woman. It's been said before. But there is nothing better in this life than being able to change your own tire and make your own tea. Self-love is the new long-term relationship. Hadn't you heard?"

"But people do things for other people because they want to, not because the other person is incapable. Like that guy." Claudia watched as he walked away from them toward the inn. "He looks like the steady, reliable type. The sort that isn't going to run in a crisis. He's carrying logs because he cares about someone. He wants them to be warm and comfortable."

A young woman appeared in the doorway and greeted him with a few words and laughter.

"Judging from the look on her face and his, I think he's taken," Anna said.

"He's probably carrying logs because he is being paid to do it. And of course he'd run in a crisis. That's what men do." Erica unclipped her seat belt. "Now, can we stop this conversation and start our vacation?"

Claudia watched as the man disappeared through the door at the back of the inn.

She didn't believe he'd run. She thought he'd stand fast and handle whatever was barreling toward him. But she wasn't really interested in him. She wasn't interested in a relationship at the moment, but it was a relief she could still admire an attractive man when he crossed her path. That felt like another step forward.

Whoever that man loved, she thought as she grabbed an armful of gifts, was a lucky person but nowhere near as lucky as the woman who owned the inn.

Claudia had never believed in love at first sight but looking at the shimmering windows and snow-covered roof of the Maple Sugar Inn, she suddenly did.

Forget the man; what she really wanted was the inn. If the inn belonged to her, she was sure she'd live happily ever after.

NINE

Anna

The inn was warm and welcoming. As Anna stepped over the threshold and saw the tall Christmas tree sparkling with lights and ornaments she thought, *I wish I were here with Pete.*

He'd suggested that the two of them go away together several times lately and she'd always found a reason not to. It was one of the few points of tension between them. He didn't seem to understand that she needed to be around for the kids. It was hard to find the time. Now she was wondering if she should have made the time.

"I want to live here forever." Claudia gazed at the tree. "You're a vacation genius, Erica."

"Yes." Anna was about to ask Erica if she was happy with everything when a young woman emerged from a room at the back. It was the same woman they'd seen greeting the man with the logs. Her cheeks were flushed and her hair formed a cloud of curls around her smiling face.

"Hi there, you must be Erica, Anna and Claudia. Welcome. I'm Hattie."

This was Hattie?

She looked so young. Too young to have a child and be running the inn.

And then Anna remembered she would have been around the same age when she'd had the twins.

She glanced at Erica, expecting her to take the lead as she'd made the reservation, but Erica was standing frozen, staring at Hattie.

Anna had no idea what the problem could be.

Erica was often blunt and efficient, but she was never rude. Also, she was rarely silent. Usually, she would be taking charge by now, not because Anna and Claudia were in any way less competent, but just because she couldn't help herself.

Anna waited another beat, and then stepped forward and stretched out her hand.

"Hi there, I'm Anna. This place is incredible. I feel as if I'm on the set of a Christmas movie."

She had no idea what was wrong with Erica, but she didn't want Hattie thinking it was anything to do with the quality of the establishment.

Hattie dragged her anxious gaze from Erica's face. "I'm pleased. We really want your stay to be special, so if there's anything at all you need, please let me know. Now, let me get you checked in and show you to your rooms." She leaned forward and hit a couple of keys on the computer. "You have three rooms together. I have Erica in the River Room." She glanced up and Anna gave Erica a prod in the ribs.

Erica seemed to wake up. "You're not from around here, are you?"

"I'm British. Born and raised in London, but I moved here when I met my husband." Hattie saw Erica staring at the photographs on her desk. "That's my husband with our daughter, Delphi—you'll meet her at some point, I'm sure. She's five and often manages to be where she's not supposed to be. Here's the key to your room."

Erica reached to take it and in doing so knocked over the other photo on the desk.

"I'm sorry." She picked it up and Anna waited for her to set it back in its place, but instead Erica held it and stared at it in silence.

Finally, she looked at Hattie. "Who is this?"

Anna felt a rush of embarrassment, but Hattie was warm and friendly and seemed not at all offended.

"That's me, with my dad."

"Your dad? He's holding you. Swinging you in the air."

"That's right. He loved to do that. This is my favorite photo of him. He passed away seven years ago. I miss him every day. I was around four years old when that photograph was taken, but the weird thing is I remember that day clearly. It's my earliest memory."

Erica stared at the photograph for a long time. "You two were close."

Anna shifted uncomfortably. This was becoming awkward. Why the personal questions? Since when did Erica show so much interest in a stranger? What was going on? Maybe this had something to do with Christmas. Maybe she was thinking about family. Although she rarely admitted it, she knew Erica had been deeply scarred by the way her father had treated her and her mother. His actions had pretty much defined her life.

Maybe hitting forty had affected her more than she thought it had.

"We were very close." Hattie looked puzzled, but was still sweetly polite. "My mother died just after I was born, and my dad raised me alone. It was a special relationship. I feel lucky to have had that. Anna, you're in the Forest Room. I hope you like it. Let me know when you'd like to hold your book club discussions and I'll reserve the library for you. The only time it isn't free is Wednesday evening." She handed over a key, and then did the same for Claudia. Her gaze skated nervously back to Erica, who was still holding the photograph. "If you'd all like to follow me, I'll show you to your rooms and have your luggage brought up."

"We can handle our luggage, no problems," Claudia said, grabbing her bags and Erica's. She gave Erica a gentle push.

Erica looked at her blankly as if she'd forgotten where she was.

"Luggage. Checking in. Vacation," Claudia muttered. "Any of these words ringing a bell?"

Erica put the photograph carefully back on the desk.

She looked pale and tired and Anna felt a twinge of real concern.

Was Erica unwell? Did she have some sort of health crisis going on?

It would be just like Erica to support all of them through a crisis and fail to mention her own.

"You've been so kind." She smiled at Hattie, doing her best to compensate for Erica's unusual behavior. "We're all in dire need of a good break as you can probably tell, and we're excited to be here. Lead on."

They followed Hattie toward the stairs and wound their way up one flight and along a corridor.

"These three rooms are yours." Hattie gestured. "The library is decorated for Christmas and there's a log fire going in there, so if you wanted to have tea once you've unpacked, I could arrange that."

Anna took a quick look at Erica's frozen expression and decided they might need something stronger than tea.

"Thank you, but we might go for a walk. The town looked so pretty." She decided that the sooner the three of them were alone, the better. "I'm sure you're very busy, so don't let us keep you."

As soon as Hattie walked away, Anna removed the key from Erica's numb fingers and unlocked the door.

"Let's get inside." She pushed open the door and sighed with delight. The room was light and airy, thanks to two large windows, which had views toward snow-covered mountains. There was a fire, a comfy chair for reading and a small desk tucked under one of the windows. "It's gorgeous. What a dreamy place. Is this room okay for you, Erica? Do you want to check out the others in case you prefer one of them?" Maybe Erica was just thinking that the place wasn't for her. It was quaint and quirky, and Erica's preferences leaned toward sleek and modern.

Erica didn't even look around her. She just sat down hard on the bed.

Anna looked at Claudia.

Claudia closed the door firmly so that they were alone.

"Okay, tell us what's going on. And don't say it's nothing."

"It was something to do with that photograph, wasn't it?" Anna sat down next to her and put her arm around Erica. "Tell us."

"Or is it this place? You've been acting strangely the whole journey. Tense." Claudia sat on the other side of her, protective. "If it's just too quaint and Christmassy, we can leave. Find somewhere else."

Erica made a sound somewhere between a laugh and a sob. "You'd do that?"

"Of course." Anna ignored the twinge of disappointment. The place was perfect, but this week was about people not places. Her friends. If it wasn't perfect for Erica, then they would leave. "We love you. This is our special week. We want you to be happy and have fun. Is that what's wrong? Is it this place?"

"Yes. No. Not exactly. Not in the way you think." Erica rubbed her palm over her cheek and only then did Anna realize she was crying.

Erica. Crying.

Anna cried frequently. She cried at movies. She cried over books. She cried when she looked at photographs of the twins when they were little because they looked so cute, and those days had been so happy, and she was never going to have them back. She cried when Pete bought her flowers because it meant he'd

thought about her during his day, and she cried whenever she drove away from her parents' house after a visit because she loved them and they were growing older and she hated leaving them.

Erica never cried. She munched popcorn in sad movies; she shook her head in disbelief when her friends cried over sad books.

Anna's heart split in two. "Please don't cry."

"It's your fault for being kind. Stop being kind." Erica sniffed. "Does anyone have a tissue?"

"Anna will have a tissue," Claudia said. "Anna has everything in that bag of hers. She could feed you and save a life."

Anna dutifully produced a tissue and Erica took it from her.

"Thanks. Sorry. This is supposed to be a lighthearted getaway and I'm ruining it."

"You're not ruining anything." Anna gave her shoulders a squeeze. "Whatever it is, you can tell us. We're your family."

Erica gave a watery smile. "Pete and the kids, they're your family."

Anna heard the tremor of insecurity and was shocked by it. This wasn't Erica. "Yes, but so are you. And I've never given you reason to doubt that. Neither has Claudia. The three of us have been a family since the day you stomped into our room and claimed the top bunk."

"Is it a man? Is it Jack?" Claudia was scowling. "Because I can punch him. I've been practicing my punches. I'm good. I'd welcome some real-life practice."

Erica pressed the tissue to her eyes. "It's no one you can punch. It's not Jack." She drew in a quivering breath. "I shouldn't have come. It was stupid of me. Bad decision. I should have been honest with you guys, so that you could have talked me out of it."

"So it is this place. Right, that's it." Claudia pulled out her phone. "We're going to find somewhere else right away. Where's the nearest town, Anna? We'll find somewhere to stay tonight, and then drive to Boston tomorrow. A week in Boston will be

great. We can run alongside the Charles River, linger in coffee shops and pretend we're young college students again."

"It's not this place. Not exactly." Erica blew her nose and Anna handed her a fresh tissue.

"The photograph upset you. Hattie obviously had a close relationship with her dad." She hesitated. "Did it make you sad, seeing her with her father?"

"Yes." Erica screwed the tissue into a tiny ball. "Yes, it did."

"He looked like a good guy." Claudia glanced up from her phone. "A good dad. Hattie was lucky. Except that her husband died, so maybe not so lucky…" Her voice trailed off and she glanced at Anna for help.

Anna badly wanted to say the right thing, but didn't know what the right thing was.

She wasn't sure what this was about.

"It must hurt seeing a caring, loving dad when your own walked out when you were only minutes old."

"It does hurt."

"Hattie's dad was a good person. Your dad wasn't and that sucks." Claudia paused. "I'm no good at this. I'm saying all the wrong things. I'm sorry."

"No, you're not. It really does suck." Erica screwed the tissue into a tiny ball. "Mostly because Hattie's dad and my dad are the same person. The same guy."

There was a long silence.

"What? What are you saying?" Anna's head spun. "Hattie's father?"

"Yes, Hattie's father. That caring, loving dad." Erica took the whole packet of tissues from Anna's hand. "He was also my father. My dad. The one who walked out when I was eight minutes old."

TEN

Erica

Erica stood up and walked to the window. Hattie was right. The view was incredible, but she wouldn't have cared if she was looking at a parking lot. The feelings churning around inside her were new to her. She wasn't used to feeling confused. She wasn't used to admitting weakness, and right now she felt both weak and vulnerable.

Seeing that photograph had felled her. She felt as if someone had taken a baseball bat to her heart. As if everything inside her was being squeezed. She didn't know this feeling. It might have been panic, except Erica had never panicked in her life so it couldn't possibly be that.

She felt as if the walls of the room were closing in on her.

She'd arrived here thinking that she'd be able to take it slow, observe, find out what she needed to find out and then make a measured decision based on the facts. She hadn't expected to be plunged deep into emotions so visceral she'd been robbed of breath.

Her thoughts and feelings about her father had all been acquired secondhand, given to her by her mother.

Some men can't handle responsibility.

You can't trust a man to stick by you when times are tough.

Those were the answers she'd been given whenever she'd asked questions about her father. Her mother had placed all the blame squarely on him.

Some men aren't built to be fathers.

But now she had evidence to the contrary. Maybe her father hadn't been able to handle the responsibility of her, but he'd handled being a father to Hattie. Maybe some men didn't stick around when times were tough, but her father had stuck around for Hattie. He'd stuck by her in the toughest of circumstances. He'd been a great father to Hattie.

So what did that mean?

Erica wrapped her arms around herself.

Had her father ever thought of her? In all those happy years with his second daughter, had he thought of his first? When he'd swung Hattie into his arms, had he ever felt a twinge of regret or guilt that he hadn't ever put those same arms around Erica?

She leaned her burning forehead against the glass.

She was forty years old for goodness' sake, and she'd been taking care of herself for as long as she could remember. Even as a child her mother had insisted she solve her own problems. There was no reason to be standing here with shaking legs, feeling as vulnerable as a child. Definitely no reason to cry. It was pathetic.

She felt embarrassed. She couldn't understand why something so far in her past could cause such emotional havoc in her present.

It took a moment for her to register the silence behind her.

She turned to find both her friends staring at her stupidly.

They didn't know what to say. She didn't blame them. She didn't know what to say, either.

She gave an awkward shrug. "This is a first, isn't it? Me crying?"

Claudia spoke first. "I don't understand."

Erica shrugged. "I don't understand, either. Apparently, I'm more emotional than I thought. It's a disturbing discovery."

"Not that part." Claudia waved a hand. "I mean, I don't understand how Hattie's father can be your father."

"Neither do I. This makes no sense." Anna looked confused. "Hattie is British. She grew up in London."

"Yes, she grew up in London. She was born there, and her mother was British. But her father—" Erica drew in a breath "—her father was from New York."

"How do you know all this?" Claudia stared at her. "Your mother refused to ever talk about him."

"That's right. She never did talk about him, except when she held him up as an example of the folly of relying on anyone other than yourself." She should have confided in her friends sooner. She wished she had, but opening up had never been easy for her and the right moment to talk about this hadn't arisen. "You remember when I cleared out my mother's house after she died?"

"Of course we remember," Claudia said. "We were there."

"I know. It was a horrible job, and you were incredible, both of you." They'd both insisted on joining her, even though she hadn't asked. They'd brought food, and most important of all they'd brought friendship. She'd needed the second more than the first. "I found something. Hidden away in my mother's things. I almost missed it."

"What did you find?"

They'd forgotten about the room, the views, their luggage, the book they'd read specially, the purpose of their trip. They were both focused on her, and Erica felt a twinge of guilt because this was supposed to be a fun week, and right now it was anything but fun. She'd ruined their special vacation. She should have warned them, so that they'd had the choice. They could have said *no way do we want to waste our book club week digging into your past. It's supposed to be relaxing. Pick a different hotel.*

But even as she thought it, she dismissed it. If she'd told them, they would have wanted to come and be with her. They would have insisted. That was who they were.

"I found a card," she said. "A birthday card. For me."

"From your dad?" Claudia glanced at Anna and then back at Erica. "And you didn't tell us? Why not?"

"It's fine." Anna touched her arm but Claudia shook her off.

"No, actually, it's not. This is huge. We're your closest friends. Why wouldn't you share something like this?"

"I don't know." Erica had asked herself the same question. "I was shocked. I was processing it."

"Okay, that might explain why you didn't tell us at the time, but it was two years ago and you haven't said a word to us?"

"I blocked it out. Tried to forget it. It's what I do. You know it's what I do." She felt the emotion rising and didn't know what to do. She never felt like this. She had no experience of this. "I didn't mean to upset you."

"You haven't upset us," Anna intervened. "It's now that's important, not what has gone before. This card…your mother never gave it to you, or mentioned it to you?"

"No." And she'd asked herself why. She'd conjured up so many possible scenarios, but she'd never know for sure because her mother was gone and with her all the answers to the questions Erica was never going to be able to ask.

Claudia bit her lip. "What did it say?"

"Nothing. Just his name."

"Which name?" Claudia showed her usual forensic attention to detail. "His actual name or—Dad?"

"I don't remember." She remembered perfectly. It had said *Jeff, your father.* It was telling that he felt he needed to introduce himself. Of course if he hadn't walked out shortly after she'd drawn her first breath, it might not have been necessary.

She didn't tell them that when she'd found it she'd ripped the card into four pieces. Or that she'd then stuck it back together.

Anna wouldn't have torn it up. Anna would have folded it

neatly and stored it in a file. Anna would have thought carefully about the best way to deal with it.

Claudia probably would have set fire to it.

Anna slipped off her boots and curled up on the bed, settling herself in for a good heart-to-heart. "But if he sent a card, then that means he was thinking of you. He hadn't just walked away and forgotten about you. Maybe it didn't happen exactly as your mother said."

"Or maybe it happened exactly as she said, and he had second thoughts." Claudia frowned. "Were there more cards?"

"No, just the one."

"But why go to the trouble of sending a birthday card and then never send another one? That doesn't make sense. Not that I expect male behavior to make sense." Claudia paced across the room, as she always did when she was thinking. "I mean, he walks away. Your mother doesn't hear from him. Then he sends a card. Why?"

Erica had been asking herself the same question. She'd asked it over and over again.

"Maybe he had a moment of guilt, and after that it was easier not to bother."

"Was there a date on it? Do you know when it was sent?"

"He sent it when I was twelve. A single card."

"But why—" Claudia stopped pacing and exchanged looks with Anna. "Well, whatever the reason, it's rough. I wish you'd told us."

"I wish you'd told us, too, but only because we would have wanted to support you and be there for you." Anna spoke softly. "Do you need a hug?"

It was so very Anna, that Erica almost smiled. "I don't need a hug, but thank you."

Claudia was still processing the information. "All these years you thought your father just walked out and never looked back. That he didn't think about you once. But clearly the guy thought about you."

"For as long as it took to send the card, at least."

Claudia tapped her fingertip on her cheek. "Are you upset with your mother for not showing you the card?"

"At first, I was confused. Maybe a little angry. But then I thought about it from her point of view. The man left her when she was at her most vulnerable. She put all her trust in him. So I could hardly blame her for protecting herself when he got in touch after so long. I assume it was out of the blue."

"I don't think she was only protecting herself." Anna stood up and poured a glass of water from the jug on the table. She handed it to Erica. "She was protecting you. Her baby. He hurt you both. He let you down. She couldn't risk him doing it again. At least that's how I'd feel if Pete had walked out when the twins were born. She was trying to be strong for you both."

Erica felt her heart miss a beat. "I hadn't thought of it that way."

She took a sip of water. Was that what had happened? She'd tried to imagine how her mother must have felt when that card had arrived. Tried to imagine her making the decision about how to respond. She'd been twelve years old. Had her mother considered giving it to her or had she just made up her mind right away not to ever show Erica?

Anna poured water for herself and Claudia. "But how does Hattie fit into this? Did your mother know about her existence?"

"I don't know. I assume not. There was nothing in her things to suggest she'd had any contact with him at all. That she knew anything about his circumstances."

"I still don't understand," Claudia said. "You found the card two years ago. So what did you do? You tracked him down?"

"At first, I did nothing. I was missing my mother horribly. I decided that if she didn't want me to know about the card, then I'd forget I ever saw it. I wanted to respect her wishes. Also, I was angry—thinking back about how very hard her life was back at the beginning and blaming him." Her head started to ache. She finished her water and handed the glass back to Anna. "But I couldn't forget it. And then a few months ago I decided to find out more so I hired someone. I wanted to know if my father was alive, and what he was doing. I didn't have plans to get in touch or anything. I just wanted to know what happened to him. It felt like unfinished business."

"I can't believe you hired a private investigator." Claudia was fascinated. "I've only ever seen that happen in the movies. I didn't know people did that in real life."

Anna was focused on Erica. "How much did you find out?"

"Quite a bit." Erica thought of the file on her computer. "He moved to England right after he left my mother. I guess if you're going to run, you might as well run far. He worked there for a while, then quite a few years later met a woman who he married. They had one child. Hattie. His wife died a week after giving birth. Blood clot."

"Oh, that's tragic." Anna sat down hard on the edge of the bed.

"Yes. He was left with a newborn." And the irony of that hadn't escaped her. "I suppose if he was going to run from fatherhood a second time he would have done it then, but he didn't. He raised the child alone. Those were the facts, but facts don't tell you anything really. They didn't tell me if he ever thought about his other family. They didn't tell me if he was sorry for the way he treated my mother."

"And you," Anna said softly. "He didn't just abandon your mother. He abandoned you."

It was typical of Anna to understand the full emotional impact of any situation.

"That's true. Those facts didn't tell me how he reacted when his wife died. Didn't tell if he was a good father, although he obviously stayed, so that was a start and a very definite improvement on his performance with me."

Claudia thumped her empty glass back on the table. "We're not ready to give him an A plus yet."

"I had more questions than I had answers. And then we walked into this inn, I saw that photograph downstairs and the answers were right there." There was an ache in the center of her chest. "However he felt about us, his first family, he loved his second family. He didn't walk out on them the way he did us. This time he didn't run from the challenge. He raised his child on his own. He was a good dad."

"Maybe he was." Anna swung her legs off the bed and walked across to her. "And that's good in one way, but hard in another. It has to hurt."

"I'm still processing." She couldn't make sense of her feelings, or maybe it was simply that she didn't want to. She didn't want to feel this much about anything. She preferred to skim along the surface of life, never dipping deeper.

"Wait—" Claudia joined them at the window. "That means Hattie is your half sister. You have a half sister."

The ache in Erica's chest grew more intense. "That's right."

The three of them absorbed the implications of that.

"Well—" Claudia swallowed. "I mean, she seems nice. Don't you think so, Anna? Warm and caring? Also, she has great taste in boots. And a good eye for interior design if the inn is anything to go by."

"Yes." Anna pressed her hand to her chest. Her eyes were shining. "Erica, you do realize what this means? You have family. Actual family. And Hattie has a daughter, which means you're an aunt."

"Stop it. You know that word freaks me out."

"I know. You refused to let my kids call you Aunt Erica."

Erica tried not to recoil. "Too heavy. Too much responsibility."

"Being an aunt freaks me out, too. Mostly because it's expensive," Claudia warned. "I told my sister to stop at two, but did she listen? No. Start saving now."

"But *family*." Anna emphasized the word and Erica sighed.

"Only in your world is *family* the equivalent of an all-weather down duvet ready to protect you from everything. Hattie and I are not family, Anna. We're strangers."

"But not for long. You're going to fix that. When are you planning to tell her? Do you want us to be there when you do it? How can we support you?"

Erica rubbed her hand over her chest. She couldn't ever remember feeling this stressed. "I'm not planning to tell her."

There was a shocked silence.

"Wait—you're not planning to tell her at all?" Claudia enunciated the words carefully. "Not ever?"

"That's right." Erica turned back to the window. Her legs were shaky and she felt a little sick.

"But if you're not going to tell her," Anna said slowly, "why did you come here?"

It was a reasonable question and one she'd been asking herself constantly. "Because I only now this minute made that decision. Before arriving here, I hadn't made up my mind what I was going to do. I was just doing the research. I read about her in the report. I read that she was widowed, and on her own with a child, and I thought about how she might be struggling, the way my mother struggled. And I thought I'd come here and check things out, see if maybe I could—" She stopped. Could what, exactly? Saying it aloud made her realize how ridiculous the whole situation was. "I thought maybe she needed help, but honestly it was a crazy idea. What sort of help would I be? What exactly would I say? *Hi, you don't know me—you probably don't even know of my existence—but I wanted to check you're okay.* Hattie is clearly okay. She has a whole community looking out for her, including the Christmas tree guy, and even if she wasn't okay, what am I going to do about it? I don't know anything about kids. I don't know anything about running an inn, particularly a country inn. I'm a city person. And honestly, she'd probably be less okay if she found out about me. It's probably best if I just slink back into the shadows and stay as my father's dirty little secret."

Claudia frowned. "You don't think she knows?"

"She doesn't know. Why would she know? It was forty years ago. My father had a different life then. He clearly reinvented himself, very successfully, it seems." The more she thought about it, the more she could see she'd made a big mistake. Some things were best left alone, and this was one of them. "I shouldn't have come here. I think you're right about leaving, but I don't have the energy to go anywhere right now. We'll stay one night, then check out tomorrow and go to Boston as you suggested. We'll think of an excuse and let Hattie keep the money. I'll pay for the next place, and I'm really sorry I've ruined our vacation." And she felt terrible about that because she knew how important this week was to them all.

"You haven't ruined anything," Anna said. "And if you want to leave, then of course we'll do that."

She felt a rush of love for her friends. "Thank you. You probably think I made a bad decision coming here."

"No." Anna shook her head. "I think coming here was absolutely the right thing to do. Also, it's so typical of you to want to check on Hattie even though you don't know her and the whole thing is painful. It's caring."

Erica had a feeling that leaving without telling Hattie who she was would be more caring.

"What I keep wondering," Claudia said, "is why your mother kept that card? If she didn't intend to share it with you, which she obviously didn't, why keep it?"

"I've asked myself the same question. I don't know the answer."

Anna was watching her. "At least if we stay tonight that will give you some time to reflect and be sure of your decision."

"I'm already sure." The more she thought about it, the more confident she was that she was making the right decision. "To Hattie, I don't exist. And it's better if it stays that way."

"She doesn't remember her mother, and she lost her father

years ago, then her husband." Anna's voice was soft. "She might be pleased to discover she has family."

"I don't think so, but that's because you and I are different. You see family as this wonderful positive force." Erica paced to the fireplace and stared at the flames. "Sometimes it isn't that simple."

"You are her family." Claudia was logical. "Whether you tell her or not doesn't change that."

"But it changes the actions. Enough." Erica turned to look at them. "I'm not telling her. That's my decision."

"Whatever you want."

She was grateful that they hadn't argued with her. "And now I need stress relief. There's no gym, and it's too early for a glass of wine. Any suggestions?"

"There are acres of trails around the place." Claudia glanced out the window. "We have at least an hour before it gets dark. Shall we go for a walk?"

"We could walk to that bookstore. Books are always a stress reliever," Anna said and Erica nodded.

Anything to get out of here and clear her head. She didn't like this version of herself. This unsure, shaken, indecisive version. She needed a dose of normal, and visiting a bookstore with her friends sounded suitably normal. It was a tradition when they met up for their book club. They always found the nearest independent bookstore and spent a few happy hours browsing and buying.

"The bookstore sounds like a good distraction. Let's do it." She looked at the room properly for the first time. Saw the size of the bed, the fur throws, the velvet sofa, the stack of carefully chosen books on the nightstand and the small Christmas tree sparkling in the corner of the room. It was stylish and comfortable and she felt a momentary twinge of regret that she was going to be checking out the next day. The feeling surprised her. She'd stayed in more hotel rooms than most, and generally she didn't ever feel an inclination to curl up and move in forever. But that was the way this room made her feel.

It was welcoming. They could have relaxed here. They could have had a good time.

Who had chosen the decor? Was that Hattie—she wasn't ready to think of her as *my sister*—or her husband?

What sort of person was Hattie? It gave her a jolt to think that there was someone in the world that she was related to but knew nothing about. All she knew about her was that she'd moved to the US with her husband, and that they had a daughter. Facts. She knew facts, but facts weren't what made a person. She didn't know what made her laugh. She didn't know if she was a city person or a country person—presumably country, or she wouldn't be living here? She didn't know if she loved chocolate and could mix a good cocktail. She didn't know what Hattie wanted out of life.

And she never would, she reminded herself, because it wasn't her business. Hattie's life, however that looked, would continue without her intervention or interference.

All she knew about Hattie was that she'd loved her father, that they'd been close, and that was something she and Erica definitely didn't have in common.

ELEVEN

Claudia

Claudia watched as Anna slung her bag over her shoulder and buttoned up her coat.

"Let's go straight out," Anna said. "Right now. Let's not even bother taking off our coats."

Thank goodness for Anna, who was a master at handling delicate situations.

Erica eyed their luggage. "You don't want to unpack and settle in first?"

Claudia nudged her suitcase to one side. "No point in unpacking if we're leaving tomorrow." She'd fallen in love with the place and the thought of leaving was depressing, but after everything Erica had done for her there was no way she was going to voice that thought.

"I can't wait to explore the town." Anna pushed her feet back into her boots. "It looked so pretty driving through."

Erica looked guilty. "Better than Boston."

"Boston will be great, too. I love Boston. I'm excited about Boston. We will have had the best of both worlds."

Claudia wondered if Anna was laying it on a bit thick; they

all knew Anna only loved Boston for very short trips, but Erica seemed grateful.

"I know what a big sacrifice this is." Her voice was thickened. "I saw your faces when I pulled up outside the inn. You both fell in love with the place. And I'm making you leave."

"You're not making us," Anna said. "We're the ones suggesting it."

"Right." Erica gave a wan smile and reached for her purse and her car keys. "Let's go. And hope we don't bump into Hattie on the way out."

Claudia hoped for that, too. The last encounter had been awkward, to say the least.

They slunk out like criminals, all relieved that there was no sign of Hattie as they walked out of the inn.

Claudia glanced back at the inn and felt an inexplicable sense of loss. The place was tugging at her, in a way that nowhere ever had before.

But friendship sometimes required sacrifice, and this was a sacrifice she was prepared to make for Erica. What would she have done in Erica's position? It was impossible to say. Her family was boringly normal. She called her parents weekly, and they met up for all the key holidays if they were in the country. After Claudia had left home, her parents, taking advantage of their empty-nest status, had expressed their intention of traveling, and since then they'd done exactly that. They took two major trips a year, and much of their remaining time was spent in the planning.

It was snowing again, so instead of walking they trudged through the deepening snow to Erica's car and took the road back into town.

She managed to park on the street, right outside a gift store with festive windows and pretty lights. Next to it was a café, its windows misted from warmth and conversation, and farther down the street was the bookstore. Wreaths hung on doorways and greenery was wrapped around lampposts, until the whole place was a blur of festive green and red against a background of softly falling snow.

The place was bustling. Some of them locals, Claudia thought, but a large chunk of them tourists who posed for selfies in front of windows decorated with snowflakes and fairy lights.

"This place is ridiculously quaint." Anna pulled out her phone and took a few photos. "Let's have one of the three of us as a reminder of this visit."

Was that a good idea? Was Erica going to want to remember this when they left, or did she want to put the whole thing behind her?

Erica backed away. "You know I hate photographs."

"Just one. As a memento for me." Anna slipped her arm through Erica's and pulled her close as she raised her arm to take the photograph. "I promise not to post it anywhere. Or add a filter that makes you look like a rabbit. Smile."

Erica bared her teeth. "How did I come to have such sentimental friends?"

"Because you have good taste. Also, we're not easy to shake off because we like you." Anna slipped the phone back into her pocket but kept her arm through Erica's. "Now the question is am I going to visit that little store with the lights and garlands selling gingerbread, or am I going to head straight to the bookstore? Choices, choices."

"In normal circumstances I could be tempted by gingerbread," Claudia said, "but before we left I happened to glance at the menu for this evening—professional interest, you understand—and now I'm saving myself." She'd thought the menu was a little fussy, but she knew Chef Tucker by reputation and was interested to taste his food.

"How about mulled cider?" Anna gasped and pointed farther down the street. "There's a sleigh ride! Shall we take a sleigh ride?"

"Are you six years old? We're not taking a sleigh ride. Look at the queue of kids. It would be mean to take up a turn."

They walked along the street and Anna stopped in front of the window of a boutique.

"That sweater is gorgeous. Slightly sparkly and such a pretty shade of blue."

"You do not need another sweater." Claudia tugged at her arm. "You already have too many sweaters."

"It isn't possible to have too many sweaters."

"We agreed to visit the bookstore."

"Fine." Anna allowed them to move her on. "But if someone buys that sweater in the meantime I might have to kill you."

Erica guided them both toward the bookstore and pushed open the door.

A bell rang, and they stepped into warmth and the scent of cinnamon and cloves.

Claudia unwrapped her scarf from her neck, thinking that there was nothing better than the scents of winter. If she ever owned her own restaurant—a girl could dream, couldn't she?—she'd pay attention to atmosphere. The place she'd worked in California had been sleek and modern with acres of glass. Claudia had sometimes felt as if she was working in a dental office. As far as she was concerned a meal in a restaurant wasn't just about the food; it was about the whole experience and that included the people and the atmosphere.

"Welcome." The woman standing behind the counter gave them a friendly smile. She was wearing a reindeer sweater and a pair of glittering earrings shaped like Christmas trees. "You've picked the right place to warm up. We have a wide range of books and we serve the best hot chocolate in town. Whipped cream and cinnamon, no extra charge."

"I'm in." Claudia stuffed her scarf into her bag. "This place is cute."

"Thank you. It's my grandmother's store, but she had a fall recently so she's not here as much as she'd like." The woman placed a fresh stack of bookmarks on the countertop. "This place was her dream and she loves it as much now as she did when she set it up all those years ago."

"I can see why." Anna unbuttoned her coat and glanced around her. "I need to buy gifts for the twins and Pete. Looks as if I might get lucky here."

"I hope so, but if not, I'm sure you'll find something in one of the other stores. You've picked the perfect week to visit. It's our Christmas Fair. From tomorrow there will be stalls along Main Street, and there's a competition for who has the most festive store window. Take a look at Gaynor's Gifts just along the street to your right. She has a good eye. Her jewelry is always a hit with teenagers. And now I'll leave you to browse. Each room is themed. There's crime, romance, biography, history, poetry, literature—I'll let you explore. I'm Judie. If you need help, shout."

Anna thanked her and immediately headed to the romance section.

Claudia stayed close to Erica, who was staring at the bookshelf closest to the door.

"Are you all right?"

"I'm not sure." Erica lowered her voice. "I can't stop thinking about her. She lives here. This is her life. Does she come into this bookstore, do you think? Does she wear jewelry from Gaynor's Gifts?"

Claudia assumed that *she* in that sentence was Hattie.

"I'm sure she does. It's a small town. The sort of place where everyone knows everyone. Which is both good and bad." She glanced over her shoulder but the woman behind the counter was focused on the two children waiting patiently to buy the stack of books they were carrying.

"Alison and Tara, what do you have there?"

"Grandma gave us money to choose books. We can't read them until Christmas Day." The taller of the two girls took her sister's books and placed them on the counter.

"What a perfect gift. Shall I wrap them for you? That way you won't be tempted."

The two girls glanced toward a woman, presumably their mother.

"Thanks, Judie. That would be great." She put two more books on the stack, then added two scented candles, a board game and a silver necklace. "Every year I promise myself I'm going to get ahead and do my shopping in September but it never happens so I'm doing the whole lot right now. How's your grandmother? Has she recovered from her fall?"

"The bruises are fading but she's still stiff and not moving well." Judie rang up the purchases, swiped the woman's card and handed it back.

"It knocks your confidence, a fall like that. And it doesn't help with the weather as it is. Everything out there is so icy."

"We're driving her everywhere at the moment, which she hates. Thank you for the casserole, by the way. Much appreciated. Will you be at book club on Wednesday?"

"Definitely. Lynda called." The woman slid her purchases into a bag. "We're meeting at the inn. Did you hear that?"

"I did. I saw Lynda at yoga on Monday and she told me." Judie offered both children a sticker. "It will be perfect, particularly as it's a festive book we're discussing. I heard it was Hattie's idea. Are we supposed to bring something? Food? Drink?"

"Hattie said not to bring anything, even when Lynda insisted that we didn't want to make more work for her. How that girl copes with everything, I have no idea. What with running the inn and caring for Delphi single-handed, she must be exhausted."

"She looks better than she did two years ago, though," Judie said. "I was worried about her."

"We all were. Devastating. And no family to support her. I don't know where I'd be without my family, even though there are times when I wish they'd all move to California and give me peace. I'll take two of those pretty bookmarks while

I'm here. Actually, make it three. They make great stocking fillers. Thanks, Judie."

No family to support her.

Claudia winced inwardly and glanced at Erica. She was staring at the books on the shelf without seeing them. "Maybe we should go—"

"No." Erica shook her head. "I want to listen."

Claudia closed her eyes. She had a feeling listening was a very bad idea.

"Lynda is keeping an eye on her. She adores that girl. And Noah is always there, of course."

"He's a good man." There was a pause. "Sometimes I wonder—"

"I wonder the same thing. But Lynda asked me to wonder it quietly so that's what I'm doing."

Who was Lynda? Noah? And what were the two women wondering about?

They clearly knew each other well. Were part of the same community.

Claudia had grown up in a small town, but she knew Erica had never experienced that. Her mother believed in keeping herself to herself. Not relying on anyone. Erica had once told them that even when she'd broken her arm, she wouldn't ask anyone for anything. *We'll manage,* she'd said to Erica as she'd gritted her teeth and did her best to cook one-handed.

It was a story that had stayed with Claudia, mostly because her own experiences were so different. She'd lived in a neighborhood where you only had to sneeze and someone would be making you a casserole and offering to take the kids to school.

No one had ever offered Erica and her mother a casserole. No one had known her mother was working three jobs. No one had known they were struggling.

Erica's mother had been determined to manage alone, and Erica had learned that resilience was keeping going even when you thought you couldn't take another step.

Claudia remembered the first time she'd opened up to them in college. It had been a turning point in their friendship.

Knowing how hard it was for Erica to ask for support, Claudia reached out and gave her arm a squeeze.

"This is a lovely bookstore. Let's explore."

Erica finally stirred. "Yes," she said. "Good idea."

They stepped farther into the store, away from the conversation. They didn't need to hear more about Hattie, Claudia thought. They didn't need to hear that she was exhausted. What was Erica supposed to do anyway? If Hattie's life was stressful then Erica announcing her existence would surely only add to the stress.

Erica was probably right to walk away. Hattie clearly wasn't alone and struggling. She had a whole community of people to support her. She had Lynda and she had Noah. Was Noah that gorgeous guy in the truck who had delivered the logs? She didn't need anyone else.

"There you are!" Anna suddenly appeared. "I was talking to you both for at least five minutes before I realized you weren't there. I've found this stunning art book. I think Meg would love it. And I've found a book on battlefields for Pete—are you two all right?"

"Yes," Claudia said. "We're fine. Just browsing."

Anna glanced at the bookshelf next to Erica. "Since when were you two interested in notebooks?"

Notebooks?

Claudia took a closer look at the shelf in front of her. Notebooks. She hadn't even noticed what she was staring at.

"We thought maybe we'd start journaling."

"You're kidding."

"Yes, she's kidding," Erica said. "We've been eavesdropping shamelessly. Who knew that the local bookstore would be the perfect place to gain insight into the community? It's the equivalent of the office water cooler."

Anna studied her carefully and then gave her sleeve a tug.

"Come and see the thriller section. It's brilliant. All crime tape and blood-spattered walls. You'll love it."

Erica allowed Anna to propel her into the next room. Claudia followed.

In normal circumstances she would have admired the business brain behind the store. The whole place was designed to draw people in. She was desperate to explore the cookery section but she didn't want to leave Erica.

Anna pulled Erica into a corner away from other people. "You're upset. Tell me about the conversation you overheard."

"They were talking about Hattie. Everyone seems to know her."

"Small town." Anna paused as a woman passed them on her way to the romance section. "Did you learn anything interesting?"

Erica paused. "I learned that life has been tough for her."

"Right. But you assumed that. It's why you came looking for her, isn't it?"

Erica was silent and Claudia wondered if she even really knew why she'd come looking for Hattie.

Anna frowned. "You can change your mind and stay if you want to?"

Claudia held her breath. She so badly wanted to stay but Erica immediately shook her head.

"I don't want to stay."

"Are you sure?" Anna was watching her closely. "I wondered if hearing them talk about her might have changed your mind."

"On the contrary, it's clear to me that she has a big support network here. There's no reason to stay."

Anna hesitated. "You're her family, Erica. That's a good reason."

"We both know there's more to family than DNA. She doesn't need me, Anna."

"Maybe she does." Anna spoke softly. "And maybe you need her."

"That's absurd," Erica said. "I've made it to forty without her in my life. I'm sure I can survive the next few decades."

"I'm sure you can. But there's a difference between surviving and thriving. Maybe the risk would be worth it. Maybe," Anna said, "those decades would be richer for having her as part of your life."

"I don't need the emotional complication," Erica said. "And your problem is that you're too much of a romantic."

Anna smiled. "I don't see that as a problem."

"How are we friends?"

"I don't know, but you held my hair back the first time I drank too much and was sick so we're bonded forever. There's no escaping me." Anna glanced at the cover of the book next to them and shuddered. "Why do people read this stuff?"

"Because it allows them to experience the darker side of the world without taking personal risk. And that was the only time you've ever drunk too much."

"It wasn't an experience I wanted to repeat."

"Your bad-girl credentials are lacking." But it was a reminder of how well they knew each other, how deep their friendship ran. "I just want things to go back to the way they were. I wish my mother had thrown that card away. I wish I'd never found it. I wish I'd never acted on it."

Claudia put the book she was holding back on the shelf. "Do you really?"

"Yes." Erica straightened her shoulders. "I'm leaving tomorrow. I've made my decision and I'm comfortable with that decision. So why do I feel weird?"

"Because even if you leave, things will still be different," Claudia said. "Just because you're choosing not to act doesn't mean things haven't changed. Information changes things."

"Yes. Call me Pandora." Erica stared at the chalk outline on the floor. "What's that supposed to be? A reader who died of boredom?"

Anna laughed. "Let's hope not." Another couple joined them

in the crime section and the three of them strolled through to the next room, which had the same tall bookshelves along with a comfortable seating area stacked with cushions. A deep pile rug muffled their footsteps.

Erica glanced up at the hearts hanging from the ceiling and the fairy lights twisted around the bookshelves. "The romance section? You've brought me to the romance section?"

Anna shrugged. "I'm appealing to your softer side. Also, I want to buy a Catherine Swift."

"You already have her latest. That's what we're discussing later over a glass of good red wine." She watched as Anna scanned the shelves. As students they'd spent hours in bookstores, and then rationed their purchases because money was tight. She knew that Anna would choose a book over a meal every time. Whenever she and Erica were buying a gift for Anna they always chose books.

"I'm looking for early Catherine Swift. Not murder Catherine—romance Catherine. I need an antidote for all the darkness." Anna reached high on the shelf and pulled out a book. She turned it over and scanned the back. "I think I might have read this one."

"You've read all of them."

"Most of them. There are still a few of her earlier ones I haven't read. Why did she start writing crime? That in itself is a crime. It's cruel to her readers. I can't bear to think I'll never read a new Catherine Swift romance again." She added the book to the other items she was carrying.

"Life doesn't stay the same. Isn't that what you're always telling us? Apparently, that's true for romance novelists, too. And not to preempt our discussion about the book, but I'd say her talent is still there."

"I agree. I couldn't put the book down. I'm looking forward to talking about it—particularly the part where the heroine murdered her husband instead of starting with therapy like every normal person—but to go from writing romance to

crime? That's like booking a vacation on the beach and finding yourself in a freezing ski resort." Anna pulled another book
from the shelf. "They have such a good selection. I think this
might be my new favorite bookstore."

"They've done a good job," Erica said. "And I feel guilty
dragging you away from this place, because it's perfect for you.
Particularly you, Anna. It's probably your Christmas dream and
I'm being selfish, asking you to leave."

"You're not asking. It was our suggestion." Anna put the
book she was holding back on the shelf. "It won't be any fun
if you're worrying the whole time. We need to relax and that's
what we're going to do. Claudia has already found a cute boutique hotel in the Beacon Hill area. It looks cozy. We were
going to show it to you before we booked because you're the
hotel expert."

It was true. Claudia had found somewhere on the car ride
into town and it did look cute. But it was a long way from the
festive Maple Sugar Inn.

And Erica clearly knew it. "I still feel terrible that I'm spoil-
ing your special trip."

"Why? You'd do the same for us," Anna said. "In fact, you
have done the same. Remember the time the twins were sick?
We'd only been on vacation for two days and you drove me to
the hospital and stayed with me the whole time."

"That's different. Your kids were sick. It's not as if you had
a choice."

"No, but you did. You didn't have to come with me, and
having you there made all the difference." Anna gave her arm
a squeeze. "We should get out of here. Go back to the hotel.
Take a bath and relax, then have a glass of wine together before dinner. Or we can leave before dinner if you prefer. Drive
to Boston tonight."

"No. We'll leave in the morning as we planned."

Claudia seized the moment. "If it's okay with you, I might
just have five minutes in the cookery section before we leave."

She left them in romance debating the merits of authors switching genres and immersed herself in the expansive cookery section. It took her less than five minutes to pick out three cookery books and a box of cookie cutters shaped like fir trees.

If I lived here, she thought, *I'd come here every day.*

She returned reluctantly to her friends, and Anna raised an eyebrow when she saw the books.

"I thought you'd given up cooking."

"I'm not going to cook from these. I'm going to read them."

"Read them?" Erica frowned. "You mean like a novel?"

"Yes, she does mean that. It's what she does when she's stressed," Anna reminded her. "You know the story—when she was eight she discovered all her grandmother's old French cookery books and read them cover to cover."

It was true. She'd sat cross-legged on the floor of her grandmother's bedroom, reading her way through dusty books, with a French dictionary by her side. Her grandmother had discovered her there and invited her to join her in the kitchen.

I will teach you the five mother sauces of classical French cuisine.

At her grandmother's side she learned about the great French chefs, Marie-Antoine Carême and Georges-Auguste Escoffier. With her grandmother's hand over hers, she'd learned to make *béchamel*, *hollandaise*, *velouté*, *espagnole* and *sauce tomat*.

Those lessons had served her well when she'd started training and she'd been grateful, but what her grandmother had really given her was a love of cooking.

And although Anna was right that reading cookery books was usually a stress buster for her, she hadn't picked one up for six months.

Now, for the first time, she wanted to. Maybe that was progress.

"Cookery books fascinate me. They tell you so much about local culture. These are local Vermont cookery books. I know we're not staying," she said quickly, "but I'd still like to read these."

"And the cookie cutters?"

"I collect cookie cutters like a writer collects notebooks. I thought they were cute, but I don't suppose I'll ever use them."

Erica glanced at Anna. "Want to bet that she uses them before the end of the holidays?"

Anna shook her head. "I never bet on a certainty."

They paid for their purchases and headed back to the car. It was dark and the street sparkled with Christmas lights.

"Everyone is having fun," Claudia said as they picked their way through the snow to the car. "Do you think they're this happy in January or is it part of the Christmas festivities? Maybe you're only allowed to take part if you smile."

They arrived back at the inn to find Hattie checking in a young couple who were keen for information on local ski trails.

Erica kept her eyes straight ahead and headed to the stairs.

"Shall we meet in two hours for drinks before dinner?" Anna followed her into the room and she and Claudia collected their luggage. "That should give us time for a relaxing bath and some personal time."

Personal time for Anna would mean calling Pete. Claudia imagined her snuggled on the bed in her dressing gown, face pink from the bath, telling Pete everything that had happened because she and Pete always discussed everything.

Claudia felt a twinge of envy.

No matter what happened, Anna always had Pete.

What did Claudia have? She needed to fix her life, but in the meantime, she was going to make the most of her one and only evening in the Maple Sugar Inn. A relaxing bath sounded like a good idea, so she would do the same and then curl up in front of the fire with her cookery books and indulge in a comfort binge read.

TWELVE

Hattie

Hattie stood outside the door for a full minute before she finally knocked.

This was possibly a big mistake, but there was only one way to find out.

There was a pause and then the door opened.

Erica stood there. She was wearing a red wool dress and a pair of boots that made Hattie want to cry with envy—it was good to know they had at least one thing in common! Her dark hair fell to her shoulders in a smooth, well-cut bob and her lips were a bold shade of red.

The smile on those lips vanished when she saw Hattie. She'd obviously been expecting one of her friends.

They stared at each other for a long moment.

Hattie had a whole speech planned but the whole thing flew from her brain.

"I came to check you're happy with your rooms." It was a pathetic opening, but at least she didn't stammer. "If there's anything you need—"

"There's nothing. And the rooms are great." Erica was civil, but distant. "Thank you." She kept her hand on the door as if she couldn't wait to close it. She was waiting for Hattie to walk away, but Hattie knew that if she walked away she was going to regret it always.

She stood awkwardly, feeling out of her depth. She'd expected Erica to say something, but it seemed she wasn't going to. What did that mean? Why was she even here if she didn't intend to have a conversation? Perhaps she'd just been waiting for the right moment. Perhaps she had a speech all planned and Hattie had ruined everything by knocking on her door.

"I didn't really come to check you're happy with the rooms, although of course I'm pleased that you are—" This time Hattie did stumble over the words. "There is no easy way to say this so I'm just going to say it and I hope I'm not out of line."

Erica's hand tightened on the door. Her knuckles were white. Hattie looked her in the eye. "You're Madeleine, aren't you?"

Erica's lips parted. "Erica," she croaked. "My name is Erica."

"Yes. That was what confused me. It's the reason it took me a little while to figure it out." She felt slightly giddy. This was her sister. Her *sister*. She'd gone from having no family to having a sister. This must be how it felt to win the lottery. "It doesn't matter what you're called. I'm just happy you're here now. For years I hoped this moment might come, but it never did and lately—" she broke off, choked by emotion "—lately life has been very tough and—well, I didn't expect a gift like this."

Erica was still holding tightly to the door, as if it was the only thing keeping her upright. "A gift?"

"You coming to find me after all these years. You did come to find me, didn't you? It can't be coincidence. The moment I saw you looking at the photo of our dad—"

"Stop." Erica's face was white. "Please, stop."

"I know this is awkward, but—" Overwhelmed, Hattie felt tears mist her eyes and on impulse she stepped forward and hugged Erica. She wanted to bridge this awkwardness. She wanted to get past it as fast as possible. This was her *sister*. "I can't believe you're actually here." She clung to her sister, feeling the brush of wool against her chin and breathing in her sophisticated scent. Her heart felt as if it had swollen to twice its normal size. She felt dampness on her cheeks and realized she was crying. And she realized something else—that Erica hadn't moved from her position in the doorway. She hadn't let go of the door. She hadn't returned Hattie's hug. She was standing rigid in her embrace and hadn't said a single reassuring word. She hadn't said anything at all.

Mortified, Hattie let go of her so suddenly that Erica almost lost her balance. "Sorry. So sorry. That was inappropriate." She felt as if she was standing on quicksand, being sucked downwards. "I don't know what I was thinking. I was just so pleased to see you. No, not pleased. *Pleased* doesn't begin to describe it. I never thought this day would come and that made me so sad. You've no *idea* how it feels to know you have a sister out there somewhere—a blood relative—and that you're not in touch. I'd given up hoping. I've never believed in Christmas miracles before but now I think I do."

Erica finally spoke. "You said you've waited for this moment for years—you knew about me?"

"Of course I knew about you. Dad told me everything. Not the fact that you use the name Erica—I don't think he knew about that. But I always knew I had a sister out there somewhere. And now here you are." Hattie's smile faltered. "And I can see from your face that you're not at all pleased to see me."

This was so awkward. And to make things worse, she'd been stroking Rufus immediately before plucking up courage to knock on Erica's door, and the hug had transferred a number of dog hairs from her sweater to Erica's pristine red dress.

She shouldn't have knocked on Erica's door and she definitely shouldn't have hugged her. First Noah, and now Erica. She seemed to have developed an unfortunate habit of indulging in unsolicited physical affection and it had to stop. It probably came across as disturbingly needy. She should have waited for her to make the first approach, but she'd been so unreasonably excited when she'd figured out who Erica was that she'd behaved like Rufus chasing a stick. She'd just gone for it, and damn the consequences. And now she was looking at the consequences.

Staring at Erica's frozen features she wanted to rewind the clock and do things differently.

When Erica had made the reservation, the name hadn't registered at all. Even when she'd walked into the inn, Hattie still had no idea that this was her sister. It wasn't until Erica had picked up the photograph of Hattie with her dad that she'd finally realized who she was. Erica had lifted her gaze from the photograph and Hattie had known right away, not because of the degree of interest Erica had shown in the photo, but because of the physical similarities. She'd registered her eye color, that unusual shade that hovered between hazel and green, depending on the light. Hattie's father had the same eyes. Hattie herself had the same eyes. It had been a visceral, heartrending moment.

She'd waited for Erica to make the first move, but then as the hours had passed and nothing had happened she'd changed her mind. She'd even wondered if she'd made a mistake about her identity.

But now, face-to-face with the older woman, she knew it wasn't a mistake.

There was something vaguely intimidating about Erica. She was effortlessly elegant. She didn't look like someone who was ever anything but perfectly groomed, and she had an aura of competence that Hattie envied. No one was ever going to take advantage of Erica. No one was ever going to walk over her. She probably never woke to mornings of doubt, wondering how she was going to make it through the day.

She decided that honesty was the only way forward. "What was your plan? Were you going to talk to me at some point?"

Before Erica could reply—would she have replied or would she just have carried on staring?—the door to the room next door opened, and the door opposite that one. Erica's two friends stepped into the corridor. Anna and Claudia. Hattie always memorized the names of her guests and remembered them by noticing certain characteristics. In this case, it was Anna with the brown eyes and Claudia with the short, choppy hair.

They stopped the moment they saw Hattie.

Anna spoke first. "The rooms are gorgeous. This whole place is gorgeous. I could have stayed in the bath all night. How do you get your towels so fluffy? It felt like a punishment getting dressed." She glanced from Hattie's face to Erica. "You've been talking. You mustn't think that the fact that we're checking out tomorrow has anything to do with the inn. This place is exceptional, and we'll be leaving a glowing review."

"You're checking out?" Hattie stared at her and then turned to look at Erica, expecting a denial or some words of reassurance that it was a misunderstanding. "Why would you check out? You just arrived."

Erica closed her eyes briefly. "Yes, we did. But—"

Oh, this was awful. Erica obviously never had any intention of having a conversation with her. She was running away.

"Don't worry." Hattie tried to rake together the last of her dignity. "Forget it. My mistake."

Erica finally let go of the door. "You don't understand."

"Oh, I think I do." Hattie's hands were clenched into fists by her sides. "You came here to take a look at me, and you didn't like what you saw."

Erica frowned. "Hattie—"

"If you'll excuse me, I have a full restaurant this evening and a couple checking in late so I should go." She backed away and knocked into the wall behind her, emotion making her clumsy. "If there's anything I can do to make your stay more comfortable for the one night you're here, let me know."

She was back to being an innkeeper, and not a sister. It should have been easy, because it wasn't as if she had any experience in being a sister.

Without giving Erica the opportunity to speak again she almost sprinted back down the corridor. Her cheeks burned and she felt stupid. There was humiliation, and there was also hurt. Rejection always hurt and that had most certainly been a rejection. But there was a particular type of pain that came from acknowledging that her powerful urge to know her sister wasn't returned. She felt bruised, as if someone had taken a hammer to her insides, and the intensity of her emotions made no sense. She'd lived without a sister for twenty-eight years, so why would she suddenly feel as if she'd lost something important? *Essential.* How could you lose something you'd never had? Was she really so emotionally starved that she needed a stranger in her life? No, she wasn't. She had Delphi. She had Rufus. She had wonderful neighbors and friends in the town. She stopped herself from thinking she had Noah. She wasn't sure what her relationship with Noah was, and she couldn't even think about that right now.

Her mind in a spin, she headed down the stairs and back into the reception area, which she'd left barely minutes earlier so full of hope. And because she was thinking of her sister rather than looking where she was going she slammed straight into the man heading toward her office.

"Whoa—" Strong hands gripped her arms and steadied her. And there he was. Right in front of her. Noah.

"I'm sorry—" She gasped out the words. "I was—"

"Distracted by the looks of it. Has something happened?" He kept his hands on her arms. "What's wrong?"

"Nothing. I'm being stupid."

"I doubt that." He urged her into the library. "Tell me."

She had work to do. Guests to see. But she couldn't resist the temptation to give herself just five minutes with Noah.

"You're right, it wasn't stupid." She had no intention of beating herself up over what had been a logical decision. "All the signs were there, otherwise why come here? I can't believe that was coincidence. How could it be a coincidence?"

Noah closed the door behind him. "If that question is for me then I'm going to need a little more background."

Hattie barely heard him past the noise in her head. She paced across the room, rubbing her arms with her hands.

"Have you ever just risked everything because it's so important to you that someone knows how you feel that you don't even pause and then you hand over your heart and your feelings and *wham*—just like that they drop them and everything shatters and you ask yourself if it was really worth it, and whether you should have done things differently, but you know that if you had your time again you'd do exactly the same thing because how could you not? You had to know. And now I know." She paused to take a breath and realized Noah was silent.

"What you're saying," he said slowly, "is that your feelings aren't returned?"

"That's right. And it hurts here—" she pressed a fist to her chest "—which makes no sense at all, and I keep telling myself I was fine before I said those words so I should be fine after, but it's different because before you say them there is hope and possibilities and now there's none."

"And you're brokenhearted."

"Yes." She felt the warmth from the fire burning the backs of her legs. "And now you probably do think I'm stupid."

"There's nothing stupid about falling in love, Hattie." His voice sounded rough around the edges. "And you can't always choose who you fall for. Is he a guest?"

"Who?"

"The man you're in love with."

"Man? I never said anything about—" She stopped as understanding dawned. "No. I'm not in love. Why would you think that?"

"Because you mentioned being honest about your feelings and being rejected."

"Yes, but not a boyfriend. Not a man. A woman. My—"

she paused, stunned that he'd think she was in love "—sister." The word felt unfamiliar on her tongue.

"Sister?" It took him a moment to catch up. "The sister your father walked out on at birth?"

"That's right. And when you put it like that, perhaps it's not surprising that she didn't run along the red carpet toward me. Erica. That's her name, by the way."

"You told me it was Madeleine."

They'd had long conversations about it in the months before that kiss, before their relationship had become awkward and stilted.

She missed that. She missed the days where she'd been relaxed and natural with him and said the things that she wanted to say and done what she'd wanted to do. She hadn't policed every word and every move in case he misinterpreted things.

She forced herself to concentrate. "That's what Dad told me, but she goes by Erica, which was why I didn't immediately recognize the name when she made the booking. I wasn't expecting her to turn up here, but the moment she stepped through the door I felt—it's hard to explain—I just knew. I recognized her, even though I'd never seen her before."

"Family resemblance?"

"Yes. And the way she stared at the photo on my desk. I knew. I expected her to say something, but she didn't. And I stewed on it and waited and then wondered if maybe she was waiting for me to say something, so I decided I should just go for it."

He nodded. "Generally, if there's something that needs saying it's better to say it."

"That's what I thought. But I messed it up. Badly."

"I don't see how anything you said could have been bad."

"It wasn't what I said, it was what I did. I hugged her." Remembering made her cringe. "I couldn't help it. When she opened the door I just felt so happy that she'd come here—so happy that I had family—"

"You hugged her."

"Yes." She could see the smile playing around his mouth and had no idea why he'd be smiling because as far as she could see there was nothing funny about the situation.

"You were pleased to see her," he said. "I don't see anything wrong with that."

"That's because you weren't there. It was like hugging a cat. Not Panther because she is unusually cuddly, but you know what I mean—sometimes they go all stiff and rigid and you know that all they want is for you to stop so that they can get back to doing their own thing." And now she thought about it, Erica reminded her a little of a cat. Dignified. Poised. Careful. Selective. "I handled it badly."

"You're being hard on yourself. There's no rulebook for handling a situation like this."

"True. But the fact that she hasn't been in touch in the past twenty-eight years of my life probably should have told me something."

"Slow down." He was holding her arms again, his grip firm and comforting. "Breathe."

"I'm sorry." She breathed. "I'm a little flustered."

"It seems so."

She probably should have pulled away but she didn't want to. She felt the tug of attraction, strong enough to distract her. No point in pretending it didn't exist. No point in pretending that she didn't feel anything. She felt plenty, but right now she had more than enough to deal with.

"I'm sure she resents me." She shifted her focus back to Erica. "And I wouldn't blame her. She probably took one look at the photograph of Dad swinging me and wanted to punch me."

"I doubt she wanted to punch you."

"You're right. She's elegant. Not at all the punching type."

"And she's here at the inn," he said, "which must mean she intended to make contact. I agree that it can't be coincidence."

"Maybe not, but she didn't act like someone who had been looking forward to talking to me."

"Or perhaps she had a plan of how to tell you, and she's one of these people who likes to stick to a plan."

"Possibly, although she's running out of time. They're checking out tomorrow morning." And that hurt. "They booked the whole week, but she clearly didn't like what she saw. Whatever her expectations, I didn't live up to them."

"Or it's something else entirely."

Standing this close to him was making it difficult to think, so she stepped back. "What else?"

He shrugged. "Maybe she's afraid."

"She doesn't exactly seem like the fearful type."

"But think about it, Hattie. It's a big deal for you. Presumably, it's a big deal for her, too."

"Maybe." The antique clock behind her chimed and she turned her head and felt a flash of panic. "Is that the time? I shouldn't be standing here. I need to take Delphi from Chloe so that she can get on with her work. She'll be wondering where I am."

The door opened, but it wasn't Chloe who stood there; it was Erica.

Anna and Claudia stood on either side of her.

For moral support? The fact that they thought she needed moral support suggested Erica wasn't as cool about this situation as she seemed. Maybe Noah was right.

Anna with the brown eyes gave Erica's arm a reassuring squeeze, and Erica took a deep breath and stepped into the room.

Hattie said nothing. After that last encounter, it was better to stay silent.

She felt Noah's arm brush against hers and realized he was probably waiting for the right moment to make a rapid exit.

She gave him a quick smile. "You probably need to be getting back."

"I'm in no hurry." He stood firm, and she felt a rush of gratitude to him for staying by her side in such a difficult moment. She was lucky to have Noah, and also lucky that her momentary lapse of restraint in the barn hadn't ruined things between them.

Erica gave him a long look, but that wasn't entirely surprising. Women of all ages had a habit of looking at Noah. Hattie saw it whenever the community got together to celebrate something. He was a favorite with everyone, from teenagers to grandmothers, as well as everyone in between. It could have been because he was tall and solid, with friendly eyes and a smile to match, or maybe it was because of his calm temperament that never seemed to be shaken up no matter how strongly the winds of life blew around him.

Hattie was grateful for that calm now.

"I'm Noah." He introduced himself. "I'm a friend of Hattie's."

"Erica." Erica introduced her friends and then turned her attention to the bookshelves. "This room is fabulous." Her gaze tracked along the books, took in the flickering fire and the sparkle of the Christmas tree. "This is the space you mentioned we could use for our book club meeting?"

"Yes." Hattie held herself stiffly and Erica seemed equally uncomfortable.

"I'm sorry about earlier."

"You don't need to apologize." If she thought of herself as an innkeeper, and not a relative, it would help her create the distance she needed. "It's important to me that your Christmas break is perfect. If the Maple Sugar Inn isn't the right place for you, then of course you should leave and find somewhere else. I can make some calls if that would help. There are a couple of other pretty inns close by. One of them has a good restaurant. They may be able to accommodate you."

Never let it be said that she bore grudges. Or maybe she did. Occasionally, she did curse Brent for leaving her to deal with Stephanie and Chef Tucker. But she hid it well.

Her offer of accommodation was met with silence and she saw the other woman—Claudia with the short, choppy hair—poke Erica sharply in the ribs.

"There's nothing wrong with the inn," Erica said. "It's perfect."

Which meant that she, Hattie, was the problem. Great.

She stood up straighter. "I was wrong to knock on your door."

"You weren't wrong." Erica glanced at Anna, as if this conversation was something they'd rehearsed. "You took me by surprise, and I'm not great with surprises. Also, this whole situation is complicated." She cleared her throat. "Emotionally complicated. And I'm not great with that, either." That hint of vulnerability softened something inside Hattie. She forgot about her earlier resolve to say nothing.

"If you're not leaving tonight, then would you like to sit down and talk for a while? Glass of wine? I'll ask Chef to produce a plate of his delicious nibbles." No doubt he'd scowl at her, but she'd weather it.

Erica gave a tentative nod. "I'd like that."

Hattie felt warmth spread through her. They were going to talk. That was a start.

"Great. I should just check on my daughter, and then—"

The door flew open again, and this time it was Chloe who stood there. She was holding Delphi's hand and there was panic in her eyes.

"Sorry to burst in, but Hattie, you need to come right now. It's an emergency."

Now what? The universe obviously hated her.

Delphi sprinted across to her and Hattie scooped her up. No matter that her daughter was growing taller and heavier by the day. If she wanted to be hugged, then Hattie was going to hug her.

"An emergency?" She held Delphi tightly. "Is it a guest?"

"No. Much worse. Chef Tucker threw a pan at the sous-chef and she walked out. Stephanie got involved, and had a terrible fight with Chef and he has also walked out. Actually, he drove, if we're being literal. He took his truck and was last seen vanishing toward town. Which is a problem on many levels, because the restaurant is full this evening and we have no one in charge of the kitchen. The rest of the staff are panicking. Fortunately, the guests are so far blissfully unaware, but Stephanie is having one of her rants—"

Right on cue, Stephanie arrived at the door. "That's it! I hope he has gone for good, but if he hasn't then you need to fire him and I demand an apology. He may be a creative genius, but I will not be spoken to the way that man spoke to me this evening, and in front of staff, too."

Delphi pressed her hands over her ears and cringed closer to Hattie. "Too shouty."

Hattie didn't disagree. She held Delphi close, rubbing her back with her hand.

"I can see you're upset, Stephanie, and we're going to figure this out. But we all need to stay calm."

"*Stay calm?* Would you stay calm if a man called you an uptight, frigid b—"

Fortunately, Delphi's crying drowned out the rest of the sentence. To complicate the situation further, Rufus, hearing the shouting, came shooting into the room barking, checking which of his family needed his protection.

Seeing Delphi safe with Hattie, he stopped barking and growled.

Stephanie took a step backward. "And that dog is a health hazard."

Delphi buried her face in Hattie's neck. "Shouty, shouty—"

Hattie tightened her arms protectively. "Please lower your voice, Stephanie."

"Who is running this business? You or that child? Or is it the dog? There are days when I wonder. It puts a whole new spin on the phrase *going to the dogs*, and this place most definitely is."

Hattie's head was splitting. Right now her daughter was the

priority because until she'd soothed Delphi, she wasn't going to be able to have a rational conversation, and she couldn't calm Delphi while Stephanie was shouting.

She was about to suggest that Stephanie wait in her office, when Anna stepped forward. She held a pretty decoration in her hand.

"Delphi? I found this on the floor. It must have fallen off the tree. Do you know where it was hanging?"

Delphi cautiously lifted her damp face from Hattie's shoulder.

She looked at Anna and seemed to like what she saw because she released her choke hold on Hattie's neck.

"No." Her breath came in jerks. "D-don't know."

"I love decorating trees." Anna's smile was kind. "It's my favorite thing. I'm sure you love it, too, am I right?"

Delphi sniffed. "Yes."

"That's great. Could you help me decide where to hang this?" Anna dangled the twinkling star from her fingers. "Shall I just pick somewhere?"

Delphi paused and then wriggled down from Hattie's arms. "I'll show you."

Rufus was by her side in an instant, and Anna reached down to stroke him. "He's gorgeous. I'm Anna. And I remember that when my little girl was your age, she knew *exactly* what she wanted Santa to bring her for Christmas. I bet you're the same."

Hattie decided that she loved Anna.

Delphi took the decoration from Anna's fingers. "I know, but it's a secret."

"A secret?" Anna's smile was compelling. "But you've written to him?"

"Aunty Lynda helped me. Mommy can't know."

Noah raised his eyebrows so presumably he knew nothing about it, either.

Which gave Hattie a whole new problem. If she didn't know what Delphi wanted for Christmas, how was she supposed to provide it?

Stephanie made an impatient sound. "I cannot believe we're talking about Santa when this place is falling apart. You do realize that at the moment all you have in our *award-winning kitchen* are a bunch of junior staff?"

At the mention of the staff, Hattie transferred her attention from Delphi to Stephanie. "First, is Helen all right?"

Stephanie gaped at her. "I'm telling you that you have a crisis, and you're asking after the welfare of your sous-chef?"

"Chloe said Chef Tucker threw a pan at her."

"Oh—yes, he did." Stephanie frowned. "She was crying, and he lost his temper. I don't condone hurling heavy objects, but I agree with him that she is much too sensitive to be working in a busy kitchen."

Hattie tried again, more firmly this time. "Is she hurt?"

"I don't know, and right now that is not the most important thing. It's time for plain speaking. I've done my best to support you since Brent died," she said, focusing her laser-like gaze on Hattie, "but even I have my limits and I've reached them. I'm sad for you, Hattie, that's the truth. It's been hard, I'm sure, but maybe it's time to admit you're not cut out for this. You've tried to step into Brent's shoes, but you don't come near to filling them. You'll never be Brent. And frankly, Brent would turn in his grave if he could see the way you're running this place."

Hattie felt the blood drain from her face. Her limbs felt shaky. She felt strange and disconnected.

Her first thought was for her daughter, but fortunately, Anna had Delphi occupied finding a place around the back of the tree for the ornament.

Which left her no excuse to not face Stephanie.

She was tempted to bolt from the room, but then what? There was no one else to handle this. Only her.

And Stephanie was right about one thing. She wasn't Brent. And she had been trying to be Brent. She'd been trying to carry on his dream for the inn. And that was the problem; she could see that now. She'd been trying to keep things going the way he'd wanted, and in doing so hadn't followed any of her own instincts. She'd done what was right for him, not what was right for her. And this was where they'd ended up.

And it wasn't a good place.

Hattie felt Noah's hand on her back, warm and protective.

She heard him draw breath and knew that if she didn't speak soon, then he would. And what sort of example would that set for Delphi? That she needed other people to speak for her? To defend her? She didn't want her daughter growing up thinking her mother couldn't stand her ground when she needed to or, worse, that she wasn't able to defend herself when someone spoke to her in such a disrespectful way.

"Stephanie, we need to talk in private. Let's go to my office."

"If you want to talk to me, I'll try and find time for you tomorrow. I'm leaving for the evening."

"Leaving? Stephanie, we're in a crisis."

"A crisis of your making. A crisis that is not my problem. There is nothing in my contract that says I have to donate my personal time to a lost cause."

"What about your colleagues? The people you work with?" Hattie's mouth was so dry she could hardly form the words. Anger made her limbs shake. "We're a team. You're just going to walk away and leave the team to struggle?"

"I'm leaving them to do their jobs, the way I do mine. I'm going to give myself time to calm down, and then if I feel up to working I'll come back tomorrow." She turned toward the door and Hattie felt her heart rate double.

She had to do this right now.

"If you walk through that door now, I don't want you back here tomorrow." The words left her mouth in a rush. It was like jumping from a cliff into freezing water.

"Is this a joke?" Stephanie stared at her. "There is no way you'll be able to keep this place going without me."

Hattie's heart was hammering. "We'll manage."

"How? You haven't got a clue. And, she—" Stephanie gestured to Chloe "—won't be any help at all. Also, can I remind you that as of now you have no chef and possibly no sous-chef? If you lose your housekeeper, too, you might as well shut down."

The sous-chef. Hattie still needed to check on Helen, but she needed to do this first.

There was a knot of panic in her stomach.

"It's true that I've been trying to run things the way Brent did, but that ends now."

Stephanie relaxed slightly. "You're going to sell up. Wise decision."

"I won't be selling up, but nor will I be running the place following Brent's blueprint. From now on I'm making the decisions. And I need a team who share my vision for the place as somewhere cozy and welcoming. I think we both know that working here isn't a good fit for you."

Stephanie's cheeks flushed dark. "What I know is that you're not the right person to be running this business. And without me, this place will be closed within months."

"I'm willing to take that chance."

Stephanie's mouth tightened. "So that's it, then. Well, good luck to you. You're going to need it." She turned and stalked out of the room, slamming the door behind her.

Hattie felt as if her head was going to explode.

The panic in her stomach grew more intense. Bands of pressure squeezed her chest.

What had she done? She had rooms booked through until January. People had treated themselves to a Christmas stay at the inn. They expected festive sparkle, comfortable rooms and food they'd always remember. And she'd just lost two of her key members of staff.

Stephanie was right. They'd be closed within months.

The panic shifted from her stomach to her throat. She probably should have done more to placate Stephanie because now she'd made her situation worse.

It was Erica who spoke first. She stepped forward and Hattie saw kindness in her eyes.

"I don't know who that woman is, but she clearly had nothing positive to bring to the situation. Letting her walk through that door is going to turn out to be the best thing you have ever done for yourself."

"Is it?" Hattie was shaking. Part of her wanted to sprint after Stephanie and apologize, but Erica was standing in her way.

"It's fine." Her voice was steady and matter-of-fact. "Everything is fine. We can help."

"You can't. No one can help. It's a good thing you're checking out." Hattie made a wild attempt at humor. "I've just lost my housekeeper, and it looks as if the restaurant will be closed. Welcome to Christmas at the Maple Sugar Inn. It promises to be memorable, for all the wrong reasons."

What had she done? Dear God, *what had she done*?

Delphi emerged from behind the tree. "That's life," she said, in a solemn and perfect imitation of the Bishop sisters.

THIRTEEN

Erica

Faced with a crisis, Erica felt more in control than she had for weeks.

The subject of her father, making contact with her sister, the confusing emotions—that all tied her up in knots. But *this*— this, she could handle. This was a crisis that required clear thinking and action, and that was her strength. She had the ability to cut through emotions and drama and see what needed to be done. She knew she could help Hattie.

And maybe she could calm her conscience at the same time because she felt awful about the way she'd reacted when Hattie had knocked on her door. It hadn't crossed her mind that Hattie might know of her existence, but clearly she'd been told about Madeleine.

She heard her mother's voice in her head.

We each chose a name. He chose Madeleine, I chose Erica. Madeleine Erica. You became Erica the moment he walked out that door.

She owed Hattie an apology, but that would have to wait because right now she didn't like what she was seeing.

Hattie had held it together well during that unpleasant exchange with Stephanie, but now she looked as if she might crumble on the spot. Stephanie's vicious attack had made so many holes in her self-esteem you could almost see the confidence draining away. Her eyes had a glassy look and her breathing was fast and shallow.

Erica reckoned she was a few short breaths away from a full-blown panic attack.

She opened her mouth to speak, but Noah got there first.

"You handled that well, Hattie. I almost cheered. I bet everyone else did, too." He put his hand on her shoulder. "It's okay. Everything is fine."

Erica would have said the same herself, only without the shoulder rub.

Unfortunately, neither seemed to soothe Hattie.

"Everything is not fine." There was a note of hysteria in her voice and she breathed in short, rapid snatches. "I just lost my housekeeper and apparently, I've already lost my chef, only unlike Stephanie he didn't have the courtesy to shout at me before he drove into the sunset."

Noah's hand was still on her shoulder, strong and supportive. "A housekeeper who has been giving you grief for two years, and a chef who constantly behaved like a toddler midtantrum."

"Maybe, but he's a great chef." Hattie wrapped her arms around her middle. "Brent thought he was a creative genius."

"He was unpredictable and a liability." Noah was blunt. "And as for Stephanie, you did what needed to be done. Said what needed to be said. Not easy. I was proud of you."

Hattie didn't appear to hear him. She didn't seem aware of anything that was going on around her. "She's right." She muttered the words to herself. "I have let Brent down. I've tried to keep things going the way he wanted them, to do the things he would have done, but I've failed. I've lost his two key members of staff. He was excited when he appointed them. He said that they'd really put the place on the map. And they're gone because of me. And poor Helen, the sous-chef." She fumbled for her phone. "Did the pan he threw actually hit her? I need to check she is all right."

Noah glanced out the window. "Her car is still in the parking lot, so she hasn't left."

"She's fine," Chloe said, "although there is a large dent in one of the kitchen cabinets."

"I don't care about the kitchen, as long as she's all right. I'll talk to her in a minute, although I don't know what I'm going to say. Maybe she'll sue us." Hattie sank onto the sofa. "I can't do this. I don't have what it takes. I should hand it over to someone who is better than me at making decisions."

Erica decided Noah needed reinforcements.

"You're making good decisions. They feel difficult, but that doesn't mean they're not right." She used the same calm tone she used when advising clients facing a crisis. "You clearly have a vision for the inn, and it's an appealing one. This is the perfect opportunity to make that vision a reality. To shape the business the way you'd like it to look. You've made a good start. You're doing well."

Her intervention seemed to snap Hattie out of her trance. She looked at Erica as if she'd finally remembered she was there.

"But you're checking out tomorrow," she said. "So I can't be doing that well, can I?"

Erica felt a mixture of guilt and admiration. It was encouraging to see Hattie at least had some fight left in her.

"That's nothing to do with the hospitality," Claudia said. "That's just Erica."

Erica ignored that. "For now, the focus needs to be on what needs to be done to get through tonight. After that we can formulate a longer-term plan."

"We?" Noah gave Erica a cool look, which made her suspect Hattie had told him everything in the short time they'd had together before the situation with Stephanie had erupted. He was suspicious of her, and given what had transpired, he probably had reason.

Erica thought about what she'd overheard at the bookstore. The women had talked about Noah. How protective he was. And now she saw it for herself. Not just in his words, but also in the way he stood close to Hattie, as if providing a physical barrier between her and the rest of the world.

No doubt Anna was already busy spinning romantic scenarios.

That wasn't what interested Erica. "I can help. If you'd like me to."

But Noah's attention had returned to Hattie. "I know it seems daunting at the moment, but things will change for the better now. And she—Erica—is right." He said the words reluctantly. "You figure out what needs doing, and do it. You solve the problems one at a time. You're good at this, Hattie."

"Good?" She gave a disbelieving laugh. "Did you not hear a word Stephanie said?"

"Stephanie is wrong. You need to do things the way you feel they should be done and trust your instincts. I predict the place will be even more successful."

Hattie looked unconvinced. "I hope we survive long enough to find out. I can't run an inn without staff."

Someone needed to get on and do something, Erica thought, or it definitely wouldn't be successful. Every minute they spent chewing over what had happened was a minute wasted.

It was a process, she understood that, but the process needed to be accelerated.

"You're looking at what you've lost," she said. "What you need to do is consider the resources still available to you, and how you might use them most effectively."

"That's me! I'm a resource, and I'm not leaving." Chloe spoke up from the doorway. "I can handle the housekeeping. I'll work as many hours as needed. There's nothing Stephanie can do that I can't do. Except possibly the moody attitude part. I'm not great at that. I'll get so much more done without her pulling me aside to tell me where I'm going wrong all the time."

Erica liked Chloe. She was young, but Erica knew there were times when enthusiasm could trump experience, and this was one of those times. In her opinion Hattie should be making good use of Chloe.

Hattie seemed to agree. "Thank you, Chloe. But even if between us we could manage, there's still the restaurant. I can't run a restaurant without a head chef. And Chef Tucker is—was—a legend. People traveled from out of state to sample his tasting menu."

"I never understood that," Chloe said. "He cooked parts of the animal that should never have seen the light of day in my opinion. He would have had to pay me to eat that disgusting scrambled brain thing—" She shuddered and Hattie finally smiled.

"I knew there was a reason you're not serving in the restaurant. *Tonight on the menu we have a disgusting brain thing. Enjoy.*"

"Legend or not, no one is indispensable." Erica gently steered them back on topic. "There are other excellent chefs." She looked at Claudia, who rolled her eyes and grinned.

"The answer is yes. I'll do it if Hattie would like me to. I'm a chef," she added. "I can help you out."

Hattie glanced between her and Erica. "But you're leaving."

"Not tonight, and you need a chef for tonight. Those brains aren't going to scramble themselves."

Hattie looked a little dazed. "You're really a chef?"

"Yes. A good one." Claudia anchored a strand of hair behind her ear. "Don't be fooled by my skinny frame. It's not a reflection of my cooking ability. I've had a bad year."

Hattie gave a faint smile. "I know the feeling. Where do you work?"

"I've been in California for a few years, but I was laid off from my job a few weeks ago. Don't worry, I didn't poison anyone or throw a knife at them. Shouting isn't my style, although I've been on the receiving end of it. I'm a good chef. French trained. My grandmother was French and I can speak it fluently if needed. If we had more time I'd cook you some-thing to prove it, but given that you don't have a chef for this evening I suggest I prove myself on the job."

"She is a brilliant chef," Anna said warmly. "The best."

Hattie let out a long breath. She looked exhausted. "We only have a couple of hours until the restaurant opens."

"Then I probably shouldn't waste time chatting," Claudia said. "All I need is a set of whites and access to the kitchen. I assume the rest of the kitchen crew are already there?"

"Unless they all walked out with Chef Tucker." Hattie rubbed her fingers over her forehead, trying to focus. "Our pastry chef, Shelley, is fantastic. She bakes the bread, does all the breakfast pastries, the cakes for afternoon tea and desserts, obviously. Maybe we can just serve dessert."

Claudia flashed a smile. "I'm sure we can do better than that. Where's the kitchen? Left or right?"

"Are you sure about this?" Hattie glanced at the three women. "You're supposed to be guests. You probably planned to curl up with the book you're reading and discuss it."

"That can wait," Anna said. "And we are guests, just the help-ful type."

"In that case, thank you. I'd be crazy to refuse." Hattie seemed to pull herself together. "I'll take you to the kitchen and talk to the staff. Hopefully, they haven't all followed Chef Tucker. And I need to check on Helen." Hattie looked at Delphi, who scrambled onto the deep, soft sofa with a book in her hands.

"I want you to read to me."

"Could I read to you? I'd love that," Anna said. "Reading aloud is my favorite thing and I don't often have the chance because my children are older than you."

Delphi shrank back against the sofa. "I want Mommy."

"I'm a good reader," Anna said. "I do voices and actions. I'm known for my tiger impressions."

"I like dinosaurs."

"I do a great dinosaur," Anna assured her. "Can I read to

you for a little while and see how you like it? You can choose the book. Any book."

Delphi considered and then nodded and held out her book. Anna sat down next to her and Hattie gave a grateful smile.

"Thank you. I'll be back in a minute."

"While you're doing that, I'll get that final room ready," Chloe said. "And then I'll draw up a plan for tomorrow. I'll check the bookings, look at everyone's preferences and make sure every room is perfect. If I have a problem, I'll let you know. Don't worry."

"How can I not worry? You can't do the work of two people," Hattie said and Chloe flexed her biceps.

"Watch me. At least half of Stephanie's work was managing me, so I figure that if I manage myself that's a big chunk of the job done."

Erica laughed and even Hattie looked more hopeful.

FOURTEEN

Claudia

Claudia's happiest memories involved food. Sometimes when she was lying awake at night stressed, she'd let her mind fill with the scents and sounds of the kitchen. She'd remember standing on a chair helping her grandmother sift flour. She'd think about punching her fist into dough. The scent of bread, freshly baked. The sweetness of peaches, the trickle of juice on her chin. The pungent aroma of a perfect espresso. To Claudia, food was a form of expression.

But right now she was all business.

She'd heard of Chef Tucker. Knew someone who knew someone who had worked with him. Rumor had it that his food was good but his personality was as appealing as burnt toast.

That had to give her an advantage, surely? Not that she didn't have her own flaws, but she definitely wasn't burnt toast.

She walked into the kitchen and took it all in at a glance.

The staff was frozen, panicked, talking to each other in low voices. As far as she could see, nothing was getting done.

Hattie cleared her throat. "As you probably all know by

now, Chef Tucker has gone. So has Stephanie. Neither will be returning."

Glances were exchanged. Judging from their expressions, this was the first they'd heard about Stephanie's abrupt departure.

One of them spoke up. "But Chef is the most important thing about this place."

"No. The most important person in the Maple Sugar Inn is the guest." Hattie walked farther into the room. "When someone makes a reservation here, they do it because we've made them a promise. We've promised to serve them delicious food, in comfortable and welcoming surroundings. That's what they expect when they book, and that's what they're going to get. Every person who works here is important, but no one person is more important than the other. We're a team. Chef Tucker may have gone, but you're still here and I know you'll all do a brilliant job. And now I want to introduce you to Claudia. She's a top chef from California, and it's our good fortune that she'll be working with us tonight."

Top chef.

In other circumstances, modesty might have persuaded Claudia to argue with that description, but she decided modesty didn't have a place in this kitchen.

One of the junior staff frowned. "Like a guest chef?"

"Yes. A guest chef. We're lucky to have her."

Claudia gave them a friendly nod. "We'll do introductions later. The priority is to serve an excellent meal to the guests who are dining with us tonight. I'm going to change, and when I'm back we'll discuss our strategy."

She followed Hattie out of the kitchen and found her leaning against the wall with her eyes closed.

Claudia wasn't sure how to handle the moment. Shake her? Hug her? "Are you okay?"

"Fine." Hattie kept her eyes shut. "I'm fine."

"Right." Maybe she should call Anna. Anna always knew the right thing to say. "It was a great speech you made back there."

Hattie opened her eyes. "Really?"

"Yes, really. If I wasn't stuck in the kitchen, I'd be booking a table to eat." Claudia patted her on the arm. "Get me these whites and then go and do whatever you do to relax. Eat cake. Take a bath. Whatever works. This is going to be great."

Hattie swallowed. "Are you sure?"

"Yes." Claudia smiled. "I'm a top chef, didn't you know?"

"In that case I need to talk to Helen." Hattie hurried off and Claudia was back in the kitchen minutes later.

"First things first. Where are we on the menu?"

Someone handed her a menu and she saw instantly that Chef Tucker had made everything as elaborate as possible, presumably to make himself indispensable. Or maybe to feed his ego. She'd met his type. She'd worked with his type. All fuss and foam.

And however talented he was, she knew the menu wasn't going to work tonight.

"Eight courses?"

"Yes. Chef only offers the full taster menu. But there are a few problems." The sous-chef, Helen, was back from a conversation with Hattie, apparently none the worse for wear, and determined to carry on. "There is no parmesan—they didn't deliver the quantity we ordered, so Chef sent it all back."

"All of it?"

"All of it."

Great. "So no parmesan." Claudia decided it was best to have all the bad news up front. "What else?"

"He did the same with the mushrooms. It's a key ingredient for the taster menu."

"Tonight we won't be offering a taster menu." She needed to pare down the menu, and she needed to improvise. And she needed to do it fast. She couldn't make any dramatic changes, but she could simplify what they had. She scanned the menu. "We'll offer a choice of three appetizers—two soups, one of them vegetarian, and the pâté with the chargrilled brioche and plum-and-sweet-apple chutney. We need the emphasis to be on fresh and in season." She was thinking aloud. "The spiced venison already on the menu? We'll keep that. The buttermilk chicken, too."

Helen was making notes. "We serve that with parmesan crisped potatoes. There's no parmesan."

"Tonight we're serving mash. Swap out the parmesan for local aged cheddar. It will be delicious. It's snowing outside. People have been out enjoying the winter air. They need warming comfort food and that's what we're going to give them. Where are we with dessert?" She flashed a smile at the pastry chef. "Shelley, isn't it?"

"Yes. Before we move to dessert, I have a fig-and-goat-cheese tart—you could offer that as an appetizer or an entrée."

"Good. Let's add that to the menu."

"For dessert I have raspberry torte, maple-and-walnut ice cream made from our own maple syrup," Shelley said efficiently and enthusiastically, "a chocolate mousse, and a warm apple compote served with cinnamon crumble and whipped cream from our local dairy."

Claudia allocated tasks to the other members of the kitchen staff, checked everyone was happy and knew what they were doing, and then turned to find Erica standing in the doorway watching her.

"What's wrong?"

"Nothing." Erica leaned casually against the door frame. "I'm just watching someone who hates cooking fall in love with cooking again. It's entertaining and more than a little heartwarming. I'm trying hard not to say I told you so."

"I haven't cooked anything yet, and I'm not in love." But it was true she felt a buzz that she hadn't felt in a long time. It was probably adrenaline. Who didn't get a kick out of helping someone who needed help? If Chef Tucker had happened to walk in at that moment she would have told him what he could do with his brains. "Currently, I'm solving a problem. That's it."

"Tell yourself that, by all means."

"If you're going to be smug, could you do it somewhere else and not in my kitchen? If you've time on your hands, you can type up a new menu."

Erica straightened. "I can do that. Do you have it?"

"I will in five seconds." Claudia took the tasting menu she'd been given and drew a line through most of the dishes. She scribbled, amended and altered the layout. "We need to change the font. Make it easy to read and friendly. All that curly type is intimidating. Food should never be scary. Where's Hattie? Last time I saw her, she looked as if she was in shock."

"She's fine. Currently exchanging small talk with a couple from Ohio who are celebrating forty years together. Paying attention to their every need. She's good at it. I would have thrust a guide book and a local map into their hands and told them to get on with it."

Claudia handed the menu to her friend. "Which is why you don't work in hospitality."

"That could be it. But Hattie has a gift. See her with the guests and you'd never know she was weathering a crisis." Erica scanned the menu. "No brains? Shame. Chloe will be heartbroken. Leave this with me. I'll deal with it."

Claudia realized that since Stephanie's dramatic exit she hadn't given a thought to Erica's situation. "How are you doing?"

"Me? I'm still here, if that's what you mean. And you know me—handling a crisis is my comfort zone. I'd rather do that than talk about feelings." Erica waved a hand toward the kitchen. "Go and create. We'll talk later."

Erica vanished, and Claudia worried about her for a moment and then turned her attention back to the task at hand.

The team of four worked quietly, heads down. When she spoke to one of them their heads jerked up and there was a wariness in their eyes.

Expecting to be shouted at for something, Claudia thought. She'd been there, although whenever she'd been nervous or upset she'd never let the executive chef see it.

"Chef?"

It took a moment for her to realize that they were talking to her.

"Yes?"

"Do you honestly think we can do this without Chef Tucker?"

"I know we can."

"If we pull this off tonight, it will be a miracle."

Claudia reached for a skillet. "Then it's a good thing it's Christmas. It's the perfect time for miracles. Now, let's get back to work. Those carrots aren't going to peel themselves."

FIFTEEN

Anna

One of Anna's favorite memories was of reading to the twins when they were very young. Sometimes she'd managed to engage both of them at the same time, and the three of them had snuggled in the bed, taking turns to flip the pages of the book. More often she'd taken one of them and Pete the other. Occasionally over the years, she thought back wistfully to that time and she thought of it now as she was snuggled on the sofa with Delphi, cocooned by tall shelves of books and warmed by the fire.

There was a tendency to only remember the good when you looked back, but of course there had been difficult days, too. There was a relentlessness to parenting young children that sapped energy from the most robust of people. There had been one memorable winter when the twins had been ill constantly, passing germs between them until Anna had wondered if they'd ever be well again.

Still, there had been a simplicity to those days that she missed. There had been no worries about the influences of friends, no staying up late until she knew the twins were home safe, no terror at the thought of one of her babies behind the wheel of a car.

For eighteen years they'd been under her roof and under her care. They'd been her focus, *her life*.

Next to her, Delphi had fallen asleep on the cushions and Anna closed the book they'd been reading together, wishing she could stop feeling this way. She had much to be grateful for, and the fact that her children were healthy and able to leave home and lead independent lives was one of them. She knew, deep down, that this wasn't about them. Yes, she'd worry about them because that was part of being a parent, but it wasn't worry about the twins that kept her awake at night. It was worry about herself.

She wanted to look into the future and be excited and motivated. She didn't want to feel this slow, seeping sadness. She didn't want to be counting down the days until they left home.

We could have another child.

Did she want that? There was something about that conversation she'd had with Pete in the kitchen that hadn't felt quite right. She knew he didn't really understand how she was feeling, and maybe it was unrealistic of her to expect him to. Still, it would have been good to talk properly about it.

She'd tried to call him earlier and he hadn't answered, which was unlike him. Normally, whenever one of them was away, they enjoyed long phone calls.

She picked up her phone and sent him a quick message.

Everything okay with the kids?

The door to the library opened and Anna glanced up as Hattie came into the room.

Anna pushed her own problems aside. "How's it going?"

"So far, so good, I think. I just wanted to check on you and Delphi. The couple from Ohio has dietary issues. Gluten free. I need to warn Claudia."

Hattie looked like a person who had too much going on in her life. In her head.

"Claudia will already have thought of that. And you don't need to worry about Delphi." She glanced at the sleeping child. "We read two books, made up a story with Huge the dinosaur as the main character, then she told me everything she wanted for Christmas, and after that she crashed out. Should I have woken her? I know it's a little late in the afternoon to let her sleep, but she seemed to need it."

"She's recovering from a cough and it has kept her awake," Hattie said. "Let her sleep."

Anna studied the shadows under her eyes. "I'm guessing that cough has kept you awake, too. I remember those days. And you're on your own with it. That can't be easy."

"I'm fine."

Anna reached for the soft throw draped over the back of the sofa and tucked it around Delphi. "I remember saying those words while screaming inside."

Hattie gave a half smile. "I could do without all this extra pressure, that's for sure."

"Sit down for a moment." Anna patted the sofa next to her but Hattie shook her head.

"Tempting, but if I sit down I might never get up again and there is so much to do. I need to check Erica is okay."

"Is there a reason why she wouldn't be?"

Hattie glanced over her shoulder as a guest walked past. "Are you going to catch the bookstore before it closes, Mike? Be careful. It's icy out there. Call us if you need anything." She turned back to Anna. "Erica is using the computer in my office to type up a menu, and then she's going to do a job description so that we can advertise for a new chef."

"She won't need help with either of those tasks." Anna almost smiled at the idea of Erica needing assistance.

"She's been great," Hattie said. "You all have."

Anna debated whether she should say something about Hattie and Erica's situation, and decided that a little bit of gentle interference was justified in this case.

"I know Erica didn't handle the situation well earlier. I'm sure that upset you."

"It doesn't matter. I understand."

"I doubt that you do." Anna checked Delphi was still asleep. "I'm not generally considered a gossip, but there are a few things it might be helpful for you to know about Erica. The first is that she isn't easy to know—which is why I'm giving you a crash course. The second is that once you do know her you'll discover that she's the kindest, most generous person you will ever meet. Not always tactile." Anna saw the doubt in Hattie's face and plowed on. "If you want a hug and a 'there, there, poor you' from someone, don't pick Erica, but if you want someone who cares deeply for the people she loves and will offer any practical help within her power, then she's your woman."

Hattie hesitated and then joined Anna on the sofa.

"You three have been friends for a long time? You met at a book club?"

Anna smiled. "No, we met at college. Our book club happened by accident. It was our way of escaping from the heaviness of what we were reading. We were all stressed out from studying and exams and I became addicted to romance novels as a way of relaxing."

Hattie brightened. "I did the same at college. Romance novels were my happy place."

"Erica loved thrillers and crime, and Claudia biographies and cookery books—we each thought the other's reading choices were pretty awful. Erica teased me about romance and I teased her about reading crime but then we realized we'd never actually read each other's books. So that's what we did. One evening after a bottle of wine, we swapped. We each picked one from our favorites and the others read it. Then we talked about it." She leaned back against the sofa, remembering. "Those discussions were such fun. We'd pick apart everything. Why the romance heroine behaved in the way she did, why crime fiction won awards when romance fiction was ignored and denigrated. Why violence was celebrated and stories about relationships—probably the single most important thing in our lives—dismissed as froth."

"I hope you're not asking me that question," Hattie said, "because my only answer is snobbery."

"That's the conclusion we reached." Anna sat up. "Anyway, it started from there. When we graduated, we used our book club as an excuse to meet up. Once a year we book a hotel for a week. Occasionally near a beach, but often in a city because Erica loves that. It's a week to chill out, relax, do some sightseeing, catch up and talk about books."

"Always a hotel?"

"Yes. The idea was that it was a week where none of us had to do anything except relax together. No one had to cook. We could order room service. There was nothing to do but enjoy ourselves. And the weird thing is we can go months without seeing each other, and when we finally get together it feels as if we only saw each other yesterday. That's friendship, I suppose. It's the reason I look forward to it every year." And she needed it. Her friends were better than therapy. Definitely cheaper.

"But this year your summer gathering didn't happen?"

"Claudia had some personal issues back in the summer—we all agreed to push it back to Christmas. We thought it would be cozy and festive. And it is." Anna glanced from the fire to the tree. "I felt conflicted coming away at this time of year. It's a special family time. Families should be together at Christmas, shouldn't they?" Only after she'd said the words did she realize how tactless they were, but fortunately, Hattie didn't seem upset.

"It's a magical time of year. How many children do you have?"

"Two. Twins. Boy and a girl."

"That's nice." Hattie was watching Delphi. "Family is the best thing."

"Yes." And to Hattie, Delphi was family. Not Erica. Anna felt a stab of sadness, but knew it wasn't her place to interfere.

"What you've done to this place is fantastic and I couldn't feel more Christmassy if Santa dropped in for a visit. I have that same feeling that I used to have when visiting Santa."

"Good." Hattie stretched out her hands toward the fire. "But that isn't why you chose to come here, is it?"

"No." Anna tried to shift her position without waking Delphi. "It was Erica's choice."

"And she chose it because of me."

"So it would seem. Although I didn't know that at the time."

Hattie was frowning. "Why now? Why wait twenty-eight years to get in touch?"

"Twenty-eight years?" Shock made Anna respond without thinking. "She only found out about you recently—" She stopped talking, feeling suddenly disloyal.

Hattie stared at her. "She didn't know about me? Is that true?"

"Why wouldn't it be?"

"Because I've known about Erica—although I didn't know that was her name—all my life. My father was always honest about his past."

Now it was Anna's turn to stare. How honest? It was hardly a pretty story. Had he painted himself as some sort of wounded hero?

She wished she'd never started this conversation. What if she revealed something Erica would rather have kept private?

It was strange, Anna thought, to think that Hattie and Erica were related. Strange to think about all the years that they'd lived parallel lives, never intersecting. But they'd intersected now, and that was going to have consequences.

She tried to be tactful. "I think a conversation is needed, but between you and Erica."

"We're planning to talk later, although I have no idea what the outcome will be. If she didn't know about me until recently, then I'm starting to understand why it would have been an adjustment. This was helpful, thank you." Hattie stood up.

"I hope you still have a chance to discuss books, whether it is here or somewhere else. I envy you that."

Anna hoped it was going to be here. She couldn't think of anywhere more perfect to spend a week. If Erica wanted to leave, then of course she'd leave, but that didn't stop her hoping they'd be staying.

"You obviously love books." She glanced at the bookshelves, which were crammed with everything from leather-bound classics and travel guides to paperback novels. There was something for everyone, including a book she'd already bought Pete for Christmas. "You don't belong to a book club? This would be the perfect place to hold it. Or maybe in the bookstore."

"The town has a book club, but the bookstore doesn't have a room big enough to accommodate everyone. I've invited them to use this room for their meeting on Wednesday. Hopefully, that will work out and we can make it a regular thing."

"You're not part of that group?"

"No. Mostly because I don't have time to read the book before the meetings, which makes me feel as if I'm failing at yet another thing. It's more pressure."

"And you already have plenty of that."

"It's been a difficult few years. I should check Erica and Claudia have what they need—" Hattie paused in the doorway. "If Delphi wakes up—"

"Then we'll come and find you."

"I'm sure you have a million things you'd rather do than babysit my daughter."

"I really don't," Anna said. "Snuggled up here in your cozy library with a Christmas tree, a log fire, all these books and Delphi—that's as close to bliss as it comes for me."

"In that case, I'll go and finish my jobs and then come back for her." Hattie paused. "You and Erica should eat dinner in the restaurant this evening. You must be hungry after your journey."

"Would you join us?" Anna hoped Erica wouldn't kill her

for issuing the invitation. "No pressure, obviously. I don't want it to feel awkward."

"Thanks, but I have to put Delphi to bed and settle her down. Fortunately, our private rooms are just off the main hallway so I'm always available if needed, but it's the part of the day I try and keep just for her."

Anna remembered doing the same. She remembered days when she'd been so frazzled that she couldn't wait for them to fall asleep, and days when the twins had been so adorable and endearing, and warm and cuddly from their bath, that she lay down in the bedroom with them and just watched them, the love she felt for them almost too big for her body. "Sometimes that's great, and sometimes it's exhausting, and the best part of the evening is the glass of wine you treat yourself to afterward."

Hattie laughed. "Something like that. Oh, by the way, you said that Delphi had told you what she wanted for Christmas. Can you help me out with that?"

Anna thought about what the little girl had said. "That's tricky, because she made me promise to keep it a secret. But trust me, it's not something you can buy in a store so don't worry."

"I am worried! If she writes to Santa and asks for it, it's not going to arrive, is it?"

Anna thought about what she'd seen earlier. "You never know. It might."

"It wasn't to do with her dad, was it?"

"No," Anna said softly. "It wasn't."

"She was so young when he died, she has no real memory of him. I don't know if that's good or bad." Hattie gave a forced smile. "Anyway, thanks. It was good talking to you, Anna."

"Good talking to you, too."

Change, Anna thought, had a lot to answer for. But in the end everyone had to find a way to deal with it.

And that included her.

SIXTEEN

Hattie

Hattie hurried back toward the reception area, cursing herself for not pushing Brent harder to listen to her opinion when he'd employed Stephanie and Chef Tucker. It wasn't that he was intentionally forceful, more that he'd overridden her with the sheer weight of his enthusiasm. The strength of his convictions had made her doubt her own. And after he'd died, she'd been so grief ridden, so absolutely determined to keep things the way he'd wanted them, that she'd ignored her own instincts and continued to pursue his plan.

She'd built a shrine of his ideas, kept things the same, frozen time, because that had seemed like a way of keeping a part of him alive. Brent had hired Stephanie, therefore Stephanie's presence was a connection to Brent. But she saw now that living like that had stopped her moving on.

When you lost someone you loved, you only ever remembered the good parts. Or that was what had happened to Hattie. She remembered Brent's smile, his enthusiasm, the way he said yes to everything even when he didn't have time for anything else in his life. The way he swept you away with the conviction that this was going to be the best thing that had ever happened to you.

But there had been bad things, too. She felt guilty even thinking that, but it was true and it was time she was honest with herself. That confidence and conviction of his had also made him stubborn. When she'd suggested that a country inn like theirs perhaps didn't need a celebrity chef with enough stars to form their own galaxy, and that maybe an excellent chef keen to build his reputation might be a better idea, he'd dismissed it. He talked constantly about reviews and once they'd opened, he'd checked the reviews feverishly. He was determined that people would cross continents to eat in their restaurant, and stuck with that view even when she'd pointed out that if that happened then they wouldn't have room in the restaurant to feed the guests so how would that work?

He'd appointed Stephanie as their head housekeeper because she'd worked in a five-star establishment in Boston favored by corporate types and sports stars. He'd been impressed by her credentials, and when Hattie had pointed out that maybe giving ordinary people a really special, memorable break required a different set of skills, he'd again overruled her.

But now here they were, with no award-winning chef and no head housekeeper.

She had two choices. She could curl up and give up, which wasn't an option because someone had to take care of the guests, or she could throw out Brent's rulebook—his dream—and run things the way she felt they should be run.

And she knew which choice she was going to make.

All the ideas and impulses that had been held tightly inside her bubbled to the surface.

The incident with Stephanie had somehow shaken her out of her inertia. For the first time since Brent had died she'd taken a step that had been of her choosing. She'd shown a strength she didn't know she was capable of showing. And it was a step forward. If she could take that one step, then she could take others. She needed to keep moving.

"Hattie?" A young couple who had checked in the day before arrived back from a trip to town loaded down with bags stuffed with gifts. Snow dusted their coats and they looked as if they'd just stepped straight off the set of a Christmas movie. Most importantly, they looked happy and that, to Hattie, was the most meaningful review she could have had for the inn.

She stopped to talk to them. No matter what revelations were popping in her head, her guests always came first. "You seem to have had success with your Christmas shopping."

"It was fabulous. I bought gifts for everyone, including Ray's mother, and believe me, that's the biggest challenge of all because she is not an easy woman to please." The woman gestured to one of the bags, which obviously contained the precious item. "Thank you for the suggestion."

"You're welcome."

"We have a table booked for seven fifteen," the woman said, "but we wondered if we could push it back to eight? We wanted to wrap the gifts and make some calls and just enjoy being in the room. It's hard to force ourselves outdoors, to be honest, because we love it here so much. It's not often you book a festive break and don't want to leave the room, but that's how we feel. Would that annoy Chef? He seemed very put out last night when we were five minutes late."

Hattie wondered at what point the emotional state of her chef had started to take precedence over the wishes of her guests.

The man gave a nervous smile. "We wouldn't want him to have a tantrum and walk out."

A bit late for that, Hattie thought.

"That will be no problem at all," she said. "I'll let the kitchen know."

Providing there was anyone left in the kitchen. It was entirely possible that in the past hour they'd all followed Chef Tucker and left Hattie to stew in her own misery—or boil, or flambé, depending on whether you preferred your crisis to be well-done or medium rare—although hopefully Claudia would have persuaded them against that course of action.

She wished Claudia was staying.

"If there is anything I, or my team—" *what's left of it* "—can do to make your stay more comfortable, please don't hesitate to let us know."

The couple headed toward the stairs, and Hattie watched them for a moment and then walked to her office.

Erica was pulling some pages from the printer and looked up as Hattie walked into the room.

"I've retyped the menu—changed the layout as Claudia requested. Take a look and let me know what you think." She handed them over and Hattie took the menu, trying not to be distracted by the fact that this was Erica and the whole situation was beyond weird. She had no idea how she was supposed to react, but that was true of so much of life, or so she was discovering.

She scanned it. "You've called it the Winter Warmer menu?"

"It's no longer a taster menu, so I thought we should present it as something different. Confidently. Not as something we've thrown together in last-minute desperation. It's snowing outside. People enjoy comfort food when it's cold, and also at Christmas. I thought tomorrow's menu could be Festive Feast. And maybe later in the week we could have Santa's Supper."

Hattie was so focused on simply surviving the evening, she hadn't given a thought to the rest of the week. But Erica had thought about it. Winter Warmer. Festive Feast.

"I wanted to do something similar in the beginning—fun themed evenings. I thought we could do a Swiss night, with fondue and other traditional Swiss dishes. I even thought about offering posh afternoon tea, the way they do in the big hotels in London. Finger sandwiches and amazing cakes, maybe a glass of champagne—" She stopped and shook her head. "Sorry.

Getting carried away and I need to stay focused. Thanks for the menu."

"Wait—" Erica tapped her finger against her lips. "So what happened to your idea for Swiss night and afternoon tea? It wasn't a success?"

"We didn't try it. Brent didn't think it would work. He wanted to offer a gourmet tasting menu with wine pairings. And that was popular. His idea was a good one."

"But that doesn't mean your idea was bad," Erica murmured. "There is more than one good idea in the world. I've heard a lot about what Brent thought, but what about you? What does Hattie think?"

No one ever asked her what she thought. Everyone had just assumed she'd keep things going the way Brent had. Except Noah, of course. He'd always shown confidence in her and encouraged her to forge her own path.

Noah.

She wasn't sure what she would have done without his support earlier. Just having him there had made things easier.

And she badly wanted to show the courage he seemed to think she possessed.

"I think I like what you've done with this menu. I think that once things have settled down, I'd like to explore being more creative with our dining options."

"Good. If you want to toss around a few ideas, I'm a good listener."

Hattie felt a flicker of excitement. It was slowly dawning on her that she could do whatever she liked. Make whatever decision she wanted to make. No one was going to stop her or tell her they had a better idea. It was both freeing and scary. The responsibility for success or failure was all hers.

She looked from the menu to Erica. "You were on your way out the door. Why are you helping me?"

"You look like someone who could use some help, so let's start with that as a reason and tackle the rest later." Erica tidied up the paper stacked by the printer. "We need to get this menu to Claudia for approval and then print them. After that, you can tell me what else needs to be done and we can throw around some ideas if that's helpful. Do you want me to take her the menu?"

Hattie had no idea what Erica did for a living, but she was willing to bet she was good at it.

"Thank you, but I'll do it. I should probably check on things."

She headed to the kitchen. No matter how good Claudia was, the staff had been unsettled to have lost Chef Tucker and were probably upset by all the conflict and concerned for the future.

Braced to give another motivational speech, she pushed open the doors of the kitchen and stepped inside.

She felt the energy instantly. Everyone was busy, food was being prepared, the smells so delicious that for a moment she wished she were a guest and not the owner. And in the middle of it all was Claudia, who appeared to be everywhere at once, encouraging, demonstrating, praising and smiling.

Hattie felt a sudden burst of optimism. The ball of tension in her stomach eased.

Claudia noticed her and strode across the kitchen. "Are those our menus?"

Hattie liked her use of the word *our*. With Chef Tucker and Stephanie every conversation had been dominated by *I*. *I need this. I want this.*

"Yes. Erica has done a great job."

"No surprise there." Claudia took the menu and scanned it, checking for mistakes. "All looks good. Winter Warmer. I love it. Are you fine with all the menu changes?"

Hattie realized she'd barely looked at the content. "You're the one in charge of that. If you think it works, then it will work."

Claudia gave her a curious look. "Right. Good. It's going to work, trust me." She handed the menu back. "Erica can print these up for the tables and I'll get back to work."

"I don't know how to thank you." Hattie touched her arm. "You've saved the day."

Just this one day, but it was a start.

"You're the one who saved the day." Claudia patted Hattie's hand. "You got rid of Stephanie, and you trusted a stranger in your kitchen. Big decisions, but good ones. You need to have more faith in yourself. You've got this."

Was that true?

For the first time since Brent had died Hattie felt that maybe, just maybe, she did have this. She just needed to believe in herself and stop listening to the negative voice in her head.

SEVENTEEN

Erica

Erica stood outside the door to Hattie's private rooms.

She rarely felt awkward in situations, but she wondered now if that was because she avoided situations that made her feel awkward. She stayed in her comfort zone. But didn't everyone, up to a point?

Having printed the menus, placed them on tables in the restaurant and checked on Anna, she'd contemplated returning to her room. But somehow, here she was, outside Hattie's door.

Maybe this was a bad time. Anna had always hated being called in the middle of bath time when the twins were little. Erica glanced at her watch. Was this bath time? She had no idea. She wasn't only outside her comfort zone, she was also outside her zone of expertise.

She knocked and waited.

There was no response, or sounds of movement, and she was about to walk away—at least no one would be able to say she hadn't tried—when the door opened.

Hattie stood there. Her hair was loose over her shoulders and in her hand was a children's book. She looked soft and maternal and more assured than earlier in the day facing Stephanie.

"I'm disturbing you." Erica backed away, but Hattie shook her head and opened the door wider.

"No, you're not. I finished the story half an hour ago, but it took a while for her to go to sleep. Too much excitement today. Come on in."

Left with no choice, Erica stepped over the threshold.

"This is where the innkeeper lives." Hattie led her into the living room. "We have two bedrooms, this room and a small kitchen. We're a little cramped for space, but it's cozy."

It was cozy. The sofa was stacked with cushions, and a soft mohair throw was folded over one of the arms. The coffee table was reclaimed wood, and a vase of eucalyptus sat in the center. Everywhere she looked there were signs of Delphi. Coloring books, a child's picture of a house in the country complete with snowman. A pair of tiny shoes peeped from under the sofa, and on the table were the remains of a glass of milk and half a cookie. On almost every surface there were photographs of Brent. On his own, looking windblown and handsome on a ski slope. Swinging Delphi above his head. Smiling with his arms wrapped around both Delphi and Hattie. Action man. Family man. The many facets of Brent.

Erica stared at those photos. Growing up, her father hadn't had a presence. Her mother never talked about him. There were no physical reminders. It was as if he'd been deleted from their lives.

That wasn't the case here. Brent still had a place in Hattie and Delphi's life.

She pushed down emotion that she didn't entirely understand. "It's a beautiful room."

"Thank you." Hattie lifted an armful of clean laundry from one of the sofas and put it on the table. Then she gathered up two soft toys and a plastic dinosaur. "Sit down wherever you can find room. Check you're not sitting on a toy or anything squishy first."

Erica settled herself in the armchair. "You were probably looking forward to a few hours off."

"I don't know what that is." Hattie scooped up two paintings and rescued a crayon from the floor. "My priority is always to put Delphi to bed and spend that time with her, and I've done that so I'm happy."

"I thought, maybe, we could have that conversation we should have had earlier."

Hattie added the crayon to the stack on the table. "I'd like that. Can I get you anything? A drink?"

"I'm fine, but thank you." Erica kept her hands clasped in her lap. She had no idea how to start the conversation. "You probably—"

"Mommy!" Delphi appeared in the doorway. Cheerful robins danced across her pajamas and she had her dinosaur tucked under her arm. "I can't sleep."

Hattie put her glass down and went to her daughter. "That's because you're standing in our living room. To sleep you have to be in your bed. I'll take you back." She scooped up the child and Delphi buried her head in her shoulder.

"Can I stay here? I want to be near you. And I like the tree and the fire."

Erica liked the tree and the fire, too. Like the rest of the inn, Hattie had turned her own living accommodation into a sanctuary. She seemed to think she'd added little to the inn, that it was all down to Brent, but it seemed to Erica that her mark was everywhere.

Hattie was patient. "If you don't go to bed, you'll be tired."

"I don't like my bed." Delphi's arms tightened around her neck. "I want to sleep in your bed."

From the flush on Hattie's cheeks, Erica assumed that happened a lot.

Erica had never been allowed to sleep anywhere but her own

bed. If she was sick, or had a bad dream, her mother would sit with her for a while but she would never allow Erica to curl up next to her, and on the few occasions Erica had crawled into her bed in the night, hoping to remain undetected, her mother had immediately lifted her and carried her back to her own room.

"You're fine right here," she would whisper. "If you feel lonely, all you have to do is think comforting thoughts."

Out of nowhere Erica thought about Jack. About the last time they were together. He'd suggested staying, and she'd been the one to remind him that that wasn't what they did. That wasn't how their relationship worked. He hadn't argued, and she'd watched him dress, pulling on his discarded clothes and shrugging his broad shoulders into his wool coat. It was what she'd wanted—*wasn't it what they both wanted?*—but the moment the door of her apartment had closed behind him she'd felt bereft. As if she'd lost something important. Which was ridiculous, because she'd been sleeping through the night on her own since she was an infant. She didn't need anyone else in her bed to be happy. For the first time in her adult life she'd had to try to find comforting thoughts, but they'd proved elusive.

There was a tap on the door and Hattie sighed and settled Delphi on the sofa next to Erica. "Stay there while I see who that is." She hurried to the door and Erica heard low voices and then Hattie returned looking stressed.

"That was Chloe. One of the guests has a question I need to deal with." She crouched down in front of Delphi. "I need to go and help someone. Will you stay here with Aunt Erica? I'll be quick."

Erica almost looked over her shoulder to see who else was in the room, but then realized she was Aunt Erica.

It was an uncomfortable thought.

She'd always refused to be Aunt Erica to Anna's children, but she could hardly object this time, could she? Technically, she was Delphi's aunt.

Hattie shot her a look of apology. "Do you mind watching

her for a moment? I won't be long. She's so sleepy she'll probably crash out. I'll carry her to bed when I'm back." There was a soft throw over the arm of the sofa and she tucked it around Delphi. "Close your eyes."

Delphi closed her eyes, scrunching them up tightly.

"I'll be just a few minutes." Hattie grabbed her phone and left the room.

Delphi opened her eyes. "Do you like sharks?"

"I—it's not something I've ever thought about."

"I like sharks. My favorite shark is a hammerhead. Do you know how many sleeps there are until Santa comes?"

"No. I haven't counted."

"It's sixteen."

"Oh." Erica blinked. "Well, thank you."

"If you don't go to bed at all on Christmas Eve, it's fifteen. But if you're awake, Santa might not come so you have to pretend to be asleep."

Was she supposed to know all this? She found herself suffering from a major attack of imposter syndrome.

She had virtually no experience with children. Unlike Anna, she wasn't one of those people who loved children just because they were children. In her opinion children were like any other humans. They had to earn her respect and friendship. Anna's children were different, not only because they'd turned into interesting people, but also because Erica saw them as an extension of Anna and Pete, whom she already loved.

To steer the conversation onto more familiar ground she thought of the most safe, generic question possible. "Do you know what you'd like for Christmas, Delphi?"

"I'd like a sled. A small one is fine, and also one of Panther's kittens, but a pet is a big responsibility—" She stumbled over the word, clearly reciting something she'd been told. "You have to care for it and love it always, not just when you feel like it. And you have to feed it and keep it warm and if it's sick you have to take it to the vet. Also, you have to clean up poop. It's a *lot* of work."

"That's true." Erica was reminded of all the reasons she'd chosen never to have a pet.

"You can't change your mind and give it back, so you have to be sure. And we already have Rufus. My daddy chose Rufus when he was a tiny puppy and now he's one of the family and he's ours forever and ever."

The mention of her father was so natural it was obvious that she and Hattie talked about him frequently.

Erica was thinking about that, and the difference with her own mother's approach, when she realized Delphi had asked her a question. "I'm sorry, could you say that again?"

"Would you like one of Panther's kittens?"

"Me?"

"Yes. I can't have one right now. You could have one, but you'd have to be sure because if you're not sure you can't have a pet."

Erica's head was spinning. "Right." She definitely wasn't sufficiently briefed for this conversation. She would rather have sat in front of an auditorium of CEOs. "I definitely can't have one of Panther's kittens, but thank you for thinking of me."

"There's something else I want for Christmas but it can't be bought and it can't be wrapped." Delphi lowered her voice to a conspiratorial whisper. "I would like Noah to live here. With us. But I'm not sure Santa can fix that. Do you know?"

"Do I know what?"

"If Santa can fix for Noah to live with us?"

Erica knew nothing about Santa, and she knew nothing about Noah, but she did know when she was in over her head. "Santa's job description is not one of my areas of expertise." She could imagine Anna frowning at her for that response and made a valiant attempt to do better. "You seem to like Noah a lot."

"Yes. He's funny and kind. Rufus likes him. And Mommy is always happy when he is here, although sometimes she drops things."

"She drops things?"

"Yes. Yesterday she dropped a glass when he walked into the room. Last week she dropped Rufus's food. But it didn't matter because he ate it anyway." Delphi studied her with frank interest. "What do you ask him for?"

"Who?"

"Santa. When you wrote your letter. What did you ask him for? If it's a secret, you don't have to tell me."

Erica shifted in her chair. "I haven't written to Santa."

"Why not?"

"Well, because—" What was she supposed to say? If she was sticking to the truth then she'd say that there had never been a time when she'd believed in Santa. Her mother hadn't believed in sugarcoating life. Santa had been a fantasy figure, along with the tooth fairy and the Easter bunny. Also, in her mother's case, men who knew about responsibility. But it wasn't her place to ruin Delphi's fantasy. "I'm sure he is busy. And I can't think of anything I need."

"Do you have a dog?"

"No, I don't have a dog. I don't have pets."

Delphi wrinkled her nose. "If you promise Santa that you'd care for it really well forever, you could ask for a dog."

If she hadn't known better Erica would have thought the child was in league with Anna.

"I'm away from home a lot so it wouldn't be fair to have an animal. I'm sure Santa would agree."

Delphi snuggled deeper into the sofa, deep in thought. "Are you really my aunt?"

"Yes, I'm really your aunt." It was a relief to be moving away from the topic of Santa.

"I've never had an aunt." Delphi rested her chin on the dinosaur's soft head. "What does an aunt do?"

Assuming that *no idea* wasn't an acceptable answer, Erica rooted around for something that might work. "Well, I—"

"You don't know, do you?" Delphi cuddled the dinosaur.

"That's okay. Mommy always says it's okay not to know, but you always have to say so."

Erica gave the same advice on a regular basis to her senior executives. "That's wise advice."

"If you like, we can figure it out together."

"Oh—well, that sounds like a good idea to me." Erica looked at the tangled golden curls and the big eyes and felt something shift inside her. "What would you like an aunt to do?"

Delphi curled her legs under her and thought. "You could read to me?"

Erica relaxed a little. "Reading sounds like an excellent idea. Fun."

"And you could take me to Disneyland. Do you like roller coasters? My friend Jamie was sick on a roller coaster but that was because his daddy gave him ice cream right before he went on the ride."

"Delphi!" Hattie arrived back in the room at that moment. "You can't ask strangers to take you to Disneyland."

"But you said she isn't a stranger. She's Aunt Erica."

"You're doing too much chatting and not enough sleeping." Hattie scooped Delphi up along with the dinosaur. "Say goodnight to Aunt Erica."

"But—"

"There is no *but* in 'good night, Aunt Erica.'"

Delphi grinned and waved. "Night night, Aunt Erica."

"Good night, Delphi. Sleep well."

Hattie was gone for less than five minutes and when she returned she had a bottle of wine and two glasses in her hand.

"Sorry about that. Did she talk you to death?"

Erica thought about the conversation. "She certainly did have a lot to say. She's very confident. Not that I know much about what children say at various ages but she seems ahead of her age."

"She talked before she walked." Hattie put the wine and the glasses down on the table. "And she always has plenty to say— she's five going on fifteen. That's my fault. Because it has been

just the two of us, I talk to her about all sorts of things I probably shouldn't. I try not to use her for emotional support, apart
from occasionally letting her sleep in my bed and pretending I'm
doing it for her—" She gave a wry smile. "That's what Rufus
is for, isn't it, Rufus?"

Rufus lifted his nose from his paws and wagged his tail across
the rug.

"Whatever you're doing, it seems to be working. I enjoyed
Delphi's company." And no one was more surprised by that than
she was.

Her words seemed to cheer Hattie.

"You have no idea how good it is to hear that. I worry that
she has a slightly strange life, living here, but at the same time
she has lots of experiences she wouldn't have in a conventional
family unit. And the guests are always entertained by her, so
she gets more fuss and attention than she should. But she's
pretty sensible."

"Yes, I witnessed that. She gave me a long and almost disturbingly rational explanation as to why she probably shouldn't
have one of Panther's kittens for Christmas. Who is Panther,
by the way?"

"Panther is one of the farm cats," Hattie said. "She's still
going on about Panther's kittens? I thought that moment had
passed."

"Don't worry. She can't face clearing up the poop. You're
off the hook."

Hattie laughed. "Phew."

"I suspect if everyone thought it through as deeply as your
daughter there would be fewer abandoned pets."

"I'm big on emphasizing responsibility. Or maybe I'm just a
killjoy. I worry sometimes that without Brent around to balance it out, I'm making her cautious." Hattie opened the wine.
"Brent was more of an impulse person. Act now, and deal with
the consequences later. He'd get these great ideas and plow
ahead without thinking through the detail. *We'll figure it out,*

Hattie was his favorite phrase. But I prefer to figure things out before we do them. I think about the consequences first. Brent said it was like going through life with the brakes on. Wine?"

"Please. Considering consequences is part of being an adult, surely?" Erica watched as Hattie poured the wine carefully into the glasses. As someone who was instinctively guarded with people she didn't know, it surprised her that Hattie was so open with her. She felt as if she knew her already. As if she'd been given a shortcut to everything she was. The who. The why. "But maybe I'm not the best person to talk to about that. In a way, that's what I do for a living. I focus on consequences."

Hattie set the bottle down and handed her a glass. "What do you do?"

"I specialize in crisis management. I started working in public relations, and always seemed to end up at the sharp end when there was a crisis. Thanks—" She took the glass from Hattie. She felt as if she should say more about herself, but the words lodged in her throat, refusing to leave her. It wasn't natural for her to spill secrets about herself.

"I bet you're really cool in a crisis." Hattie tugged off her boots. "That explains why you were so calm when Stephanie and Chef Tucker walked out and I was in a panic."

"It's easy to be calm when it's not your problem."

"Maybe. I am bad at decision making. I'm so afraid of making a mistake that I end up not making a decision at all." Hattie picked up her own glass. "I hate that about myself. I'd like to be confident and decisive."

"Everyone has something they don't like about themselves."

"Do you?"

This was proving to be a very uncomfortable conversation.

Erica hesitated. "I find it hard to express emotions, even when I really want to express them. It's as if they are jammed inside me." She couldn't believe she'd just said that aloud. She half expected the world to collapse, and was surprised when all that happened was that Hattie nodded.

"Now I understand why you were so freaked out when I hugged you," Hattie said. "It wasn't because it was *me*, but because I was basically a stranger."

"I was outside my comfort zone, that's for sure."

"And I know how hard that is. I've been out of my comfort zone every minute of the last couple of years. Most days I feel as if I'm never going to find my comfort zone again." She pulled a face. "Do you think I'm doomed to spend the rest of my life in my discomfort zone?"

It was hard to be distant with someone so likable.

"I have a feeling you've reached a turning point."

"Let's hope so." Hattie curled up on the sofa, tucking her legs under her. "So how does your job work? Companies call you when something awful has happened?"

"Sometimes. If they're wise, they get me in before it happens. I work with senior teams to try and identify all the possible areas of vulnerability. Then we put together a plan. But not everything can be predicted. The unexpected happens."

"It certainly does." Hattie leaned back against the sofa. "Life is full of bombshells you never saw coming."

"And you've had a few of those." Erica took a sip of wine. She'd thought she didn't want to get involved, but now she discovered she wanted to know more about Hattie. "You've had a tough few years. How are you coping?"

Hattie shrugged. "I don't know. I don't ask myself that. I just deal with today's problem and then move on to the next one."

"That sounds like an excellent strategy."

"It's the only strategy, really," Hattie said. "I've learned that there's not much point in having a plan because something always derails it."

"I should imagine there are plenty of interruptions and disturbances, what with running an inn and being a single mother."

"You have no idea."

Erica put her glass down. "Actually, I do. I was raised by

a busy working single mother." She regretted the words the moment they left her mouth. "I apologize if that was tactless."

"Tactless because Dad was the one who left her as a single mother, you mean?" Hattie removed a small toy wedged behind her back. "That's not tactless, that's honest."

She'd expected Hattie to sugarcoat it. To tell a version that bore no resemblance to the real version. "You've obviously known about me a lot longer than I've known about you."

"It seems that way." Hattie leaned across and topped up Erica's glass and then her own.

"Thanks. So when did you find out?"

"About you?" Hattie put the bottle down and snuggled back on the sofa. "I've always known."

"Always?"

"Yes." She took a mouthful of wine and nodded. "This is good."

Erica was more interested in the conversation than the wine. "What do you mean, *always*?"

"Dad never kept you a secret. I can't remember when he first told me he had another daughter. I feel as if I've always known, so I suppose I must have been very young. He told me that when he was much younger he'd done a terrible thing. He had a relationship with a woman and when she ended up pregnant, he panicked. He left. It was the worst thing he'd ever done in his life, and it left him deeply ashamed. He said that there was no excuse for it. At the time, he was terrified by the responsibility. Terrified that he wasn't able to be the person he needed to be."

"He left my mother terrified, too. He walked out of the delivery room and never came back."

"I know. It was an *awful* thing to do." Hattie nursed her wine on her lap. Far from defending her father's behavior, she appeared to be in complete agreement. "Truly awful. I can't even imagine. If Brent had done that to me I would have tracked him down and haunted him forever. That's if I ever recovered sufficiently from the panic attack to leave the delivery room.

And it's no consolation at all, but Dad knew that. He never forgot it, and he never, ever forgave himself. But he did learn from it. It colored everything he did."

"What do you mean?"

Hattie pulled the throw around her. "For a start, he was determined never to let anyone down again. My mother died soon after I was born, and he said he felt that same terror because the responsibility was crushing. I suppose he had a taste of how your mother must have felt being left alone with a baby. But this time he was determined to do it right, and not only because he was the only person in the world I had left."

Erica thought about the photo she'd seen on Hattie's desk when they'd checked in. "He was a good dad to you." There was a stab of something she didn't recognize. Envy? Loss? How could she feel loss for something she'd never had?

"He really was a good dad. And I don't know if that makes you feel better or worse, but it's the truth." Hattie gave a half smile. "And maybe, in a way, I have you to thank for the fact that he was. He learned a hard lesson."

Erica felt the past change shape around her. Not a selfish man walking away from responsibility and never looking back. A youthful mistake, a terrible error in decision making. Remorse carried through a lifetime. "I think if someone learns from a mistake, makes a major change in their lives because of it, that's to be applauded. Not everyone learns."

She thought of one particular CEO she'd dealt with in the past who couldn't manage to rein in his behavior even though it was damaging the reputation of the company. He'd made excuses. Blamed everyone and everything except himself until in the end, Erica had walked away from the business, and felt sorry for his senior executives who were less able to do so.

She admired people who took responsibility. It seemed that her father had taken responsibility—the second time around.

Hattie took a sip of wine. "Dad was a good person. But he made a bad decision." She lowered her glass. "He did try to put it right. A few years after you were born, he contacted your mother, but she wouldn't have anything to do with him. She told him never to contact either of you again."

A strange feeling washed over her. Her mother had never mentioned that contact, either. She'd assumed her father had never thought of her again.

But she imagined for a moment how her mother must have felt. She'd weathered those hard early days alone, handling both a baby and the loss of her love. She'd lived with the hope that he'd come back or at least get in touch, and when he hadn't, she'd lived with the grief. She'd learned to cope with the practical and the emotional. She'd done everything she could to strengthen the places where she'd been vulnerable, including her heart. She'd accepted no help and reached out to no one.

It had been the only life Erica had known, and at the time it had seemed normal, but now she realized how very lonely her mother must have been. Between working and caring for Erica she'd had no time to pursue friendships, and by the time her father finally made contact, her instinct to protect herself and her daughter would have been entrenched. It would have taken great reserves of courage to trust him a second time.

But what if she had? If her mother had welcomed his approach, would he have become part of Erica's life or would he have been a source of more upset? It was impossible to say, and really, what was the point in speculating?

She realized that Hattie was waiting for her to respond.

Her mouth felt dry and she took another sip of wine. "After he left, she waited for him to get in touch, but he never did. She found it particularly hard at Christmas. I think it took her a long time to accept that he really had left for good, and once that sank in, she wasn't able to forgive. It was a survival thing."

"Dad understood that." Hattie paused. "He punished himself over it. Told himself that he deserved to be cut out of your life and that you were probably better off without him. After what happened with your mother, he steered clear of relationships for a long time. He focused on his work."

"What was his work?"

"He was a plumber. He set up his own company, employed a handful of people who felt the same way he did about delivering excellent customer service, and did really well. The business could have expanded, but he never wanted to lose that personal touch."

"And then he met your mother?"

"Yes. And he told me he was a different person by then. A decade older for a start, but also that early experience shaped him."

It shaped all of us, Erica thought. "In what way?"

"He was really big on responsibility. If he told a customer he could do something, then he did it, even if it meant he was out half the night fixing a frozen pipe. Whatever I started, he encouraged me to see it through no matter how hard it was. The past couple of years, when it has been so hard, I often think about him. In the beginning there were days when I almost couldn't drag myself out of bed, and I imagined him tugging back the covers and telling me to get up and do what needed to be done. Is this difficult to hear? If you want me to stop, say so."

"I don't want you to stop." It wasn't true. Part of her did want Hattie to stop, but another part—the bigger part—wanted to hear more.

This was a side of her father she'd never been given access to before. And it was real. All she'd ever had before now was what her mother had given her, and to her mother, Erica's dad was the man who had walked out on his family when they'd needed him most and he'd remained frozen in that time. A blank figure. The sum of that one single action that had blown apart her mother's life, and the image Erica had of him went no deeper than one single photograph that her mother had shown her when she'd asked to at least see him. But Hattie was describing a person, not a mistake. Her father, who had always been a one-dimensional figure in her life, was coming to life in her head.

Over the years she'd felt anger, frustration and no small degree of contempt toward the man who had played a defining role in her life and yet never been part of it. But now her feelings toward him, once so clear, were murky and ill-defined.

Hattie stood up and fed another log into the fire. "It was my mother who persuaded him to reach out to you again." She watched as the flame caught and flickered. "She was pregnant with me by then, so that probably contributed to the fact that she felt so strongly. She felt he owed you that, at least. I think he was afraid of doing it. Afraid of rejection, but he did it anyway. You were twelve when I was born. He sent you a card. He was upset when your mother told him for a second time never to contact you both again, but he wasn't surprised. He understood and he blamed himself totally, but he wanted to keep the door open. He always hoped that one day he might be given another chance to build a relationship with you. He wanted you to have that choice."

Erica's hand shook as she carefully put her glass down on the table. "I found that card when I was clearing her things after she died."

"I didn't know you lost your mother."

"Two years ago."

Hattie straightened and her eyes darkened with sympathy. "I'm sorry to hear that. All this must be very difficult for you. Do you want to stop?"

"No." It was difficult, but not as difficult as she would have expected. Maybe it was because Hattie herself was so straightforward and honest about everything. "I'm interested in the details. I've never had that."

"You must have had so many questions when you found that card." Hattie sat down again and picked up her glass. "Is that why you're here now? No, it can't be. If you found the card a while ago, why now? It wasn't a coincidence, which means you chose to find me. But then you didn't seem exactly pleased to see me."

Erica stared into the fire. Beyond the windows snow was falling, coating the trees with another layer of white. "When I found the card, I was shocked. I had a lot of questions."

"But no one to answer them."

"Right. And I had such mixed emotions." It was the first time she'd admitted it. "Part of me was upset that my mother had kept that hidden from me. But I also felt protective of her. She never did anything without thinking about it carefully. If she'd wanted me to know then she would have given me the card."

Hattie paused. "That was a big decision she made, given that it affected you, too. You weren't angry with her?"

"A little, at first. But then I thought back to what her life had been like. He left her alone and afraid. And in those early days when she might still have forgiven him, he didn't make contact." Erica felt a pang as she thought of how difficult it had been for her mother. "That panic he felt that made him run? She felt that, too. She felt the weight of that responsibility, but she shouldered it and became fiercely independent. She never wanted to feel that vulnerable again, and she raised me to be independent, too. To handle things."

"Your poor mother." Hattie spoke softly. "That card arriving when you were twelve must have shaken her. She must have been afraid that letting him back into her—or your—life, in whatever way, might threaten everything she'd built."

"Exactly. And she didn't throw it away, which suggests she was conflicted." Erica glanced at Hattie. "And I was, too, which is why when I found the card I just put it away, with a few of her other things that I kept. Not many." She gave a quick smile. "I'm not sentimental, as Anna will confirm. But putting the card away didn't stop me thinking about it. I decided I wanted to know more about my father, so I hired a private investigator."

Hattie lifted her eyebrows. "People do that in real life? I've only ever seen it in movies."

"Claudia said the same thing, but yes, it's a thing. He told me my father had died, but he also told me about you. And Delphi." Erica paused, wondering how much to say. "There wasn't much in the report except a few dates and locations. Facts. But I looked you up, read a piece about this place and everything that had happened."

"But what made you decide to come and find me?"

She'd asked herself that same question.

Erica felt a stirring inside her that might have been panic. "I'm not sure. I couldn't stop thinking about you. Maybe it's because you were raising a child alone, as my mother did."

"Or maybe it was because you were curious about me. I was definitely curious about you. And why not? We're related. Family." Hattie shifted her position. "I thought about you often. Although obviously, I didn't know anything about you, so my image of you was all in my head."

Erica's mouth was dry. "What did you imagine?"

"When I was younger I used to picture you showing up at my door. You'd love me on sight, of course, and we'd become instant best friends—" She gave a rueful smile. "My expectations were set very high back then."

Erica felt a stab of guilt as she remembered her less than friendly greeting when Hattie had appeared at the door.

"I don't tend to love people on sight. I'm more cautious than that."

"I'm sure you are. After what happened, it must be hard for you to trust. But you have such a close friendship group, you clearly have managed it."

That was true. She trusted Anna and Claudia completely.

Hattie paused. "I don't expect you to love me on sight, but I would like the chance to get to know you a little and I hope in time we might become closer. I think our dad would have liked that. More to the point, I'd like that and I know Delphi would, too." She toyed with the stem of her glass. "When I came up to your room earlier it didn't seem as if you wanted a relationship, and if that's the case then of course I understand."

Erica no longer knew what she wanted. Pursuing this relationship wouldn't be a casual thing, especially not with a child involved. It couldn't be. She remembered the loneliness of her own childhood. The nagging feeling that maybe the fact that it was just the two of them was somehow her fault. That if she'd done something differently, been a different person, maybe her father wouldn't have left in the first place, or maybe he would have wanted to come back and live with them. She didn't want to be in Delphi's life and then exit, leaving her with the feeling that she'd somehow fallen short.

So far, their interaction had been fairly superficial. She could still check out in the morning and put all this behind her, and Delphi would forget her in a week.

But was that really what she wanted?

For the first time in her life, she didn't know what she wanted. She felt cowardly. Unsettled. But she knew she owed Hattie an apology.

"I was rude earlier. I apologize. It's no excuse, but I underestimated how emotional the whole thing would be. I didn't know my father, and I didn't know you, so I didn't expect to be assaulted by so many feelings. It was—" she stared into her glass "—it *is* confusing."

"I'm finding it confusing, too. You were this shadowy figure in my life. Almost a permanent reminder of the importance of behaving responsibly." Hattie gestured to the window, where snow was swirling in the darkness. "It's snowing heavily. At this rate you may not have a choice about leaving tomorrow."

There was a wistful note in her voice, and Erica felt as if this was the point where she should say that she no longer wanted to leave, but she couldn't force the words out of her mouth. She didn't know how she felt. Staying would mean deepening the bond, and she wasn't sure she was ready for that.

Hattie broke the silence. "Tell me more about you. Where do you live?"

"I have an apartment in Manhattan. But I'm not there often. I travel a lot for work."

"Where to?"

"Everywhere." Erica relaxed a little. "Often Europe and the Far East."

"Sounds glamorous."

"It can be." Erica thought about the hotel rooms, the spas, the room service. "It can also be lonely."

"Do you have someone special in your life?"

"You mean romantic?" Did Jack count? No, their relationship was practical and satisfying but not serious in any way. "No."

"You hesitated." Hattie leaned forward and passed Erica the bottle so that she could top up her glass. "Tell me more. Leave nothing out."

"Now you're sounding like Anna."

"Well, you clearly love Anna, so I'll take that as a good thing."

Erica poured a small amount of wine into her glass. "There is someone I see from time to time, but it's casual. It's more a question of convenience. We're there for each other when one of us needs a date."

"But you like him. A lot."

Erica frowned. "I don't know how you draw that conclusion from what I just told you."

"Because you don't strike me as the kind of woman who wastes time with someone whose company you don't enjoy."

Erica shrugged. "I value my independence."

Hattie tilted her head. "How does being in a relationship threaten your independence?"

It was a reasonable question and one Erica found hard to answer. She enjoyed Jack's company. Jack hadn't asked her to give anything up or change anything. So why hadn't she let him stay the night when he'd suggested it?

"I suppose I'm set in my ways." She changed the subject. "How about you? Noah seemed—attentive."

"He has been a great friend." Color whooshed into Hattie's cheeks and Erica knew Anna would have immediately dived in with a follow-up question, but she wasn't Anna.

Should she mention that Delphi wanted him to move in? No. She knew nothing about being an aunt, but she had a feeling that betraying a confidence wouldn't be a good start.

"You're right that the wine is good, by the way." She'd been so focused on the conversation she'd only now realized just how good.

"It is good." Hattie glanced at the bottle. "Brent employed a sommelier to fill our wine cellar when we first opened. He left lots of notes for us, including when certain bottles should be drunk. I found this one when I was in the cellar last week and decided I was going to gift it to myself."

"An excellent decision." Erica took another sip. "But I feel guilty drinking your profits. Put this on my bill."

"Don't worry about it. Right now there isn't much in the way of profits, but the fact that I no longer have Chef Tucker and Stephanie on the payroll may mean my costs have gone down dramatically. They were the employee equivalent of white truffle."

Erica laughed. "You were brave tonight. You handled it well."

"Did I? I think it was more a case of being trapped in a corner, and if it weren't for the fact that you have friends with useful talents I don't think we would have made it through the evening, but what the hey—" Hattie fiddled with her glass. "I think you were brave, coming here."

Brave? She'd arranged this trip without telling anyone why she was doing it; she'd stepped into the inn, taken one look at that photo and been so unsettled by the emotion unleashed inside her that she'd almost run away.

Almost.

So far, technically, she'd only run as far as the bookstore.

She'd been so sure that she wanted to leave. But now?

Something had shifted during the conversation with Hattie. She was no longer a stranger, but a real person. She'd created a detailed picture where previously Erica had only had bare facts, a rough sketch. And then there was Delphi.

Walking away had seemed like the easy answer, but it no longer felt easy.

She could check out in the morning as planned, spend Christmas in the city and step firmly back into her comfort zone. She could go back to her old life and pretend nothing had changed. Maybe message Hattie occasionally.

But was that what she wanted?

EIGHTEEN

Claudia

"I tell you, the guy was a bully." Claudia drizzled extra maple syrup over her pancakes. "And the sort who intimidated people with his food. Food should never be intimidating. If I'd had to rename one of his dishes I would have called it *A fat slice of ego served on a bed of overinflated self-esteem.*"

Anna picked up her coffee cup. "Shouldn't that be a soufflé of self-esteem?"

"Maybe." Claudia smiled. Inside she was buzzing. She couldn't remember when she'd had as much fun as she'd had the night before. She'd had complete autonomy in the kitchen, or as much autonomy as was possible when you were working with someone else's ego-driven menu. "I've worked with people like him and trust me, it was an experience I could happily have lived without. He was the type who thought the food should be honored to have him preparing it."

The sort of chef who had put her off working in kitchens.

Anna sipped her coffee. She was wearing a cream cable-knit sweater, and her hair fell dark and silky past her shoulders. "Do you think he'll come back?"

"I hope not. You look great, by the way. Like an advert for a Christmas mini break. Is that another new sweater?"

Anna tilted her head. "It depends on how you're defining *new*."

Did she ever look as well put together as Anna? When she wasn't working she was more of a fall-out-of-bed-into-workout-gear type of person. If she wasn't working out, she more often than not pulled on her most comfortable jeans. If someone called on her unannounced, she'd apologize for her appearance and say she didn't know she'd be seeing anyone, but Anna would be able to answer the door at any time, knowing she was looking her best.

Anna always looked like an adult. Claudia always felt as if adulthood was something she had yet to attain. She resolved to make more effort.

Anna helped herself to fruit from the basket on the table. "You don't think the chef might change his mind when he calms down?"

"His sort never calms down. Hattie is better off without him. And she fortunately has an excellent breakfast chef. These buttermilk pancakes are excellent. Not always easy to make them this fluffy." She examined the texture. "And the caramelized apple and walnut is a perfect addition."

"Maybe Hattie will be better off without him in the long-term," Anna said, "but in the short-term she needs a head chef. Unless the breakfast chef can work evenings, too?"

"Different skill set." Claudia put her fork down. "Are you saying I didn't do a good job? I'll have you know I left the kitchen no fewer than eight times last night to speak to diners who wanted to thank me in person. Everyone was happy and the kitchen staff wasn't traumatized. I consider that a win."

"Since when have you been so sensitive? I'm not saying you didn't do a good job. Of course you did a *great* job. But you were standing in for the night, that's all. We're leaving today." Anna sneaked a look at Erica and then sliced into her pancake. "You're not a permanent solution and Hattie needs a permanent solution." She took a mouthful of food. "You're right. These pancakes are excellent. Is that cinnamon in the apple?"

"Yes." The idea of leaving today killed her mood. Last night had been the first time in ages that she hadn't once thought about John, or wondered what she was going to do with her future. She'd been absorbed in the moment, loving every second. The challenge of stepping in last minute to a difficult situation had given her a buzz, and she felt good about supporting Hattie.

She was enjoying the inn, and her evening in the kitchen had been the happiest few hours as a chef she'd had for a long time.

"You're smiling," Anna said. "Did you meet someone?"

"What? No! Why would me smiling mean I'd met someone? I smile all the time."

"Not like this—" Anna waved her fork. "It's a goofy smile. An 'I just fell in love' smile."

"That has nothing to do with a man. I had fun last night, that's all. And I learned that I do still love cooking." She waited for Erica to say *I told you so*, but her friend was gazing out the window. "Not only cooking. I discovered that I love being a chef if the circumstances are right. And it's a relief, because I'd lost that joy and I thought it had gone forever. It's like discovering you love your husband after all and no longer want to divorce him."

"I have no idea how that feels because I have never wanted to divorce Pete, but I'm pleased."

Claudia was pleased, too. "It changes things. I was facing a future of not knowing what I wanted to do, but now I know. I still want to be a chef, but not just anywhere. The atmosphere is important to me. I need to make sure I don't panic and take the first job I'm offered. I need to give myself time to make sure the culture is a fit."

Anna reached across and gave her hand a squeeze. "It's good to see you happy." She went back to her pancakes. "What is Hattie going to do about staffing the kitchen tonight?"

"I don't know. We're meeting after breakfast to talk through how she can simplify the menu and maybe manage with the team she has." She wanted to volunteer her services, but she wasn't in a position to do that.

She glanced at Erica again. Would she change her mind about leaving?

Hattie seemed pretty great. And okay, the initial situation and meeting had been awkward, but they'd already bumped their way over that so why was Erica so determined to walk away from it?

Erica hadn't spoken since they'd sat down at the breakfast table. Nor had she touched her food. All she'd done was sip black coffee and gaze out the window. Not that gazing out the window was a bad occupation. The snow had continued to fall during the night and they'd woken to blue skies and a deep layer of fresh snow. Bright sunshine dazzled, adding sparkle to the jewel-encrusted surface. Trees were coated, their branches bowing under the weight of fresh snow. The view added to the festive atmosphere of the inn.

"What did you two do while I was sweating away over a hot stove?" Claudia finished her pancakes, making a mental note to congratulate the chef later.

"I spent an entertaining hour with Delphi," Anna said. "Who reminded me how much I love young children. Also, how very exhausting they are."

Claudia reached for her coffee. "How old is she?"

"Five and three quarters, as she told me. We read, and she asked approximately two hundred and fifty questions in the space of thirty minutes. She also drowned me in interesting facts. Did you know that there are over five hundred species of shark? Also, they have been around for more than four hundred million years."

"Four hundred million? I'm going to stop complaining about almost being forty." Claudia suppressed a yawn. "I remember yours asking a million questions when they were that age. Don't you, Erica?"

Erica didn't answer and Anna frowned slightly.

"Erica?"

Erica turned her head and blinked. "Sorry, what did I miss?"

"Sparkling conversation and pancakes—" Claudia gestured to the untouched plate in front of her. "You should eat."

"I'm not hungry."

"You're going to eat, or you'll offend the chef."

"Yesterday you were telling me it was the guests that were important, not the chef's feelings."

"That was yesterday. And it depends on the chef. I happen to like the breakfast chef. Eat. And also, tell us what's on your mind." Claudia leaned across the table and helped herself to a bite of Erica's pancake. "Anna will get it out of you eventually, so you might as well just tell us now. Ow!" She felt Anna's foot connect briskly with her ankle and stopped talking.

"I tapped on your door last night," Anna said, "but there was no answer and you didn't reply to my message. I was worried."

"My phone was on silent." Erica took a mouthful of pancake. "I spent the evening with Hattie."

"That's good." Or was it? Claudia reached down and rubbed her ankle. "Did you talk?"

"Yes. And also shared a bottle of exceptionally good red wine. I've ordered you and Pete a crate for Christmas, Anna."

"Thank you. That's thoughtful." Anna leaned forward. "And? Give us details."

"It's a pinot noir. Pete will love it."

"I wasn't asking about the wine."

Erica put her fork down. "I know."

A few other guests started to arrive in the restaurant, smiling a greeting as they passed the three women on their way to their table.

Anna waited until they were seated and out of earshot. "You don't have to talk about it if you don't want to."

"Yes, she does," Claudia said. "If we're leaving this morning then there are plans to be made." Was it selfish of her to hope they wouldn't be leaving?

Anna was focused on Erica. "Was the conversation upsetting?"

Erica pushed her plate away. "It was strange. Unsettling. She talked about him. At length. I suppose it was the first time I'd ever thought of my father as a fully rounded human being. To me he was always the man who left us. Or the man that ran, as my mother used to refer to him."

Claudia felt guilty for thinking about herself when this was such an emotionally draining time for Erica. If Erica wanted to leave then they'd leave.

She wanted to say the right thing, but she didn't know what that was. It would be insulting to pretend she understood. Like Anna, her parents were boringly normal, whatever normal was, and for that she was grateful. They were still together after forty-five years of marriage, still fought about the same little things, still tended their garden and finished each other's sentences. She couldn't imagine being in Erica's situation.

"Of course you saw him that way," Anna said. "Why wouldn't you? You didn't have any other information." She pushed Erica's plate back toward her.

"But now I do." Erica picked up her fork again and poked at her food. "To us he was the man who ran, but he didn't run when he found himself in sole charge of Hattie. He didn't leave her. He was a single dad in tough circumstances. He made compromises that meant he could focus on his daughter."

"That's heartening. They say people can't change, but he clearly changed." Anna finished her coffee. "Does that hurt?"

"It could, couldn't it?" Erica paused, as if she was silently checking for injury. "But it doesn't. In fact, it helps to know that my father wasn't a bad person. All the signs are that despite everything, ultimately, he was a decent man."

Claudia listened while Erica told them the details of the conversation. She wondered whether, in Erica's position, she would have been angry with her mother for not responding to his efforts to reach out and make amends, but Erica was fiercely loyal to her mother and didn't seem angry. Just a little sad.

Claudia wondered what Erica's life would have been like if her father had reentered her life. If she'd grown up seeing that men might run, but also that they might then grow up and step up. Would that have changed things?

"I like the fact that he told Hattie about you," Anna said. "But it's funny thinking that she grew up knowing everything about you, whereas you've only recently found out about her. She is obviously pleased you're here."

"Yes."

Anna glanced toward Claudia, and then back at Erica. "Are you sure you want to leave?" Her question was casual, but Claudia had a feeling Anna knew just how badly Claudia wanted to stay.

"I don't know." Erica put her fork down. "I don't know what I want to do."

In all their years of friendship, Claudia had never seen Erica struggle with a decision. "What does your gut tell you?"

"I don't listen to my gut when I make decisions. I use my head. And my head tells me I can't do this. I don't know how to be what I'm supposed to be."

Claudia was confused. "Who are you supposed to be?"

"A sister. I'm not familiar with the job description." There was a flash of panic in Erica's eyes. "It doesn't help that I like her."

"Isn't that a good thing?"

"Yes, in one way. But it also increases the pressure."

Anna pondered that. "You mean because you like her, and you're afraid she might not like you back?"

Erica shifted in her seat and then scowled at Anna. "How are you so good at this? How do you always manage to see things that I can't see myself?"

"Because I know you." Anna hesitated. "You've always had a bit of a fear about being left. Deep down, no matter how much you rationalized it, a part of you always wondered if your father leaving was somehow your fault. But you know it wasn't."

"In a way it was." Erica gave a faint smile. "He wasn't ready to be a dad. If I hadn't appeared, he might have stuck around. And don't turn this into some deep philosophical discussion about why I'm not married with eight kids, because the truth is it isn't in any way linked to any residual daddy issues I may have. I just don't want that."

"Good." Claudia helped herself to more fruit. "I couldn't afford to buy gifts for eight kids."

"I really do love my life."

Anna shrugged. "No one is suggesting you change your life. Just allow a few people in, that's all."

"A few?"

"Hattie and s—Delphi." Anna stumbled slightly and Claudia had a feeling she'd just stopped herself saying *sexy Jack*. "Also, there is no reason why Hattie wouldn't like you. *We* like you."

"Speak for yourself. I don't like her one little bit," Claudia said, "but I've been too busy to find a new friend."

Erica laughed and the atmosphere lightened. "I suppose I—"

Anna lifted her hand to end the conversation. "We have company. Hello, Delphi, how are you this morning?"

"I'm very well, thank you." Delightfully polite, Delphi slid onto the vacant chair next to Erica and handed her a large sheet of paper. "I made you a painting, Aunt Erica."

Aunt Erica?

Startled, Claudia glanced at Erica's face and then at Anna, who was watching intently.

Erica said nothing for a moment and then took the painting and studied it. "This is for me?"

"Yes. It's a Christmas painting." Delphi knelt on the chair and pointed. "That's our home, and that's my mommy, and that's Rufus, and that's you standing by the Christmas tree. That's Noah, although he won't be here on Christmas Day because he lives somewhere else and he has to help his dad on the farm. Did you know that sharks don't have bones?"

"I've never thought about it. That's very interesting." Erica gave the painting her full attention. "What am I holding? A present?"

"Yes. It's a present for me. I didn't know how big to make it. If the real present you've bought me is smaller than the one in the painting you don't need to worry. It's the thought that counts." Delphi patted her hand reassuringly and Claudia turned laughter into a cough.

She had a feeling that if anyone was going to penetrate that protective wall Erica had built around herself, it would be Delphi.

"This is very special. That's really me? It's an extraordinary likeness. And I'm wearing my best boots." Erica peered closer. "There's someone on the roof."

"That's Santa. He's coming down the chimney. We're supposed to be asleep when he comes but drawing people in their beds is hard. It's just a drawing so I don't think it will stop the real Santa coming. But you need to write your letter soon because he needs time to get whatever it is you want. Do you know what you want? Because if you do then you could write the letter now. I can help you."

Claudia decided she would give a lot to see Erica write a letter to Santa. "You haven't already done it, Erica? Shame on you."

Erica shot her a look. "I've been busy. Have you done yours?"

"I did mine in November. I'm a people pleaser, and if there's one person it's important to please then it's Santa." Claudia stole the last piece of pancake from Erica's plate and gave a smug smile. "I like to give Santa plenty of time. I don't believe in creating unnecessarily tight deadlines." She had a feeling Erica might kill her later but she'd live with that.

"Santa is busy," Delphi agreed, "and just in case what you want is difficult to get it would be only fair to tell him soon."

Erica looked baffled. "Right. I'll bear that in mind."

"Do you like snow?"

"I—on occasions, yes."

Claudia suspected those occasions were usually when she was looking out the window at it, and not going anywhere.

"I love snow," Delphi said. "Rufus loves snow, too. I have a sled. Do you have a sled?"

"No. And I've never been on a sled."

Delphi's eyes flew wide. "Never? Not even when you were little?"

"I lived in a city."

Delphi patted her hand pityingly. "I can teach you. I'd like us to do that together. I have to go and walk Rufus now, but we can write that letter when I come back." She slid off the chair just as Hattie hurried into the room.

"Delphi, you're not supposed to be in the restaurant." She took Delphi's hand.

"But I did Aunt Erica a painting."

"I know, but Aunt Erica is a guest and you know we don't disturb guests."

Delphi frowned. "Aunt Erica is family."

"Yes, that's true—" Hattie floundered and sent them a look of apology. "We'll leave you to finish your breakfast."

Delphi was in no hurry to leave. "But later can Aunt Erica see my toys?"

"Aunt Erica is far too busy to see your toys, and—"

"I'd love to see your toys," Erica said, "if that's all right. Is that Rufus standing by the door? Not that I know much about dogs, but it looks as if he has his legs crossed out there so maybe you'd better take him for his walk and I'll see you later."

Delphi ran across to the dog, and the two of them disappeared.

"Later?" Hattie retrieved Delphi's hair ribbon from the floor. "You're not checking out?"

Claudia held her breath and saw Erica glance in her direction. There was a pause as their eyes met, and Claudia wondered if Erica could see how desperately she wanted to stay. Was it visible on her face?

Maybe it was because Erica gave a brief smile. "We have reservations for the whole week," she said, turning to look at Hattie. "We have a book to discuss, and wine to drink, and conversations to have. And Claudia seems to be having fun in your kitchen, so no, we won't be checking out."

"That's great." Hattie looked as if she was fighting emotion. "I'm pleased."

Claudia felt similarly emotional. She'd seen that look. She suspected Erica's reasons for changing her mind about leaving were more complicated than just a consideration of her friend's feelings, but still, she was grateful.

And she intended to make the most of the opportunity. "I am having fun in the kitchen. I don't suppose you're looking for a chef to cover this week, are you? Because I might know someone who can help."

"Are you sure?" The tension seemed to seep out of Hattie. "This is your book club week. Your vacation with your friends."

"There will be plenty of time to talk about books, and anyway, my friends are boring."

"Thank you," Anna said mildly. "We love you, too."

"Do we?" Erica raised an eyebrow. "Personally, I only love her food."

"I thought we agreed never to tell her that?"

"Well, it's out there now. She'll have to live with it. Cupboard love."

"Refrigerator love," Anna said. "Range cooker love."

Erica waved a hand in Claudia's direction. "I'm already hungry. Go to the kitchen right now and get to work."

Claudia felt a rush of love for her friends. "I'm going to do that. I have menus to plan with Hattie and a team to motivate. Let's meet up for a quick lunch later. If I start work now, I'll have time for that. What are you two going to do?"

"I'm going to take a trip into town to try and finish my

Christmas shopping." Anna reached for her bag and stood up. "While you're sweating over a hot stove, I will be sipping cinnamon hot chocolate. I might treat myself to that sparkly sweater I spotted in the window."

Erica shook her head. "Because Anna never saw a sweater she didn't want to buy."

Anna shrugged. "It's Christmas. It would be cruel to leave it there all alone, feeling as if no one cared about it. Unloved. I'm offering it a good home. And after I've made the sweater feel at home among all my other sweaters, I will be checking that Chloe doesn't need housekeeping assistance, and then I will be calling my Pete." She frowned. "Or trying to call him. He has been unusually elusive this week."

My Pete.

For once Claudia didn't feel envious. She was too excited about the week ahead. Mostly she was relieved to discover her love of cooking hadn't left her. It was like falling in love again. "Erica? What will you be doing?"

"Me? I'm going to keep Anna company on her shopping trip to make sure she buys a maximum of one sweater, then I'm going to write a letter to Santa," Erica said, "and because I have no idea what I'm doing, Delphi has generously offered to help me."

Claudia was so grateful to her that she stepped forward and hugged her. "Thank you for staying."

"Oh, a public display of affection. My favorite thing." But she gave Claudia a hug back. "You would have left for me, and I can certainly stay for you. And anyway, you're not the only reason. Go and produce something that will make our taste buds explode."

NINETEEN

Anna

Anna snuggled deeper into her wool scarf as she walked with Erica along the main street. The snow crunched under their feet, and each breath formed a cloud as it met freezing air.

"This place is so pretty."

"Yes." Erica paused outside the toy store and gazed at the window. "I should buy something for Delphi. But what? Obviously, I'm clueless. Will you help?"

"Love to." Grateful for an excuse to escape from the cold, Anna pushed open the door and went inside before Erica could change her mind. Like Claudia, she was relieved to be staying but mostly she was relieved that Erica seemed to have formed a tentative bond with Hattie and Delphi. She intended to do everything she could to encourage that, and maybe she was a little interfering, but what were friends for?

Being with Delphi reminded her of when her own children were small.

Now, standing in the toy store, looking at the kaleidoscope of colorful toys, she felt a serious pang of nostalgia. In the middle of the store a train track circled a large Christmas tree, and a train chugged steadily past a stack of prettily wrapped toys. The corner of the store had been turned into a grotto and the staff were dressed as elves.

She watched as a young mother wrangled an active toddler while trying to entertain an older sibling.

The twins had loved visiting toy shops, particularly at Christmas.

"What's wrong?" Erica looked at her. "You look sad."

"I'm fine." Anna forced herself to focus on the toys on the shelf. "Right. Let's find something."

"Yes, but what?" Erica made a gesture of despair. "What do I buy?"

"You've always been great at picking gifts for Meg and Daniel. We just have to think about the type of person Delphi is. She obviously loves painting, so you could buy her some art materials." Anna picked out various items that she thought Meg would have loved at the same age and handed them to Erica. "Stay clear of anything with glitter or that's your relationship with Hattie over before it has started."

Erica stared at the corner of the store. "That drum kit over there is cute."

"No. Nothing noisy. No drum kits, or electric guitars, or trumpets."

"Those aren't fun?"

"Not for the parents. You don't want to give Hattie a headache. Unless you happen to have a musical genius in the family or a soundproofed room, they should be considered revenge toys."

Erica picked up a jigsaw. "Revenge toys? Children think like that?"

"Not the children, the parents. One of the dads in Meg's class gave his son a drum kit after his wife divorced him for having an affair with the nanny. She spent the next month wearing earplugs. The wife, not the nanny. This notebook will be perfect for Meg's Christmas stocking." Anna popped it under her arm and walked farther into the store. She stopped in front of a rail of clothes. "How about a dressing-up outfit for Delphi? Meg went through a dressing-up stage. On the other hand we don't know what Delphi already has, so probably better to stick with art materials."

"That's not unimaginative?"

"Not if you enjoy art, which she seems to. I wonder what else she likes?"

"Sharks," Erica said. "She likes sharks."

"Good point." Anna moved to the soft toy section and picked up a hammerhead shark in plush gray velvet. "This is cute."

"I can't believe I'm saying this, but it actually is cute and I happen to know that a hammerhead is her favorite shark. But she already has a dinosaur that seems to go everywhere with her."

"Doesn't mean she wouldn't also like a shark." Anna handed it to Erica. "And you should buy her books. She loves books."

"We don't know what she already has."

"I'm sure that bookstore would change it if we buy a duplicate. How about this construction set? Both of mine would have loved that." Anna added the box to the growing pile in Erica's arms. "How much do you want to spend?"

"I don't know. The right amount, whatever that is." Erica looked lost and Anna gave her arm a squeeze.

"This isn't an exam. You can't get this wrong."

"I can. I've never been an aunt before."

"You're godmother to my children and they adore you. It's not so different." Anna pushed her toward the checkout. "Just be yourself."

"We both know that won't work." Erica stopped walking. "I don't want to mess this up. I *won't* mess this up. If I'm in her life, then I'm in it. No walking away."

Anna tried to work out where this was coming from. "You have never walked away from anything."

"I almost walked away from this," Erica said. "And the stakes are higher. I won't hurt a child."

"The fact that you're even thinking of that means that you won't. You gave it a lot of thought, which is important. Now you need to stop thinking and just do."

"What if Hattie wishes I'd never shown up?"

"Hattie is delighted that you showed up. I think Hattie is a very rounded person who understands that everyone is flawed. Apart from me, of course. I have no flaws."

"Apart from your inability to resist buying a new sweater every week."

"It isn't every week, and that isn't a flaw. It's an endearing quirk."

Erica handed over her purchases to the cheerful "elf" standing behind the counter, and added another couple of small items while she was waiting to pay. "Thanks for this. And now I need a few tips for this letter I'm writing with Delphi. What am I going to ask Santa for?"

"A long steamy night with sexy lawyer Jack? Two steamy nights, breakfast included?"

"There are children present," Erica muttered, taking her credit card back from the elf. "You might want to keep your voice down."

"It's a letter. How hard is a letter?" Anna leaned against the counter. "I've never seen you this uncertain about things before."

"Yes, well, I'm out of my depth and prepared to admit it." Erica took the bag from another girl dressed as an elf and gave her a smile of thanks. "This is important. I'd really like to stay in touch. Build a relationship of sorts." They walked back through the store to the entrance. "Maybe one day Delphi could come and stay with me in Manhattan and we can go shopping together. Not toys. Clothes. Do you remember when Meg did that?"

Anna decided not to point out that Delphi wasn't yet six, and that Manhattan shopping trips were a long way in the future.

It was good that Erica was even thinking that far ahead. "Meg loved every minute. She still talks about it."

"Right. So maybe that would be fun for Delphi. We could hit all the main tourist hot spots. Have lunch somewhere fancy. Do you think she'd like that?"

"I'm sure she'd love it."

Anna felt a strange sensation in the pit of her stomach. Whether she realized it or not, Erica's future was changing. She'd taken an important step. A huge step. Claudia's future was looking brighter, too. They both had things they were looking forward to.

When Anna looked into the future, she saw change she didn't want. She didn't feel excited; she felt sad. And for the first time ever she felt that Pete didn't really understand. She'd mentioned it again in their conversation the night before but he'd been unusually quiet. She had a feeling something wasn't quite right. It was all very unsettling.

They stepped out onto the street and Erica held the door for her.

"Thanks for your help. I appreciate it." She stopped as she saw Anna's expression. "Is everything okay?"

"Everything is great." She needed to pull herself together. "I'm pleased this is working out for you. Hattie is great. And it's good to see Claudia happy."

"Yes. We both knew she still loved cooking, but she needed to rediscover it for herself and fortunately, she has. And Hattie has a temporary chef, so that's two problems solved in one go." Erica stepped to one side to allow a couple to pass. "Where next? Bookstore?"

"Yes. We'll choose some books for Delphi and then we'll go back to the inn." She wanted to talk to Pete and try to find the connection that seemed to be missing the night before.

They spent an hour in the bookstore, left with yet more purchases along with wrapping paper and ribbon so that Erica could reproduce the parcel Delphi had drawn in the picture, and then headed back to the inn.

"Give my love to Pete." Erica was almost staggering under the weight of her parcels. "I'm going to wrap these while you're catching up with him."

Anna unlocked the door to her room. "I'll see you in an hour for lunch."

She closed the door and tugged off her boots. Then she walked to the bathroom and stared into the mirror. She should be grateful that the twins were able to leave home and live independent lives. The fact that they were excited about it meant she'd done a good job as a parent. They were confident and self-reliant.

But whenever she thought about dropping them off at college and then returning in an empty car to an empty house, she felt sick. She was going to miss keeping the fridge stocked, and miss listening to their funny observations about the world. She was going to miss seeing multiple pairs of oversize running shoes in the hallway when Dan had friends over. Who was she going to nurture once they'd gone? Where was she going to put all this love that was inside her?

Her eyes filled and she scowled at her reflection. *Pull yourself together.*

Feeling vulnerable, she settled down on the chair next to the window and called Pete.

He answered after a couple of rings. "Hey. How are things? I thought you'd be deep in book discussion. Or cross-country skiing."

"I'm meeting Claudia and Erica for lunch in an hour. I wanted to hear your voice." She gazed at the trees outside the window, their branches bowing under the weight of new snow. "How are the kids?"

"They're fine. Meg is upstairs finishing a project and Dan is over at Alex's house rehearsing."

"That's good."

"Everything okay?"

"It's fine." She tightened her grip on the phone. "The place is fantastic. So Christmassy. I'm glad you encouraged me to come. We've only been here a day and so much has happened. Do you remember that I told you I thought there was some reason Erica picked this place?" She told him about Erica and her relationship to Hattie and he listened without interrupting.

"That's huge," he said when she finally stopped talking. "And Erica didn't tell you?"

"Not before we arrived. And we were ready to check out and go somewhere else because that was what she wanted, but then everything blew up." She told him about Stephanie and the chef walking out.

"It sounds as if you've been surrounded by drama."

"Yes, but in a way it was a good thing because it forced Erica to get involved. You know how good she is in a crisis, although to be fair, Hattie was pretty good, too, so maybe it's a family trait."

"I'm still trying to imagine Erica writing a letter to Santa."

Anna smiled. "I know. But Delphi is adorable, and you know how it is with children—they don't respect boundaries or tread gently. They just say it how it is, and Erica's pretty much like that herself."

"So she's happy, and so is Claudia."

"Yes. I think this is just what she needed."

There was a pause. "And how about you? Still thinking about the kids leaving home?"

Anna walked across the room and curled up on the bed. "Yes. And I wish I didn't feel this way." She badly wanted to make him understand. "You should have seen Claudia's face when she was working in the kitchen last night. She was energized and excited. And this morning at breakfast I could see she was just dying to get back into the kitchen. And Erica has this great job, and is planning how she can build a relationship with Delphi and Hattie. They have so much to look forward to."

"Have you given any more thought to the conversation we had?"

"The one about having another baby?" She leaned back against the pillows and stared out the window. "Was it a serious suggestion? Do you want another baby?"

"I want you to be happy, Anna." He sounded tired. "If having another baby will make you happy, then I think we should at least talk about it."

Would it make her happy?

"I don't know. When I think about the kids leaving home, I just want to freeze time and somehow stop it happening. And I know this is life, and that it changes all the time for everyone. It is changing for Claudia, and Erica. And Hattie, as well. This is normal, but it doesn't make it easier to handle. I don't know how I'm going to cope when they're gone." And her friends seemed to be better at handling change than she was. Even Claudia, who had been struggling for half the year, seemed excited and upbeat. It took her a moment to realize that Pete hadn't spoken. "Are you still there?"

"Still here."

She felt suddenly guilty.

"Am I moaning? I don't mean to moan. I know I'm lucky. And that's half the problem. I love my life a little too much. I don't want it to change."

"I know."

Something in his tone wasn't right. "What? I know you're thinking something, so just say it."

There was an extended silence. "I know how much you love being a mother, and you're a great mother—"

She was holding her breath. "But?"

"But it's not very flattering to know you're dreading the kids leaving. I know you'll miss them—I'll miss them—but you seem to be forgetting that we still have each other. I know empty-nest syndrome is a thing, and I get it, but there's a difference between missing them—which is healthy and natural—and dismissing what's left of your life. When you say you don't know how you'll cope when they're gone, I feel hurt because you're basically saying our relationship isn't important to you anymore. That I don't count."

Anna felt as if all the air had been sucked out of her lungs. "Pete, that's not true. You know it's not true."

"I'm telling you how I feel, Anna. You're anxious about how you're going to cope when they leave, but not once have you seen it as an opportunity. You focus on what will be missing from your life, not on what is left. And that's me, by the way. Us. We're what is left, but you don't seem at all excited about that."

She opened her mouth to point out how wrong he was, but when she tried to find evidence that would refute his accusation, her mind blanked. He was right. She did think about what she was losing, and not what would still be there. She hadn't been able to see it as an opportunity. And she felt a rush of guilt because only now could she see how it might have felt to him. As if the two of them being left alone together was a bad thing. Something she was dreading. And she was dreading the moment the twins left, but not because she didn't want to be with Pete. She loved him. She adored him.

And now she'd hurt him. Pete, who had been there for her through thick and thin. Pete, who always listened and paid attention to her feelings. Since when had she been so careless with his? She'd made him feel as if he wasn't enough and the mere idea that she'd caused him pain made her chest ache.

She gripped the phone, wanting badly to put things right, wishing they were having this conversation face-to-face. "Pete—"

"I've lost count of the number of times this year I've suggested going away together. I even booked that weekend for our anniversary, but Meg had something going on and you wanted me to cancel."

Her guilt intensified, which might have been why she felt the need to defend herself. "She had an exam on the Monday.

I wanted to be around for her. It didn't feel like the right time to go away."

"No, the truth is that at some point we stopped being a priority. Our relationship is something that gets slotted in around the kids. Before the kids were born, before they were part of our lives, we enjoyed being together." He spoke quietly. "Remember that trip to Paris we took after we left college?"

She hadn't thought about the trip in years. "We had no money. We stayed in that place with the bed that squeaked so badly we could only have sex on the floor."

"We couldn't afford to eat in restaurants, so we took French bread and ham back to our room."

She closed her eyes and let her mind go back there. They'd drunk cheap red wine and studied the guide book trying to work out how long it would take to walk to the Eiffel Tower because they couldn't afford a metro ticket. "You're forgetting the cheese."

"I've never forgotten the cheese. And we could only go to places that were free. We walked everywhere—"

She smiled. "I wore through a pair of shoes."

"But we had fun. We laughed a lot."

They *had* laughed a lot. How could she have forgotten that trip? "The wine was terrible."

"It was truly terrible, although that could have been because we used the cup from the bathroom. I seem to remember that was your idea."

"I think it was." She couldn't imagine doing it now, but back then she'd felt as if she was living her greatest adventure. It had been a perfect trip, and the reason it had been perfect was because she'd been with Pete. Something uncurled inside her.

"Do you remember when the twins were young, and your mother used to babysit so we could go out for dinner?" He was reminding her of those early days when time together had been rare and precious.

"Of course I remember."

"You said you loved it because it gave you an excuse to dress up and feel like something other than a mother."

That was true. She'd treasured those moments when she and Pete had stolen time together.

"We made a rule that we couldn't talk about the kids. The evening had to be about us. We were the priority. The first time we did it we sat in silence for the first half hour because neither of us could think of a single thing to say that didn't involve the children."

"I know. And at the beginning of our relationship we couldn't stop talking. You had opinions on everything, and I loved hearing them." He gave a soft laugh. "Once the twins arrived it took us a while to remember how to communicate about something that wasn't sleeping, feeding or keeping them alive."

"We were so tired."

"Don't remind me."

But somehow they'd weathered those sleepless nights and the relentless demands of small children. They'd taken it in turns to get up early at weekends, each allowing the other a lie-in. They'd shared. They'd figured it out together.

And they should be figuring out this next step together, too.

We were the priority.

"Pete—"

"I know things are changing." His voice was quiet. "Life, relationships—they constantly evolve. But I still remember that first time I saw you in the library. I think about that first night we spent together when you told me in detail what you would have changed about the book you were reading. About all the plans you had for the future and I was so desperate to share that future with you. We built our little family together, and we will always be a family even if we're not all living under the same roof. That's enough for me, but it seems it's no longer enough for you. I want to help, but I don't know how."

There was a pressure in her throat. "Pete—"

"I have to go, Anna. Lola is running in circles waiting to be let into the garden and then I have to cook lunch."

"Wait—" She felt something close to panic. "Call me afterward. I love you."

There was a pause. "This is your time with your friends. Enjoy your lunch and your book chat, Anna. We can talk when you're home."

She waited, expectant, but then realized that he'd ended the call. Pete had ended the call without saying those words back to her. *When had he ever not said them back?*

She paced to the window, trying to calm herself by looking at the snow that coated the world outside, but all she could think of was Pete.

Pete was hurting, which was bad. Worse was the fact that she was the one who had hurt him.

Her mind ran back over the conversations they'd had recently. The things she'd said. She'd thought only of herself, and how she felt about the twins leaving. The sense of impending loss had enveloped her like a fog obscuring her future.

Because she trusted him implicitly, because they'd been close for so long, had she committed that ultimate and clichéd sin of taking him for granted? Unintentionally, maybe, but yes, she had.

We were the priority.

They should be the priority again. Pete was right that instead of thinking about what they were losing, she should think about what they were gaining. She should think about all the things they would be able to do as a couple. Guilt shot through her along with a clarity that had been missing until now. He was right that lately she'd prioritized the kids over their relationship, even when the twins' needs had been less important. It had been the easy thing to do. And now she wished that she'd said yes to his suggestion of a weekend away, if only because it would have shown him how much he meant to her.

She took a slow breath and tried to calm herself.

They weathered everything together. There was nothing they couldn't handle. They'd sort this out.

Everything would be fine.

But why hadn't he said *I love you, too*?

Had he forgotten? No, Pete never forgot.

She grabbed her phone and called him, but he didn't pick up and her call went to voice mail.

She left a message. "I'm so sorry I hurt you. I love you. Call me back when you get this."

She sat there, holding her phone until there was a tap on the door and she realized that it was Erica, and that it was time for lunch. For a wild moment she considered saying that she couldn't join them, but she knew that was ridiculous.

Pete was cooking lunch, too, which was why he hadn't answered his phone. Or maybe he'd left his phone in a different room and forgotten about it, as he sometimes did.

He'd call her later, she reasoned, and when he did she'd apologize and find a way to make it up to him.

TWENTY

Hattie

Hattie stared at the dress in the mirror. It was black, well-cut and—safe? She'd bought it when she was in college and had found it useful in all kinds of situations. But was it right for her evening with Noah?

Just dinner, he'd said. As if it was nothing. And maybe to him it was nothing. But to her? She didn't know exactly what it was, but it certainly wasn't nothing.

She'd pushed it to the back of her mind while she was dealing with the fallout of Stephanie's and Chef Tucker's departures, but now she needed to deal with it.

Was it a date? If it was a date she should be dressing up. But if she dressed up and he was thinking of it as a casual evening with a friend, then she'd be wearing the wrong thing. And she had no idea what the right thing was. She lived in her "uniform" of a short skirt worn over thick tights, and her favorite pair of boots. She hoped she looked businesslike, but also friendly and approachable. On Christmas Day the year before, she'd added a sparkly sweater, but that was as close as she got to dressing up.

She rifled through her clothes, rejecting everything she

touched. This was ridiculous. There had to be *something* she could wear.

She needed a girlfriend's opinion, but she didn't have any girlfriends. She thought about Erica, Anna and Claudia and felt a stab of envy. They were so comfortable with each other. Supportive. They'd all been willing to check out if that had been what Erica wanted. They teased each other in that way that only people who knew each other really well could get away with. No doubt if one of them needed a second opinion on what to wear, they wouldn't hesitate to call each other.

Hattie didn't have a close girlfriend she could call. She'd had plenty of support from the local community and she knew lots of good people, but there was no one she could talk to about something like this. Brent had been her closest friend, and since his accident she hadn't had time to cultivate friendships.

There was Lynda, but she could hardly ask Lynda what she should be wearing for a night out—she still couldn't think of it as a date—with her son. And of course there was Noah himself, who had been an excellent friend to her—but that simply raised the stakes. If she made a mistake, she might damage a friendship and she'd rather have something than nothing.

Delphi wandered into the room with Rufus at her heels and her dinosaur tucked under her arm. "Why are you wearing a dress?"

"Because I'm going to dinner with Noah on Thursday and I need something to wear."

Delphi clambered onto the bed and sat there, all curls and innocence. "You're going on a date."

"It's not a date." Hattie's pulse took off. "Who told you it was a date?" She wondered what their conversations would be like when Delphi hit her teenage years.

"Lynda. She told me she is going to look after me so that you and Noah can go on a date. Are you going to marry him?"

"What? No, of course I'm not going to marry him. Wherever did you get that idea?"

"Eddie's mom just got married. It's her second time, and she hopes it will be the last because her first husband—that's Eddie's biological daddy—was a loser. Eddie heard his mom say so." Delphi frowned. "I don't know what he lost. Eddie doesn't know, either, although his toy car did go missing so it could have been that."

Eddie was in the same kindergarten class as Delphi, and clearly talked too much.

"I don't think we should be talking about Eddie's family. It's not kind to talk about people when they're not around. What are you going to do when Lynda is here?"

"We're going to read, and make Christmas decorations. And I'm going to be really good so you can enjoy your date."

"That sounds like fun. I hope you're also going to go to bed at some point and sleep. And it would be good if you could stop calling it a date." Hattie turned sideways. "What do you think of this dress?"

"It's too black. It needs more glitter. Or maybe feathers. I have some in my art box. We could stick them on."

Glitter? Feathers?

That was what happened when you asked a five-year-old for fashion advice.

"What do you think I should wear?"

Delphi didn't hesitate. "I think you should wear your princess dress."

"My princess dress?" Hattie didn't know she owned such a thing, but Delphi slid off the bed and padded to the clothes that Hattie had been rifling through.

"This one." She tugged at a sequin dress in dark green and it slid off its hanger. "It's like a Cinderella dress."

"I assume you don't mean the part when she is cleaning the kitchens. And since when have you been reading fairy tales?"

"Our teacher read it to us."

"I hope she also told you to work hard, get a proper job and not wait around for a prince. In my favorite version of that story, Cinderella sets up her own cleaning company and goes global." Hattie rescued the dress. She'd bought it years before and worn it once for a night out with her girlfriends in college. She hadn't thought about it for years. "I'm too old for this dress."

"I like it," Delphi said emphatically. "I think Noah will like it, too. It's very happy. What do you think, Rufus?"

Rufus gave an obliging bark and wagged his tail.

Great. The dress had the vote of a five-year-old and a dog. Based on that alone she should put it right back on the hanger. And anyway, it was far too dressy. Noah would probably have a heart attack if she wore it.

"It won't fit."

"Try it." Delphi was insistent so Hattie took off the black dress and slid into sequins. Instantly, she was transported back to that night of the college ball. Music thumping, hair down, drinks flowing. It had been before her father had died, before she'd even met Brent. She'd been young and living in the moment. Another life.

Delphi smiled. "It fits. And it looks like Christmas."

Surprisingly, it did fit. Maybe that was what stress and being too busy to eat did for you. And she could see why Delphi thought it looked festive—all she needed was a red bow in her hair and she'd look like something that had fallen off the Christmas tree.

She smoothed the fabric over her hips.

"I can't wear this to dinner with Noah."

"Why not?"

How to explain to a five-year-old the nuances of dressing for an evening out that definitely wasn't a date?

"It's too sparkly."

"Sparkly is good." Delphi grabbed her hand. "We need to ask Aunt Erica."

"Excuse me?"

"You always say that if you don't know something then you

need to find out." Delphi tugged her toward the door. "Aunt Erica is in the library."

"I know, but she's with her friends and they're having lunch and talking about a book. I don't want to disturb them—" But she was talking to herself because Delphi was already sprinting ahead, leaving Hattie with no choice but to follow.

Delphi knocked on the door of the library, but didn't wait for an answer before entering. Hattie made a mental note to talk to her about being a little too comfortable intruding on guests' spaces.

She heard laughter and the sound of Delphi's voice and then Erica's.

Feeling self-conscious, she followed her daughter and saw Erica, Anna and Claudia seated around the low coffee table. In front of them was a plate of freshly cut sandwiches and a pot of coffee. There were three copies of the novel they were reading, one of them peppered with pieces of paper covered in scrawled notes.

"I'm sorry to disturb you—" Mortified, she reached to tug Delphi away but Erica stood up.

"You're not disturbing us. And that dress is incredible. Delphi was telling us you have a date on Thursday."

She'd said that? Now they'd ask her who with, and then they'd make more of it than they should. And what if Delphi accidently said something to Noah? It was a meal; that was all. People had to eat, didn't they?

Hattie felt her cheeks burn. "It's not a date exactly. It's more of an evening out. I haven't been out in a while and I was trying to find something to wear and—"

"And I think you've found it," Claudia said. "That dress is gorgeous. And perfect for Christmas."

"It's just dinner."

"No reason why you can't look pretty to eat dinner." Erica studied her from all angles. "That dress wants to be taken dancing, but I'm sure it would settle for dinner."

Hattie smoothed the fabric over her hips. "I'm not sure it's right."

"Mmm." Erica narrowed her eyes. "I have just one question. Does wearing it make you feel good?"

It did make her feel good. More than that, it made her feel human. Like someone who had a life, and might actually go dancing on occasion.

Hattie felt herself weaken.

She *did* love the dress so perhaps she should wear it. It was Christmas, after all. So maybe Noah wouldn't think she was overdressed or trying to dazzle him. Maybe he'd just think she was taking advantage of the season.

"If you think it's okay, then I'll wear it."

"Good decision." Erica sat down and helped herself to a slice of cheese. "You should let us help you get ready for the evening. There is nothing we love more. Anna is good with hair."

Delphi brightened. "Can I do your makeup?"

Hattie had a horrifying vision of how she'd look if Delphi was allowed to do her makeup. "That's kind, but maybe we will save that for another day." Preferably a day when she wasn't going to be seen in public.

"I'm in charge of makeup," Erica said, "but I could use an assistant if you're available, Delphi."

"I'm available!"

Rufus whined from the doorway and Delphi shot toward him. "He needs to pee. I'll take him outside. Come on, Rufy. Hold on to it." She disappeared, leaving Hattie with the others.

"Eat your lunch." She waved a hand at the table. "Enjoy. If you need anything, shout."

"Don't rush off." Claudia patted the empty space on the sofa next to her. "Please tell us that the date you're going on is with the gorgeous Noah."

"Yes, but it's really no big deal. I don't think it could be described as a date. It's not romantic or anything." But he *had* called her several times since the incident with Stephanie, to check that she was okay.

"But it's a big enough deal that you're thinking hard about what to wear."

"That's because I never go anywhere. I mean, obviously I go to plenty of places—" she corrected herself, hopefully before they could think she had a very sad life "—but mostly it's the farm with Delphi, or shopping with Delphi, or we go for pizza or milkshakes or ice cream. We don't go to fancy places that require you to dress up."

"But Noah invited you to dinner."

"Technically, it was his mother who did that." And because they were so friendly, and looked so interested and sympathetic and because she couldn't possibly talk to anyone in the local community about this, she told them what had happened.

"I like Lynda already." Anna cut a slice of cheese and added it to her plate along with a few grapes. "And Noah doesn't strike me as someone who is going to do anything he doesn't want to. If he agreed, then I suspect he wanted to take you out."

"Maybe, but the whole thing feels so awkward." She clenched her hands in her lap. "Probably because I'm out of practice." And because she'd kissed Noah, although there was no way she was sharing that piece of information. "The last man I dated was Brent, and that was a long time ago."

Anna put her plate down. "You're nervous."

"Terrified."

"Understandable."

"Yes," Claudia said. "When you've been with someone for a long time, the idea of starting again is daunting. You get comfortable with someone, life has a rhythm and a predictability—you know them, they know you and you share a kind of emotional shorthand, which makes everything easy and then *wham*, suddenly that's gone. Dating feels like arriving in a foreign country where you don't speak the language." She eyed her friends.

"What? I'm just saying I understand, that's all. It's hard. Sometimes it feels easier to stay home."

Hattie saw Erica give Claudia a sympathetic look. "You've lost someone?"

"Not like you," Claudia said. "But my relationship ended after ten years. I can't imagine dating someone else, although I admit to not having the more complicated emotions you're probably feeling."

"Ten years is a long time."

"Yes. I'm trying not to think about the fact that I wasted a decade." Claudia gave what was supposed to be a casual shrug but wasn't at all casual. "And I'm not pretending for a moment that my situation is the same as yours. Losing someone you loved and who loved you back—that's a whole different level of hard."

"It's complicated. Being with someone else feels like a betrayal." She hadn't said that to anyone before, and she wasn't sure why she was saying it now except that these women were so easy to talk to. "It feels as if by showing interest in someone else, I'm saying I don't care for Brent anymore."

Claudia frowned. "That's not what you're saying at all and I'm sure Brent wouldn't want you to feel that way. He'd want you to be happy."

"If something happened to me, I'd want Pete to find someone else," Anna said. "Although she'd also have to love my children or I'd come back and haunt her."

Hattie smiled. Talking to them about it somehow made her feel better. Maybe the situation wasn't so complicated really. She was the one who was making it complicated by tormenting herself with feelings of guilt. But it was unnecessary because they were right about one thing—Brent would have wanted her to be happy.

"We always expect feelings to be simple and straightforward," Anna said, "but it's never like that."

"That's true." Erica reached for a grape. "Which is why I usually avoid relationships."

Hattie was curious. She knew so little of Erica and she badly wanted to know more. "But then you miss out on so much. Not that I'm saying we were the perfect couple, but being with Brent was an adventure. Even with everything that has happened, I wouldn't change the past."

Anna leaned back against the cushions. "What was he like?"

"Brent? He was larger than life. If he was in a room, you'd know it. You could hear his laugh across in the next county. He wasn't afraid to take risks—he just didn't seem to need the guarantees that I always wanted out of life. He followed his instincts and he was impulsive, which occasionally drove me crazy and often scared me to death, but it was also good to be with someone like that. Left to my own devices I would have played it so safe, and then I would have missed out on so much."

Claudia took an apple from the bowl. "Like what?"

Hattie thought back to all the times Brent had made her step out of her comfort zone. "Without Brent, I wouldn't have the inn. I wouldn't have Rufus. I might not even have Delphi. I was determined to wait until exactly the right moment to have a child because I wanted to do it right." That decision had been particularly hard to make, probably because of her father's influence. "It was Brent who made me see there was never really a right moment. His mantra was always *go for it and we'll figure it out as we go along.* Being with him made me braver."

Erica put her plate down on the table. "That's a nice thing to say about someone."

"Yes. And when he died, I forgot how to be brave. For the last couple of years I've been playing it safe because I didn't have the belief in myself that he had. I relied on him to tell me everything was going to work out. I suppose I'd let myself believe that he was the one who was going to make it work out. Instead of building up my own confidence, I leaned on his. And after he died I told myself that I was keeping things the way he'd wanted them because it was a way of keeping him close." She paused, suddenly seeing things more clearly. "The truth is I kept things the way he'd wanted them because I was afraid. I was afraid to do things the way I wanted to do them, in case I messed it up. There would only be myself to blame."

Anna stirred. "And now?"

"I'm not proud of the fact that it took Chef Tucker walking out and Stephanie being her usual inflexible self to make some changes, but at least I did it." She sat up straighter. She shouldn't need Brent in order to be brave. She should be able to do that for herself. "I feel better for it. More in control. Ready to make decisions and take responsibility instead of needing someone else to tell me what to do. I'm grateful that the three of you were here." She was sure she wouldn't have done it if they hadn't been there. "I don't think I'm good with change. You cling desperately to the familiar, to what you know, because even if it's not great it seems more appealing than the unknown. I've always taken what I believed to be the safe option, but I was deluding myself. There is no *safe*, because life continually throws in the unexpected. Does any of this make sense?"

"Yes." Erica spoke quietly. "It does."

It felt good to talk about it. "Being a mother increases the pressure. If I get it wrong, it affects Delphi, too. I'm not just responsible for the inn, and for myself, I'm responsible for a child. And sometimes that feels huge."

Anna's smile was wistful. "It certainly does."

"It isn't only the practical stuff, like worrying if I'll make such bad decisions I go out of business. It's the emotional side of things. The way I handle myself. Children see everything. And they copy. They see the way you react to things. They learn from it." She thought how much she'd learned from her father. "It's important to me that Delphi sees me being resilient, but also I need her to see me handling change even when it feels scary and hard. And change often is scary and hard, isn't it?"

The three women were silent and she had a feeling she'd struck a chord.

"Yes." Anna's voice was thickened. "Change can be very

hard, particularly when it's something you haven't chosen. You want to freeze time."

Hattie saw Erica glance at Anna and had a feeling there was more to the comment than simply an astute observation on human behavior. Either way, Anna was right about sometimes wanting to freeze time. That was essentially what she'd done since Brent had died.

And she realized that everything she'd been applying to the inn applied to the rest of her life, too. She'd been standing still, as if by not moving on she could somehow keep Brent with her.

"Obviously, I didn't know Brent," Erica said, "but I'm sure the man you describe wouldn't have wanted you to be feeling this way. He sounds as if he was the bold, adventurous type. He'd want you to get out there and live life to the full."

"Yes, he would." And it was what she would have wanted for him, too, had their situations been reversed. She wouldn't have wanted him to pause his life. She would have wanted him to make the most of the life he'd been given.

And finally, she saw it clearly. It wasn't a betrayal to him to make small steps forward, to move on. It would have been a betrayal not to. She owed it to him to live a full life and not let her decisions be driven by guilt or fear.

She felt lighter inside. "It's good to talk to you. Thank you."

"Good to talk to you, too. We, the Hotel Book Club, are always available for advice and bonding sessions. So this date with Noah—" Claudia cleared her throat. "Sorry, I mean this not-a-date with Noah, where are you going?"

"I don't know. He said he'd book somewhere."

"That's romantic."

Hattie laughed. Noah was more down-to-earth and practical than romantic. "He probably just didn't know at the time. Which brings us back to this dress." But she no longer had doubts about the dress. She didn't want to melt into the background. She didn't want to play it safe. She wanted to wear a dress that made her feel happy, and this dress most definitely did that.

Anna waved a hand. "The dress works wherever you end up eating. It's agreed. We're doing hair and makeup and you are going to enjoy a guilt-free evening."

"And if he kisses you," Claudia said, "you are going to kiss him right back. I bet that man is a seriously good kisser."

This time Hattie said nothing. She already knew he was a seriously good kisser, but that wasn't something she was willing to share. Some feelings were hers and hers alone.

But maybe instead of hiding from what had happened, it was time to address it.

TWENTY-ONE

Erica

Erica hauled the sled to the top of the bank, following Delphi, who was, quite evidently, a great deal more experienced at this than she was. The padded jacket she'd bought for the trip felt bulky and unfamiliar. It wasn't flattering and it was a long way from her usual choice of clothing, but at least it was doing a good job keeping out the cold.

She paused to draw breath, feeling the freezing air fill her lungs. All around them were trees and beyond the trees the mountains. Below her the ground fell away in a gentle slope all the way to the gardens of the inn, the fresh layer of snow turning hedges and plants into frozen sculptures.

Erica had never been on a sled and couldn't quite believe she was doing it now. When she'd suggested Delphi pick an activity, she'd expected to find herself coloring, or reading, or enjoying some other quietly thoughtful occupation. But Delphi had wanted to go outdoors.

"She loves it out there." Hattie had tucked Delphi into multiple layers and helped her pull on snow boots. "She's an unstoppable bundle of energy. After a day at kindergarten, it's what she needs."

Erica had managed to pretend that playing in new snow in temperatures capable of freezing human skin was exactly what she needed, too.

Fortunately, Anna had been keen to join them and the three of them had trudged round to the back of the hotel and then up to the top of the slope, which Hattie assured them provided first-class and very safe sledding. Anna had gone first, whooping her way down the hill while Delphi cheered. And now it was Delphi's turn.

Trying to be a responsible aunt, Erica turned to warn her to be careful but Delphi was already on the sled and speeding down the hill toward Anna. A kaleidoscope of possible catastrophes filled Erica's head, but Delphi made it to the bottom without mishap and then it was Erica's turn.

Hoping that next time Delphi would pick coloring as an activity, Erica straddled the sled. From this angle the slope seemed steeper than she'd first thought. For a second she felt something close to fear, and then laughed at herself. A five-year-old had just gone down the same slope without hesitating, and here she was wondering if it was a good idea. It made her realize that her life was far too sanitized and controlled. She spent too much time inside soulless glass offices and luxury hotels.

She breathed in the sharp, cold air and decided she needed to get outdoors more. Maybe instead of hotel gyms, she'd start running. Maybe she'd learn to ski. Jack skied and was always talking about how the concentration required meant that, for him, it was the ultimate form of relaxation.

Feeling thoroughly unlike herself, she pushed off. She could see Anna and Delphi at the bottom, waving, and behind them the inn with its pretty windows and balconies.

For the first couple of seconds the sled crawled and Erica thought *this is fine*, and then it suddenly gained speed. How was it going so fast? She whooshed down the slope, gasping and then giggling because she felt thoroughly out of control and she never, ever felt out of control. Was she going to stop? Had Delphi gone this fast? She heard Anna yelling something about using her feet as a brake but before she could do anything she somehow hit a bump and finished the run on her back with the sled on top of her.

She lay there for a moment, the air knocked from her body. Snow found the gap between her jacket and her skin and slid in frozen rivulets down her neck.

Delphi was clapping her hands and dancing with delight. "Isn't it *fun*, Aunt Erica?"

Erica pushed the sled away and stared up at the sky, trying to work out what she'd broken. "So much fun."

And then she started to laugh because actually it had been fun and she couldn't believe she was lying here, covered in snow, with a five-year-old grinning down at her. And having started laughing, she couldn't stop. Her sides ached and she couldn't breathe properly but still she laughed in a way she couldn't ever remember laughing before.

Delphi started laughing, too. "You have snow in your hair. You look silly, Aunt Erica."

"Do I? Good. It's a good thing to not take yourself too seriously."

And she did that a lot. Everything in her life was serious. Instead of focusing on the moment, she focused on consequences. And it was her job to do that, to look into the future and predict what crisis might derail a client's long-term plan, but since when had she lived that way in her personal life? *Since always.*

Anna hurried over, concerned. "Are you all right?"

"I've never been better."

And she realized with a disturbing flash of clarity that she didn't have enough fun in her life. She enjoyed reading, she loved relaxing in a spa, she enjoyed the theater and she was addicted to the rush of adrenaline that was part of winning a big piece of business, but the only thing in her life that came close to giving her that feeling of dizzying lightness that had come from rushing down that slope against a backdrop of Delphi's excited yelling, was the time she spent with Jack.

"You need to steer," Delphi said helpfully, "then you won't fall off. I'm going again." Without waiting for either of them to reply she shot up the slope again, all energy and determination, dragging her sled behind her.

Anna was shaking her head. "What happened to you?"

"According to Delphi, I didn't steer."

"I'm not talking about your skill on the mountain, I'm talking about all this laughter. I can't believe you're enjoying this. It's not you at all."

"I know. Which just goes to show we don't always know what's good for us, because I can't remember when I had more fun." She held up her arm for help. "Remind me, where is the nearest hospital?"

"You're in the middle of nowhere. No hospital." Smiling but bemused, Anna tugged her to her feet. "You're really having fun? I assumed you'd be fantasizing about shoe shopping in Manhattan."

"Shoes are nice, but shoes have never made me laugh so much my sides hurt." Erica tried to brush the bulk of the snow from her jacket but it was a losing battle. "I'm having a good time."

Anna watched her with a strange look in her eyes. "You look like a different person."

"No, I'm the same person—just colder than usual. I'm not used to taking lessons on something from a five-year-old."

"She's so funny and adorable." Anna glanced up the slope toward Delphi, who was getting into position for another run. "And you're great with her."

"You mean she's enjoying my humiliation?"

"No. I mean the fact that you were prepared to join in even though this was the last thing you wanted to do says a lot."

"And the fact that I'm having a good time says a lot, too. It tells me I need to do more of this." Erica stamped the snow from her boots and Anna looked at her curiously.

"More winter sports?"

"More things that make me laugh." Erica removed her gloves and shook out snow that had managed to wedge itself inside. "I need to do more things that bring me joy."

Anna checked on Delphi, gave her a wave and then turned back to Erica. "You mean like spending more time in bed with sexy Jack?"

Despite the snow, Erica felt warmth spread through her. "Maybe. And maybe also time out of bed."

Anna's eyes widened and she pressed her hand to her chest in an exaggerated gesture of shock. "You don't mean—a relationship?"

Erica accepted the teasing. "I enjoy his company, which is the very reason I've been reluctant to see more of him."

"That only makes sense to me because it's coming from you." Anna slid her arm through Erica's. "You're scared that you might end up needing him."

"Relationships are scary." Erica turned to her and shrugged. "I don't expect you to understand. You make romance look easy."

Anna's smile faltered. "I do understand. There are so many things that can go wrong, and when you love someone the stakes are so much higher. And romance—love—is never easy."

It wasn't the response she'd expected.

Erica stared at her friend. "Is everything all right?"

"Fine." She waved at Delphi again, who was positioning herself to attack the slope again. "You struck the jackpot with this place. The views are incredible."

Romance—love—is never easy.

In all the years she'd known Anna, she'd never heard her say anything like that before.

When it came to relationships, Anna was everyone's role model.

Erica peered closer and noticed how tired Anna looked. Why hadn't she noticed it before?

"Are you sleeping okay?"

"Me?" Anna turned. "Fine. You?"

Erica floundered. Anna was usually so open. "Great. Comfy bed." She knew something was wrong but didn't know how to encourage Anna to talk about it. Was this how her friends felt about her? She made an instant promise to herself to try to be more forthcoming. But as for Anna, she'd just have to wait and hope that eventually she'd tell them. "It's a pretty place, although I might need to rethink my clothing if these outdoor activities are going to be the norm. How long does it take for frostbite to form?"

"What you need is a hot bath, and fortunately, you have time for one before dinner."

Erica liberated another chunk of snow from the neck of her jacket. "A hot bath sounds good. Claudia won't be joining us for dinner because she's cooking, but we could meet in the library for a drink before we eat? I know you'll want to call Pete first."

Anna said nothing and when Erica glanced at her she saw she had tears in her eyes.

"Anna?" Concerned, she took Anna's arm. "Tell me what's wrong."

"With me?" Anna rummaged in her pocket for a tissue. "I'm not the one that managed to fall off a sled on a baby slope." She pulled her hand out and her shoulders sagged. "I don't have a tissue."

Erica dug into her own pocket and pulled out a packet. "Here. Take the lot."

Anna sniffed and pulled one out. "You never carry tissues."

"I thought I might need them as I'm looking after a five-year-old. I'm following your example of being prepared for all things. Tell me what's going on. You were quiet at dinner last night, and again at breakfast this morning. And you went for a long walk on your own this morning."

"Well, you had to make work calls, and Claudia was in the kitchen so I thought I might as well get some fresh air." Anna blew her nose hard.

"Aunt Erica! Anna!" Delphi's voice carried through the cold air. "Watch me!"

Anna immediately beamed and waved her arms. "We're watching!" She brushed away the tears and whooped as Delphi shot down the slope toward them.

Erica marveled at her ability to always set aside her own feelings and put on a bright smile for the child.

"Are you missing home? Thinking of Christmas?" She started in the obvious place, a wild stab in the dark, but Anna shook her head.

"No, not at all." She kept her eyes on Delphi. "This place is so festive and being with you two, my best friends—" she cleared her throat "—it's perfect."

Now she was sure something was wrong.

Erica wished she were more intuitive. She needed Anna's skills. "Is this about the kids leaving home? All that talk about change with Hattie has upset you?"

"No." But this time Anna's smile was a pathetic imitation of the real thing. Seeing raw misery, Erica put her hand on her arm.

"Anna—"

"Ignore me. It's just something Pete said a few days ago. Oh, look at her go! She has no fear. Meg was exactly like that. Nightmare." Anna clapped her hands as Delphi careered toward them.

Erica wanted to ask what Pete had said, but Anna was running to meet Delphi, all smiles and encouragement, and Erica followed, accepting the fact that Anna clearly didn't want to talk about it.

She watched her friend with Delphi, seeing the warmth and the interest. Anna was so natural with children. So completely happy and absorbed by them. It wasn't hard to understand why she'd be sad at the prospect of her own children leaving home.

She frowned. Was Pete annoyed that Anna had come away with them so close to Christmas? No. Pete was the most laid-back person ever, and he'd never tried to control Anna. So what had happened?

She wanted to ask but at that moment Delphi came barreling toward her.

"Aunt Erica! Did you see me?" She wrapped her arms around Erica's legs and hugged her tightly.

Erica felt a rush of warmth. It was impossible not to respond to Delphi's affection. "I saw you. You were brilliant."

"I love going fast. Shall we go again?" Delphi's pleading look was hard to resist.

Erica glanced at Anna, who gave an overly bright smile.

"Why not? It will be dark soon. Let's do it."

They hauled themselves back to the top of the slope for a final run, and this time Hattie met them at the bottom with Rufus and deftly persuaded Delphi that it was time to come indoors.

Delphi insisted on holding Erica's hand. Erica had no idea what she'd done to deserve such unreserved acceptance and was surprised by how good it felt.

"Aunt Erica," Anna whispered into her ear and flashed a quick smile as she headed toward the stairs and the sanctuary of her room. Erica looked at the slump of her shoulders and saw Anna check her phone quickly and then put it away again.

"Anna, wait—" Erica wanted to talk to her, but Anna didn't pause.

"See you for drinks." And then she disappeared around the curve of the stairs and Erica couldn't follow because Delphi was tugging at her hand.

"Do you like hot chocolate?"

Erica tore her gaze away from Anna. It was no use pretending she wasn't worried. Anna was the steady one, the one who soothed them when they were in a crisis. Even with her friends, she sometimes played the role of mother. If there was a problem, she talked about it. She was straightforward and easy to read. Which added to Erica's anxiety, because right now she couldn't read her.

"Aunt Erica?" There was another tug on her hand and Hattie crouched down in front of her daughter.

"Aunt Erica is here on vacation with her friends, so we have to let her have some time on her own."

"I'm her friend, too, and I like playing with her."

Erica felt pressure in her chest. "Hot chocolate sounds good." Anna had made it clear that she wasn't ready to talk about whatever was bothering her, so she might as well enjoy a little more time with Delphi. "Let's do that. Then I'll go and take a hot bath and get ready for dinner."

For the first time in her life she was starting to understand the pleasure Anna derived from simple interaction with young children. To be with Delphi was to witness unfettered happiness in the moment. Whether it was careering down a slope on her sled, coloring a picture or making hot chocolate, she managed to turn each activity into a moment of joy.

Adults, Erica thought, *could learn a great deal from children*.

Hattie rose to her feet. "You drink hot chocolate?"

She hadn't had hot chocolate since she was a child, but what harm could it do? She was freezing, so at least it would warm her up. "On snow days, I most definitely do."

By the time she made it back to her room it was dark outside and the snow was falling again. Erica stripped off her outer layers and hung them to dry and then went to run a hot bath. As steam gathered she sat on the edge and added bubbles.

She'd always lived an independent, single life. When Anna had talked about wanting a family, Erica had simply wanted to be able to focus on her career. She'd never been able to imagine deriving the same satisfaction from a family that she did from her job. But now she was wondering.

Aunt Erica.

Hearing those words should have unsettled her, but oddly enough they hadn't.

Reflecting on that, she stripped off the rest of her clothes and slid into the bath. The heat warmed her frozen limbs. If playing in the snow was going to be a more frequent occurrence, then she needed to rethink her wardrobe. So far, she hadn't given any thought to what happened beyond the end of this week.

It seemed strange to think that only a few days before she'd been planning to leave without ever even introducing herself to Hattie. She'd been longing to get back to her uncomplicated life in Manhattan, but she no longer felt that way, although she still had to figure out what should happen next.

Aunt Erica.

She grinned and added more hot water to the tub. She had no idea how to be an aunt. So far, she'd followed all Delphi's leads, but she should probably try to do better. There had to be books on the subject, surely? Was an aunt supposed to be fun and do all the things a mother would frown at, or was she supposed to be firm and a disciplinarian?

She stepped out of the bath, wrapped herself in a large towel and stared at her phone.

The urge to call Jack was almost overwhelming. Should she invent a function she wanted him to attend with her? Think of a different excuse?

No. This was ridiculous. She was forty. Too old to play games. Jack was a straight talker and so was she. If she wanted to call him, she should simply call him.

And say what? That she was regretting not letting him stay that last time they'd been together?

Impatient with herself, she walked back into the bedroom and dressed for dinner.

She took time over her hair and makeup and then took a deep breath and picked up the phone.

He answered almost immediately. "Erica?"

Hearing his voice made her stomach flutter and sent a slow warmth through her veins.

"Hi."

"How's your week with your friends? Are you painting each other's toenails and having midnight feasts?"

The image made her smile. "Is that what you imagine we're doing?"

"I have no idea what you're doing, but I'm having fun picturing you lounging around in your underwear, so don't ruin my day by telling me you're wearing a ski jacket zipped to the neck."

She'd forgotten how much she enjoyed talking to him. There were few people she felt so comfortable with.

"I'm sorry to break it to you, but a few hours ago I was wearing a ski jacket zipped to the neck. Also, I went on a sled. And no, I'm not joking."

There was a pause. "Why would I think you were joking?"

"Because we both know I'm not a sled type of person. I doubt I would have agreed to it if the person I was with hadn't been so persuasive, but they were, so I did. And I had fun." She walked across the room and chose a pair of boots for the evening. "Are you surprised?"

"That you're capable of letting go and enjoying the moment? Not at all. I've always known you have hidden layers." He paused. "Tell me more about the person who persuaded you to get in touch with your inner child—is he a six-foot-four ski bum with overdeveloped shoulders and bulging arms? I want a description of my rival. Would I win in a fight?"

Her skin tingled. The word *rival* suggested that she and Jack enjoyed an intimate relationship. She was surprised how much she liked the sound of that.

"That depends." She pulled on her boots. "What's your weapon?"

"A laptop and a fountain pen. I slay with both. Also a photographic memory and words. I win with words."

She imagined him in his office, seated behind a large desk with acres of glass behind him and the whole city spread beneath. His shirt would be crisply ironed, and his jacket would fit his shoulders perfectly. Jack was always immaculate. When he walked into a room people noticed, although he had a gift for putting them at ease. He was always calm and in control. She couldn't imagine him being wiped out on a sled or threatened by a rival.

"My companion is five years old. Unless you happen to know a lot about sharks or dinosaurs, you won't win in the conversation stakes."

"I happen to have an encyclopedic knowledge of dinosaurs, and I am confident I would be able to hold my own in an interrogation on the Jurassic era. So, Ms. Chapman, what's your favorite dinosaur?"

"Excuse me?"

"Your favorite dinosaur. Everyone has one."

She walked to the window, smiling. "They do? In that case, tell me yours."

"Velociraptor." He didn't hesitate. "They're smart, quick on their feet and not afraid to kill."

"You mean they are the lawyers of the dinosaur world."

Jack laughed. "Maybe. Now it's your turn."

"I don't know. I'm new to this. Help me out. The only one I know is a T. rex, but it's a savage meat eater, which is frankly gross, and I've always been put off by tiny arms."

"No tiny arms. Noted. I'm going straight to the gym after this conversation. Hold on a moment—" There was a pause and she could hear voices in the background and then the click of a door closing. "Sorry about that. There are people who think I'm here practicing law, so I have to keep up the pretense. Where were we? Oh yes, dinosaurs. I think you'd like the diplodocus."

"Is that a savage meat eater?"

"No, it's a herbivore. Intimidating on the outside, but gentle on the inside. A bit like you."

"You find me intimidating?"

"You're forgetting I've seen you naked. No one is intimidating when they're naked."

She hadn't forgotten. In fact, she'd thought about it a great deal more than she would have liked.

"I had no idea you were a dinosaur expert."

"If you'd asked me when I was seven I could have told you anything you wanted to know. I wanted to be a paleontologist for a short time, until I realized that the ratio of digging versus drama was heavily loaded toward the former."

Their conversation was still light, but they both knew they were dancing around something much more serious.

"So—" He broke the silence. "I assume you called for a reason. Give me the date."

"The date?"

"Of the event you want me to attend. Black tie?"

She was invited to so many things, most of which she didn't accept. It would be easy to pick one and use it as an excuse to get together.

But she didn't want to make an excuse.

"I don't have a specific event in mind. That wasn't why I called."

"Then why don't you tell me why you called?" His voice was like a caress, and she pressed her fingers to her neck, imagining the brush of his mouth against her skin.

"The last time we saw each other—" She paused, swallowed. "I've been thinking about it."

"Mmm?"

She stared out the window, wondering why she was finding this so hard. "I was thinking that next time we get together, you could leave a few things at my place. A toothbrush. Whatever."

There was silence, and for a moment she wondered if he'd heard her.

"Jack? Are you still there? I said—"

"I heard what you said, Erica." The way he said her name made her catch her breath and then she felt a moment of breathless panic.

"You probably don't want to. You're very independent and you like your own space as much as I do and—"

"Erica." There was a smile in his voice. "Breathe."

"Oh." She pressed her hand to her chest. She could feel her heart thudding. "I'm breathing."

"Why would you think I don't want to?"

She felt as uncertain as a teenager embarking on her first relationship. "Because that isn't what we do."

"That isn't what we've done up until now, but I seem to recall being the one to suggest I stay last time we were together." His voice was low-pitched and intimate. "Remember that evening?"

She closed her eyes. "Yes."

Thinking about it brought a rush of heat to her cheeks. Jack, his mouth on hers in the shower. Jack's hands spinning magic over her quivering body. It had been overwhelming and she'd wanted him to stay almost as much as she'd wanted him to leave.

"I wanted to stay," he said. "I've wanted to stay for a long time."

She opened her eyes, feeling as if she was seeing the world for the first time. "How long?"

"Months."

"And you didn't say anything?"

"I was playing it cool. I know you're cautious about who you let into your personal space."

Her legs felt wobbly and she sat down in the chair. "Jack?"

"Yes."

She licked her lips. "What if I were to invite you into my personal space?"

"You have no idea how long I have waited for that invitation. Where are you now? Vermont. How long would it take me to get to Vermont? Too long, dammit, and I have a meeting in an hour and I'm in court tomorrow morning. Anyway, you're with your girlfriends and if you haven't had a pillow fight yet you probably still need to schedule that in. I don't want to intrude on your book club week. When we're together, I want your full attention."

She felt awareness tighten in her stomach. "I have a suggestion."

"Make it."

She took a deep breath. It was a crazy idea. "You don't have to say yes." And it suddenly occurred to her that there was so much about his life of which she knew nothing. "For all I know you're seeing someone else—"

"There isn't anyone else, Erica. Just you. And I'm saying yes. Now you just need to tell me what I've said yes to."

Just you.

She closed her eyes. Maybe it was a crazy idea, but she was going with it.

TWENTY-TWO

Claudia

"I've connected with two of our suppliers this morning. You have a brilliant network here." Claudia sat in a corner of the kitchen with Hattie, going through plans for the week.

"It really mattered to me that we kept things local as far as possible. And it's a way of supporting and becoming part of the community. We all need each other." Hattie took a sip of her coffee. "This cappuccino is delicious, by the way. And the chocolate Christmas tree on top is art. Did you do it?"

"I have hidden talents." Claudia opened a file and pushed it to Hattie. "I was thinking that we should make more of what you're already doing. Tell people about it. At the moment we tell people where their food is coming from, which is great, but we could do more."

Maybe she shouldn't have said *we*. After all, the inn belonged to Hattie, not her.

She held her breath as Hattie picked up the file and turned the pages.

"You've done a detailed background of each supplier. Photographs. Their story. It's so human. Real." She turned another page. "A map of how to reach their farm."

"Only the ones who offer tours and sell to the public," Claudia said quickly. "I'm not suggesting we encourage stalkers. And obviously, we would need to check with them first. It would be collaborative. I thought maybe in the summer we—you," she corrected herself, "could have evenings when you showcase the produce of a particular supplier. And maybe offer cookery classes to small select groups. Just an idea."

"It's a brilliant idea." Hattie flipped the page and smiled. "You've included the Petersons."

"Good photo of Noah, don't you think?" She saw Hattie's cheeks turn pink.

"Yes."

Claudia didn't probe. It really wasn't her business and she was the last person to offer advice on relationships.

"Are we inviting suppliers to dine in the restaurant? Because we should."

"Involve them more?" Hattie was scribbling frantically. "You're right. This is all great, Claudia. Can I ask you another favor?"

"Of course." Claudia finished her coffee. "Anything."

"I've written a job description for the head chef job. Would you take a look?"

Claudia felt her bubble of enthusiasm deflate. She hated the idea of someone else taking over the kitchen at the Maple Sugar Inn, which was ridiculous because she was on vacation and leaving in a few days. "Sure. Email it to me. I also thought maybe we could—" She broke off as her phone rang. "Sorry. I thought I'd switched it off." She picked it up and saw "John" on the caller display.

John?

Her mouth dried and her fingers shook slightly. They hadn't spoken since the day he'd walked out on their shared life six months earlier.

"Take it. We can finish this later." Hattie stood up. "I'll give you privacy."

Claudia didn't ask how Hattie knew that this phone call needed privacy.

She waited for Hattie to leave and then took the call.

She said nothing, because she honestly didn't know what to say.

"Claudia? Claudy?" His use of his pet name for her made her wince. Pet names were for people who cared for each other, and he'd made it clear he didn't care for her.

"What do you want, John?" All the misery and insecurity she'd spent six months blocking out came rushing back.

"It's good to hear your voice."

Her knees shook and she felt a rush of longing and immediately hated herself for it. This man had treated her with no respect. "If you'd wanted to hear my voice, you could have contacted me at any time."

"I'm sorry. I behaved badly and I know I have a lot of work to do to persuade you to forgive me. How are you?"

How was she? She'd been doing just fine until she'd answered this call. And what did he mean, forgive him? What made him think she'd forgive him? And why did he want her to?

"What do you want, John? Why are you calling now, after six months of silence?"

"You're angry. I can understand that. I wasn't expecting this to be an easy call. I deserve everything you throw at me."

If he'd been in the room there were plenty of things she might actually have thrown at him. "I'm busy. Can we make this quick?"

"Where are you? I expected you to be in the apartment when I arrived, and my key isn't working."

She tightened her grip on the phone. "You're in the apartment?"

"Outside our apartment, which apparently, I can no longer access. Is there a problem with the locks?"

"I had them changed." She sent silent thanks to Erica, who had arranged it. "And the apartment ceased to be *ours* when you moved out with no warning and stopped contributing to the rent." For the past six months it had been a roof over her head, nothing more. "As for where I am—I'm away with Erica and Anna. Book club."

She had no idea why she'd told him that, except perhaps to prove that she was still living her life. That his actions hadn't broken her.

"Doesn't that happen in the summer?"

"We couldn't arrange it in the summer." *You left me. I was a mess.* "You still haven't told me why you're calling."

And suddenly she wondered. Was this about Trudy? Was he calling to say he was getting married? Her stomach lurched.

"I want you back, Claudia."

The room spun. She must have misheard, surely? "Sorry?"

"I want us to be together. And I know this is probably a shock."

A shock?

She wanted to say something cutting but her mind was blank.

"Claudia? I know you're mad with me. I don't blame you. I don't know what happened to me, but I'm going to spend the rest of our lives making it up to you."

The whole conversation was unbelievable.

"Where does Trudy fit into this little arrangement?"

"Trudy was a mistake. But maybe I needed to be with Trudy to realize you were the one for me."

Was she supposed to send Trudy a thank-you note?

"Claudia? You've gone quiet. I'm saying that I want us to be together again. Forever."

Forever.

She was being offered her old life back. She could move back into their apartment, get another job and settle down to California living. With John. Her John.

She stared out the window. Except he wasn't her John, was he? The past few days with her friends had made her realize that their relationship had been far from perfect. She'd mistaken the length of a relationship with quality, but now she could see all the ways in which it had fallen short.

She thought about him slamming the front door on the day that he'd left, ignoring her entreaties that he at least talk to her. Despite their years together, he hadn't even shown her that basic courtesy. Respect, affection, consideration—where had they been on that day?

Where were they now? Surely he didn't really think that all he had to do was make a call and she'd come running back?

"I'm sure you're overwhelmed," John said. "Take a moment. I love you, Claudia. We're good together."

"You love me?" She tried to keep the sarcasm out of her voice. "When did you decide that?"

"I've always loved you."

Anger mingled with incredulity. "You cheated on me. You betrayed everything about our relationship." And she knew now with absolute certainty that she didn't want him back. She didn't want to reconstruct her old life. She was excited about her new life. The one she'd tentatively started living. And John wasn't part of that. She'd had no choice in any of the things that had happened to her this year, but now she had a choice.

She pressed her fist to her mouth, not knowing whether to laugh or cry. She felt ridiculously powerful for the first time in her life.

"Claudia?"

"Ellen and Tilda in the apartment above us have a spare key. I'll message them and tell them to give it to you. Do what you want with the apartment, John. Keep it. Don't keep it. Whatever. I don't care. I won't be coming back there. I'll send someone to pack up my things."

"You can't mean that."

"I do mean that."

He made an impatient sound. "Is this some kind of petty revenge because I did the same thing?"

"No. This will no doubt deliver a bruise to your ego but I'm not even thinking about you right now. I'm thinking about me." She stood up, smiling. "I don't want to fly all the way to California simply to leave again once I've packed up my things. I can outsource that, but thank you for giving me the idea. You taught me how to take all the emotion out of a breakup."

"I made a mistake, Claudia, I admit it." He sounded desperate now. "And I wish I could explain why I did it, but—I don't know," he breathed. "Maybe it was hitting forty. Shook me up a little, you know?"

"Age isn't a reason to cheat on your partner."

"I regret that deeply. And I don't expect you to forgive me overnight. I know I'll have to work hard to earn back your trust."

"Don't bother. I really don't care what you do or who you do it with. Sleep with who you like. We're not together."

"Is there someone else? Are you in love with someone?"

It was typical of John to assume that the only reason she wouldn't want to be with him was because she'd found someone else.

"There's no one else. I'm not in love." Or maybe she was, in a way. She thought about the past few days, the fun she'd had with her friends, the excitement of stepping in and working in the kitchen, the buzz she felt discussing ideas with Hattie. The hope she'd felt when she thought about the future. She was in love with the idea of a new life.

"But you wanted to get married—"

"I'm pleased we didn't. You weren't the right man for me. I should probably thank you for making me see that. Now I have to go—I have a job to do. Don't call again." She ended the call and blocked his number. Then she read the email she'd been waiting for and went in search of Hattie.

She was talking to Chloe, but excused herself as soon as she saw Claudia.

"Are you okay?"

"I really am." She felt as if she'd taken a massive step forward. "I need to talk to you about that job description."

Hattie studied her face. "You don't think it works?"

"It works." Claudia took a breath and channeled all her newly discovered energy and confidence. "I'd like to apply."

Hattie stared at her. "You?"

"I realize that you'll want to see who else is interested," Claudia said, "go through an interview process, although I do advise that whoever you consider offering the job to, you ask them to cook something for you because the proof of the pudding really is in the eating in this case. But I'd like to be considered."

"Wait—" Hattie rubbed her fingers across her forehead. "Your home is California."

"It's not my home. I have a rented apartment, which is easily dealt with. I'm free to go anywhere I'd like to go—" she paused "—and I'd love that to be here. And I don't want you to feel pressure. It's important that this time around you hire exactly the person you think would be right for the job. Someone who can make your vision for this place come alive."

"Claudia—" Hattie interrupted her. "If you're telling me you'd like the job—that you want our arrangement to be permanent, then the answer is yes." She gave a disbelieving laugh. "A big yes."

"Really? You probably want to think about it."

"I don't need to think about it. I'd love you to join the team. How could you doubt it? We think alike. We want the same things. We're both excited to try new things. I can't wait to brainstorm more ideas with you." Hattie's eyes shone. "You coming here is the best thing that has happened to me in ages."

Claudia felt a lump form in her throat. She hadn't been anyone's best thing in a long time.

"You need to get out more."

"I intend to." Hattie gave a smile. "My big date is tomorrow."

"Right. Hair and makeup time." Claudia straightened her uniform. She felt energetic and ready to go, as if someone had changed her batteries. "So you're interested in making this permanent?"

"More than interested. I'll sort out a contract right away. What about accommodation? After you and your friends check out, we're fully booked but you're welcome to stay in the Sugar Shack behind the inn. It's not fancy, but it's warm and comfortable. Brent intended to do it up and turn it into a rental to give us another strand of income, but Chef Tucker insisted that we provide him with accommodation as part of his package, so he was living there. You're welcome to it."

"I don't want to deprive you of an income generator."

"For now it's sitting empty. I'd love you to use it. I'll ask Chloe to make sure it is cleaned and stocked."

"Chloe has enough to do. I'll do it myself this week. It will be fun. Thank you." She was already planning what she could do with it to make it feel like home.

"I'm the one who should be thanking you." Hattie sighed. "You've saved me."

Claudia thought about the kitchen, with its gleaming pans and spotless work surfaces. She thought about the first moment she'd seen the inn, cloaked in snow and dressed for the holidays.

In a way, she hadn't been honest with John. She was in love, but not with a man. She was in love with a place, this special, wonderful place and the people who worked here. She was in love with the promise of a future, a future that excited her.

She took a breath and smiled at Hattie. "I'm completely sure that you're the one who has saved me."

TWENTY-THREE

Hattie

Noah picked her up—not in the family truck with *Peterson's Christmas Trees* emblazoned on the side, but in his own car, which was sturdy enough to cope with all weathers and all challenges. A bit like Noah himself, Hattie thought as she slid into the passenger seat. She was sure that somewhere behind her Lynda and Delphi had their faces pressed to the window, watching. She didn't look. This was nerve-racking enough without acknowledging her audience.

"Are you warm enough?" Noah looked at her, gloved hands on the steering wheel as he waited for her to fasten her seat belt. The streetlight sent a wash of light across the interior of the car, highlighting the thick layers of his hair and his broad shoulders. His gaze lingered on hers for a moment and then he smiled. "You look great."

"Thank you." She decided not to admit that Erica and Anna, with Delphi acting as chief assistant, had spent an hour on her hair and makeup.

"You also look nervous. It's just dinner, Hattie. A relaxed evening with a friend. And it's no one's business but ours." He reached across and squeezed her hand and she sat for a moment, feeling the reassuring pressure, and thinking about that night in the barn, remembering the heat, the need, the sheer desperation and the giddy realization that she was still capable of feeling something that wasn't sad or dark.

And she realized that she wasn't nervous of what people would think, but of what she might feel.

"A relaxed evening sounds good. Just what I need." She croaked out the words, feeling a delicious rush of anticipation. Would she even be able to eat? There was so much tension in her stomach she doubted there was room for food. "How is your mother?"

He let go of her hand, started the engine and headed toward the road. "Annoyingly interfering, but don't worry about that. Hopefully, she won't follow us to the restaurant and spy on us through the window."

She laughed at the thought of it. "I love your mother."

"She loves you back." He stopped at an intersection. "But that doesn't mean she isn't capable of overstepping."

She remembered her dad telling her that it didn't matter how old your child was, they were still your child. "I expect she does this to you all the time. Tries to engineer dates."

"This is the first time." He kept his eyes on the road, leaving her to handle that revelation.

If Lynda had never interfered before, why now? Why her?

She stared at the side of the road, focusing on the gleam of snow picked out by the headlamps. She was overthinking things as usual. Dinner with a friend. That was it.

And it was good to leave the pressures of the inn behind for an evening.

Good to be with Noah.

The interior of the car was snug and her coat was thick and warm. Underneath those layers of wool she could feel the sensual slide of the green dress against her skin.

"I thought we'd get away from town," he said, "that way we

can both relax, and you won't be worrying about who might be watching."

"I don't care who is watching." She turned to look at him and saw the hint of a smile tug at the corners of his mouth.

"That's a relief, because no matter how careful we are we can probably guarantee that next time we're in town for something, we're going to be asked if we enjoyed our evening."

"I'm sure you're right."

"I turned my back on big city living a long time ago, but I'm still getting used to the fact that folks around here know everything about you, and most likely everywhere you have visited in the past couple of weeks. Take yesterday—" He adjusted his grip on the wheel. "On my way to deliver a couple of trees to a family who lives on the other side of the valley, I called at the pharmacy to pick up painkillers for my father. His shoulder bothers him when the weather is cold. There were only two other people in the place, but by the time I returned home he'd had several phone calls, a casserole delivery, a tray of freshly baked brownies and several offers of help on the farm."

She had no trouble believing him. "That's great, but imagine if you'd been picking up something embarrassing."

"Obviously, I'd drive to Boston. If it was *really* embarrassing I might have to fly to Alaska."

She found herself relaxing. "When I discovered I was pregnant, Brent and I decided to keep it to ourselves for a while, but someone had seen me buying the pregnancy test."

"Don't tell me—you arrived home to find a baby outfit on your doorstep?"

"Almost. On my next trip into town, four people asked me how I was. And one actually pointed out that it would be a lot of work having a baby while trying to renovate the inn and start a business."

"I bet you wish you'd thought of that."

"Indeed. It's sometimes aggravating, but more often it's heartwarming." She preferred to focus on the positive. "I like the human connection. It makes me feel as if I'm part of something. Maybe it's harder if you have something to hide."

"I'm sure it is. It would be hard to conduct an illicit affair, for example. If you tried climbing out of someone's window to avoid being seen, you can be sure someone local would be standing there with a ladder."

"Are you speaking from experience?"

He smiled. "I prefer relationships where I can walk through the front door. And now tell me about the rest of your week. I was half expecting you to cancel. Too busy."

She'd almost canceled a million times, not because she was too busy but because she was afraid. Afraid of herself. Afraid of where this might go, or where it might not go.

She knew instinctively that Noah could change her future.

"Not too busy. In fact, tonight is the first night in a long while that I've felt confident that I can leave the place without worrying that someone will walk out while I'm gone. Thank you for your messages checking on me. That was kind." She didn't tell him that she'd kept her phone with her constantly, and reread those messages multiple times.

"I was worried about you. I wanted to know you were all right. And you do seem all right." He took the road that led to the next town. "Fill me in."

She told him about Erica, and how Delphi had somehow bridged the awkwardness between them. And then she talked about Claudia and about how Chloe had blossomed in the few days she'd had full responsibility. "Stephanie thought I should fire her, but she's proving to be more than an asset now that Stephanie's gone."

"People are often capable of more than they think, particularly when they're given responsibility and allowed to use their initiative."

"Yes." She wondered if they were still talking about Chloe. "How about you? Christmas is your busiest time."

"It is. Everyone wants a Christmas tree, although this year

we've done well in the shop selling wreaths and the small pot-grown trees."

They were driving along snowy roads, through small towns and past houses coated with snow and framed with lights.

Hattie felt a warm glow of contentment, and for a brief moment she felt the same childlike rush of excitement she'd had when she was young and contemplating Christmas, and it cheered her to know she could still feel that, that it was still there, because for so long she'd been afraid it had gone forever.

"I used to love Christmas. It was my favorite time of year."

It was a moment before he responded. "And now?"

"I'm looking forward to it. And Delphi is beside herself. Pretty soon she'll be counting hours, not sleeps."

"Will Erica be staying on now that you're getting to know each other?"

It was something she'd wondered herself. "I doubt it. She is a busy woman. She probably has plans. I get the impression she's not the type of person who gets dizzy about the holidays. She wrote a letter to Santa. Her first one ever."

"She did that?"

"Yes. She did it for Delphi, who was shocked that she'd never written."

"She's gone up in my estimation." He glanced at her, curious. "What did she ask for in this letter?"

"I don't know. They wouldn't tell me. Nor do I have a clue what Delphi asked for." And it was bothering her. "If I don't know, how can Santa bring it?"

"I hope that's not a question you're expecting me to answer because we've definitely strayed beyond the scope of my expertise."

"I don't know why she won't tell me. She always tells me." She frowned. "I just have to hope she loves what I've chosen for her."

"And how about you? What do you want Santa to bring you?"

The question made her smile. "I think I'm low on Santa's list of priorities."

"You're always thinking about other people. How about thinking about yourself for a change?"

For the past few years she hadn't had the luxury of being able to put herself first. Even before Brent had died, they'd been so busy renovating the inn and then building the business that all she'd wanted Santa to bring her was a good night's sleep.

But tonight, for the first time, she had no one to think about but herself.

And it had been so long since she'd had an evening that was all hers, not shared with the inn, or even with her daughter, whom she loved deeply but whose presence allowed little in terms of personal space. And while being busy was good and had helped her to get through each day, she wondered if it had also kept her stuck in the same place. It was so much easier to do what needed to be done than contemplate an alternative.

"I am thinking of myself," she said. "That's why I'm here."

But why was *he* here? She didn't know much about his dating life, but it was impossible to live in a town like this one and not hear things. There had been rumors about Noah and one of the local doctors, and she knew from comments she'd overheard that plenty of women were interested, but she'd never seen him with anyone. She didn't know if he'd loved and lost, or never loved at all.

"We've arrived." Noah swung the car into a space outside a restaurant that glowed with festive charm. Surrounded by pine trees, the mountains rose behind it, the snow luminous in the moonlight.

Hattie sat for a moment, absorbing the atmosphere. "What a perfect place. It looks like a log cabin. I feel as if I'm in Switzerland. How did I not know about this?"

"You haven't exactly been getting out much. But hopefully, we're going to change that."

She looked into his eyes and felt a jolt of heat. *A relaxed evening with a friend,* he'd said, but she was pretty sure he didn't look at any of his friends the way he was looking at her at that moment. And he was making it sound as if this dinner wasn't a one-off. As if this might be the beginning of something and not just a single night.

She was surprised by how much she hoped that was the case.

"Careful." He closed the car door and extended a hand. "The path might be icy."

She took his hand, thinking that the heat currently pounding from her would melt any ice in a moment.

"You've been here before?"

"A couple of times. In the summer they have tables out on the deck, overlooking the river and the mountains. It's a pretty place and the food is excellent."

Who had he come here with? Had he sat across from the doctor, looking at her the way he was looking at her now?

She pushed the thought away. They were both too old to be bringing the past into the present. That was life.

He opened the door to the restaurant, and they stepped inside. Instantly, she was enveloped by the cozy atmosphere. Delicious smells drifted from the kitchen. There was an open fire, and fairy lights and foliage artfully twisted over thick wooden beams.

"This is wonderful." She felt the heat from the fire and unfastened the buttons on her coat. "The only place I've eaten in the past year that isn't my own home or yours is Delphi's favorite pizza place. I hope I can remember how to order something that doesn't have toppings and come ready sliced."

She caught a glimpse of her reflection in the large mirror that stretched the length of one wall behind the tables and stared for a moment because she didn't recognize this glamorous version of herself. It was like meeting an old friend after years of absence and searching to find those aspects that were familiar.

Her eyes looked bigger thanks to Anna's expertise with makeup, and her hair, usually close to unruly, tonight looked artfully creative.

She handed over her coat to the girl who was hovering, and saw Noah looking at her in a way he never had before. Or maybe he had, just once, on the night of the Halloween party. She'd seen the same hungry look in his eyes in the fleeting seconds before she'd kissed him, when two glasses of "witches' brew" and a deficit of human contact had eradicated all traces of self-control.

She rubbed her palms over the fabric of her dress, feeling suddenly self-conscious. "Too much? You can blame Delphi. I started with my standard safe black dress, but she said it was boring. You've probably noticed that five-year-olds aren't subtle. To win her approval, something must either glow in the dark or sparkle."

"You're doing both." His voice was husky. "Remind me to thank Delphi when I see her next." Before he could say anything else they were interrupted by a woman who appeared from the kitchen.

"Noah?" She approached with a bouncy stride and gave him a warm, unselfconscious hug. "This is a treat. Why didn't you tell us you were coming? We would have reserved you our best table."

"Didn't want to make a fuss. And all your tables are great, Sophie." He kissed her on both cheeks and introduced Hattie.

She liked the fact that although he obviously knew the place well, he hadn't asked for any favors. That was Noah. Quiet. Decent.

"You brought a date? Welcome." Sophie studied her, and Hattie saw the curiosity there, but it was friendly curiosity.

"Thank you. This place is wonderful."

"And now it's my turn to thank you." She beamed. "Wait— are you the same Hattie who owns the Maple Sugar Inn?"

"Yes."

"Congratulations. That place is incredible. My partner and I stopped by for breakfast just yesterday before we went to the Christmas market. Your new chef is a treasure. If you weren't a friend of Noah's, I might try and steal her from you." With a wink, she gestured to a table in a quiet alcove by the window.

"You should take this table." The girl who had been waiting to seat them started to say something, but Sophie waved her away. "It's fine. I'll deal with it."

They sat down and Hattie wondered whose table they'd just taken.

"Menus." Sophie provided them with a flourish. "Or you could just ask me what I recommend, and I'd tell you to go for the seafood bisque, followed by the beef."

"She's a control freak," Noah said mildly. "You don't have to agree."

"Seafood bisque and beef sounds perfect." Hattie handed the menu back and Sophie smiled her approval.

"Allergies?"

"None."

"Good. What can I bring you to drink?"

Noah looked at Hattie. "Champagne?" There was something in his eyes that she couldn't read, and not being able to read him unsettled her. She was used to feeling comfortable with Noah.

"Champagne would be great." She felt a little breathless, as if she was balanced on the edge of something.

Sophie walked away and Hattie watched her for a moment. "She's friendly. You know her well?"

"Pretty well. We've been supplying the restaurant for years, and they buy their Christmas trees from us. She's a good customer. Took over the place from her parents a few years ago, and has been gradually making changes. That was tough at the beginning. They'd built this place from nothing and didn't understand why she needed to change anything."

"They took it personally?"

"It's always delicate working with family." He paused as Sophie delivered two glasses of champagne with a smile and then melted away discreetly.

Hattie watched the bubbles rise. "Are we celebrating something?"

"The moment. Christmas. A night off." He lifted his glass and smiled. "Take your pick."

"The moment sounds good to me." She took a sip. "I remember you telling me you had some lively discussions with your father when you first joined him."

"That's true, although I'm the first to admit I didn't handle it well." He put his glass down. "I wince when I think about it. My dad probably does, too. I like to tell myself I was young, but I know that's a pretty poor excuse."

"You were twenty-three?"

"Twenty-four. After I graduated I worked at a tech startup in Boston. In those first few years I thought I was going to change the world."

"I can't picture you living in a city."

"When I was growing up, it was all I could picture. This place felt—" he paused "—small. Compressed. I lay awake at night dreaming of escape."

"Was your father disappointed that you didn't want to join him in the business?"

"Maybe a little, although he never showed it. He and my mother were very supportive. They knew I needed to follow my own path. They were wise." He stroked his fingers along the stem of the glass. "I think they knew I'd be back. It was just a question of when. It took a couple of years for the shine to come off city life. I realized I was coming home more often, to ski and hike. I missed the mountains and the trails. The clean air. I missed having family close by. Then Dad had his accident and that was that. I decided to come home. It wasn't something I needed to think about. I knew right away." He gave a half laugh. "I think it was the excuse I'd been looking for. It saved me having to admit that the city wasn't for me after all."

"But you tried it. You had a dream, and you followed that dream. That's important. If there's something you want to do, you should do it and if it doesn't live up to expectations then—" she shrugged "—at least you know. Better that than spending your life wishing you'd done something and wondering if you would have been happy or not. But I'm guessing it wasn't an easy transition."

"I tried too hard. Wanted to prove myself. When I came back they had a computer, but barely used it. I changed all that, which led to some friction until I managed to show Dad how much time I was saving him. The turning point was when I persuaded them to buy a drone, so that they could monitor crops and our small dairy herd. Dad thought it was great. It was a game changer. I think that was the point where he realized I could bring something to the business, and I realized how much he knew. We started listening to each other."

Their food arrived, deep bowls of creamy seafood bisque with walnut bread served fresh from the oven.

"Do you think you'll ever go back to Boston?"

"To live? No." He picked up his spoon. "This is home now. I love it. It started as an escape, but now it's where I want to be. Demand for organic produce has grown, and I enjoy being involved in the whole process—in this area it really is farm to table. How about you? How are you feeling about everything now?"

She gazed at him and a feeling of warmth spread through her body. "Despite everything that happened with Stephanie—or maybe because of it—this week has been the most I've enjoyed work in a long time. Working with Claudia has been brilliant. We've already made some changes. It's exciting."

"It's good to hear you talking about the place as if it's yours." He looked at her across the table and she felt something shift and wondered if he felt it, too. She'd known Noah for years, but somehow tonight felt different.

She felt glad to be here. Not guilty, or uncomfortable, or even sad, and maybe those emotions would come back later, but right now they were absent and it gave her hope that when she fell down into the hole of grief again, she'd be able to pull herself out.

"Buying the inn was Brent's idea, but I fell in love with it, too." It was time to be honest with herself. "We viewed it in spring and it was glorious. Moved in the summer and spent a few happy months working on the place and hiking the trails. It was idyllic. And then our first winter we had that crazy nor'easter and lost our power. Then there was a bomb cyclone. I was pregnant with Delphi—"

He pulled a face. "I remember that winter. We lent you a generator."

"You did, and I'm forever grateful because without it we probably would have frozen to death. I'm British and we're not used to extreme winter weather so the whole thing was a bit of a shock. But it also taught me the strength of community. We'd only moved in that summer, but people treated us as if we belonged."

They talked about that winter, and more about Noah's experiences learning about the farm, and Hattie shared how hard those early days had been when Brent had been driven more by enthusiasm than knowledge.

"After he died, I didn't know how I was going to cope. I didn't know how I could give Delphi the attention she needed and keep it all going. It felt like too much."

"And now?"

"This week I've had a glimpse of how the future could be. Some of that has been working with Claudia. She has so many ideas, and talking to her has reawakened all the ideas that I had back at the beginning."

"Maybe you should offer her a permanent job."

"I did. And she said yes." She still couldn't quite believe it. "We agreed to it yesterday. We have big plans."

"I'm pleased." He leaned back in his chair and smiled. "It's good seeing you like this."

"Like what?"

"Energized." He hesitated. "I can't really imagine how difficult the last couple of years have been for you."

"It has been difficult. I'm grateful to have Delphi. And grateful to have people like your parents, and the rest of the community."

And him. She was grateful for him but this didn't feel like the right moment to tell him that. She'd wait until they were alone, until they were no longer surrounded by people.

Instead, she focused on the meal as they ate their way through a menu of delicious food. After the bisque there was rib of beef, slow roasted with vegetables sourced from the Peterson farm, and for dessert they shared a wickedly indulgent chocolate cake, with cinnamon cream and fresh berries.

They talked about the farm, and the inn, and about family and how life so rarely worked out the way you thought it was going to, and by the time she'd finished her coffee Hattie had forgotten that she'd ever felt self-conscious or unsure about this evening. She didn't want it to end.

They headed to the car and she settled herself in the passenger seat.

"I'm glad we did this tonight. I had a brilliant time. You've been a good friend, Noah. The best." On impulse she leaned across, intending to kiss him on the cheek, but he turned his head and his lips brushed against hers.

She felt a sharp jolt of awareness and pulled back. "Sorry. I didn't mean—"

"Why are you sorry?" His mouth hovered close to hers. "I was the one who kissed you. And I did mean it."

She looked into his eyes and saw something that made her stomach tighten. "Noah—"

"That night of Halloween—" he stroked his thumb across her jaw "—maybe now would be a good time to talk about it."

"Did you just say...?" She broke off, replaying his words in her head. *I did mean it.* Her heart was hammering. "I thought you regretted it. I embarrassed you. I grabbed you—probably because I drank the witches' brew on an empty stomach."

A smile touched the corners of his mouth. "Deadly stuff.

Remind me to give you a crate of it for Christmas." He slid his fingers through her hair. "What made you think I regretted it?"

"You never mentioned it again. We've been avoiding the subject."

He eased away so that he could look at her properly. "Because I thought that was what you wanted. You seemed—conflicted. I didn't want to do, or say, anything you weren't ready for. I didn't want you to feel at all awkward around me."

"That was why you never mentioned it?"

He gave a faint smile. "Honey, if it had been up to me I'd have been kissing you a hundred times a day since that moment in the barn." His hand was still in her hair, his thumb still tracing a seductive line across the edge of her jaw.

Her heart almost punched its way out of her chest.

"You would?"

"Yes, Hattie, I would. You really didn't know that?" He studied her face for a long moment. "Maybe our nonverbal communication isn't as good as it could be."

"That's entirely possible."

He paused. "We should probably work on that."

"Yes." She felt breathless, and when he slowly lowered his mouth to hers she stopped breathing altogether.

Memories of their last kiss were alive in her head, but this time the uncontrolled wildness was replaced by leisurely discovery. He cupped her head with his hands, holding her steady while his mouth tantalized and teased. Heat ripped through her. Her body ached, and she kissed him back with the same hunger he was clearly feeling. She felt his fingers on the buttons of her coat, followed by a rush of cold air and then the skilled touch of his fingers on her breast.

Her heart was pounding against his hand, her mouth urgent against his. She tried to shift closer but their movements were restricted by the car. She heard him curse and then ease away from her.

"You're shivering—I'm sorry." He tugged the coat around her and switched on the engine.

"Don't be." She tried to tell him that right at that moment she would have been happy to roll naked in the snow with him, but her brain didn't seem capable of forming a complete sentence.

He grabbed a blanket from the backseat and tucked it around her and then he pulled her against him again, but this time to warm her up.

"The car will heat up soon."

"I don't care." She was pressed against his chest and could happily have stayed there forever. Sadly, that wasn't an option. "We should probably get back."

"I know." He released her reluctantly and sat back in his seat. There was tension in his shoulders and he let out a long breath. "I suppose there's no point in me telling you that there's a route to my barn that doesn't go past the main house?"

Never had she been so torn between duty and desire. "I said I'd be straight home after dinner. I don't want to take advantage of your mother."

"And now I'm wishing we'd skipped dinner and settled for a bottle of wine and a bag of potato chips at my place." His voice was low and rough and it was obvious that his frustration matched hers.

She thought about how much she enjoyed his company, their conversation, his quiet humor, the way he loved Delphi. She thought about the way he made her feel when he kissed her and she thought about how much she'd enjoyed the evening they'd just spent together and how she didn't want it to end.

And she smiled and touched his face with her hand.

"A bottle of wine and a bag of potato chips sounds like the perfect second date."

TWENTY-FOUR

Anna

Anna stared into the fire, wondering why she didn't feel warm. She was wearing the sparkly sweater she'd bought on her shopping trip with Erica but so far she didn't feel remotely festive.

"This has been the strangest, most surreal book club week ever." Claudia stretched out on the sofa in the library and put her feet on Erica's lap.

Erica pushed them off. "Our friendship has limits."

"I thought you loved me?"

"Not enough to have your feet on my lap."

Claudia rotated her ankles. "My feet are tired. I've been standing on them all day."

"Exactly." Erica moved to the sofa next to Anna, leaving Claudia to stretch out full length. "Right. Do we have anything more to say about the book or are we done?"

On the low table that sat between the two sofas was a bottle of wine and glasses, a cheeseboard and their copies of the novel.

"I'm done." Anna had said all she wanted to say about the book. Right now she was clinging to her belief in love and romance. She didn't want to think about relationships that had gone wrong.

"I'm done, too," Claudia said. "And I have something to tell you."

Erica reached forward and poured wine into the glasses. "I hope it's something profound and life-changing."

"It is. Anna, are you okay?" Claudia waved her hand in front of Anna's face. "You're quiet. Is it the book? Next time we'll pick a romance. Your choice."

"I'm fine." She could feel Erica looking at her, waiting for her to tell them what was wrong, but she still wasn't ready to talk about it. Instead, she focused on Claudia. "Tell us your news."

"It's major." Claudia rubbed her calves. She looked tired but happy. "First, I have a new job."

"What?" Anna was stunned. "Where? What?"

"Here. You're looking at the new chef for the Maple Sugar Inn. Good food guaranteed and produced in a wholesome, tantrum-free environment." Claudia was almost glowing. "I've had so much fun this week. Working with Hattie has been brilliant. She's smart and full of ideas. We think the same way, and we're a good team so we're making it permanent."

Erica was smiling. "That's *great* news. Congratulations."

"Yes." Anna was delighted for her friend. "So this means you won't be going back to California?"

"That's my second piece of news. I had a phone call earlier. John."

Erica spilled wine on her skirt. "After six months of silence? You hadn't blocked his number?"

"I wasn't ready to cut him out of my life, and I'm glad I didn't. It was a good phone call."

Anna handed Erica a napkin for her skirt. Like Erica, she was worried about Claudia, but she was determined not to judge. All relationships were complicated; she knew that. And Claudia had needed some closure. "It must have been upsetting for you to talk to him after all this time and everything that has happened."

Erica was less tactful. "You shouldn't have taken his call." She pressed the napkin to her skirt and watched as it slowly turned red. "I've ruined my favorite dress. Why did you tell me that when I had a glass in my hand?"

"At least your dress is black. And I'm pleased I took his call."

Erica made a sound that was somewhere between a grunt and a growl. "What did he want after all this time?"

"He wanted to get back together."

"Oh, Claudia—" Anna bit her lip to stop herself expressing her horror at the very idea.

"No need to *oh, Claudia* me. That isn't happening."

"Good." Erica reached for a fresh napkin. "But why didn't you say so right away instead of creating all this tension? And why is it that a glass of wine feels like nothing when you're drinking it and a massive lake when you spill it?"

"Hush." Anna put her hand on Erica's arm so that Claudia could finish her story. "What happened?"

"I know you think I shouldn't have talked to him, but it was the right thing to do. When he walked out, he was calling all the shots. I felt as if I hadn't been given a choice."

"You hadn't." Erica dropped the napkin on the table. "He walked out without a discussion."

"I know. And it has been hard, and then losing my job, too—" Claudia took a deep breath. "It made me feel helpless and out of control. But being here this week, spending time with you two and falling in love with cooking again, I realized that I have plenty of control over what I do next."

Erica examined the stain on her dress. "I can't believe you took his call."

"We were together for ten years. We had no closure, and I wanted to hear what he had to say. And it wasn't what I expected."

"Don't tell me—he loves you," Erica did a fair imitation of a breathy voice "—he made a big mistake, he wants you to forgive him so that you can both live happily ever after."

Anna nudged her. "Of course he didn't say that. Drink your wine, Erica, instead of spilling it on yourself."

"Actually, he did say that," Claudia said. "Or pretty much that."

Erica stared. "Seriously?"

"Yes. I was shocked, too. I wasn't expecting him to come crawling back. And it was strange, because my thoughts have been so tangled up and all over the place lately. I've been angry, I've been sad, I've been confused—but while he was talking, everything cleared in my head."

"And? There are more cliff-hangers in this story than in Catherine's book."

Claudia snuggled into the cushions. "After you've been with someone a while, it's easy for everything to become a comfortable habit. It's not like the first flush of romance, but you tell yourself that's normal in a long-term relationship. I thought I was happy—" she frowned "—maybe *content* is a better word, and when he walked out it was a terrible shock because I didn't see it coming, but now I realize there were plenty of things wrong with our relationship. Things I just accepted and didn't think about. Being with you two this week brought that home to me. The things you've said about Pete and Jack have made me realize that what I had with John wasn't as great as I thought it was. And really, I should have known things weren't right. The fact that he changed the subject whenever I mentioned marriage should have given me a clue. And I never forced the issue, which should probably tell me something, too."

Anna had often wondered about that. "If he had asked you, would you have said yes?"

"I don't know. The truth is we had settled into a comfortable habit. Our life together was okay, but not great. My work paid the bills, and it was what I was trained to do. And I never challenged that, either. Like my relationship, I accepted *okay* in my work as normal. People don't get excited about their jobs when they've done them for a while, right?"

Erica reached for her glass. "I'm usually excited by my job."

"You're not normal," Claudia said. "Anyway, I was approaching forty, and I suppose I thought that excitement is for the young. And then John left, and I lost my job. But now I can see it was the best thing that could have happened. Without all that I'd still be living that life instead of being here at the beginning of something new and exciting."

"Slow down!" But Erica was smiling. "You need to breathe."

"I suppose what I'm saying is in a way he did me a favor. If he hadn't made the move, would I ever have done it? I'd like to think I would, but if I'm honest I think I'm too much of a coward to make those big changes myself," Claudia admitted. "I'm not the sort who walks out of a job when it isn't working. I stick with things. I needed change to be forced on me. And now here I am."

"Did John really expect you to welcome him back?" Erica shook her head. "Unbelievable."

"I know. He actually sounded broken up when we finished the call. And I'm obviously a horrible person because I was a tiny bit pleased about that. Not that I wanted him to meet a sticky end." Claudia gestured to Catherine Swift's book. "He wasn't *that* bad."

Anna's head was throbbing. "He hurt you."

"And also cost you a lot of money." Erica was ever practical. "He left you with an apartment that was too expensive for one person."

Anna frowned. "Is he going to move back there permanently?"

"I don't know and I don't care. That's for him to sort out. My new home is the converted Sugar Shack in Hattie's backyard. And the new love of my life is this place." She gestured to the bookshelves and the flickering fire. "Hattie and I are going to have fun."

Erica sat up straighter. "We should celebrate your new job

properly. Congratulations." She reached for her glass and Anna did the same.

"Congratulations." She didn't want to be a killjoy and admit she had a headache, so she took a tiny sip. "So no more relationships?"

Claudia shrugged. "I'm not saying never, but if it happens then I'll be more discerning. I suppose I aspire to have what you and Pete have. Sure, you've been together a long time but there's still a spark. You make each other laugh. You tease each other. You're pleased to see each other. You always treat each other with respect and do thoughtful things. Pete even cooks for you sometimes. Do you know John never cooked a meal for me in all the time we were together? You're the perfect couple." She spread her hands. "Even saying all this aloud is making me envious."

The perfect couple?

Anna felt emotion rise up so quickly she couldn't contain it. It overwhelmed her, pushing past her defenses.

"Anna?" Claudia sat up and swung her legs off the sofa, horrified. "What's wrong? What did I say?"

"We're not the perfect couple. I've hurt him." Anna covered her mouth with her hand, giving up all pretense that she was fine.

"Who have you hurt?"

"Pete. He thinks about me constantly and I've been thoughtless, and careless of his feelings. I've done that terrible thing— I've taken him for granted." She felt regret and something close to panic.

"How? Anna, you adore Pete." Claudia's tone was calming. "We all know that. Pete knows that."

Did he? She frequently told him that she loved him, but what mattered more was showing it. Making him *feel* how much she loved him. And it seemed she hadn't done that.

She felt the sofa dip as Erica shifted closer and put her arm around her.

"Do you want to tell us what happened?"

"It's my fault. You know how much I'm dreading the kids leaving." She reached forward and grabbed the only tissue that hadn't been used to mop up wine. "And I've talked to Pete about it because we always talk about everything." She blew her nose. "And he listened, as he always does, but lately something felt off in our conversations."

"Off?"

"Little things. I didn't feel as if we were connecting in the way we usually do. And after our toy shop visit I was feeling a bit down so I called him and—" she could hardly bear to talk about it "—he basically said I was making him feel irrelevant."

"Irrelevant?"

"As if he doesn't matter. When I told him how much I was dreading them leaving, he took it personally. As if I was saying there was nothing left in my life. As if, once the kids have gone, that's it. He'd obviously been feeling it for a while and hadn't said anything. And I do focus on the kids a lot. I know I do. Probably too much. He's not wrong."

"The kids are a huge part of your life."

"I know." She paused. "It was so important to me to be a good mother."

"And you are. You have a great relationship with your kids."

"But at what cost? Pete and I used to be disciplined about date nights and spending time together but lately, whenever Pete suggested a weekend away, I almost always found a reason not to go. I think, subconsciously, I wanted to make the most of this time with the kids. Why do something just the two of us, when we could do it as the four of us? And I didn't even think about it. Everyone talks about work-life balance. Getting it right. But I didn't balance things in my family. And I can see that now, but I can't undo it."

"You're shaking." Erica put her hand over hers and squeezed. "So you had this conversation after we went to the bookstore. How has it been since then?"

"We haven't talked since. And that's unusual for us." Anna blew her nose again. "We've exchanged a few messages, but every time I call he doesn't pick up. Then he sent me a message saying he'd call when he had a spare moment. A spare moment? What does that even mean?" She could feel herself spiraling and tried to calm herself.

"Maybe he really didn't have a spare moment," Claudia said and shrugged when they both looked at her. "What? This is Pete we're talking about. Pete isn't a sulker."

"That's true." Erica gripped Anna's hand firmly. "One of the things I've always admired—envied—about you and Pete is your ability to always find a solution that works for both of you. I remember a conversation we had once when you told me that it's important to choose your battlegrounds. You told me that there were things about Pete that infuriated you—"

"The way he leaves his bowl on top of the dishwasher." Anna sniffed and tried to smile.

"And things that infuriated him about you."

"I'm always at least ten minutes late for everything."

"Exactly. But you both know when to let things go. The most important thing is that the two of you are good at resolving problems."

That was true, but this time she was the problem.

"Erica is right," Claudia said. "There's nothing you and Pete can't fix."

"I don't know." Anna used to believe that, but her confidence had been rocked. She was ashamed of herself, but also confused. "The thing is I *am* dreading the children leaving, and I can't pretend I'm not." But she could see now that she could have been more sensitive about it. She'd stomped in without once thinking how Pete might interpret her reaction.

Erica was silent for a moment. "You can love Pete and enjoy being with him and still feel sad about the kids leaving," she said finally. "He's a smart guy. Surely he doesn't think one emotion cancels out the other?"

"I don't know. But I can see why he'd be hurt." It was painful to admit it. "I've never once talked about the positive, only the negative. I've never said *Hey, Pete, we can go on a cruise, or spend a month in Paris learning French.*"

"Well, he has a job," Claudia said briskly, "so a month in Paris would be difficult."

"I need to fix this." Anna rubbed her throbbing head with her fingers. "I don't know how."

"You could book a posh hotel and buy new lingerie?"

"I think it's more complicated than that. I need to look at things differently. See opportunities instead of black clouds. Take this Christmas, for example. We have so many traditions and they're gradually slipping away. Instead of being excited, I'm thinking *what if this is the last time?* It feels like an ending." She extracted her hand from Erica's and poured herself a glass of water. "I don't know what to do. What am I going to do?"

"Don't ask us," Claudia muttered. "You're the relationship expert. You and Pete, you're—"

"Yes, except we're not." And she realized how badly she needed her friends to tell her everything would be okay. She needed to hear that from someone, preferably from Pete, but if not him then her friends.

But they didn't. They were silent, as if this tremor in the foundations of the one relationship they'd always regarded as rock solid had somehow shaken them, too.

Claudia shrugged helplessly. "I don't know, Anna. Erica? You're the crisis expert."

"Not a marriage crisis expert." Erica ran her hand over the back of her neck and breathed. "We all need to stay calm. Maybe if you did a couple of things differently, it would show him you'd paid attention to his feelings."

Their concern escalated Anna's own feelings of anxiety.

"Like what? I can hardly lie and say I can't wait for the kids to go to college."

"I don't know," Erica said. "But maybe it's to do with not clinging on to the little things. Claudia?"

"Why are you looking at me? My relationship fell apart without me even noticing it was happening. I'm the last person to help."

Erica floundered. "You were upset about the tree—the kids had plans, you wanted to stick to the usual. Pete suggested lunch."

"And that was thoughtful." Anna covered her face with her hands. "And I snapped at him. I should have been flexible. And appreciative that he was trying so hard."

Erica rubbed her back gently. "Maybe it is time to make new traditions instead of clinging to the old ones."

Anna let her hands drop into her lap. She felt exhausted. "Any suggestions?"

Erica shrugged. "Have an adventure."

"At Christmas?" Anna took a sip of water. "What sort of adventure?"

"I don't know. But do something different," Erica said. "That way you won't be sitting around wondering if this is the last time you're going to be doing it because it will be the first time. Take control."

"Also, you're seeing your life as this big empty void but there is so much you could do. You're great with kids," Claudia said. "Can't you do something with that? Volunteer at a school. Work in a library. You know every book there is. Set up a children's book club or something."

Anna stared at her. "A children's book club?"

"Yes, I'm sure your library would host it. They'd love it. Or maybe you can travel around schools. Be a mobile book club."

Anna felt something stir inside her. A children's book club. "I like that idea. No idea how it would work, but it's something to think about."

She was about to discuss it further when her phone buzzed. She picked it up and felt her heart beat faster. "It's Pete." Her fingers were so sweaty she almost dropped the phone. "He wants me to call him if I'm not busy."

"You're not busy. Call him. And then come back and tell us what happened because the stress is killing us." Claudia waved a hand toward the door. "We'll stay here and eat, and drink and discuss all the reasons women might kill their husbands."

"If we've finished talking about this book then I'd like to end the conversation by saying that I'm surprised she didn't kill him sooner." Erica picked up the book and gave Anna a gentle push. "Go. And give our love to Pete. Now then, Claudia, you and I are going to talk about how to kill a man and get away with it."

"I've always favored using food."

Anna rolled her eyes. "You two are delightful." But she appreciated their attempts to lighten the atmosphere.

She grabbed her room key and her purse and headed to the door.

"Hope it goes well." Claudia tried hard to sound casual and Anna could tell that her friends were now almost as tense as she was.

"Thanks."

She walked back to her room, wishing she'd had more time to think through exactly what she was going to say.

Her hand shook as she closed the door behind her and tugged off her boots. She'd been with Pete for more than half her life. He was her best friend and it was ridiculous to feel nervous, but still, she felt nervous as she held her phone and braced herself for the call.

In all the years they'd spent together, they'd never hit a bump as big as this one. Right now this felt like the most important conversation she was ever going to have. What if she said the wrong thing? And it shocked her that she could know someone as well as she knew Pete, and love someone as well as she loved Pete and yet still get it wrong. She closed her eyes, took a deep breath and called him.

"Hi there."

"Hi. Sorry I haven't been in touch before. It's been a little pressured here. Hold on a moment. Lola has found one of Meg's shoes and she's chewing on it. Lola! Drop it. I said—" There was a pause and the sound of Lola barking happily. "Damn. I thought nothing could go wrong in the five minutes it took me to call you. Where did she find that? I was careful. Sorry."

Anna wanted to ask which shoes, but then she decided she didn't care. Meg's shoes were Meg's problem. She didn't want to talk about Meg.

"If Meg left the shoes where Lola can grab them, then that's on her."

"It wouldn't have happened on your watch."

"Of course it would."

"We both know it wouldn't, Anna. You're great at all this. You're the perfect mother."

She sat down on the edge of the bed. She wasn't a perfect anything. "I've tried calling you a few times."

"I know, and I'm sorry it has taken me so long to call you back. You make running the household seem simple, but I'm not you. Things take me a while. And that's embarrassing to admit because how hard is it to wash a load of laundry without flooding the kitchen?"

"You flooded the kitchen?"

"Don't worry, we managed to dry it out, but when you messaged me there was no way I was taking your call and admitting to my incompetence."

That was why he hadn't responded? "But I messaged you yesterday, too."

"Yes, and I couldn't answer because I'd left my phone in the house."

"If your phone was in the house, where were you?"

"Not in the house." He sighed. "Locked out of the house."

"Locked—"

"Yes, locked. I closed the front door and forgot to pick up the keys. And I know you never do that because you're organized and great at doing nine things at once, but I'm a one-task-at-a-time kind of guy, and I was trying to get Lola out for her walk, and the phone rang as I was leaving and I was distracted—do you know what? It doesn't matter. But it meant that it was too late to call you by the time I was reunited with my phone."

"Sharon and Mike next door have our key."

"I remembered that half an hour after I broke in through the downstairs window."

She winced. "You seem to have had an eventful time while I've been away."

"Not my best week. And poor Daniel is having girl trouble, so I've been trying to be supportive."

"Girl trouble?" Even though she was determined to focus on Pete, she couldn't help feeling a flicker of anxiety for her youngest child. "Did he talk about it?"

"A bit. Not much. But I've got it covered. Don't worry about it."

"What did you do?"

"We played computer games. He destroyed me, naturally, something that Meg won't let me forget in a hurry."

She imagined them, side by side on the sofa, and the tight knot inside her slowly unraveled. Pete had shown Daniel that whatever happened he was right beside him. In his corner, always.

A lump settled in her throat. Sometimes she felt as if the kids were her responsibility, but that wasn't true, was it? Right from the moment they were born Pete had been looking out for them, too. And he was still looking out for them.

"Why didn't you tell me all this when we spoke?"

"About Daniel? Because I didn't need to. I knew you'd worry and I didn't want you to worry. I handled it. As for the rest of it, I'm proud and stubborn and I like to think I'm a modern man. But apparently, there are certain household tasks which defeat me, which is humiliating to admit. Somehow we've fallen into traditional roles. I take out the trash, sort out winter tires for the car and fix windows that won't open and clear the snow. You do everything else."

Anna felt love seep through her, filling every corner of her. "I'm glad you do those things, because I hate doing them. And who cares if we're ridiculously traditional when it comes to the domestic stuff? It works for us. We're happy with the arrangement. That's all that matters." Her eyes filled. "And you're forgetting to mention all the years you've trekked to the office even when the job has been horrible. You did whatever it took to support us, so that I could have my dream and stay at home with the kids." She thought about all the times he'd been there for her. All the times his calm, unflappable nature had made a bad situation better. He was strong, and kind, and good. And he was hers. "Oh, Pete—" The relief was so intense she felt shaky. "I'm so pleased."

"You're pleased I'm incompetent?"

"You're not incompetent. I'm pleased that's the reason you didn't call."

"What other reason would there be?"

"I upset you. Because all I've thought about lately is the kids leaving."

"I was upset, but that was my problem. Seeing you distressed about something I can't help with makes me feel helpless. Inadequate."

She was stunned. "Inadequate? How?"

"Because this is our family. It's my job to make sure everything is stable and everyone is happy. If one of the kids has an issue, I'm going to do what I can to fix it or help them fix it themselves. Same for you. But I couldn't see a way to help you with this."

Things suddenly started to make more sense. "Is that why you suggested another baby?"

"Desperate measures. I didn't know what to do, Anna. I wanted there to be a simple solution. I wanted us to be enough."

It was a struggle to hold back the emotion. "We are enough. More than enough."

"Remember that conversation we had in the kitchen when we were talking about the Christmas tree? You said you didn't regret having the kids. You said they were the best thing that ever happened to you and I agreed."

"Yes." She wondered where he was going with this.

"I was wrong." He paused. "The kids aren't the best thing that ever happened to me, Anna. You're the best thing that ever happened to me because without you there would be no kids. There would be no cozy, welcoming home. There would be no laughter and warmth. It's you, Anna. For me, it's always been you. You're everything."

You're everything.

She gave up trying to fight the emotion. Tears slid down her cheeks.

"You're everything to me, too. And I owe you an apology. A big one. I hurt you—" her voice cracked "—and I feel terrible about that. I was thoughtless and careless and I will never do that again. I don't know when I became so focused on the kids, but that's going to change. Yes, I feel sad about the fact that everything is changing, but I'm also excited. I'm excited about all the things we're going to get to do that we couldn't possibly have done when we had kids living at home. And I should have said that before now. I'm sorry, Pete." She'd used up all her tissues on Erica's wine accident, so she wiped her tears with her sleeve.

"Don't cry, honey." His voice was soft. "Honestly? It's good to know you're not actually perfect after all."

She gave a choked laugh. "What are you talking about? Of course I'm perfect." It was a relief to joke about it, a relief to feel that warmth between them once again.

"In fact, you are pretty perfect. After this week I think I'm understanding more about why you feel the way you do. This home stuff is all-consuming and sometimes I forget that. It's your whole world. It's more than losing your job, because normally, if you lose your job you still have a home. But in your case, home fills your life. I'm sorry I didn't really get that."

She finally found a tissue and blew her nose. "And I'm sorry if I made you feel for one second that you weren't enough. Or important. Or that I wasn't looking forward to exploring a new life together." Her voice cracked. "I love you so much."

"I know you do. And I love you." His voice softened. "What I said about having another baby—I know it was a wild suggestion, but I meant it. If that's what you want, let's do it."

This time the answer was easy. "It's not what I want, but thank you for always paying attention to my happiness."

"In that case, we need to start thinking about how we can make this transition easier for you."

She leaned back against the cushions, wondering whether to mention the children's book club idea. No. She wanted to think about it a little more first. "This week away has been good for that. It has given me some perspective. I need to accept that it's going to be an adjustment, and I need to just go with it and focus on other things. Maybe we can go back to Paris, and this time stay somewhere with a view and eat in romantic bistros instead of having a carpet picnic."

"I love that idea. We'll book the trip for just after we take them to college. That way we won't sit around the house moping."

"You think you'd mope, too?"

"I might, although obviously I'd do it in a manly way. I'd tinker with the car engine or barbecue something and I'd pretend to be the strong one. I definitely wouldn't confess that I'd messaged Meg five times to check she was okay."

She laughed. "Paris sounds like a good idea."

"And I was thinking more about how upset you were about our Christmas tree trip. I was too casual about it. I know how much you love our traditions, particularly at Christmas, so I'm going to try harder to make sure we keep those going."

"You weren't casual. I was clinging too tightly to tradition. What does it matter when we fetch the tree? I've been thinking a lot about Christmas generally, and I have a suggestion." The idea had come to her while she'd been talking to Erica and Claudia and the more she'd thought about it, the more she was convinced it was the perfect solution.

She hoped her family thought so, too. And as for the future—when the children finally left for college they'd learn to be Anna and Pete again.

Catherine Swift may have given up on romance, but Anna definitely hadn't. Sometimes when handling change you didn't need to do something dramatic or big. Sometimes you just needed to shift the emphasis.

TWENTY-FIVE

Erica

Erica zipped her suitcase and put it by the door. It was hard to believe a week had passed. Hard to believe that less than seven days ago she'd been looking for ways of escaping this ordeal.

There was a tap on the door and she opened it to find Anna standing there looking fresh and happy in a sweater the color of holly berries.

"Is that yet another new sweater?"

"Maybe. Possibly." Anna turned pink. "Suits me, don't you think?"

"It's the big smile that looks good on you." Erica picked up her coat and closed the door of her room behind her. "You actually had us worried for a moment. We're relieved to know that you and Pete are back to your normal state of sickeningly idyllic marital harmony."

"I can't wait to see him, although I'm going to miss you and Claudia."

"You'll see us again soon." She looked up as Hattie appeared in the corridor. "Any luck?"

"Yes." She beamed at Erica. "Just had a cancellation. A couple flying in from San Francisco has had a family emergency and they've had to postpone their trip, so I have a room for three nights. Does that work?"

Erica felt a little flicker of nerves. No turning back now. "It works."

Anna looked at her curiously. "You're coming back?"

"I am. Jack and I are coming here for a mini break over Christmas."

"What?" Anna's shriek carried along the length of the corridor. "That's the most romantic thing I ever heard."

"This is me we're talking about, so it probably won't be," Erica said. "You know I don't do romantic."

"That's a shame." Hattie was grinning. "I was planning on filling the room with giant pink heart-shaped balloons and I've already asked Claudia to make a cake—*Erica loves Jack*."

"Don't forget to fling rose petals over the bed." Anna was smiling, too. "This is great news. If you get lucky, you might even be snowed in for Christmas."

"I wonder if it's too late to check in somewhere else?" Erica wondered what sin she'd committed to end up surrounded by romantics. "And I don't want to be snowed in. That would be inconvenient."

"You're far too practical."

"And you're too much of a dreamer, particularly for a woman of forty."

"*Almost* forty." Anna lifted her chin. "And those forty years have taught me that romance doesn't have an age limit."

Erica thought about herself, and about Jack, and thought that Anna might possibly be right.

Not that she was going to admit that.

Instead, she looked at Hattie. "You see what I have to deal with?"

"I've given you the Mountain Suite," Hattie said. "It has an incredible view. I'll stock a fridge with champagne. You won't have to leave the bed."

Erica didn't know whether to laugh or scream. "Are you in league with Anna?"

"Not exactly in league, but like Anna, I'll take a happy ending wherever I can find one."

Erica had seen Hattie arriving back from her date with Noah and had a feeling her own happy ending wasn't too far in the future.

"The champagne is a nice touch but if I see a rose petal anywhere I'm checking out." She turned to Anna. "We're going to drive from Manhattan. Apparently, Jack often does that trip to ski in Vermont. We could visit you and Pete on the way if you're around, providing you promise not to interrogate him."

"I can't promise that," Anna said. "It so happens that we won't be around. We're going away."

"For Christmas? You always stay home for Christmas."

"Wasn't it your suggestion that I change some of our traditions? I decided that instead of Christmas at home, we'd come here. The kids are excited, and I'm even more excited now that I know I'm finally going to meet sexy Jack."

Erica's idea of a quiet, discreet few days away was vanishing into the ether. Was it a good idea to introduce Jack to her friends at this delicate point in their relationship? Maybe not. But on the other hand, if this really was a relationship, then it was going to have to include her friends. "Are you going to embarrass me?"

"I will try very hard not to, but it would be wrong of me to promise." A dimple appeared at the corner of Anna's mouth. "Apologies in advance."

"Claudia is planning a special Christmas lunch menu," Hattie said. "I can seat you separately, unless you'd rather share a table?"

Erica gave her friend a look. "If Anna promises to behave, we can share a table. If Jack is going to get to know me properly, he might as well know the truth about me early on. Including my questionable taste in friends."

"The kids would love that," Anna said. "Meg will fight to sit next to you, although she will do it discreetly while trying to look outwardly cool."

"I'd like to sit next to Meg." Erica glanced at Hattie. "Where will Delphi be sitting?"

"I always make myself available for guests," Hattie said, "so Delphi usually tags along with me. It's pretty informal. She and I usually eat in the evening, when everything has calmed down."

"Why doesn't she join us at the table? That way you can focus on work without worrying about her. She can sit on the other side of me." Erica tried to sound casual, but she could see Anna gaping at her. "What? I'm relying on her instruction to know how I'm supposed to behave on Christmas Day."

"You're sliding comfortably into the role of Aunt Erica." Anna winked at her. "I'll sit next to sexy Jack so that I can get to know him better."

"In that case, I'm sure our relationship will be over by the evening." It felt strange talking about Jack as if they were a couple, although if she was honest with herself they'd been a couple for a long time. It was just that she'd refused to acknowledge it.

There isn't anyone else, Erica.

"So that's decided, then." Hattie reached for Erica's suitcase. "Technically, you are still here as a guest, not as a family member, so I will take your case downstairs for you."

"Don't be ridiculous." Erica took the case back. "If you want to help someone, you could help Anna carry all her new sweaters."

They headed along the corridor and down the stairs, where Delphi was playing with Rufus.

"Aunt Erica!" She sprinted across to Erica and put her arms around her, squeezing tightly. "I hate it when people leave."

Erica ruffled her hair and felt a lump in her throat. "I hate leaving." She crouched down so that she was eye level with Delphi. "But I will be back for Christmas." Rufus put his paw on her cream coat and she made a mental note to buy herself a more dog-friendly wardrobe.

Delphi held on to her. "Do you promise you'll be back?"

Erica didn't hesitate. "I promise."

"Did you know that veggie eating dinosaurs had eyes on the sides of their head?"

Erica smiled. "I didn't know that, but I'm going to study hard before I see you next."

She was already looking forward to it.

TWENTY-SIX

Hattie

"Sorry I took so long. *One more story* turned into about ten more stories and I need to learn to be firmer. I know it's Christmas Eve and I wasn't expecting it to be easy, but I didn't think she'd ever go to sleep." Hattie collapsed onto the sofa next to Noah, who was stretched out comfortably. Her heart gave a little thump. She saw him all the time, but not like this. Not sprawled in her living room as if he was part of their lives. "What are you reading?"

"Delphi's dinosaur book." He closed the book and put it back on the table. "Did you know that a stegosaurus had a very small head compared to its body?"

"Yes. I know every word of those books by heart." Hattie leaned her head back against the sofa. "Please don't bombard me with any more dinosaur facts. Sometimes I dream about dinosaurs."

He raised an eyebrow. "You dream about dinosaurs?"

"They play a big role in my life. No ballet or dolls for me."

"Is that right?" He put his arm around her and pulled her closer. "Maybe it's time we gave you something else to dream about." His mouth hovered close to hers, and the look in his eyes was enough to make her forget the subject of their conversation.

Dreams. They were talking about dreams.

"I'd like to dream about something else." She felt as breathless as a teenager. "Did you have something particular in mind?"

He gave a slow smile. "How about sharks?"

She started to laugh but then he covered her mouth with his and kissed her, and she kissed him back until her heart was hammering and her stomach melting. She wrapped her arms around him, feeling the hard muscle of his shoulders under her hands. His kiss was raw and skillful, an intimate prelude to something deeper, more intimate, but they both knew that wasn't going to happen tonight.

Even consumed by pleasure, Hattie was acutely conscious of Delphi sleeping in the next room.

She pulled away reluctantly. "Delphi—"

"I know." His voice was roughened, and he pulled back and closed his eyes for a moment. "Give me a moment. Talk about something unsexy."

Unsexy?

"Er—did you know that a T. rex weighed around seven thousand kilograms?"

He opened his eyes. "Had he tried time-restricted eating?"

She smiled and snuggled closer, gazing into the fire. "I used to love Christmas."

He closed his hand over hers. "And now?"

"This year I love it again." She shifted so that she could look at him. "That's because of you. I can't believe you're here, in my living room, on Christmas Eve. It feels—"

"How does it feel?"

"It feels good. It feels the way Christmas is supposed to feel." She lifted her hand and traced his face, the roughness of his jaw, the silk of his hair.

He took her hand and kissed her palm. "It feels like Christmas to me, too."

"Delphi was so excited that you were here this evening. And you were adorable with her."

"Adorable?" Still holding her hand, Noah gave a mock frown. "I don't think of myself as adorable. I think of myself as a tough outdoorsman who can light a fire by rubbing sticks together while fighting off a bear."

She widened her eyes. "You've fought off a lot of bears lately?"

"About ten a day. Twenty on some days."

"Aren't bears supposed to be sleeping at this time of year?"

He shrugged. "They get excited about Christmas, just like the rest of us."

She leaned her head against his shoulder, feeling content, relaxed, for the first time in ages. "Do you remember when Delphi used to call you the Christmas tree man?"

His fingers tightened on hers. "I do. I was pretty happy with that title. Who wouldn't want to be Christmas tree man?"

Hattie paused, feeling as if she was balancing on the edge of something momentous. "She loves you, Noah."

"I love her back." He said it easily, without hesitation, and then pulled her gently to him. "I love you, too. Just in case you were wondering."

The words drove the breath out of her body. "Noah—"

"I don't have an agenda." He slipped his fingers under her chin and raised her face so that she was looking directly at him. "I'm telling you the truth, that's all. And now you're going to tell me you're worried about Delphi being hurt, but you know I'd never hurt her. I'd never hurt you, either, but I understand that it's complicated and that you're probably not ready. But I wanted you to know how I feel, so that if and when you feel ready, you can let me know."

"I love you, too." She had no hesitation in saying the words because they were true. She loved Noah. She knew that now just as she knew that the relationship wouldn't be easy, that she couldn't just delete her feelings for Brent, that guilt would ebb and flow. She hadn't thought she'd fall in love with another man, but it had happened and she could ignore that or she could embrace it as a gift and be grateful that happiness had come her way twice in a lifetime. "And I know you'd never hurt Delphi. You've been the very best friend to both of us." And she knew she'd never have to hide how she felt when she was with him. Never have to pretend that she was fine if she was having a moment of sadness, or guilt, or pain. Noah never tried to offer suggestions or *fix* as so many people did. He didn't minimize her pain. He didn't tell her that all she needed was time. He seemed to accept that some things in life were tough, and sometimes there were no shortcuts and you had to find your own way through it, and all anyone else could do was to listen and offer support.

"Hearing you say that is the best Christmas gift I could have had. I hope, one day, maybe there will be a place for me in your little family." He kissed her again, but slowly this time and she could have stayed like that forever, with his lips on hers and his words in her heart.

"You're already in our family." But the mother in her was still on duty and eventually, she eased away. "It's late, and Delphi will be up before dawn. You should leave, but I don't want you to leave. I don't want the evening to end." She was torn between her own needs and her responsibility as a mother.

"Me neither." He stroked her hair, holding her close. "What are you doing tomorrow?"

"It's just like any other day, but with Santa and presents and an overactive, overexcited child."

He raised his eyebrows. "I assume you're talking about yourself?"

"Naturally. Delphi is the restrained, adult one." She marveled at how conversations with him almost always made her smile. "After I have ripped open my presents with abandon, I will probably drink several large mugs of very strong coffee in order to set me up to serve Christmas lunch to a dining room full of guests, including my sister and sexy Jack."

"Sexy Jack? You think he's sexy?"

"Why? Are you jealous?" It was her turn to tease him.

"I don't know. Can he wrestle bears and chop down a tree?"

"I have no idea. I've never met him. Chloe was here when they checked in and they haven't emerged from the room since."

"Then how do you know he's sexy?"

"I don't. But that's what Anna calls him. I'm waiting to make my own judgment." And she was sure that whatever the mysterious Jack was like, he wasn't going to be as sexy as Noah.

"That decides it. I'm going to be here tomorrow, helping." He leaned toward her, intending to kiss her again, when they both heard a sound behind them. They jumped apart guiltily.

Flustered, Hattie smoothed her hair and jumped to her feet. "Delphi! What are you doing? You're supposed to be asleep."

"I tried but it didn't happen." Delphi ran to her, arms outstretched, and Hattie scooped her up, feeling the weight and the warmth of her, and her heart felt full.

"You have to sleep."

"I can't because I'm not sleepy. And anyway, Noah is here, which means Christmas has started."

"Christmas hasn't started and Noah was just leaving," Hattie said quickly and Noah obligingly stood and reached for his jacket.

"That's right. Just leaving."

Delphi shook her head. "He's not leaving. He can't leave."

"What do you mean?"

"He won't be leaving because he's going to be here in the morning when I wake up and that's likely to be very early." Delphi was breathless with excitement. "I knew that if I wrote to him, it would happen."

"If you wrote to who?" Hattie was thoroughly confused. "And Noah is coming to see us tomorrow, but he won't be here when you wake up. Unless you happen to sleep late." And they both knew that wasn't likely to happen.

"Yes, he will." Delphi was emphatic. "Because that's what I asked Santa for."

"You asked Santa?" Was this the mysterious *gift* that she'd been worrying about? "What exactly did you ask him for?"

"I told Santa I would like Noah to live with us. And because his gifts are waiting for me on Christmas morning, I guessed Noah would be here sometime during the night. And here he is." She squeezed her eyes tightly shut. "I'm not supposed to see my presents before the morning."

"In that case, I'd better take you straight back to bed. Say good-night to Noah."

"Good night, Noah."

"Good night, Delphi. See you in the morning."

Head spinning, Hattie carried Delphi back to her room and tucked her safely back into bed with her dinosaur. "Now, keep your eyes closed and you'll fall asleep. I love you." She bent and kissed her daughter and then tiptoed out of the room, leaving the door slightly ajar.

Noah was standing where she'd left him, in the middle of her living room with his coat in his hand.

"Apparently, you're her Christmas gift." She looked at him curiously. "Did you know about this?"

"No. If I'd known, I would at least have made sure I was gift wrapped. Worn a ribbon or two." He tugged her against him. "Does this mean I don't have to go home? If she's going to wake around five-thirty, it means I have to be back here by five. It's already almost midnight."

Hattie was still getting her head around the fact that her daughter wanted Noah to live with them.

"Why didn't she say anything to me before?"

"Probably thought it was between her and Santa." He wrapped his arms around her. "How about a compromise? To-night I'll sleep in here on your sofa. That way I'll be the first thing Delphi sees when she comes to find her presents under the tree in the morning. And after that? Well, let's just take this a day at a time."

"I'm not sure I'll get much sleep, knowing that you're just on the other side of the wall."

"That makes two of us. But I promise to keep my eyes shut so that Santa doesn't know I'm awake."

She laughed. "You're a real hero, Noah."

"I like to think so."

She slid her arms around his neck and kissed him, making the most of the moment. The present. And she was going to keep doing that. She was going to make the most of each day, not just because she knew it was what Brent would have wanted, and not just because she wanted to set a good example for her daughter, but for herself. Brent was gone, but she was still here. Damaged, bruised, but still here. She had Delphi, and the inn, and a whole community ready to offer support.

And she had Noah.

She smiled and buried her face in his neck.

That was the best gift.

EPILOGUE

Hattie

"That's the first time in my life I've eaten a Christmas lunch that I haven't cooked for myself. And what a lunch." Lynda folded her napkin neatly. "What do you think, Roy? Is it the best meal you've eaten?"

"Do you honestly expect me to answer that? Do you think I haven't learned a thing or two after all these years of marriage? If I say it's the best meal I've eaten then I offend you, and if I say it isn't the best meal I've eaten I offend Hattie and Claudia. So I'll simply say it was an excellent meal." Roy smiled at Hattie and glanced around the dining room. "And I'm not the only one to think so. All your guests look happy."

"Good." Hattie had been rushing between the kitchen and the dining room, checking everyone had what they needed. She was pretty sure her face was the same shade of red as Santa's suit. "Sorry to neglect you."

"You're not neglecting anyone. You're doing your job, and

you're doing it well." Lynda took a sip of her wine. "I've been talking to your sister. Impressive woman."

Hattie glanced across the table to Erica, who was laughing at something Jack had said. It turned out that Jack had an encyclopedic knowledge of dinosaurs, which had made him an immediate hit with Delphi. He, Noah and Erica had kept Delphi entertained during lunch, leaving Hattie to tend to the guests.

It had only been a short time since Erica and Anna had driven away from the inn after their book club week, but Erica had called Hattie every day.

She knew those daily calls would probably become less frequent once Christmas was over and Erica was traveling for work, but still, she treasured each conversation and was enjoying learning more about her sister. They'd moved past the awkwardness of exchanging facts on their past lives and experiences—to Hattie it resembled the beginning of a TV show where they did a recap of what had happened in previous episodes—and their relationship was gradually becoming more comfortable and natural. Erica had confided in her that her relationship with Jack was getting serious so quickly that it terrified her, and Hattie had in turn confessed her true feelings for Noah. She was nervous, too, but if life had taught her anything it was that if you shut out risk you also shut out happiness, and she was determined not to do that. Protecting yourself emotionally meant missing out on so much. For Hattie, love was a risk worth taking and presumably Erica was starting to feel the same way.

Through the large windows of the dining room she could see Noah bending down to scoop up Delphi from the snow where she'd fallen. He'd given her a new sled for Christmas, but Hattie knew that all Delphi really wanted was Noah in her life and it seemed she had that.

And suddenly, she longed to be out there in the snow, playing with her family. Because Noah *was* her family, she knew that, as was Erica, and she thought about how life could seem so bleak and you hardly knew how to go on, and then somehow managed to deliver something magical that made you appreciate being alive. She knew that there would be days where she would feel sad and miss Brent, but also days when she would feel as happy as she did today. She'd accept both. That was life, as the Bishop sisters would say.

The two women were seated now at their usual table in the window, watching indulgently as Delphi played in the snow with Rufus and Noah. They'd arrived armed with gifts and had already booked another week in both the spring and the summer.

"This place is our second home, honey," Ellen had said as Hattie had shown them to their favorite room, carefully decorated by Chloe, who had demonstrated a remarkable ability to deliver exactly what each guest needed.

She felt a hand on her arm and turned to see Lynda smiling at her.

"Fetch your coat and go outside. Have some fun. You've earned it. We can call you if you're needed."

Hattie was about to say she couldn't possibly do that when Delphi pressed her face against the glass of the dining room and waved at her mother, gesturing for her to join them.

Hattie waved back. They'd woken early and opened presents under the tree, and Noah had cooked breakfast and supplied plenty of strong coffee, which both of them needed after a night where sleep had not been a priority.

"Go." Lynda gave her a gentle nudge. "Take some time with them. You've worked hard all morning, now it's time to enjoy your own Christmas."

"I really shouldn't—"

"You definitely should." Erica added her voice to Lynda's. "We can handle this. Go and play in the snow."

"Go." Anna added her voice to the others. She was wearing a new sweater, this one apparently knitted by her daughter, who was currently engaged in spirited banter with her brother.

Hattie could see what a close family they were by the way they communicated, and the love between Anna and Pete was clear to see. Anna had brought the kids stockings from home, and Chloe had helped her stuff them with gifts at midnight. It was a way of incorporating the old traditions with the new.

Change was unavoidable, Hattie thought, and it was better to embrace it than fight it. Better to see the future as an opportunity rather than a threat.

"By the way, your new chef is not only a genius in the kitchen but she loves reading," Lynda said. "I've already enrolled her in our book club. Our next meeting will be in January. We're holding it here, in the library, as that worked so well. I hope that's all right with you. We're all hoping you'll join us."

"It's more than all right." She imagined expanding that idea, and welcoming small groups of readers to stay at the inn. "And I'd love to join you."

"Claudia was telling me that the pair of you have designed a special book club menu. You should rename the place The Book Club Hotel."

Hattie smiled. "That's not a bad idea."

There was so much she could do and the infinite possibilities were exciting rather than daunting. Perhaps it was because she no longer felt alone with it. She had Claudia and Chloe, she had Erica and Lynda. Most of all she had Noah.

Her gaze met his through the glass and she saw something in his eyes that made her breath catch.

Without waiting to be told again she left the dining room, closing the door on the laughter and the celebrations. She grabbed her coat and stepped outside into the winter wonderland, appreciating the blue skies and the icy sparkle of fresh snow in the few seconds before Delphi spotted her. The child sprinted across as fast as she could, her movements restricted by her outdoor clothing. Hattie scooped her up and held her tightly and then Noah arrived and put his arms around both of them.

Hattie closed her eyes for a moment, breathing in the scent of him and feeling her daughter's hair tickle her cheek.

The child and the man. Her present and her future.

★ ★ ★ ★ ★

ACKNOWLEDGMENTS

Publishing a book is a team effort and I owe many people thanks. I'm grateful to my publishing teams CSP in the US, and HQ in the UK, for their dedication and creativity. I'm fortunate that the support they offer is not only for the book but also for me, the author. I couldn't ask for a better publisher.

Thanks to my brilliant editor, Flo Nicoll, who makes every book better and does so with generous enthusiasm.

I'm grateful to my wonderful agent, Susan Ginsburg, Catherine Bradshaw and the entire team at Writers House.

To all the booksellers, librarians, bloggers, reviewers—thank you for championing my books. And to my readers, many of whom have read my work from the beginning, thank you for continuing to read my stories and for your encouraging messages. I love hearing from you.

Finally, to my friends and family for their unfailing support. You're the best.

Turn the page for a sneak peek of
USA TODAY *bestseller Sarah Morgan's next novel,*
coming this summer from Canary Street Press!

Lily tightened her grip on the handlebars and pedalled harder. Here on the northern tip of Cape Cod while the rest of humankind were still sleepy and had barely reached for the coffee pot, she felt as if the place was hers.

All around her were sand dunes and the ocean stretching as far as she could see. She cycled this same route every day, and every day was different. Today the sky was a vivid blue, but she'd seen burnt orange, flame red and smoky silver.

It was a place favored by migratory birds and tourists and generally she preferred the first to the second. The day before she'd seen a blue heron and two snowy egrets. As far as she was concerned the fewer humans the better, but she owed her job to the influx of summer people so she wasn't complaining.

She breathed deeply, letting the salt air fill her lungs and her mind. She felt free here on this windblown, sunbaked strip of seashore. For the first time in months she felt better. Stronger. As if she might survive after all.

She felt something close to happiness and then her phone buzzed and the feeling left her in a rush.

She pedalled faster, trying to outrun its insistent demand. She didn't have to look to identify the caller. It was ten in the morning exactly. Only one person called her routinely at that time.

Goddamn it.

Guilt made her brake and she pulled over, breathless, and dug out her phone. If she didn't take the call now, she'd be taking it later and the thought of it looming in her future would darken the skies of an otherwise cloudless day. This was the price she had to pay for living virtually off grid.

"Lily, honey? It's Mom."

Of course it was.

She'd been expecting this call, ever since she'd declined their invitation to come home and "talk things over." Still, every time she saw her mother's name pop up on her phone screen she felt sick. They'd made huge sacrifices for her, and she'd as good as slapped them in the face. And she hadn't even given them a reason.

She was a bad daughter.

"I'm on my way to work, Mom. I can't be late." Never had dirty pots and pans and other people's laundry seemed more appealing. She'd rather deal with that any day than talk to her parents. Every conversation left her so twisted with guilt she was almost convulsing. "Is everything all right?"

"No, it isn't. We're so worried about you, Lily." Her mother's tone was shaky. "We don't understand what's going on. Why won't you tell us?"

Lily tightened her grip on the phone. "Nothing is going on, Mom. And you don't need to worry."

"Can you blame us? We have a bright, brilliant daughter who has chosen to throw away the life she worked hard for. And with no reason."

There was a reason. She just hadn't shared it.

"I'm fine, Mom."

"Are you eating? Have you put on some weight? You were skin and bones when you left here."

"I'm eating. I'm sleeping. I'm good, really. How are you and Dad?"

"We miss you, obviously. Come home, Lily. We can cook for you, and spoil you and look after you."

She knew what going home would mean. She loved her parents, but they'd hover over her with frowning concerned faces until she ended up worrying more about them than herself. The pressure of pretending to be okay had been exhausting.

"I'm happy, Mom. I just need some space. It's beautiful here. You know I always loved the ocean."

"I know. I remember when you were six years old and we couldn't drag you away from the sand castle you'd built." There was a pause. "Honey, Dad made some calls. He thinks it's not too late for you to go back to medical school if you want to."

Interference, even well-meaning interference, should be designated a crime.

"I don't want to. I know you and Dad are disappointed—"

"It's not about us, it's about you. We tried so hard to give you all the opportunities we didn't have. We never wanted you to struggle the way we did."

Lily stared at the ocean and tried to find her inner calm, but it had fled the moment the phone had rung.

They'd made huge sacrifices for her, and she'd thrown it in their faces. She wasn't just a bad daughter, she was a horrible person.

"This is difficult for me too, Mom." The lump in her throat made it difficult to speak. "I know I'm hurting you and I hate it, but this is where I want to be. And this is what I want to do. I want to be an artist."

"But, Lily, you're cleaning houses."

"To earn money while I pursue my passion." While she tried to loosen the knots of stress in her body and untangle the mess in her head. "There's nothing wrong with cleaning houses. It's a respectable way to make a living. You did it."

"If I could have been a doctor, I would have been one."

Guilt, guilt, guilt.

Her mother sighed. "Do you need money? We still have some savings."

And she knew just how hard it would have been for her parents to pull that together after everything they'd already spent on her. She'd vowed never to take another cent from them.

"I don't need money, but thank you." She tried not to think about the dire state of her bank account. She was one punctured tire away from financial disaster but there was no way she could admit that or ask for help. She'd already wasted enough of their money. She was determined to manage on her own now.

"Lily—" her mother's voice was gentle "—your father would kill me for asking because I know I'm not supposed to ask, but did something happen, honey? Was it the work? Was it too much? Or was it something else? Did someone hurt you? Your dad and I always thought you'd make a wonderful doctor. You're such a kind, caring person."

"Nothing like that. I just wasn't cut out to be a doctor." Lily's throat burned. She badly wanted this conversation to end. "Could we talk about something else?"

"Of course we can. Let me think…not much has happened here. Your father has been busy in the garden, of course." Her mother spoke in a cheery *I'm changing the subject to a safe topic* voice. "The hydrangeas are beginning to bloom—they're going to be stunning. I made the most delicious orange cake last week. No wheat. You know your father. Ground almonds instead of flour."

"Sounds yummy." She felt a pang imagining them at home together. She missed them. Part of her just wanted to run home and be looked after but she knew she couldn't do that.

"I'm sure there was something I wanted to tell you." Her mother paused. "What was it? Oh, I remember—I bumped into Kristen Buckingham last week. She's always so charming and friendly. So normal."

The last person Lily wanted to think about now was anyone with the name Buckingham.

"Why wouldn't she be friendly and normal, Mom?" Lily knew how self-conscious her mother was around her friends and she hated it. It reminded her of being back at school and feeling like second best.

Her parents had scrimped and saved and worked multiple jobs in order to send her to the best school. They'd believed she'd have a great education and make influential friends. She would absorb their greater advantages by osmosis. It would be her ticket to a better life. They imagined her living her life in a bubble of success, mixing with people whose parents owned mansions and yachts and jets. People whose fridges were loaded with food and never had to worry about making it stretch to the end of the week. People who had drivers, and housekeepers, and staff who cleared the snow from their yard.

And she had met people like that, but most of the time Lily had felt like a stray dog that had somehow wriggled its way into a litter of pedigrees. She'd been badly bullied. She'd also felt crushed by the pressure of work and parental expectation. Panic had hovered close to the surface, threatening to suffocate her. The only thing that had got her out of bed in the morning was the knowledge of her parents' sacrifice and their pride in her. She hadn't felt able to tell them how unhappy she was, or that locking herself in a cubicle while having a panic attack didn't feel like success to her.

She'd been thoroughly miserable, and then Hannah Buckingham had rescued her from a bully who was trying to remove her ponytail with a pair of scissors and everything had changed.

Hannah was a champion of the underdog. She had a fierce urge to protect anything threatened. She wanted to save the whales, and Sumatran tigers, and Antarctica. Lily was added to the list, and they'd become best friends from that moment. Hannah had said Lily was the sister she'd never had. Hannah hadn't cared about the differences between their household incomes.

Hannah hadn't cared that Lily didn't have her own bathroom, or a housekeeper to keep her room tidy, or tutors to make sure her grades were the best they could possibly be. Hannah had found Lily interesting. They'd been inseparable and they had stayed that way. Protected by Hannah, the bullying had stopped and Lily had flourished. With Hannah as her friend, her confidence had grown. She no longer felt like a misfit.

They'd gone to the same college, where they'd both studied biological sciences, and then they'd applied to the same medical school. When her acceptance letter arrived, Lily's parents had cried. They'd been so proud and thrilled. It was the happiest day of their lives. Lily was happy and relieved that she was everything her parents wanted her to be.

When the pressure started to crush her brain again, she tried to ignore it. She was going to be fine. There were so many different branches of medicine. She'd find one that suited her.

Hannah had known from the start that she wanted to be a surgeon like her father, Theo. Hannah wanted to save lives. She wanted to make a difference.

On the few occasions she'd met him, Lily had found Theo to be terrifying, or maybe it was more accurate to say that she found his reputation terrifying.

Hannah's mother, Kristen, was equally intimidating. She was an art expert, a whirlwind of brisk efficiency.

And then there was Hannah's older brother Todd, who was smart, handsome and kind, and the object of lust among all Hannah's friends. Lily was no exception. Teenage Lily had fantasized about Todd. Twenty-year-old Lily had kissed Todd in a dark corner during an out of control student party.

Lily was in love with Todd.

Todd was the reason that Lily and Hannah were no longer speaking.

Lily had trained herself not to think about Todd.

"I just mean that Kristen is very important, Lily, that's all," her mother said. "But she always takes the time to talk to me when I see her."

"She's just a person, Mom. A person like the rest of us."

"Well not really like the rest of us," her mother said. "Her father was Cameron Lapthorne. I don't pretend to know anything about art, but even I know his name."

Hannah had taken her to the Lapthorne estate once and Lily had gazed at the paintings hungrily, studying every brushstroke, envious of the skill and envious of anyone who could build a life as an artist. Hannah had given her a catalog of her grandfather's work from an exhibition that was running, and it had become Lily's most treasured possession. She thumbed the pages, studied the pictures and slept with it under her pillow.

Ever since she was old enough to hold a paintbrush, Lily had loved painting. She'd painted everything in sight. When she'd run out of paper, she'd painted on the walls. She'd painted her school bag and her running shoes. She'd said to her parents *I want to be an artist*, and for a while they'd looked worried. They'd told her no one made money that way and that she was smart enough to be a doctor or a lawyer. Lily knew how much they wanted that for her, and she knew how much they'd sacrificed. She owed them. So she dutifully took up her place at medical school and maybe she might even have stuck it out if it hadn't been for what happened on that one particular night.

"Lily? Are you still there?"

Lily tugged herself back into the present. "Yes. So how was Kristen?"

"Busy as ever. She was in the middle of organizing a big event at the Lapthorne estate. Celebrating her father, the artist. It's happening today, I think. Todd will be there with his fiancée—I forget her name. And Hannah will be there of course. Kristen invited us, and you, which was so generous of her."

Todd would be there with his fiancée.

Lily imagined Todd in the rose garden with a glass of champagne in his hand and Amelie gazing up at him with that self-satisfied look, a large diamond glinting on her finger.

Amelie.

Amelie was the girl who had tried to cut off Lily's ponytail with a pair of scissors. And now she was marrying Todd.

Todd had broken Lily's heart.

Her palms felt sweaty. "Are you going to the party?"

"No, of course not. Your father wouldn't know what to say and I wouldn't know what to wear. They're your friends really, not ours. Kristen mentioned that Hannah is about to start her clinical rotation, but you probably know that as she's your best friend."

Lily didn't know that. Lily and Hannah hadn't spoken since that terrible fight on the night Lily had packed her bags and left medical school for good.

Every time Lily thought of Hannah she wanted to cry. When they were young they'd sworn that nothing, and no one, would ever come between them and they'd truly believed that.

They'd been wrong.

"I have to go, Mom. I'll be late for work and I don't want to let people down." She winced as she said it, because she was all too aware that she'd let her parents down. "I'm sorry you're worried but you don't need to be. I'm happy. I like my life."

"We just don't want you to waste your talents, honey, that's all. You're capable of so much. You could be curing cancer—"

Curing cancer? *No pressure then.*

"I hated medical school." She didn't expect them to understand. They believed that if you were smart enough to be a doctor, why wouldn't you be one? "I want to be an artist, Mom. That's all I've ever wanted. You know that."

"I know, but where's the future in that? Your dad and I just don't want you to struggle financially as we did. Life can be hard, Lily."

Lily closed her eyes. She knew that. She knew how hard life could be.

"Stop worrying, Mom." She tried not to think about the tiny amount of money in her bank account. "I'm managing fine. And I'm going to pay you and Dad back."

"That's not necessary, honey. We love you, and remember there's a home and a welcome here whenever you need it."

Lily's throat felt full. "Thanks, Mom. And now I have to go. Give my love to Dad."

She ended the call, wondering why big life decisions had to feel so difficult and wondering why, when there were so many people her mother could have bumped into, she'd had to bump into Kristen Buckingham.

But she wasn't going to think about that now. And she wasn't going to think about Hannah, starting her clinical rotation. Twice in the last few months she'd almost texted her. Once she'd even typed out a message, but then she'd deleted it. What was the point?

The friendship that they'd believed could never be damaged, had been damaged. Smashed. Broken. Amelie might as well have taken her scissors to it.

But that was in the past now.

Hannah was living in the city, and Lily was here on the Cape, and if it wasn't as blissful as she'd imagined it would be when she'd left the smothering security of her parents' home, then at least it was her choice.

Eyes stinging, she dropped the phone back into her bag and pedalled hard. The call had cost her ten minutes, but if she worked fast she'd still get the work done.

The breeze blew into her face and dried the dampness of tears. One day she'd make it up to her parents. She'd find a way to make them proud, even though she wouldn't be curing cancer.

She turned into the driveway of a large mansion and cycled up to the house, her sudden stop creating a small shower of gravel. Grabbing her backpack, she sprinted to the front door and waved to Mike, the gardener, who was hauling trays of plants from the back of his truck.

This particular house was a prime beachfront property and was booked solid throughout the summer months. It slept fourteen, and those fourteen had clearly had a good time if the state of the kitchen was anything to go by.

The company she worked for catered to the luxury end of the market (people with more money than sense, the owner was fond of saying) and it always surprised her that those people seemed never to have mastered the basic art of clearing up after themselves.

She scooped up empty pizza boxes, removed a discarded lobster shell from one of the kitchen chairs (she could be curing cancer, but instead she was clearing up lobster shells) and cleared half a dozen empty champagne bottles into the recycling. She wiped, she spritzed, she mopped, she polished and once she'd restored the kitchen to its usual pristine state and reassured herself that there was no lasting damage, she headed towards the bedrooms.

By the time she'd finished it was mid afternoon.

She took a large drink of water from the bottle she kept in her backpack and retrieved her bike.

"I'm all done." She pushed her bike across to Mike, who was bent over a flower bed.

He straightened, stepped over a clump of petunias and walked over to her. "Where are you off to next?"

"Dune cottage."

"That place is a mystery." He pulled his hat down to keep the sun from his face. "I fixed the deck last summer, but the place was empty. Have you ever seen anyone staying there?"

"Never. Easiest cleaning job I do all week. A bit of light dusting. Clean the windows, sweep the deck. Change the sheets in the master bedroom once a fortnight. Report anything that needs repairing."

"Why change the sheets?"

"Apparently they like to keep the place ready, just in case."

"In case of what? Who do you think owns it?"

Lily shrugged. "I'm guessing some billionaire from Manhattan who can afford to keep it empty."

"Isn't it a bit small for a billionaire?"

"Maybe he's a small, single billionaire."

Mike grinned. "A single billionaire. Does such a thing exist? Money is a powerful aphrodisiac."

"Not to everyone." In her experience, money didn't always bring out the best in people. "I have to go. See you tomorrow, Mike." She climbed onto her bike and pedalled down the drive and onto the cycle track that led to a remote part of the outer cape. The trail took her over sandy dunes and past salt marshes and then finally the cottage appeared, nestled among the dunes, separated from the ocean by soft sand and whispering seagrass. Its white clapboard walls and shingle roof had been weathered by the elements, but still the building stood firm, and it had become as much a part of the landscape as the shifting sands that surrounded it.

Whoever owned it was the luckiest person in the world, Lily decided. Also maybe the most foolish, because who would own a place like this and not use it? It was a criminal waste.

She and the people she worked with occasionally played guessing games. It was owned by a rock star who had ten mansions and never quite got around to using this one. It was an FBI safe house. The owner was dead and buried under the deck (that wasn't Lily's favorite theory).

Whoever it was had made sure that they couldn't be identified. The management fees were paid by an obscure, faceless company. Occasionally over the years they'd give instructions that the cottage was to be inhabited and the staff should stay away, but no one could remember when that had last happened. It was as if it had been forgotten, abandoned, except not quite abandoned because it was maintained as if the owner might be coming home any day. And Lily was responsible for keeping it that way.

It was, in her opinion, the perfect job, and if she was ahead of her workload she occasionally sneaked an hour or more to paint because the light and the views in this particular corner of the Cape were spectacular.

She leaned her bike against the wall where it would be protected from the elements, hoisted her backpack onto her shoulders and headed up the wooden steps to the deck that wrapped itself snugly around the cottage.

If Lily had been asked to name her dream house, this would have been the one. Not for her, the mansions that were dotted along the coast from Provincetown to Hyannis. She didn't want marble, or hot tubs, a games room or a cinema room.

She wanted this. The ever-changing light. The views. The feeling that you were living on the edge of the world. When she was here, some of her misery lifted. Some of her energy returned and she just wanted to grab her sketchbook and her paints and record the view so that the memories would stay with her forever.

She delved into her pocket for the keys and opened the front door. Every time she stepped into the place she fell in love all over again.

She tugged off her shoes (she didn't believe in making more work for herself) and left the door open to allow the air and sunshine to fill the place.

The interior was simple but sophisticated, every item carefully chosen to complement the ocean setting. The sofa was cream, the armchairs facing it upholstered in the same shade. There were hints of nautical everywhere. The cushions were marine blue and turquoise, bringing the summer skies indoors. The coffee table was made of timber salvaged from a shipwreck, no doubt a casualty of the dangerous waters and shifting sandbars. It was stacked with books and sometimes Lily curled up in the evening and read them with the sounds of the ocean floating through the open windows.

The living room opened onto a wide veranda that Lily was continually sweeping. At the back of the cottage there was a studio, north facing, with large windows overlooking the ocean and the wide expanse of sky.

Upstairs was a master bedroom with glorious views across the dunes and the ocean, a large second bedroom and a third bedroom built into the eaves. No one had slept in the cottage for at least a year, probably more. At least not officially.

Lily headed upstairs and dropped her backpack in the smallest bedroom. She felt a stab of guilt and had to stop herself glancing over her shoulder to check that no one was watching her.

Just one night, she'd told herself the first time she'd stayed here. And then one night had become two, and two had turned into a week and she was still here two months later. At first she'd felt so guilty she hadn't even slept on the bed. She'd unrolled her sleeping bag and slept on the sofa in the living room and woken when the morning light had shimmered across the room. She'd used the shower in the smaller of the two bathrooms, and told herself that occasionally running the shower and flushing the toilets was an important part of her caretaking responsibility.

Over the winter she'd shared a room with two other girls in a house in the town, but then the tourist season had taken off. Every bed was needed for visitors and Lily's funds didn't stretch far enough to cover the cost of a new rental.

That was what she told herself, but the truth was she couldn't bear to leave this beautiful place. She sometimes felt as if the cottage needed her as much as she needed the cottage. And who was ever going to know? No one came out this far once the sun had set, and she'd already decided that if someone found her here during the day she would simply say that she was cleaning the place.

Gradually the cottage had embraced her, and made her feel at home. She'd graduated from the sofa to the smallest bedroom in the eaves (the master bedroom was taking it too far) and now her sleeping bag was stretched on top of the bed and she even kept a few toiletries in the shower room.

And over time she'd started to think of the cottage as hers. She cared for it as lovingly as a family member. When she'd noticed that one of the stairs down to the beach had rotted, she'd told the management company and they'd had it replaced. Nothing escaped her. A window that didn't quite close after the winter. Paint peeling away on the front door. Lily noticed it and arranged for it to be fixed. Sometimes she even talked to the cottage as she was shaking out cushions and dusting down surfaces.

Why does no one come and stay in you? What sort of people are they that they'd leave you alone like this?

Whenever anyone asked her where she was living she gave a vague response, leading them to believe that she was couch surfing until she found somewhere permanent. The truth was, she'd stopped looking. Partly because her days were so full, and partly because she couldn't bring herself to leave and saw no reason to do so as the place was empty.

She loved being alone here. She loved the fact that she could cry and not worry that someone might see her and worry. She loved the fact that if she couldn't sleep she could switch on the light and read without anyone asking her if she was okay. She could eat, or not eat, knowing that no one was policing her food intake. She could feel what she wanted to feel without the added pressure of knowing she was worrying someone.

She didn't have to pretend to be fine.

Because she wasn't fine. She hurt, inside and out, and until she stopped hurting she didn't want to be anywhere but here. She couldn't think of a better place to be wounded.

The cottage nurtured her, tempting her to sit on its sunny deck, or venture into the cozy kitchen to make herself a sandwich or a mug of creamy hot chocolate. With its hand-painted cabinets and butcher block countertops, the kitchen had a warm, welcoming feel that was a contrast to the sleek, modern kitchens that graced most of the homes she cleaned.

But the biggest comfort for Lily were the paintings. There were sketches, and oils, and pastels—she'd studied them all closely, examining every brushstroke and every line. Her favorite was the large watercolor hanging above the fireplace in the living room. She'd stared at that painting for hours, seduced by the subtle blend of colors, intrigued by the figure of the woman standing on the sand, staring out to sea. Who was she and what she was thinking? Was she simply admiring the view, or was she planning on plunging into the freezing waters and ending her misery?

Every time she looked at the painting it seemed different. The shadows. The soft flush of light across the ocean. It was as changeable as the scenery that had been its inspiration. Looking at it made her chest ache and her throat close. It wasn't just a painting, it was a story. It made her *feel*. Whoever that woman was, Lily felt an affinity with her.

And she couldn't believe that a painting like this one was hanging on the wall of an almost abandoned beach cottage, because this wasn't any old painting. It wasn't one of the prints that sold by the thousands in various shops along the Cape. She was sure—or as sure as she could be—that it was an original Cameron Lapthorne. His initials were in the corner. CL. And if it was an original then it was worth *millions*. But she didn't care about that side of it. For her it was all about the art. Its value was in its beauty. Being able to gaze for hours at that painting was a privilege. It was like having a private view of the *Mona Lisa*, or Monet's water lilies. Looking at it made her think of Hannah (and also Todd, but she tried not to go there).

She suspected Mike was wrong when he assumed the cottage wasn't owned by someone with pots of money. Maybe not a billionaire, but whoever it was had enough money not to care that they were leaving an original Cameron Lapthorne unattended.

Or perhaps it wasn't an original.

She'd studied his work in depth, but she'd never seen any mention of this particular painting. It captivated her, but it also inspired her, and she tore her gaze away from it now and headed for the studio where she kept her paints and canvases carefully hidden in one of the cupboards.

She realized that she'd missed lunch, but she didn't want to waste a moment of the light on preparing a meal for herself, and anyway the conversation with her mother had chased away her appetite. Instead of eating, she reached for her pad and her oil pastels and headed towards the deck.

She wanted to paint. And even if nothing she produced ever came close to capturing the magical light of the Cape in the way Cameron Lapthorne had when he was alive, she would keep trying.

Food could wait. And so could finding alternative accommodation.

There was no urgency. After all, it wasn't as if anyone was using the place.